1

Bloody Rattenkrieg

By Andrew McGregor

Prologue

Late November 1942 on the banks of the River Volga. The German advance into the Caucasus Mountains in search of the Russian oilfields has ground to a halt as the bitter fighting in Stalingrad takes centre stage.

The Germans, desperate to take the city that holds Stalin's namesake, strip their flanks of troops to bolster their forces fighting inside the city.

The Russians seize their opportunity, launching a counteroffensive in the north on November 19th and in the south on November 20th, smashing through the Romanian armies defending the weakened flanks of the German Sixth Army.

The Russian armies strike west, moving behind the beleaguered city and desperate street fighting to cut off their enemy, stranding them on the banks of the Volga. In bitter, freezing temperatures, survivors of the offensive desperately try and escape the roaming Russian units.

This is the story of one such group. Isolated and cut off in the south after the Russian offensive, they fight and bluff their way through enemy lines and positions in an attempt to reach the city in the belief it provides safety.

Finally reaching the river, the survivors join a small pocket of resistance on the south bank, within sight of German lines and potential safety further round the Volga bend. Barricaded into only two storage towers on the banks of the river, the small group of Axis soldiers attempt to hold off overwhelming enemy numbers to buy time to get away.

Realising the only way of saving the men was to escape, Leutnant Hausser leads a small group of soldiers along the riverbank and around the Volga bend in an attempt to re-join German lines inside Stalingrad.

One this escape was established, the plan was to assist the remaining men in the storage towers to escape along the same route.

Shortly after their departure, Russian infantry and flamethrowers attacked the defenders in the storage towers with the aim of wiping the small Axis force out. With ferocious Russian attacks intended in finally destroying the last pocket of the enemy on the south bank, one final escape plan is interrupted as the defenders lose the ground floor of one of the storage towers. There may now not be enough time left...........

Character Overview.

Leutnant Hausser

A serving officer in the 76th Infantry Division, Leutnant Hausser has had a varied military career for his 27 years of age. Having been born in Dusseldorf, his parents moved to Potsdam, a suburb of Berlin when he was a teenager. His father served in the previous war and also fought in Russia. Leutnant Hausser has seen action in the Crimea and central Russia before the unit's participation in the drive on Stalingrad. Due to his language skills, speaking Romanian and Russian as well as his native German, he has been deployed across Army Group South during the ongoing months of Operation Barbarossa.

Quartermaster Sergeant Tatu

Tatu is in his early forties and originates from Bucharest. He has been close friends with Petru and his family for some considerable time and they used to work together in a furniture business in their home city. Enlisting in the army, he was deployed to the Romanian 20th Infantry Division.

Corporal Petru

Petru is in his mid-forties and also originates from Bucharest, where he worked making furniture with his close friend, Tatu. He is a family man and has three children, one of which, the youngest boy has some medical problems. Joining up with his friend, Tatu, he also joined the Romanian 20th Infantry Division.

Private Meino

Born in Sinj in Croatia, Meino's parents owned an Inn in the town. As an experienced soldier in the 369th Infantry Regiment, he was deployed to the southern front of Stalingrad after a call for Romanian speakers was announced. He is thirty two years old.

Private Udet

Udet is twenty two and from Potsdam in Berlin and also a member of the 76th Infantry Division. Assigned to the southern front of Stalingrad with Leutnant Hausser.

Private Nicu

Nicu is nineteen years old, and the youngest of the group. A member of the Romanian 14th Infantry Division, his unit was virtually destroyed in the initial Russian assault south of Stalingrad. Nicu is from Hotin near the Russian border.

Private Luca Barsetti

Luca is in his late twenties and assigned to the 248th Autieri Group (Transport) after an argument with his commander. The 248th drove supplies into Stalingrad from outside the city, and he was unfortunate enough to be directed with his supplies to the southern suburbs just before the Russian offensive began, being 'cut off' during the attack in the storage towers. On his own admission, he is an excellent shot, but this is yet to be seen in battle.

'Hase'

Little is known about this soldier. A Russian 'Hilfswilliger' ('Hiwi' for short) or volunteer grew up in Kiev. He has been with Hausser for some time and it is currently uncertain where they originally joined forces, but this probably happened in the Crimea. At 28 he is a year older than the commander, and seems to respect him immensely, displaying considerable loyalty.

Introduction

Luca hammered his fist on the warehouse door facing the river, 'Open up, it's Luca!' His Italian voice raised as he pressed the side of his face to the thick wooden door.

The echoes of bullet fire surrounded the buildings and he shivered, the cold breeze from the river enveloping him on the top of the slope that descended to the river's edge. An explosion on the front of the building next door, caused him to hammer on the door once more. 'Open the door, someone, it's time to leave!' He coughed as the cold caught in his throat, forcing him to swallow hard.

He leant back, looking up at the dark hulk of the building, straining his ears to try and distinguish any sound from inside the building. His exhaled breath formed in clouds of condensed air around him and through the mistiness he could make out the long frozen icicles hanging from the upper window sills, their openings long since bricked and boarded up. Then a smile crossed his face as he recognised a cautious muffled voice on the other side of the door replying to his shout, 'Is that Luca? What's going on?'

Lifting his rifle and pulling the strap over his shoulder, the Italian's eyes narrowed in frustration as he realised the fear in the man's voice, 'Open the damn door, Alessio! Let me in!'

The bolts on the top, middle and bottom of the inside of the sturdy wooden delivery door were drawn slowly back, the crisp sound of the cold metal grinding against their steel housings initially making him relax slightly, then a large explosion on the roof of the storage tower next door drowned the sounds out. He turned abruptly, startled, seeing debris dropping onto the iced snow from the roof of the neighbouring building.

The right side of the double doors slowly creaked inwards as the soldier on the other side pulled the sturdy delivery door towards him, creating a small opening. Luca side stepped through the opening into almost complete darkness, the large room illuminated by only one oil lamp. Seeing two silhouettes before him lower their rifles, he breathed a sigh of relief, realising the men were at a high state of alert.

The door was closed behind him and the bolts pushed back into place, his eyes struggling to adjust in the gloom. A hand grasped his right shoulder and he turned to look at his countryman in the darkness, the Italian soldier shorter than him, grinning in the dim light.

'So what's the plan?' The man spoke in the darkness. 'We have little time left here now as the Russians are about to attack in force.'

Luca walked forward towards the two other soldiers as they lowered their rifles further, eventually holding them by their sides in one hand. He cleared his throat, 'The Leutnant is moving along the river bank with a group to secure an escape route for us. He sent me to get you. How many of you are in here?'

Alessio spoke from behind him, turning to push the door as a final check that it was secure, 'Only nine of us now, Luca. We sent the others across to the other building. The rest are upstairs providing cover fire for the tower next door.'

Luca nodded grimly, 'Ok, let's have a look at the Russian positions from upstairs. We will choose six men to leave with me and then come back for the rest.' He walked forward boldly, heading for the doorway in the right corner of the room. As he reached the doorway, he turned and started to climb the stairs to the first floor, hearing rifle shots from the floors above echo down the stairwell. A distant muffled explosion from outside prompted him to increase the speed of his ascent, pushing his legs up two steps at a time.

Reaching the first floor, he glanced into the room to his left, seeing three soldiers at the barricaded windows facing the street, their positions at an angle to look out into the thoroughfare before the building next door. As he turned on the landing to begin to climb the next set of stairs, he heard an adrenalin fuelled shout from the room he had just looked into, 'Smoke in the street, the Russians are starting their attack!'

Luca turned, making eye contact with his younger countryman, Alessio, the soldier stood on the flight of stairs below him. The young man's eyes were wide with excitement, his breathing becoming shorter as his fear rose within him. They both ducked instinctively as an explosion outside startled them.

As Luca climbed the next few steps, he began to breathe heavily in the cold stairwell from the exertion and stress, the chilled air seeming to grasp at his chest. Reaching the second floor, he saw two further soldiers aiming out at an angle, and as he turned to ascend the next flight, a shot rang out as one fired into the smoke diagonally down the street.

The muffled gunfire from outside seemed to intensify as he ascended the next few steps, his breathing becoming laboured. He grasped the metal handrail and started to pull himself up the last few stairs, his legs aching at the strain. Alessio drew level with him on the stairs, grasping his left elbow tightly and pulling him upwards. As he did so, the younger Italian leant towards him, his lips near Luca's ear, 'Don't worry, it's the change in temperature from outside to inside, it messes with your breathing. It seems us Italians are not suited for the Russian winter.'

Luca nodded, coughing, his right hand pulling on the metal handrail, he gulped in air, 'Just get me to the fourth floor. We can check the street from there.'

Reaching the next landing, the two men glanced into the storage room to their left before turning to climb the next set of stairs. Two soldiers were stood pensively against the walls, the outline of their German steel helmets in the gloom distinctive with the glow from the oil lamps on the floor. Both were looking out diagonally from the boarded windows, their rifles in their hands.

Climbing the next few steps, Luca' breathing became more laboured, the tightness in his chest causing him to grasp the handrail with both hands. Alessio leant into him, his voice concerned, 'Are you alright Luca? Normally it's not this bad.......shall we stop for a moment?'

Luca shook his head, swallowing air, 'N..No, let's keep going...I...I should be alright in a moment.' His breathing was becoming wheezed, the stress of the climb and cold temperature playing on his chest.

Gunfire echoed around the stairwell as the riflemen on the floors below fired out into the smoke billowing in front of the next door building. A muffled explosion from outside the other storage tower startled them, the gunfire outside rising in intensity again. The two men struggled up the stairs to the fourth floor, Alessio pulling Luca upwards with the tight grip on his left arm.

As they reached the fourth floor, a Romanian soldier emerged from the office to the right, his eyes wide with excitement, 'Russian infantry are storming the ground floor in the next building.......we will be next!'

Alessio's eyes narrowed, frustration crossing his face, his voice raised, 'Hold your nerve! They are not here yet! The building is secure!'

The Romanian's eyes dropped, his expression becoming solemn, 'Yes, Alessio, I...I am sorry.' Seeing Luca lean forward the Italian clutching is chest, he moved forward concern on his face, 'Luca, are you alright?'

Luca coughed deeply, his hand outstretched to the soldier, 'I will be ok, just need a minute. Have we a good view from this floor?'

The Romanian shook his head, 'No, better from above. One of the windows is half open up there.'

Luca grimaced, 'Ok, let's go Alessio...next floor.'

Turning the two Italians began to climb the next set of stairs, Luca leaning on Alessio and breathing heavily. The Romanian slowly stepped up behind them, watching Luca pull on the metal handrail, his body nearly bent double in an attempt to make breathing easier.

The men slowly reached the fifth floor, half carrying Luca into the wide dark storage area to the left of the stairs. Luca leant against the wall, breathing heavily and reaching into his tunic breast pocket for some cigarettes. He watched as the Romanian lit an oil lamp half way along the front wall of the room, the light struggling to illuminate through the darkness.

Cold air and the occasional snowflake drifted in through the furthest window, the opening only half covered. The sounds of gunfire in the street below echoed through the room, the fighting persisting on the ground floor of the neighbouring building.

As Luca twisted the lighter in his hands, the flame caught and he drew greedily on the cigarette, the warm smoke drifting through his narrowed bronchial tubes, relaxing them. The cigarettes a special issue for soldiers with his identified medical condition.

He glanced around the long room, the dim light casting shadows across the walls as the flame in the oil lamp flickered in the breeze. The front of the room was relatively clear, with some debris and thick plaster dust from the ceiling lying across the cement floor. Along the back of the room the wall was obscured by what he presumed to be a large quantity of supplies or machinery, covered entirely in tarpaulin. The objects and tarpaulin came up to shoulder height and covered approximately half the floor of the storage area, with most of the back wall and end of the room in darkness due to the obstruction.

Alessio was further down the room, cautiously glancing out of the half boarded window, his fear of potential sniper fire evident in his stance. The Romanian, having lit the oil lamp, rose from his crouched position and lit his own cigarette, blowing the smoke across the width of the room.

Luca began to feel his breathing become easier, his bronchial tubes opening with the warm smoke and relaxing, allowing the air easier access into his lungs. Looking across the room at his countryman, he pushed himself from the wall, 'What can you see Alessio?'

Alessio turned, stepping back from the opening, 'It's not good, I think the Russians are on the ground floor. The shooting seems to be inside the building now.'

Luca moved forward along the wall, slowly taking the rifle from his shoulder, 'Is there still smoke?'

Alessio turned to him, the light flickering across his unshaven face. 'Yes, can't see anything in the street, but some of the firing is muffled, the Russians must be inside.'

Passing the Romanian who was glancing out through a crack in the window next to him, he cautiously approached the opening. Alessio stepped back to let him past, 'How will they get out now?'

Luca shook his head, feeling his chest more relaxed, his breathing easier. 'I don't know, it looks bad for them. Let's have a look.'

The Italian glanced out of the opening at an angle, looking down into the street. The smoke extended around the base of the building next door, billowing up to the second floor level. Silhouettes moved through the smoke towards the building, the Russian troops reinforcing their gain of the ground floor in case of counter attack and in readiness to attack the first floor.

Luca sighed, pulling back from the window and resting his back on the wall. Reaching for another cigarette, he wondered how long the men in the adjacent tower could hold out against the mass of Russians swarming towards the building. Pulling his head forward to light the cigarette, he sucked as the tobacco lit, his head slowly moving backwards, stopping when his helmet rested against the wall.

He blew smoke across the room, watching the cloud swirl as it drifted and swirled over the tarpaulin. Then he tensed and leant forward, straining his eyes through the gloom, his alertness rising.

Luca turned to Alessio, a puzzled expression on his face, 'What's under the tarpaulin?'

Alessio shrugged, 'Supplies I think, we have never really looked. We've only been here a short time, there was never the need...they are probably rotten.'

Luca pushed himself from the wall, his voice distant as his curiosity rose, 'Bring the oil lamp. Let's have a look at these *'supplies'*.'

Chapter One: As the curtain begins to fall

In the small fourth floor office in the storage tower, Tatu scanned the bank of the river bend with binoculars through the shell hole in the wall. Below him, sporadic gunfire echoed in the stairwell as the Russians tried to gain an understanding of the strength they faced before attacking the first floor. The occasional explosion within and outside the building indicated the grenades the defenders were using to deter the attackers, a stock of grenades that were now beginning to run out.

He tensed, lowering the glasses for a second as he heard a grinding noise above him in the building. The noise becoming slightly louder, then silence. Hearing boots on the stairs behind him, he raised the glasses again. He scanned the ice as it bent around the river, looking for shadows or silhouettes. Seeing nothing, he began looking along the river wall in shadows from the fires beyond.

A smile crossed his lips as he thought he glimpsed something against a gap in the wall, then he ducked his head as shells exploded above him on the roof, a shower of dust falling from the ceiling above him. Raising the glasses he looked again, seeing nothing, he reluctantly dismissed his earlier thought.

As he lowered the binoculars from his eyes, he heard Udet's shouting in the stairwell, a desperation in his voice, 'Tatu, come quickly, we need your help.' Dropping the binoculars, he ran his shaking hand over his moustache and grasped his PPSH 41 machine gun. Turning abruptly, he ran from the office. Seeing a soldier at the end of the room opposite, he realised he was grimly checking the bodies for any survivors from the blast that had occurred earlier. He averted his eyes as he approached the doorway, seeing the torn and broken bodies of the wounded that had been caught in the explosion as it burst through the ceiling.

As Tatu turned to descend the stairs from the fourth floor, Meino's voice boomed from the stairwell above, 'Not down, up…come and help!' Gunfire echoed up and down the stairwell, the defenders on the floors below them desperately trying to deter the Russians from attacking upwards.

Tatu glanced upwards, seeing the Croatian turn the corner of the staircase above him. Meino's eyes were wide with excitement, 'Come on, quickly! There is not much time!'

Tatu grasped the handrail and turned abruptly, stepping up two steps at a time as the Croatian disappeared from view upwards on the staircase. Tatu pulled himself up the steps, his gloved hands grasping the handrail tightly. As he turned the bend in the staircase, he saw Meino and Udet stood on the upper fifth floor landing, their weapons held menacingly.

As he climbed the last few steps, a blast of cold air hit him from the left doorway leading to the uppermost storage room. The ceiling mostly completely collapsed, some rubble and broken beams had come to rest near the doorway, almost blocking it. Flames flickered and burned in the room behind the rubble, the remaining stores and oil being consumed by the fire. He glanced through a gap in the debris, seeing the open dark sky where the roof had been, the stars bright and clear in the freezing temperatures. Broken machinery lay along the left wall, a metal step ladder at the end, the only route to the sixth floor that had now collapsed inwards.

Turning on the dimly lit fifth floor landing, he faced Meino and Udet, realising they stood before a closed double doorway, the flames from the room behind him casting broken light into the stairwell through the rubble. The sturdy bolted wooden doors obstructing the area that would have been the small side offices on the floors below, he blinked in surprise, 'What is it?'

Meino turned his head slightly, his eyes fixed on the door. 'I came up to check the wounded on the floor below after that explosion. Then I heard noises…I thought perhaps there was someone trapped up here.'

Udet turned to look at Meino, his expression curious, 'That noise just now….was that from the other side of the doors?'

Meino nodded, 'I think so, what do you think it is? Is someone in there?'

Tatu shook his head, hearing the gunfire below, he raised his voice in frustration, 'We have not got time for this! We are all trapped here!'

Realising his reaction had startled the two soldiers, he lowered his voice slightly. 'Let's get back downstairs and help the others. The Russkies are getting ready to attack. We will need all the men we can get to hold them off.' Turning, he began to descend the stairs. Udet shrugged and slowly stepped past Meino to follow the Romanian.

Meino turned to them sharply, his face determined, 'Wait! What was up here, what was on this floor?'

Tatu stopped halfway down the staircase, glancing up at the Croatian, he sighed, 'Look, it doesn't matter now. We are cut off. Petru is alone with the other men down there, we need to help them and hold off the Russians now, not waste time up...' His voice trailed off as the bolts 'clunked' against their metal housings. His eyes moving abruptly to the locked double doors.

Udet had stopped and turned to observe the conversation. His slowly raised his rifle, pointing towards the doors, his eyes widening, 'The doors moved! Someone is behind them!'

A volley of bullets from the floors below echoed up the stairwell, then an explosion as one of the last grenades detonated on the ground floor, the defenders attempting to deter the gathering Russian forces from rushing the stairs.

Tatu stepped up two stairs cautiously, raising his machine gun to point at the double doors. He indicated for the Meino and Udet to remain silent, pressing his finger to his lips, the gun in his right hand. Meino stepped back from the door carefully, wary of blocking the Romanian's line of fire.

A shuffling came from behind the thick wooden doors, then silence. Then a muffled voice from behind the thick wood cried out, 'Anyone there?'

Tatu's solemn stare broke as a grin formed across his face, his recognition of the Italian accent in the voice, 'Luca?'

Further shuffling from behind the doors, then the muffled voice again, 'No, it's Alessio. Will you open the doors please, it's freezing out here!'

Meino lowered his MP40, a sigh coming from his mouth. He stepped forward and reached up for the highest bolt at the top of the door, near the doorframe. Pulling the bolt, he reached for the other steel bolts.

Tatu spun round as he heard boots on the stairs below, a young German infantryman looking up at him from the landing below, his face excited, 'The Russians seem to be withdrawing from the ground floor, Sergeant. Perhaps we may be able to escape after all?'

Tatu looked at the man for a second, seeming to struggle with what the soldier was telling him, his eyes narrowing with suspicion, 'Withdrawing? Why?'

The soldier shrugged, 'There seems to be a lot of movement on the ground floor, but they are not attacking or even looking out. Shall we wait and try and retake the ground floor?'

Meino pulled the last bolt at the foot of the double doors and the right door slowly moved inwards, its base scraping against the floor as he forcefully yanked the wooden obstacle, the Italian pushing from the other side. Alessio slipped through the opening, his eyes glowing with achievement, the rest of his face covered by a thick scarf. The seams of his overcoat and uniform lined with frozen condensation as the warmer air from the building opposite had reacted to the outside temperature.

Freezing air drifted in through the opening, Alessio's exhaled breath was condensed from the far lower temperature outside, the cloud drifting across the landing. His five feet nine frame covered in an Italian overcoat, he had blond hair and was unshaven. The Mediterranean looks of the twenty five year old weathered by the cold and lack of sleep, with darkened lines under his eyes.

Glancing past the Italian into the darkness, Meino patted Alessio's shoulder, 'How long have you been behind there?'

Alessio smiled, 'Not long. We found how the Russians delivered coal to the generators on this floor, it came from the next building. We found a hatch on the other side. There is a simple conveyor that links the two buildings, it's not very safe for the weight of a man, but it will do if you men want to escape?'

Udet turned to the Romanian Quartermaster next to him, seeing the man was distracted, 'What do you think, Tatu?'

The older Romanian seemed deep in thought, then he jerked his head round to face Udet. 'I think we need to get out of here quickly, the Russians are planning a surprise for us I suspect.' His face becoming stern, his hand running over his moustache, 'Udet, Meino, get over the link if you can. I will get the others from downstairs. Be quick, I am not sure we have much time.'

With this he turned and started descending the stairs two at a time, his hob nailed boots crunching on the broken plaster and debris on the steps. As he reached the perplexed German infantryman on the landing below, he slapped the man's shoulder, 'You go too, get across to the next building now!' Then he disappeared from view, descending the cement steps.

Chapter Two: Beneath the Stars

Udet gingerly stepped out through the sturdy double doors, moving to the side of the conveyor. The blast of cold air that hit him almost took his breath away, the freezing temperature catching in his throat and making him instinctively attempt to hold his breath. Pulling his scarf up over his mouth, he cleared his throat, the cold air stinging his insides as it warmed to his body temperature.

The doors had concealed a relatively wide offloading section about two metres in depth, with a rope tied across the edges at waist height as a makeshift safety measure. Beyond this platform was a narrow wooden ledge to enable labourers to step forward and grasp items from the belt if it stopped. The cement platform was covered in frozen flattened snow, trampled by Alessio as he attempted to gain access through the doors.

Opposite him, some twelve metres away across the alleyway between the two buildings, Luca raised his hand in greeting. The Italian crouched outside the hatch on the narrow ledge on the other side, his rifle held pointing down towards the sewer exit below.

Studying the basic machine, he realised the conveyor was hand operated from the other building. The simple conveyor belt approximately half a metre wide, with worn rectangular wooden sections attached to the top and base of the extended mechanism. Small wooden strips lined the outside of each section, providing some edges for the bags of coal or supplies, preventing them from slipping or falling to the ground below as the operator in the opposite building wound the handles, the conveyor then slowly moving items between the buildings. The conveyor had obviously been used frequently as there were many cracked and half broken strips around the sections that the coal or transferring items would rest upon.

Slowly leaning forward, Udet peered over the edge of the platform, his eyes blinking in the stinging cold. He swallowed hard as he looked down the five stories into the dim light below, just making out the snow covered debris on the ground at the foot of the storage tower. Dispersing smoke slowly drifted across the ground below him, reducing his view of the broken sewer roof beneath. Stepping back, he glanced across the divide again at Luca before looking right over the river. In the distance across the snow covered Volga bend and freezing river, he could see the fires burning in the city beyond, the tracer fire rising into the air above the ravaged battlefield. Shells burst above the city streets and on the buildings below as Russian artillery fired from the eastern bank into the lower part of the city.

Alessio stepped out through the half open doorway, distracting him from the view over the river bend. The Italian turned to the younger German, 'Best get across, Udet. The longer you wait, the colder your body will become. There is a chance you might fall if you get too cold.'

Udet looked at the Italian, nodding slowly. 'I understand, how did you get across?'

Alessio looked out over the river, 'Best go on your hands and knees, the conveyor shakes as you go across. I think they will slowly wind it towards them as you cross, this may help. Grasp the sides carefully and not for too long, the wood is virtually frozen now.'

Udet looked back across the divide between the buildings again, his apprehension rising as he lifted his rifle onto his shoulder. Pulling his gloves at the base with each hand, he slowly lowered himself, grasping either side of the conveyor on the wooden strips. As he raised his right knee across onto the first wooden plate on the conveyor, he felt the cold from the wood seep through his uniform and felt underwear.

The condensation in his breath was now beginning to congeal on the scarf over his mouth, the clouds of exhaled air swirling around his face as he forced his breath through the freezing material.

Behind him, Alessio leant forward, his voice lowered to a hiss, 'Hold on tight comrade, they will start to move the conveyor in a second.' Leaning back, the Italian waved to Luca opposite. Udet glanced up, seeing Luca turn and speak through the open hatch opposite, at the end of the conveyor.

He tightened his grip on the wooden strips, the conveyor jolting as the cogs started to turn, startling him as he moved slowly forward on the belt. Inside the building opposite, two soldiers wound the thick metal handles anti-clockwise, the belt slowly moving in response, the cogs and wheels squealing under the strain.

As Udet began to move out high above the alleyway, he felt the conveyor strain below him. The worn ageing machinery struggling to support his weight. Moving into the middle of the expanse below, he closed his eyes as he felt the conveyor begin to sway slightly, then move gradually up and down with the motion. The wood creaked beneath him as he tried to shift his weight slightly to adjust to the movement, then the swaying of the conveyor settled as Alessio sat on the end behind him, straddling the belt with his legs.

As the conveyor movement reduced, he stole a glance through his clenched eyes, seeing Luca now only some five metres away, the Italian's concentration on the ground below, his rifle raised. Udet closed his eyes again, the fear rising within him. Had the Italian seen something? Was he visible from the street opposite and the Russians about to open fire? His feeling of isolation and exposure to fire now intense, he held his breath.

Muffled firing inside the building behind him made him flinch, his cold hands tightening on the wooden strips he grasped. Then gunshots echoed through the hatch before him, the soldiers in the building firing out at movement in the streets opposite the building.

His body instinctively jumped again as Luca's hand grasped his back, the grip tightening around his collar and steadying him on the conveyor. Udet opened his eyes in response, the freezing air biting at his exposed vision. Then he ducked as the hatch opened up before him, his body moving forward into the darkness beyond. He breathed deeply in relief as the conveyor jolted to a halt. Slowly lifting his legs, he stepped down off the wooden platform onto the cement floor of the second storage tower.

Turning he saw Luca look through the hatch, staring into his face, his voice strained, 'Get on the handles, Udet. One of the men will come out here, I am freezing now.' The Italian coughed. Beyond the Italian through the darkened gloom, he saw Meino cautiously lower himself onto the conveyor opposite, his MP40 slung over his shoulder.

Luca glanced back down to the street, hearing the 'puffs' of further smoke grenades as they exploded around the base of the building next door. Through the swirling mist that rose from the grenades, he saw shadowy figures of some Russian infantry retreating from the adjacent storage tower.

Amongst the trees on the eastern bank across the frozen expanse of the Volga River bend, a young Russian sniper fastened the second thickly insulated waterproof sleeping bag around his body. The temperature was dropping further in the small wood he was concealed in, a thin mist creeping through the trees and foliage he had chosen for a hiding place. Having just consumed his rations for the evening, he adjusted the branches around his body to provide further insulation against the creeping frost. Leaning forward, he retrieved his binoculars and began to slowly survey the bank opposite for any potential targets.

Chapter Three: In the shortness of time.

Tatu had descended the stairs quickly, staying back from the edges in case of enemy fire from below. As he descended the floors, he shouted into the rooms to the sides, urging any soldiers to climb the stairs behind him, to reach the potential escape route. Only two soldiers had answered his call, one Romanian and a German Military policemen, their faces ashen as they had emerged from the large storage rooms they had been firing out from.

Reaching the landing between the third and second floor, he had become more cautious, slowing his descent. Turning the last bend in the staircase, he stepped carefully over the body of a German policeman, the blood seeping out from beneath his helmet. The man was lying face down and had been hit in the face as he leant out to fire at the attackers below. Tatu had started to lean towards the wall, his caution for what was below and rising tiredness from the descent causing him to breathe heavily.

Glancing over the metal hand rail quickly, he spotted a Russian soldier duck his head back through the doorway on the ground floor below him, the man trying to see if the Germans and Romanians above were still defending the first floor. Rifle bullets whipped around the doorframe as the defenders fired at the Russian, the plaster splattering across the opening as the bullets impacted on the wooden surround, the walls streaked black from the explosions.

A Romanian soldier crouched on the next set of stairs looked up at him as he turned the corner. The man seemed quite young, almost childlike in the large uniform, helmet and overcoat. His eyes were wide in near panic, and Tatu noticed the tight grip he had on his rifle, his nerves tense. The quartermaster passed him slowly, walking between him and the metal rail. As he passed, he indicated for the soldier to go upstairs. The young man needing little encouragement, he rose and ran up the staircase behind him.

Reaching the second floor landing, Tatu saw another Romanian on the next set of stairs. The man leant against the wall holding his shoulder, his eyes closed, blood seeping through his clenched fingers. Tatu sighed, passing the man slowly, he turned and saw Petru on the next staircase, his rifle aimed at the doorway below. On the next landing, two German infantrymen were crouched next to the metal rail, their rifles held menacingly, pointing down into the stairwell.

Tatu stopped on the turn in the staircase just above Petru, drawing breath, his face flushed with exertion. Gulping air, he glanced over the rail down to the ground floor before speaking, his voice distorted from his heavy breathing, 'Time to leave now.'

Petru glanced from his weapon, a slight smile passing his lips as he recognised his friend, 'We can't just let them in Tatu.'

The Romanian quartermaster indicated to the two Germans below him, raising his voice, 'You two, get up to the fifth floor, we will hold here!'

The Germans looked up startled. Regaining their composure, they nodded in response and backed away from the metal rail before starting to hastily climb the staircase behind Petru. As they passed Tatu, he indicated to the wounded man on the next staircase, 'Take him with you and check the upper floors for survivors.'

'Yes Sergeant,' one of the Germans uttered as he passed, crouching down to help the wounded Romanian to his feet as they ascended the next flight.

Tatu stepped down two of the concrete steps to stand next to his friend, taking his machine gun from its strap and resting it on the metal hand rail. 'We will give them a couple of minutes, then slowly make our way up, Petru. There is a possible way of escape now.'

Petru nodded, not taking his eyes from the doorway below. 'I understand. Will we get out?'

Tatu paused, his mood deflated, 'I hope so, there is little time left now and perhaps too many men to get out.'

'I see.' Petru swallowed, closing his eyes for a second. 'Is Udet away? He is too young to die here.'

Tatu smiled grimly, 'I hope so, though what he will escape to, I don't know. I am beginning to think we will all be ending our days in this god forsaken city, my friend.'

A smile crossed Petru's lips, then his face hardened, 'The Russian adventure is nearly over? I don't think so, Tatu. We have come too far to give it up now.' He turned his head slightly, looking at his countryman, 'Let's get out of here, Tatu.'

Movement in the room below caused the men to freeze, raising their weapons to point at the door beneath them. Then a clicking noise from the room below and sounds of boots on the concrete floor, a light flickering inside the ground floor doorway.

Tatu' thoughts accelerated, then he grabbed Petru's shoulder, yanking him backwards. The jet of flame surging upwards from the doorway below, engulfing the handrail they had been leaning against a second earlier, the flames shooting past.

Both men turned their faces instinctively, feeling the intense heat on their cheeks and backs as the jet of flame passed them in the stairwell. As quickly as it had risen, the flame subsided, seeming to pull the air downwards as it fell.

Tatu pulled Petru upwards, his rough grip awakening his countryman from his shock. They struggled up the stairs, their backs against the wall, pushing into it. Both men trying to limit their exposure to the flamethrower below. The smell of burnt dust and plaster was overpowering, sticking in their nostrils and mouths as they struggled up the stairs. Burning plaster fragments fell from the sides of the staircase above them, down into the foot well below.

Hearing boots on the staircase below, Petru grasped the last stick grenade from his belt, twisted the base and pulled on the cord, dropping it over the landing edge as they struggled upwards. Another whoosh of flame passed them between the stairs as they moved against the wall, the roar of the chemical flame terrifying as they shielded their faces from the heat.

The explosion three floors below rocked the stairwell as the flamethrower tanks ignited, the subsequent fireball sweeping out and upwards engulfing some of the Russian soldiers on the stairs and in the foot well, their skin burnt from their bodies instantly with the intense heat. The explosion of fire rose three floors between the stairs, burning the soldiers on either side as they advanced.

Tatu pushed Petru in front of him as they carefully stepped over the outstretched body on the landing and began to climb the steps to the fourth floor. Plaster dust and burning debris fell all around them as they struggled on. Tatu turned, raising his jacket across them as he glimpsed the flames rise past them in the stairwell. They turned their backs, shielding themselves behind the thick leather overcoat, feeling the heat on their uniforms. Then Tatu cautiously looked out through the fingers of his hands as the fireball descended, having burnt the fuel remaining in the flamethrower tanks. The intoxicating smell of the chemicals burning mixed with scorched flesh filled their mouths and nostrils, almost making them retch. The screams of the soldiers below echoed up and down the stairs, the chilling sounds of the wounded spurring them on, upwards.

In between the screams, Tatu could hear shouting below, the barked orders to leave the building quickly filtering between the cries of the wounded. The hairs on the back of his neck twitching as his mind realised the possible intention of the Russian commander below. His recollection of his experiences in Odessa and other towns where he had fought this enemy, the final outcome being usually anything but favourable.

Tatu looked up as they ascended the steps to the fourth floor, seeing Alessio glance down over the metal rail, the fear on his face. Straining to shout, the Romanian coughed, then pointed to Alessio as he struggled to clear his throat, 'Get out now!'

The Italian disappeared from view as Tatu followed Petru onto the fourth floor, their boots smacking against the cement as they propelled themselves forward. Grasping the hand rail, they pulled themselves up onto the next flight of stairs, their chests heaving with the physical strain.

As they turned on the landing, Tatu's heart dropped as he saw five soldiers on the top floor, the Italian, Alessio struggling to get the Romanian and German infantrymen and policemen to understand his urgency. Before him were two wounded men, the Romanian holding his shoulder, his sleeve now covered in blood. Next to him, the German soldier Tatu recognised from the ground floor, the side of his face bandaged heavily after the burns from the flamethrower in the sewer, his face having swelled up considerably. Alongside them stood two other soldiers, one Romanian, the other German, their rifles in their hands. He shouted in frustration, his voice booming in the enclosed space at the top of the stairs, 'Get across now, there is no time!'

Alessio turned, his adrenalin rising with the shouting of the Romanian quartermaster, 'There is still someone on the conveyor! The cogs have frozen, we need to climb across now!'

Tatu rounded the top of the stairs behind Petru, noting the silence from the stairs below them, realising the Russians must be out of the building. Pushing Petru forward, his voice urgent, 'Get them across Petru!'

Petru turned to his side and slipped through the doors, then stopped as the freezing air enveloped him, the conveyor before him leaning on the ice covered ledge.

Tatu moved forward, glancing through the doorway. Looking across the dark divide, he saw Udet through the gloom, the young German with his foot on the conveyor, aiming his rifle down towards the street. Between them, an infantryman was slowly and cautiously progressing across the belt on his hands and knees.

Tatu hissed across the divide, 'Move faster!' Watching as the young man half looked over his shoulder, then attempted to move his body quicker, Udet outstretching his gloved hand towards him, beckoning the frightened soldier forward.

Tatu pointed to the conveyor, but Petru was already moving to place his weight on top, steadying the narrow platform. Petru turned as he saw the infantryman on the other side disappear through the hatch, 'Tatu, we will have to run across!'

Tatu turned back into the stairwell, 'Who's first? We need to go now!'

The German and Romanian soldiers looked at each other, then Alessio pushed past them, 'I suppose it best be me, I have already gone over once. Let's see if the Italians can pull you out of this mess.'

A gunshot from the other side of the alleyway startled them, Udet having fired into the street at the end, 'They are taking up positions, get moving....now!

Alessio pushed past Tatu in the doorway, patting him on the shoulder as he slipped out into the cold. The Italian moved to the side of Petru, stepping gingerly onto the first panel, the conveyor lowering under his weight as his body rose onto the wooden sheets. Moving his feet to either side of the section he was stood on until they touched the strip, he stepped forward onto the next section, the conveyor creaking under his weight. Waiting for the conveyor to settle, he then moved his other leg forward.

Tatu smiled briefly, turning abruptly to the men in the fifth floor stairwell, 'Who's next?'

The two unwounded men shook their heads, the Romanian stepping forward, his face determined, 'This is madness! We will never all get across, I am going downstairs to surrender!' He turned, starting to descend the steps, the nails on his boots clicking on the cement. His face half turned as he descended, 'This is over now!'

Tatu frowned, his exasperation rising, 'Are you mad? The Russkies will shoot you the moment they see you.' Seeing the German infantryman turn and begin to follow the Romanian down the stairs, his voice escalated, 'They are probably getting ready to blow up the building! That's what they do!'

The Romanian soldier disappeared from view, descending down to the fourth floor landing. The German soldier stopped briefly on the landing to look up at

Tatu, tears in his eyes, 'I think we have lost Sergeant.' Then he turned and started to descend the steps moving out of sight.

Tatu shook his head, 'Fools.' Turning to the two wounded men, his eye brows raised, 'You two having second thoughts, or can we go now?'

Petru's voice drifted through the open doorway, 'He's nearly across Tatu, next man now!'

The wounded and bandaged German stepped past Tatu and out through the doorway, joining Petru on the ledge, a cold breeze sweeping in from across the Volga.

The wounded Romanian stepped forward, clutching his shoulder, his unshaven face serious, 'I am not going to make it. I am bleeding heavily and will only slow you down. I will go downstairs and plead with the Russians, try and delay them.'

Tatu nodded in defeat, his eyes dropping. Placing a comforting hand on the man's uninjured shoulder, 'I understand, go quickly then, there is no time left.' The soldier saluted painfully, and turned to descend the stairs. Tatu returned the salute as the man turned to look one last time at him, his face ashen. Tatu nodded to him, 'Good Luck.'

The man forced a smile, 'I hope you see our Romania again sergeant, I think my war ends here. You can't save everyone.' He nodded once, his face grim, then turned his head and started to descend the cement steps, disappearing from view.

Tatu stood for a second, looking at the empty staircase, then turned and slipped through the open double doors. As he stood on the ledge, he felt the cold air sweep across his features, his body slowly adapting to the temperature as he breathed in through his nose. He looked across the alleyway, seeing the wounded German half way across the conveyor. Petru turned slightly to acknowledge him, 'How many more, Tatu?'

The Romanian quartermaster glanced down at his countryman, his voice lowered and distant as his mind cleared, 'Just you and I now my friend, let's get away from this place....'

Petru nodded, noticing the German approach the hatch across the conveyor, 'Your turn, Tatu, time for you to leave.'

Tatu shook his head, 'No, you first my friend. I will hold the belt steady.'

Petru's eyes narrowed, his voice rising, 'No! You are heavier, get on the belt now.'

Tatu's eyes widened in surprise at the outburst. Shaking his head slowly in disbelief, he realised there was little time to argue. 'Very well comrade, you be right behind me!'

Their eyes met as Tatu stepped forward and placed a boot on the first wooden plate, Petru smiled briefly, 'Get across quickly my friend, it's time to leave.' Tatu lifted the strap of his machine gun over his head, pushing the weapon onto his back.

Stepping forward, Tatu swallowed and held his breath as he heard the conveyor beneath him creak with the strain. He slid his boots forward, wary that the wooden panels were now covered in a heavy frost. He looked forward, seeing Udet in front of him, just over ten metres away. The young German beckoning him with his gloved hand, hissing at him, 'Keep your eyes on your footing, Tatu.'

Tatu looked down again, carefully lifting his right boot forward onto the next panel, testing its strength then bringing his other foot to join the first. He could feel his breathing, deep in his chest, the cold air drifting into his lungs. His heart was beating hard, a sickly feeling rising from his stomach. The outside world seemed surreally distant as he concentrated solely on his footing, the movement of the ageing machine beneath him as it reacted to his weight.

Distant shouting in Russian from the ground on the left startled him slightly, then a burst of machine gun fire. He stopped briefly, realising his arms were now outstretched to his sides, in an attempt to provide additional balance.

Looking back at the panels beneath his boots, he stepped forward again, the wood creaking beneath his weight. Then he slid his left boot onto the next panel, a cracking sound from beneath him as his weight was transferred from his right boot onto the panel below his left. He licked his lips in fear as he stepped forward again, the conveyor shaking slightly at the movement.

Stepping again across the next panel, the wood beneath him moved slightly, then settled as his full weight bore down upon it, glancing up, he reached out and grasped Udet's outstretched hand, stepping across the last wooden panel onto the ledge, he crouched down and slipped though the hatch into the second storage tower.

Petru breathed heavily in relief, seeing his friend reach safety. Then the apprehension within him began to rise dramatically, his vertigo beginning to escalate the fear in his stomach. He rose slowly from the end of the conveyor, his breath becoming rapid as he realised he had to face the walk the others had achieved, across the conveyor high above the alleyway. Picking up his rifle from the ledge, he slung the strap over his helmeted head, the rifle now resting across his back.

Breathing sharply, the cold in his muscles beginning to complain, he stepped back from the ageing and worn conveyor, briefly looking over the fires and fighting in the city to his right. He watched as a shell burst in the distance, the bright light flashing at the explosion, then the burning debris falling to the ground.

Another burst of machine gun fire from the left startled him from the scene over the city, the returning rifle shots from the building opposite at Russian infantry in the streets focussing his mind on the job at hand. Looking across the divide, he saw Udet staring at him, his eyes wide I desperation, 'Come on Petru, we are out of time!' The young German hissed across the alleyway.

Petru turned, facing the double doors, his fear almost intoxicating, and his mind conflicted. He briefly considered running down the stairs, trying to get out through the building, but realised almost immediately this was unrealistic, not knowing where the Russian infantry were.

Bullets flew through the alleyway below him, a couple ricocheting off the walls. He swallowed, feeling complete fear in his chest, his heart beating faster with every second that passed. His mind fought against the fear, the terror even of his childhood nightmares. He had often tried to overcome his fear of heights by standing on balconies, or the tops of buildings as a boy and youth, but this had just added to his phobia.

He lifted his hand, placing his glove on the rough, weathered thick wooden door in front of him. The urge to stay where he was had become almost overwhelming, the terror in his mind of the open expanse behind him becoming heightened.

In the distance he could hear the desperation in the German voice calling to him, 'Petru! Petru, come on. Move across now!' Slowly he turned, tears forming in his eyes as he resolved to face the fear that had plagued him all his life.

Udet had started to become apprehensive at the Romanian's lack of movement, then as the man turned in the darkness across the alleyway, his concern rose. Their eyes met as Petru forced himself to look across the divide, his inner mental struggle obvious to the young German. Then the stare was broken as Tatu thrust his head through the hatch, his voice stern, 'Petru, get across here now!'

Petru glanced up and across at his countryman, the fear spreading through him as his muscles tensed. An explosion below them in the sewer broke his inaction, forcing his boot onto the conveyor, he swallowed and pushed his body forward.

A further muffled explosion came from the other side of the building behind him, then another. He stepped out over the alleyway, his breath held. Another explosion below in the sewer, then one in the building behind him, his mind cleared to form one thought, 'The Russians were about to demolish the building, his time to escape had nearly run out.'

Adrenalin forced its way through his body, the fear being overcome briefly as he realised he had only seconds left. Forcing his eyesight onto the wooden panels beneath his feet, he stepped out onto across the conveyor, his movement becoming more rapid. The conveyor shuddered as another muffled explosion behind him in the building unsettled the foundations, then he felt the belt move. He stepped further, bending his knees to counter the belt shaking, then he stepped across two panels, his body pushing him forward. Smoke and dust rose from the open sewer roof below, rising towards him as he stepped again, then he pushed his body forward, his boots stepping along the shaking conveyor.

He felt the wood beneath him shake as another explosion from behind him unsettled the building, he felt his body move further, his boots pushing onto the panels below and in front of him. His senses blurred as a large explosion from the building behind and another below sent a ball of fire through the sewer, propelled out through the tunnel and over the river.

Looking at the panels below him, he forced himself to focus as he lifted his boot and placed it quickly on the next panel, then the next, then he saw another pair of boots come into view, an outstretched gloved hand as the conveyor beneath his footing began to fall away. A loud escalating rumbling behind him, becoming almost deafening, the intensely high pitched sound of metal and wood stretching then breaking, his footing slipping. He threw himself forward, his hands outstretched, flailing to grasp something as he felt his body falling downwards.

Dust and smoke filled his vision, blinding him as he grasped something in front of him, his gloves slipping slightly. He felt the back of his jacket tense as a hand grasped the material, two further hands grasping his jacket by the shoulders, then his legs swung forward, the front of his boots and legs hitting the side of the building.

He gasped, the pain spreading through his legs, his eyes closed tightly, then he felt his body rise as the rough grips on his overcoat lifting him upwards. His boots slid on the wall as he tried to push upwards, the hands pulling him up the wall as bullets whipped through the alleyway, the Russian infantry emerging from their cover after the series of explosions.

As he stole a look through his clenched eyes, he saw Tatu and Udet's faces just above him through the swirling dust and smoke, the strain of holding his weight clear in their expressions, their eyes closed. Then his body rose up as he was pulled forward. Opening his eyes again, he saw a black hole before him as he was pulled through the open hatch into the darkened room beyond.

Udet breathed heavily, alone on the ledge. His heart was beating hard in his chest, the exertion and shock from what had happened taxing his body in the freezing temperatures. He looked down at the broken conveyor beside him, the belt having snapped and shattered as the support on the other end had fallen away. He had held the wooden frame around the hatch as he had grabbed Petru's greatcoat, almost falling forward with the weight until Tatu had grasped his countryman's shoulders.

Below him, the dust and smoke concealed the smashed machinery, obscuring most of his vision. As he looked across the alleyway his eyes widened, the dust in the air beginning to fall away. The building opposite had collapsed completely, the bitter breeze from the east now unobstructed, the freezing air enveloping him in his exposed position. Looking down the alleyway through the smoke and settling dust, he saw Russian infantry emerging from cover in the distance, then he heard Tatu call to him from inside.

Across the river bend, on the frozen east side of the river, the sniper's search for targets had been disrupted completely by the explosions on the other side of the river. He had panned his binoculars around just in time to see flames shooting out of the sewer tunnels. Then smoke and dust had obscured his entire view of that side of the river. As the dust slowly cleared, he spotted a lone German infantryman crouched on a ledge on the side of a building through the mist and smoke. Not believing his luck, he had double checked that the figure was indeed German. Realising an opportunity, he quickly reached for his rifle, raising the scope to his eye and squinting through the sight. Moving the rifle across to where he had seen the soldier, his finger across the trigger, his excitement rose. He sighed, the air drifting from his body, the weapon steady.

Slowly he lowered the Mosin Nagrant rifle from his eye, shaking his head. The German was gone.

Chapter Four: The Chase......

'Hase' had sat under the pier for some time, his body beginning to ache with the cold. As the time had passed, his mind had become more conflicted, his consideration that the longer he waited the more alone he felt. The distant gunfire from both sides of him around the river bend making him feel as though he was not contributing, that his comrades may have needed him. He thought of Hausser, had the commander reached safety and forgotten him perhaps? The young German's commander's instruction for him to wait at this point for the others seemed a distant memory now as he sat alone on the frozen snow, his rifle in his gloved hands.

He had pulled the Russian balaclava he had saved around his face, re-adjusting the scarf he had round his mouth as protection against the creeping cold. The freezing breeze slipping through the pillars of the jetty seemed to bite at his flesh beneath the uniform and Russian felt underwear.

He could just make out the subdued chatter of the Russian sentries above him, the men complaining about the cold and the state of their rations. He determined there must be three of them at least, with two speaking mostly, the other adding occasional observations to the others conversation.

His senses had heightened as the gunfire from the storage towers had seemed to escalate, but then had died down, the shooting inside the buildings becoming more muffled. Concern rose within him as he looked out down the snow and river wall to the east, seeing no movement, his comrades still perhaps fighting in the towers? When the shooting subsided more, he had become deeply concerned, had they been killed? Had the Russians taken the towers? Were his friends now prisoners?

He had tensed as the explosions had begun, initially a few distant 'crumps' behind the buildings, then he had stood up, ducking his head below the pier as a larger explosion occurred. His eyes widened in shock as he saw the fireball shoot out from where the sewer pipes must be, then his mouth opened in awe as the storage tower further from him had shook, then collapsed inwards, the dust cloud and smoke billowing outwards and upwards.

He became more confused, should he leave and try to join Hausser's group or go back and investigate? Then the voices above him became louder as the Russian sentries had ventured out onto the pier to investigate the explosions. The sounds of their boots on the thick wooden beams above echoing around him as they moved. With the Russians above him, he decided to wait a little longer, emerging from the safety of the pier now would probably alert them to his presence.

As he stared back down the river wall, he strained his eyed to try and see any movement, the pier between his position and the storage towers restricting his view. He moved from side to side to try and see between the pier supports, the darkness and gloom reducing his vision. Then his heart leapt, seeing a figure emerge from the area of the second remaining tower and run along the river wall towards him. Then he saw another figure emerge behind the first, then another. Finally he saw a tall stocky figure emerge wearing a large cumbersome jacket, the figure waving for the other men to move quickly. A smile crossed his face as he recognised the silhouette of Tatu through the dim light.

The figures were running towards him, their bodies crouched against the river wall. As the men in the distance began to negotiate the supports of the first pier, a charge of excitement ran through his body. His adrenalin began to race as he realised the Russians above could not determine whether the approaching figures were German or Russian. Hearing the Russian sentries ready their weapons, he desperately thought how to warn the approaching men.

Turning, he slipped across the snow, making his way to the back of the pier. Looking around desperately, he spotted a ladder leading up to the pier surface attached to a support pillar half way along the jetty. He carefully approached the ladder, hearing the Russian voices above become heightened as they tried to decide whether to open fire or not.

As he pulled himself up the ladder, he felt the cold of the steps through his gloves, the exposed structure freezing in the temperatures. Reaching the top, he peered over cautiously, seeing the three Russian soldiers all had their backs to him, two knelt on the pier slowly raising their rifles. Glancing right, he checked the alleyway leading to the pier was empty and rose silently from the ladder.

As he crouched on top of the pier, he realised the men on the snow below were only about one hundred metres away, their urgency to escape and the darkness preventing them from seeing the Russian sentries on the top of the wooden pier. The adrenalin surged through him, his excitement rising as he briefly considered what to do, then running his tongue across his lips he stepped forward silently.

As he moved, he slowly raised his rifle, aiming at the furthest sentry. As he cautiously approached, one of the sentries turned to his countrymen, 'They must be enemy soldiers! We should fire!'

'Hase' raised his rifle higher and pulled the trigger, the weapon jolting in his hands. The furthest Russian sentry was hit just behind his shoulder, the bullet shattering his ribcage and collar bone, he spun round with the impact and fell backwards off the pier, rolling down the snow bank below.

The nearest Russian turned sharply, shouting an alarm as he realised the impending attack. As he turned, 'Hase' was almost behind him, bringing the butt of his rifle up hard under the soldier's chin, hearing a crack as he broke his jaw and knocked him back unconscious. The soldier falling backwards roughly onto the pier's surface.

The third Russian spun round, his rifle at waist height, raising it to point at 'Hase'. The men's eyes met as 'Hase' closed in on him, knocking the man's rifle back to the side with his own and hitting the man in the chest with his rifle butt, winding him. The Russian's rifle clattered onto the pier and he fell backwards grasping his torso.

'Hase' ducked as sporadic fire from the riverbank flew over his head, the approaching men alerted by the gunshot. He fell to the pier's surface as the fire intensified, seeing the Russian soldier he had just attacked scramble away on his hands and knees towards the alleyway.

Breathing heavily, he lay there with his face on the cold wooden beams of the pier, then he shouted hoarsely, 'Tatu, it's me, Hase! Don't shoot!'

There was a short pause as two more shots echoed out across the riverbank, the bullets flying harmlessly above him, then he heard the Romanian Quartermaster's voice, 'Hase? Don't shoot men, he is with us!'

A brief smile spread across 'Hase's' lips as he slowly pushed himself up onto his elbows, seeing the group of men hurriedly approaching the pier. Then his eyes narrowed as he looked back down the riverbank beyond the first pier, seeing movement in the darkness. As he watched, many more men ran out onto the snow where the original group had emerged. Two dropped to their knees and raised their weapons, his mouth dry, he tried to call out, the sound muffled, 'Enemy infantry!'

Shots rang out from further down the river, the bullets hitting the pier. 'Hase' grasped his rifle tightly, pulling the bolt back to push another bullet up into the chamber. Raising the weapon, he moved his head to the sight on the rifle and pulled the trigger, the weapon recoiling backwards into his shoulder. As the soldier he had aimed at fell backwards onto the snow, he heard shouting to his right, the escaped sentry calling for help.

Pushing himself backwards across the pier, his body sliding across the cold wood, he heard muffled gunfire from beneath the structure as the Germans and Romanians turned to face their pursuers. Glancing round, he saw the top of the ladder and pushed his body back towards it. Feeling the handle of the ladder on his boot he glanced right, seeing silhouettes of soldiers at the end of the alleyway, his heart sank.

He swung his body over the edge of the pier, grasping the side of the ladder as he did so. He felt rough hands on his legs as he slipped down the ladder, the hands steadying him and preventing his fall. As his boots impacted on the snow, he turned round, seeing Petru's face before him, holding his shoulders. Petru's eyes seemed moist, the emotions welling within him.

'Hase' nodded to him, a lump in his throat, 'Thank you.' Petru's eyes seemed to sparkle briefly in the darkness, then he turned away, leaning against the thick pier support. As the Romanian pulled the bolt on his own rifle, he glanced round the obstruction, seeing the numerous Russian infantry in the distance.

'Hase' ran to the river wall, approaching Tatu who was ushering the men under the pier. 'There are Russians in the street above Tatu! They are coming!'

Tatu turned to face him, his eyes tired but determined, 'Thank you, young 'Hase', now run with the others, get to the next pier!' Turning back, he shouted, 'All of you run now! Stay along the wall and keep the pier top clear! There are too many of them to fight!'

'Hase' glanced back down the river wall, seeing perhaps nearly thirty Russian infantry on the snow further down the river, with more emerging behind them. He swallowed, turned and ran along the wall, hearing the firing behind him as Petru and some others fired at the Russian infantry in the distance.

Tatu walked forward, grasping the wooden ladder and stepping onto the bottom rung. Lifting himself up the steps, his PPSH machine gun in his right hand, he reached the top, the rungs frozen beneath his gloves. Glancing over the top of the pier, he saw several figures running towards them down the alley to his right. He lifted his weapon, resting the metal ammunition drum on the thick wooden surface of the pier. Squinting along the barrel, he fired a burst towards the oncoming Russian infantry. Two silhouettes fell, the rest darting to the side walls of the alleyway for cover. Grinning in satisfaction, he ducked down the ladder, hearing the distinct sound of an MP40 firing beneath the pier into the distance.

'Hase' ran along the river wall, his breath laboured and cold legs aching with the strain after his inaction. Before him, two soldiers were also running half crouched. Bullets whisked past them wide of the wall, the Russians firing from behind them. As he approached the next pier, he saw the first soldier drop to his knees, turn and raise his rifle. Recognising Udet, he ran up to him, dropping by his side to lie on the frozen snow, lifting his rifle to aim at the pier.

As he watched, Udet slapped his back, 'Good to have you back, 'Hase', now let's get away from these persistent Russians!'

As 'Hase' looked into the distance, he saw Tatu drop to the ground from the ladder, turning to beckon the men from the pier. As they turned to run, he saw a man collapse between the piers supports, the Russian bullet entering his back as he left cover. Tatu bent down briefly to examine the fallen German, then turned away, running up the slope to the wall.

'Hase' tensed as he heard shouting from above, the Russians in the building next door becoming aware of the firefight below, their view obstructed by the wall. Nudging Udet, both men backed slowly beneath the pier, glancing round as they became aware of the frozen bodies around them.

The small group was approaching them, the fleeing soldiers running half crouched along the wall. Udet fired his rifle into the distance, seeing movement around the pier in the distance. As he reloaded, 'Hase' fired, the rifle kicking back into his shoulder.

Further round the Volga bend, Nicu had just finished helping the medic carry the unconscious Leutnant Hausser and placing him on the floor of the Hanomag armoured carrier. He bent down and picked up the binoculars the commander had dropped, the firing in the streets south of him intensifying as the Russians prepared to launch a counter attack.

As he lifted the glasses to his eyes, he narrowed his eyes to scan the riverbank. Seeing figures in the snow, he scanned along the bank to determine the situation. Seeing the Russians looking out from the buildings above the pier, he lowered the glasses, his adrenalin rising as he realised the fleeing group would be exposed to fire from the buildings as they turned the bend further in the river.

He glanced round desperately, seeing a German officer at the other side of the narrow street, outside an open doorway. Shouting to him, the man looked up from the wounded soldier he was talking to, a puzzled expression on his face, not understanding Nicu's shout in Romanian. Nicu looked through the binoculars briefly once more, then turned and ran to the officer, desperation on his face.

Tatu reached the last pier, ducking under the gap between the roof and the first support. He froze as he heard a thud above, then an explosion, dust and ice dropping from the underneath of the pier surface. Shaking his head, he realised the Russians above were dropping grenades from the windows, unable to see the targets below.

Another grenade bounced onto the ice before them, then rolled down the slope from the wall before exploding, showering the soldiers with iced snow and dirt. Raising his weapon he fired a burst towards the pier to the east, seeing Russian infantry massing amongst the pier supports.

The last group reached the pier as another explosion echoed around them, the grenade blasting above them on the pier's surface. Tatu looked around quickly, realising the next part of the escape route was exposed to fire from the buildings above. His stomach twisted as he looked back towards the previous pier, seeing three bodies lying in the snow. There seemed to be no way out now.

He turned, his face screwed in desperation, 'Take cover, we have to hold them here!'

Another grenade bounced down the iced slope, rolling down the slope to explode on the ice that lead out to the river. Tatu glanced around the men huddled beneath the pier in the dark, crouched between some frozen bodies. He paused slightly, his despair rising as he realised the corpses were of children.

He pushed his eyes from the bodies, the sadness filtering into his thoughts. Forcing himself to count, he estimated, there were approximately thirteen or fourteen soldiers under the pier, two of which seemed to be wounded. Tatu sighed, pushing the picture of childhood innocence in death from his thoughts, his mind struggling for a solution.

'Hase' fired again, the rifle shot echoing around the underside of the pier. Udet also fired, seeing a Russian soldier fall under the next pier, but also glimpsing there were a lot more behind the fallen soldier. Beyond the next pier he could see many figures on the snow, running towards them. Turning, he saw Tatu in the darkness, 'We have to go Tatu, there are too many of them!'

Petru leant out from one of the supports, seeing a Russian infantryman above the previous pier leaning out to fire. He fired at one, the bullet hitting the wall before the Russian, the man ducking back, his face scratched from the flying cement the bullet had caused.

Tatu was mentally struggling for the solution, his mind darting from idea to idea. Then he turned, shouting, 'Some of you, get along the wall towards that opening.' He raised his hand to point at the opening in the river wall, some one hundred and fifty metres way. 'Stay low and watch the windows above us, they will be able to fire on you when you turn the bend further along the river.'

Another grenade bounced off the pier surface, rolling down the iced snow to explode at the foot of the slope, the soldiers ducking their heads instinctively. Meino patted two of the defenders backs and ushered them with him, beginning to run along the iced snow next to the wall towards the bend in the river.

Tatu turned to Petru desperately, 'Drag the frozen bodies up and build a barricade with them, that's all we have!'

Petru's eyes widened in shock, then he nodded in the darkness, reaching out for the first corpse, about a metre from him.

Bullets whipped around the pier supports and a scream echoed around them as one of the soldiers fell backwards, clutching his stomach.

Tatu shook his head, realising it was only a matter of time before the Russian machine gunners arrived at the previous pier, that then their escape would really be over. He turned, panic rising within him as another grenade exploded above them. 'Udet, Petru, 'Hase' stay with me, the rest make your way along the wall. Good Luck!'

Alessio and a Romanian soldier crouched down, grasping and dragging the wounded man with them, the rest turned and ran from the pier as another grenade bounced down the slope. One man fell to his knees, clutching his leg, the Russian rifle bullet piercing his thigh, Luca and the man next to him grabbing his arm and half dragging him away.

Petru pulled the third frozen corpse up the slope, tears streaming down his face at the task. He realised the children, the eldest in their early teens, were all dead, but the gruesome task was beginning to overwhelm his emotions.

'Hase' and Udet fired in unison, aiming at the underside of the pier further back down the bank. Bullets splattered onto the pier supports and platform as the Russians returned fire, the defenders ducking in behind their prospective pillars.

Tatu looked round again, seeing Meino had stopped the escaping men at the furthest point he could without exposing them to fire from above. They were some fifty metres away, before the final bend in the river wall. The Croatian was getting the men to lie along the wall, aiming their weapons towards the group under the pier, a final defensive position perhaps. Looking further along the wall, Tatu felt defeat rising from his stomach as he saw the distance to the ladder was too great. The hundred metres remaining too far for any of them to achieve against such a strong Russian force firing from three different points. He glanced back along the wall, seeking a closer escape point, but there was not one. The only street nearer, adjacent to the escape route, had no gap in the wall, there was no ladder and the wall was too high.

Another grenade bounced down the slope in front of him, rolling out onto the ice and exploding. He looked around, seeing Petru pull another frozen body towards the front of the defenders. Bullets sprayed around the pier structure as the first Russian DP-28 machine gun opened fire from the pier further along the river bank. The defenders ducking behind pillars as the bullets thudded into the pier supports and frozen corpses they cowered behind.

Tatu bit his lip as he realised the futility of their position. The escape route out of reach and the defenders pinned down, the probability of escape now worsening. He strained his ears, hearing the distant 'Hurrah' as the Russian infantry emerged from the next pier, their advance now covered by machine gun fire, the defenders unable to fire back effectively.

Then he froze as he heard a machine gun firing from behind him, glancing round, he saw the top of the Hanomag emerge above the gap in the river wall, the front mounted MG34 machine gun spraying bullets down the riverbank past them. Startled, his vision moved along the wall, seeing the turret of a Panzer III tank appear in the adjacent street, then shudder as it fired over their heads. The 'whoosh' of the shell passing over the pier and hitting the wall of one of the buildings, the explosion throwing shell fragments and debris onto the Russian infantry below.

Glancing back round the pillar, he saw the first wave of Russian infantry falter as the machine gun bullets splattered across the snow in front of them, the aim short. The Russians stopped, then turned and started running back towards the next pier, another burst from the German MG34 hitting several as they ran.

He looked down at the three men with him, the grins appearing on their faces beneath their scarves, 'Let's go!' He shouted.

Rifle shots rang out as the soldiers of the German 71st Infantry Division further along the river wall fired from the streets at the buildings above them, the half-drunk Russians ducking back inside the warehouse they were in.

The four men rose from their hiding place and ran from the pier, grenades thrown out of the buildings above bouncing down the slopes next to them and rolling down the iced snow bank. The explosions spurring them on as their cold legs pushed them forward.

As he ran, Udet saw Meino gather the men up in front of them, the small group struggling with the wounded towards the ladder.

The Panzer III fired again, the smoke canister landing just short of the pier the Russians were sheltering under. The shell exploding and smoke billowing outwards, the Russian machine gunner now firing blindly towards the next pier.

As Meino ran along the wall, he heard the breach of the Panzer above 'clunk', and the gun fire again, the shell whistling out across the frozen landscape, exploding on the iced river bank near the Russian held pier.

As the small group of four soldiers ran along the wall, several more shells passed overhead, the tank now firing blind into the smoke that covered the pier further along the riverbank. Bullets whistled around them as the Russians fired back blindly through the smoke, several hitting the walls above their ducked heads.

Smoke grenades landed on the snow beside them as Meino reached the ladder on the wall, 'puffing' as they ignited, and the smoke swirling from the canisters. He stopped, pushing the cold men one by one up the ladder, then climbing it himself behind the soldiers struggling with the wounded.

As Meino reached the top, he hesitated, looking down, seeing Tatu below him at the foot of the ladder, beginning his ascent, the Romanian half covered in smoke. Turning back, Nicu grabbed his shoulder and pulled him forward, his face concerned, 'Get away from the edge, a Russian sniper has killed two infantrymen!'

Meino nodded, walking briskly behind the Hanomag, ducking his head as he heard a bullet ricochet off its metal plate. A German officer stood at the back of the carrier, indicating to another Hanomag further down the narrow street, shouting at him, 'Get your men in that carrier, we are pulling back. The Russians are about to counter attack!' He shouted officially, his face grim.

As the soldiers sat exhausted in the overcrowded carriers seats and floor, they heard the engines rev and the metal tracks grind on the cobblestones as the vehicles reversed out of the street and accelerated north, into the burning city.

Behind them, the Panzer III fired south as the Russians began to launch their counter attack. Bullets 'pinged' off the rear of the vehicle as it drove from the battlefield, the burning buildings to either side casting flickering light across the occupants within.

Most of the soldiers sat in stunned silence in the vehicle as it drove northwards, the cold and their experience numbing their personal thoughts. Tatu sat at the back of the Hanomag opposite 'Hase' looking up into the distance, seeming deep in thought. After a while he leant forward, tapping the young Russian's leg, 'Do you know what that building is?' He pointed to a tall multi-storey structure in the distance, the flash of an explosion on the outside of the building drawing his attention to it.

'Hase' turned slowly to look where the Romanian was pointing, nodding tiredly he turned back to face him, 'That's the Grain Elevator...........Hausser and I were there two months ago.'

Chapter Five: Recuperation

Hausser stirred in his deep sleep, his body aching from the strain of the last week. The fever he had experienced over the last couple of days had escalated his temperature at times, the orderly assigned to him wrapping him in blankets to protect him from the cold outside.

In the small room he had lain in, the breeze through the boarded up shattered windows had occasionally swept across his face, the cold air disturbing his deep slumber. On the occasional times he had awoken, still concussed and confused, they had forced him to drink water collected from the snow outside and boiled.

Whilst he had slept, he had been visited a number of times. The lone solitary figure sitting on the only wooden chair in the corner of the room by the door watching him. The man had a peaked nose and was in his late fifties, the hair receded over time from his head, covered by his officer's cap. He had sat smoking his looted American cigarettes continually, usually spending an hour in silence with the patient each time he visited.

Hausser lay on the floor, his bedding an assortment of worn blankets and a mattress full of straw. His pillow was a rolled army blanket, the improvised bedclothes now containing the strong odour of his days of sweating, his exposure to cold and the stresses of combat overcoming his body initially.

The military doctor had reported to the visitor that the patient required time to rest, that his body was providing this through the slumber. The doctor had stressed that the patient was initially weak after his ordeal, but that the recuperation had allowed the soldier to become healthier and stronger.

On this morning, the visitor sat as before, watching the prone soldier. As he smoked, his thoughts had drifted to the past, of a younger less experienced soldier. A man he had grown to respect and care for, despite the trials of the war and his experience contradicting this behaviour in his mind. The many campaigns and difficulties they had struggled through and overcome, albeit with setbacks, flooded through his mind. He had watched as the soldier had gained experience and the respect of his men, becoming a valued junior commander in the field.

The visitor sighed as he thought of his decision two months earlier. The strain of combat had begun to show on the young commander and he decided to post him with a couple of men to what he considered a quiet part of the front, to the south of Stalingrad to rest. The man's language skills making it easy for him to convince more senior commanders of the need to move him. It had taken a few days to gain the decision, but their confidence to release him had been sealed as the decision to move German units into the city for 'one final push' had been made. Strong commanders were needed on the flanks to bolster their weaker allies resolve, he had convinced them this was one such commander, a commander with language skills never the less.

The orderly walked briskly into the room, startling the visitor. His urgency to attend to too many casualties and wounded sparing him the usual military forms of address.

'Good morning,' the visitor stated, leaning back in his chair.

The orderly turned to face him as he knelt by the sleeping man, 'Oh, erm, sorry Major, I did not see you there. How are you today?'

The major crossed his legs, his large overcoat falling either side of his knee. 'I am fine today, lots to do, so I thought I would come here early, see how our young patient is progressing.'

The orderly nodded, wiping Hausser's face with a damp cloth. 'I think he should be awake soon, he seems quite well now, if a little undernourished. We will need to feed him when he awakes,' the orderly grinned, 'I think he will have quite an appetite.'

The major nodded, drawing on his cigarette and turning to look at the boarded window, the light from outside forcing its way through the gaps in the wooden obstructions. The sounds of distant gunfire and explosions from the nearby city drifted through the streets towards them, their position in a small factory building in the west of the city some distance from the fighting.

The orderly looked across at the Major, 'How did you find him, sir?'

The Major smiled briefly, clearing his throat, 'I sent a message to the units in the southern sector requesting immediate information on troops re-joining the city. This proved successful after a bit, I imagined he would try and get back to us.'

The orderly nodded, checking Hausser's pulse. 'I see. A bit of luck there then, it seems he has been through quite an adventure.'

The Major rose from his seat, walking towards the window and looking out through one of the gaps. Drawing on his cigarette, he blew the smoke through the wooden strips across the window, watching the cloud spiral and twist against the breeze outside. 'Escaping from one trap to another perhaps.' He replied thoughtfully, watching a wounded soldier limp across the newly fallen snow outside.

The orderly looked down at the patient, studying the man's eyes as they flickered. 'I think he may be awakening Sir.'

The major turned his head to look at the prone man, seeing his eyes flicker open, the wet cloth awakening him. 'Ah, Herr Leutnant, I am glad you could join us.' A grin beginning to form on his face as his previous deep concerns for the patient's welfare ebbed away.

Hausser struggled with his senses, the pain across the back of his head dulling his understanding. Slowly he blinked several times, the morning light cascading through the wood across the window initially painful to his sight. Breathing heavily, he looked slowly around the room, lifting his head slightly. A silhouette at the window, the dirty walls with broken plaster, the lone chair in the corner and the open doorway.

The orderly looked down on him, 'How are we today sir?'

'Wh..Where am I?' Hausser struggled to speak, his mouth very dry from the days of sleeping, his senses groggy.

The silhouette at the window turned to face him, a smoke cloud billowing across the room. 'You are near Stalingradski flight school, on the western side of the city young man. You seem to have had quite an adventure.'

Hausser blinked again, his eyes beginning to focus, 'Major Schenk? Is that you?'

'Yes it is Hausser, a surprise to see you again perhaps, but a welcome one never the less.' The major replied. 'How do you feel?'

Hausser's mind was confused, his memories beginning to crowd through his senses, 'My...my men? Where are my men?'

The orderly rose from his crouched position, 'I will get him some clean water to drink and some rations. He will need them.'

The major nodded, 'Yes, that's a start.' Turning back to Hausser he stepped forward, standing over the prone man. 'Your men are just fine. Quite a rag-tag bunch you seem to have found in the south. I have had them transferred to my.....er, your command.'

Hausser lifted his hand to his forehead, the dull pain crossing his forehead as he lowered his head onto the makeshift pillow. 'D..Did they all get away?'

The major crouched down over the young commander, 'They told me to tell you not to worry, that they all got out. Now tell me how you feel Hausser?' His voice becoming firm.

Hausser's mind cleared slightly with the Major's tone, 'I feel alright I suppose, a bit confused.'

The major nodded, retrieving a packet of cigarettes from his overcoat pocket, 'Good. I will give you the day to recover. Report to me first thing tomorrow, we need every man now, Hausser. Things are not good.'

Hausser nodded slowly, his confusion rising, 'Where will you be?'

The major smiled, placing the new cigarette between his teeth, 'Not far. The orderly will tell you later.' He leant his head as he lit the cigarette. 'You and your men have perhaps had enough rest now, I have some jobs for you to attend to.'

Hausser squinted, his eyes adjusting to the light as the major rose to his feet. 'Yes Sir. Have they rested too?'

The major stepped back, adjusting his overcoat, 'Yes my friend, they are rested, well as best they could. Now, I must go, I have work to do. I will see you tomorrow, yes?'

Hausser nodded slowly, 'Y…Yes Sir. Tomorrow first thing.'

The Major smiled, 'Good, till tomorrow then.' He turned and walked from the room, his long boots clicking on the cement floor.

The orderly passed him in the corridor, carrying a metal canteen of water and some food. Nodding to the Major he walked into the room, hearing the officer behind him, 'Feed him well medic, we will need him to be fit tomorrow, any problem with the rations, give them my name.'

The orderly turned his head sharply in reply, 'Yes S..' But the Major had gone, turning out of sight at the end of the corridor, a plume of smoke hanging in the air where he had once been.

As the orderly knelt next to the patient, Hausser lifted his head to drink from the metal canteen. Pausing before he drank, he looked up at the orderly, a curious expression on his face, 'How long was I out for?'

The orderly looked down at him, a sadness in his eyes, 'It's December the first, Herr Leutnant. I think you had better try and rest today, there will be little time for relaxing from tomorrow.' He wiped the cold wet cloth around Hausser's unshaven chin, 'Welcome to Der Kessel.'

Chapter Six: Situation Report

Hausser clicked his heels, saluting the Major by raising his right hand sharply to his helmet. 'Leutnant Hausser reporting as ordered, Sir!'

Major Schenk smiled, returning the salute, his steely grey eyes sparkling, 'Glad you could join us Hausser,' the major then turning and indicating for the officer behind him to come forward. 'You remember my adjutant, Oberleutnant Baumann?'

Hausser nodded, a smile passing his lips, 'Yes Sir.'

The major waved his hand at him in a scolding fashion, 'For heaven's sake, relax Hausser, in these circumstances we need a more friendly approach I think. I see you have shaved and had a wash...good, it will freshen you up. How's the head?'

Hausser shifted his stance uncomfortably at the scrutiny, seeing the major grin as he realised, 'Still a little sore, Sir. I am bandaged under my helmet.'

The major's grin reverted to a smile, 'Good, nearly fighting fit then, now let's not get too much of the holiday spirit, shall we begin gentlemen?'

Oberleutnant Baumann stepped forward, extending his hand towards Hausser, a smile on his face.

The major turned and retreated towards the back of the narrow bunker, sitting down heavily on a wide easy chair he had positioned some days earlier. To the right of him and further back in the narrow bunker was a radio operator, busily scribbling reports and orders that had been transmitted through the shortwave radio in front of him. To the major's front sat a medium sized table, two maps extended across it, the improvised paperweight, the officer's half-filled glass was placed across the paper overlap with a lit candle on the edge of the table. A chipped metal tea pot, the major's trade mark, sat on a small side table next to his chair.

Hausser leant forward grasping the outstretched hand of the adjutant. 'How are you *Mr* Baumann?'

Baumann's smile widened to a brief grin in return, his handshake firm, 'Good to see you again Hausser, I hear you have been busy as usual.' The grin transforming to a wide smile.

Hausser relaxed his stance, a smile flicking across his face, 'Yes, it was quite a challenge getting back to you, but I hear we may be in a bigger mess now.'

Baumann nodded, his face becoming solemn, 'Yes, this dilemma may prove just a little difficult I think.' The man stood back, rubbing his temple with his right hand. He was in his late forties with greying unkempt black hair. The lines of stress around his face from the challenges of continual organisation, fully aware that any mistake he may make could cost a life. This had played heavily on the man as the battles of the previous winter had become more costly, his personal pride in limiting casualties becoming challenged and then overwhelmed as the campaign had continued relentlessly throughout the year. Fate seeming oblivious and unforgiving towards his emotional state.

The major was becoming impatient, swigging from his glass, he stood up, 'When you gentlemen have finished your gossip, perhaps you can join me.' He indicated with his hand for the two officers to stand before the table. He then leant forward, retrieving an unlit cigarette from on top of the map and lighting it, blowing smoke into the roof of the bunker.

The two men turned, moving to the other side of the table from the major. An explosion in the distance caused the three men to look at each other cautiously for a second, listening for indications that a salvo was incoming. After a couple of seconds and no further explosions, they became more relaxed, the major retrieving a pencil from his side table.

The major cleared his throat, taking another draw on his cigarette, he looked the two officers in the eyes. 'Let's start with the overall picture. Well, there is no point in trying to give you a good version of events……there isn't one.' He smiled ironically, his eyes saddened, 'The Russians have cut us off and we are awaiting rescue, or orders to break out. There is even talk of a counter offensive to re-establish the position along the Volga, but I doubt that will occur in this weather, or indeed in the foreseeable future. Until a decision is made or actions to the effect, the Luftwaffe will supply us by air.' He paused, waiting for Hausser to digest the information.

Looking down at one of the bedraggled maps on the table, the major leant forward, turning the map with the palm of his hand to face the two officers. 'We will only be here for a short time Hausser, the adjutant and I will head northwest to form a command post near our own 76th Infantry Division. They are preparing defences and a new home on the outskirts of the pocket.' He pointed to the map with the pencil, indicating an area to the northwest of their position, then circling it with the pointer. 'However, you will be going into the city to meet with your men. I have arranged some stragglers and 'misfits' to join your little detachment, most are men cut off from their units or survivors of the Russian assault. Their morale is probably not great, but you should be able to get them together. You will have a mixture of Romanians and Germans, maybe some Hungarians.'

He paused, a frown forming on his face, he sipped from his glass. 'Now, here is the Russian Sixty Second army, still clinging onto the banks of the Volga.' He drew a narrow short line along the banks of the river on the map. 'They are the thorn in our side….perhaps our backside.' He glanced up, taking a draw from his cigarette. Seeing the solemn faces of the two officers, he resumed his briefing. 'They are a cunning unit, we drove them back from the Don bend, but the bastards refuse to give up. They are supplied from the east side of the river and are causing all sorts of problems. Fighting in the sewer, small attacks, taking buildings under our noses and sniping our troops. I will pass your command over to a Major Slusser, who is in the area opposing them.' The major stopped talking for a second, seeming to consider what he was to say next. 'He is desperate for men to contain them or drive them out, even into the river. Personally, we have not achieved it in three months of heavy fighting, so I doubt you will be able to change this, but he needs help never the less, so I have to send you for now. Once the Russkies realise they cannot start trouble because of what has happened we should be able to stabilise the situation. Hopefully we will get you back soon.'

Hausser shifted his stance, looking up from the map, the major indicating for him to speak by a nod. The young commander spoke slowly, studying the map before him, 'I presume the supplies are coming in through Gumrak and Pitomnik airfields?' He pointed at the crude aircraft drawings on the map. 'Are they vulnerable if the Russians break through?'

The major smiled, ignoring the latter question. 'Yes, you are correct. Most will land there, but a few to Stalingradski flight school. Mostly smaller aircraft and some fighters for the pocket. The Luftwaffe are attempting to repeat their success in supplying the Demyansk pocket earlier this year.' He paused, his eyes becoming strained in the candle light, 'To be brutally honest, I cannot see this myself, this is much bigger, perhaps beyond the ability of our air force. We have already had to reduce rations and our shells are limited, the fighters short of fuel, but we will see. They may surprise me.'

Hausser shook his head slowly, pursing his lips, 'The winter is upon us, Major, how will they keep flying in that weather?'

The major leant back, slowly drawing on his cigarette and looking the young commander in the eye, his expression grim, 'That is for us to find out, only time will tell.' He leant forward, placing his pencil on the map near the river, 'Now let me show you where you will be going, after which you can stay and eat with us before we all depart our separate ways. We need to build your strength up.'

Hausser stood in the snow outside the makeshift bunker, a converted wide trench dug in parkland near the flight school. Facing south, he lit a cigarette and looked up at the winter storm clouds, hearing distant artillery landing in the city to his left. Pushing his MP40 round his shoulder, he adjusted his helmet, the bandages round his head irritating him.

Hearing footsteps in the snow 'crunch' to his right, he turned his head, seeing Oberleutnant Baumann join him, buttoning his staff overcoat against the cold breeze.

'So what do you think, Hausser?' The Oberleutnant asked, reaching into his side pocket for his packet of cigarettes.

Hausser blew smoke into the crisp air, feeling the warmth in his chest. 'I don't know. Is it as bad as it was before…….last winter?'

The Oberleutnant looked away, lighting his cigarette. Turning to look at him, his face saddened, he sighed, 'I am sorry my friend, but I cannot lie to you…..it's far worse now. The Russians are throwing everything against us. Our casualties have been terrible.' He coughed, emotion rising within him, 'So many men have fallen my friend, good men, and experienced soldiers…….this is a different war now. The Russkies have learnt a lot in the last eighteen months, where as we are using units that are a shadow of what they used to be. I cannot say what will happen to us as this becomes a frozen hell.'

Hausser tried to turn the conversation, 'How about the supply situation?'

The Oberleutnant swallowed hard, trying to change his demeanour in front of his friend, his voice breaking, 'We have started slaughtering the horses for food now. Perhaps the Luftwaffe can change that with their supply drops.'

Hausser nodded slowly, uneasiness and concern rising within him, his voice low, 'Perhaps…….' Feeling dejected, the young commander's mind was surprised, seeing his friend becoming quite emotional, his eyes moist. The man he had known had usually been upbeat and confident, but now he seemed to have descended into a dark mental place, somewhere he seemed unable to escape from.

The men stood in silence for a while, smoking and looking up at the heavy snow clouds above them, the devastated city stretching across the landscape before them and to their left. Broken and damaged buildings skirted the small park, their windows and some roofs shattered in the months of fighting as the Sixth Army had advanced into the city. Sporadic gunfire could be heard in the distance to the left, the occasional explosion breaking the rattle of machine gun fire.

Above them, a twin engine German fighter slowly circled before coming into land at the nearby flight school airfield, its precious cargo, an intelligence officer with the latest instructions from thousands of miles away. A repeat of the orders received by radio a couple of day earlier, this time in writing. The instructions for the Sixth Army to 'stand firm' on the banks of the River Volga. That no breakout was to be attempted. A relief effort was being organised and would commence within days.

Chapter Seven: Returning to the Fray

Hausser had eaten a small meal with his friend before departing to head into the city, the major being called away for a situation briefing. The officers ate in troubled silence as their personal thoughts had become darker and bleaker at the situation. Small talk had been attempted, but the conversation had invariably returned to the military situation they found themselves in. The enormity of the challenges they individually and collectively perceived to face slowly eroding the will and motivation to continue the discussion.

As he prepared to depart, Baumann had given him a couple of tins of meat rations from their meagre stock, advising that he should savour the food when he could and use it to rebuild his strength. That the army only had food supplies for a short period and that rations had already been reduced to most soldiers in the pocket.

As the major and his adjutant prepared to leave to re-join the 76th Infantry Division, Hausser had made his excuses and left them, finding their company depressing. They were unable to raise each other's morale as they had done so in the past.

Walking away from the makeshift bunker, he had wondered to himself if he would ever see the two men again. The situation certainly grave, but also being parted from his unit troubled him. Had the major offered to send him into the city, knowing the situation out on the steppe outside the city was grim or even the opposite? After two hundred metres of walking, he had dismissed his mental reasoning and attempt to understand the situation, realising he would probably never come up with the correct answer, perhaps he did not even want to know.

He walked along virtually deserted devastated streets, a cold wind blowing through the city, the inhabitants and soldiers sheltering in the damaged buildings from the temperatures. The gunfire in the distance would occasional get louder as he crossed a street, or turned into an alleyway. Snowflakes began to fall as he made his way through the outskirts of the city, the roads beginning to become covered in a gathering white blanket as the temperature dropped in the late afternoon. He stopped briefly to don his gloves and adjust the scarf across his mouth, preparing for the temperatures that would surely follow as the afternoon progressed. Stepping around rubble and the through the sharp crunches of broken glass beneath his boots, he mentally ran through his orders again, considering what the future may bring for him and his men.

Shell explosions and automatic fire echoed in the distance, towards the river. Hausser headed slowly towards the sounds and as he progressed the noise began to spread across the landscape in front of him. He eventually realised the noises had become a wall of distant sound, being unable to distinguish a direction in which to head.

He passed damaged and destroyed vehicles in the streets, the gruesome signs indicating he was following the route previously taken by an advancing unit, the fighting having been heavy. The vehicles were of both sides, seemingly now allies in their destruction, exposed to the elements, their burnt hulks stripped of equipment and supplies.

He occasionally spotted civilians huddled together, busily searching for food, or combustible material to provide warmth. They viewed him with suspicion and fear as he slowly walked by. Passing sentries from several units, he saw the grim determination or underlying fear in the men's eyes, their inner thoughts betraying their concern for the situation they were all in. Their uniforms covered in a variety of clothing to provide any additional warmth, he considered the identity of individual units had now virtually ceased to exist, as if a common bond between the men, a common bond in addition to the hunger that was beginning to spread through the city on the reduced rations.

The snow gradually settled on his shoulders and arms, causing him to occasionally brush off the flakes, his insulated underwear releasing little heat for the flakes to melt into his uniform. To amuse himself he considered the compliments he would pay to the Russians they had 'liberated' the underwear from, the material was certainly superior to the German standard issue clothing.

Every now and again, he could occasionally see smoke in the distance, towards the river, but the snowfall generally reduced his visibility to a couple of hundred metres. The continuous sounds of war echoed across the streets he trudged along grimly.

At one point, a small Kubelwagen jeep had sped past him in a side street, the officer in the passenger seat looking at him suspiciously as they drove by. Unbeknown to him, the jeep carrying orders for a forward unit, their communication lines cut.

As the light began to fade in the mid to late afternoon, he realised it would take a lot longer for him to find his destination than he originally anticipated. Progress was slow in the many streets and thoroughfares through the city. He was challenged a number of times by soldiers wary of infiltrators, but all allowed him to continue after brief conversations and having shown them his orders.

Slowly as it got darker, the dim lights from oil lamps and candles in the buildings on either side began to become evident, their illumination struggling to force its way through the falling snow. The faint glows from the buildings seeming to highlight the broken and damaged window frames and doors more than in daylight, as if to emphasise the hurt the city had sustained.

Hausser progressed further towards the river and the distant sounds of gunfire. Occasionally a shell would land closer than the noise level he was used to, causing him to stop and consider whether to proceed. He was now becoming unnervingly confused as to what direction to head. He knew from the briefing he was required to head to the north east, but this had become increasingly difficult to gauge in the heavy snowfall and with the streets turning to the right and left. With the light now gone, he determined to approach the next sentry or group of soldiers for assistance.

Several lorries passed as he crossed a wide thoroughfare, the snowflakes falling gently onto the roads surface as he walked across. The vehicles slowly heading northwards, accompanied by an SdKfz 251 Hanomag, the occupants talking loudly inside. As the armoured car passed, the exposed machine gunner raised his hand in greeting having spotted him, a German Officer waiting to cross behind them.

As he ventured into a narrow dimly lit street, he saw a group of soldiers ahead through the snow flurry and slowly approached them, crossing the road. The men were stood before a half track and seemed to be preparing to move forward, an officer barking instructions nearby for them to leave the building they had been sheltering in. As he approached, he could hear the mutterings of the enlisted men as they waited in the street for their countryman to join them from the nearby building.

Approaching the soldiers, the nearest to him turned as he sensed his presence, stiffening as he recognised the officers dirt covered shoulder boards and epaulettes. He nodded as Hausser approached, moving to the side to let him pass, his rifle on his shoulder. Hausser stopped before the man as the other soldiers noticed him, their conversation falling off due to their caution of the new arrival.

The young commander smiled under his scarf, his amusement at the soldiers caution becoming evident in his eyes, 'Evening gentlemen, I wondered if you could assist me with some directions.' He reached into his tunic pocket for his orders, wary the soldiers would be suspicious.

The soldier's eyes narrowed, his voice becoming challenging, 'Which unit are you from Sir?

Hausser nodded, understanding the soldiers caution, '76th Infantry Division, now detached to the 305th Infantry Division.' Adding some emphasis to his Berlin accent.

The soldier smiled, reading his orders. 'We are the 100th Jager Division, Herr Leutnant. You are a little too far south I think. You had better ask our officer, he will know the exact location you require I believe.'

Hausser nodded, 'Thank you, are you men moving up?'

The soldier's eyes looked strained, 'Yes Sir, our company has had a days respite from the front, so now we are moving up to relieve the next company. We are on two day rotations, two days at the front, one away, but I think that may be only for a short time now.' The soldier's voice tailed off as he turned his head to look into the entrance of the apartment block. The soldier extended his arm towards the open doorway of the building before them 'There is our officer Sir, a Hauptmann Graner.'

Hausser turned to see the officer through the open doorway, a dim light flickering from within. The officer talking very closely to a soldier in the hallway, their faces some two or three inches apart.

Hausser placed a friendly hand on the Jager infantryman's shoulder as he turned to walk into the hallway, 'I am sure you will enjoy many more respites from the enemy, just take care at the front.'

The soldier nodded surprised, a brief grin forming across his face, 'Er...yes Sir, I will do, thank you.' He turned to smile at the soldiers with him, their eyes widened.

Hausser stepped into the entrance hall dusting the snow from his uniform. The officer and infantryman turning their heads as they realised his approach. Hauptmann Graner stepped back from the soldier, indicating with his hand, 'Go join the others, Beltz, and don't be late again. We need to be ready when the transport arrives, not after.'

Hausser saluted, approaching the officer. In return, the Hauptmann raised his right hand to his helmet, 'Can I help you, Leutnant?'

Hausser nodded once, 'Yes please, Leutnant Hausser, Sir. I am on my way to join the 305th Infantry, but I seem to have got disorientated. Your men told me you would have a better knowledge of where they are.'

Hauptmann Graner smiled, his face unshaven and dirty from the days of fighting, 'Yes, they are north of us, perhaps three or four kilometres. Which way were you heading?'

Hausser smiled in return, hearing a shell burst in the direction of the river, "I was heading towards the river, but have got a little lost.'

The Hauptmann stood back, resting his hands on his MP40, the strap round his neck, 'Well I am glad you stopped here, the Russians are ahead, so it is unlikely you would have got much further without 'Ivan' taking a shot at you!' He grinned, indicating to his own dirty uniform, 'As you can see, we are struggling a little to maintain our control near the river. They are a cunning enemy, snipers, fighting in the sewers, attacking sentries, they do not let us rest much.' He stopped, looking more cautiously at the Leutnant, 'So where have you been for the last few weeks if you don't know what it is like here?'

Hausser's smile fell, realising the captain's suspicion was rising, 'Apologies Sir, I have been in the south with the Romanian Fourth Army for the last two months, but now sent by Major Schenk into the city. I heard it was difficult, how are the men holding up?' He extended his hand with his orders.

The Hauptmann took the paper, holding it to the side for more light, he examined the writing and signature. He was perhaps in his mid-thirties, with dark tired lines under his eyes, the dirt and dust smeared across his face. His brown eyes nervously darting from the paperwork and resting on Hausser's uniform, a sign of his stress being stretched after weeks of bitter fighting. He licked his lips, the condensed breath escaping from his mouth, seeming satisfied, he spoke, 'This platoon is at about three quarters strength, but it is stronger than most of the others...I would say most are about fifty to sixty percent strength. I imagine it is much the same across the southern front.'

Hausser's face fell, an expression of discomfort forming, his eyes widening, 'I...I didn't know it was that bad, I am sorry.'

The Hauptmann's expression lightened, seeing Hausser's mental shock, leaning forward he placed a hand on his shoulder, 'It has been hard here, Hausser. The Russkies don't want to give the city up.' Lightly slapping his upper arm, he handed him his orders and walked past him, 'Go into the square ahead, maybe one hundred metres. Turn north, and keep walking...that should get you to your unit. Don't go much closer to the river though, the fighting is heavy there, they shoot at anything that moves.'

Hausser nodded slowly, 'Y...Yes Sir, thank you.'

The Hauptmann turned at the door, 'To the north east is Pavlov's house, the old Russian intellectual. Be careful there, the Russians have been holding out there since the beginning of this mess.' He turned in the doorway, indicating for the men to get on board the personnel carrier, then looked briefly back at Hausser, still stood in the hallway. 'Good luck Leutnant. I hope you find your unit.' The Hauptmann then turned sharply and walked out into the falling snow, the personnel carrier engines roaring into life as the driver glimpsed him exit the building.

His spirits low, Hausser slowly trudged along the street, the flickering lights of candles and oil lamps spilling from the buildings on either side. Two sentries were on the corner as the street turned towards a square, breaking their conversation and turning to face him as he approached. The air was becoming colder as the snow fell, the day progressing into the evening. The commander could feel the cold biting at his feet and ankles as he walked, the snowfall becoming thicker. In the distance, towards the river, the sounds of shells bursts and the rattle of machine gun fire became louder as he reached the bend in the street.

As he reached the soldiers, he handed one his orders, the man raising a lantern to inspect them, his rifle slung over his shoulder. The other sentry nodded to him as he stood there, his grim expression reflecting their lonely vigil in the street. The man sniffled, a scarf covering his mouth, 'Another Russian winter, Herr Leutnant.'

Hausser nodded grimly, his thoughts subdued. 'Yes another winter.' He brushed the snow from his arms and shoulders, 'How far ahead are the Russians?'

Satisfied, the sentry handed him his papers back, looking directly into his eyes. 'Maybe four or five hundred metres, Herr Leutnant. They are fighting in the houses near the river, across the square ahead.' The man leant down and placed the lantern on the step to the entrance to one of the buildings and then turned towards him, rubbing his gloved hands. 'If you go to the end of the street and turn left to the north, this will be your best route to your unit. Keep walking for a while, and ask the sentries on the way for assistance, the units are not as clearly separated as we are used to.'

Hausser nodded, 'Thank you. I will bear that in mind. Which unit are you men from?'

The soldier sniffled again, 'We are part of the 53rd Mortar Regiment, our unit is in the square for the night. We are posted sentry duty for the next hour.'

The young commander looked past the men further down the street, seeing only shadows through the heavy snow fall. 'Thank you gentlemen, I think I will continue on my way now.'

The sentries nodded, one of them adjusting the scarf across his mouth, 'Best try and get under cover soon, Sir. The Russians will probably start shelling in a while.'

Hausser turned and walked on, towards the square, 'I will, thank you.'

As he neared the wide expanse at the end of the street, he could make out the lorries parked either side of his entrance route, presuming the mortars were within the trucks. A soldier stood talking to the driver in the lorry to his right. Turning left at the corner, he started trudging north, his thoughts drifting to the men he was heading towards. Gunfire echoed across the square, the sound now much louder than before, the fighting some three to four hundred metres away towards the river. Reaching into his pocket, he retrieved a crumpled packet of American cigarettes and stopped to light one, lowering his scarf. Breathing in the warm smoke to counter the cold air, he glanced around, seeing the outline of a small circular statue some distance away in the square. Approaching to investigate, he began to make out the outline of the structure, stood about twice the size of his height and with a wide base.

As he stood before the damaged statue, he wondered what the meaning or significance of the work had been. The worn and pot holed circular wall with snow lying deep along the tops were a barrier bordering the main exhibit, set on a high circular plinth. Frogs adorned the tops of the circular wall at intervals, and he realised the structure had originally been a fountain, the water probably spouting from the snow covered frogs in peacetime. On the raised central section, six statues of children were dancing in a circle, hand in hand with the statue of a crocodile in the centre, its head raised. Parts of the individual statues had been damaged by gunfire and were slowly becoming covered in a thickening blanket of snow.

Looking into the distance, towards the river, he could just make out the outlines of the buildings that bordered the square through the heavy snowfall, their torn and broken structures exposed to the elements. Drawing on his cigarette again, he turned, walking briskly away from the statue, heading north. Throwing the cigarette onto the ground he pulled the scarf back over his mouth and hunched his body against the cold. Within a minute, he had left the square behind him, heading along a wide thoroughfare towards his new unit.

Chapter Eight: Reunion

Hausser waited in the small hallway, pacing and smoking his last cigarette. It had taken him two hours to walk the remainder of the distance from the square to where he should report, asking many soldiers along the way. The temperature had dropped further as he had walked, the cold intensifying as he passed a wide expanse to his right, the slope rising up towards the heights overlooking the city, Mamayev Kurgan.

He smiled to himself as he recalled the two children that had joined him in his walk. Their company starting just after the bitter coldness of the hill as they had seen the German officer trudge northwards. They had initially walked behind him, playfully imitating a march until he had stopped and turned asking them to explain themselves. Their eyes had widened on hearing his fluent Russian and they had smiled, informing him that they wished to join his unit.

Enjoying the game, he had questioned them as to their suitability and the boy of perhaps nine or ten years had elaborated, explaining that he and his sister would fight heroically by his side against the communists. Hausser's eyes had widened when he had asked what fighting experience they had, the boy replying cheekily that they lived in the city and that would surely be enough experience for such an officer. The boy had continued as they walked together, explaining that they would require little rations due to their age and size and would then look after him in his old age back in Germany, the three of them retiring as heroes after the war.

As they had reached the outskirts of the factory district, the snowfall becoming heavier, Hausser had explained that they should go back to their mother. That he would come and get them if they were needed for the fighting but until then they should keep safe and not stray too near the front line. As a parting gift, he had given them the two ration tins provided by Oberleutnant Baumann, wishing them well. The children had both saluted, the small girl of maybe seven or eight years holding his hand briefly, disclosing she hoped he came to get them and that he could then meet their mother perhaps staying with them for a while.

He grinned as he considered their innocence, his thoughts becoming more solemn as he realised they would probably suffer even more in the coming weeks as the battle heightened. As he finished the cigarette, the door on the right of the hallway opened distracting him, a young corporal looking through the opening, 'Major Slusser will see you now, Sir.'

Hausser walked forward nodding at the soldier who stood aside to let him past. Slipping into the warehouse office, he looked around the smallish room, seeing the Major sat behind a desk at his left hand side.

The major stood up, his chair grinding against the cement floor. 'Leutnant Hausser?' He enquired, stretching out his hand.

Hausser leant forward, shaking the superior officer's hand, 'Yes Sir, good to meet you.'

The major indicated to a chair on the opposite side of the table to himself, 'Please have a seat, I understand you have had quite a walk.'

Hausser slowly lowered himself into the wooden chair, 'Yes Sir, I may have got a little lost on the way.'

The major nodded, looking inquisitively at him, 'So I understand, I was expecting you a couple of hours ago.' He paused, scratching his nose, 'Anyway, it doesn't matter your men have had a little more rest as a result.' The major grasping some papers from the table and leaning back in his chair to study them, a candle for illumination on the edge of the desk.

Hausser looked at the major, his officer's cap on the table before him. The senior officer was perhaps late thirties, with dark black hair and brown eyes. His unshaven face was quite distinct, with high cheek bones and a red rash on either side of his neck, indicating his skin's sensitivity to the mixture of fabric. His collar was buttoned tight, the uniform dusty with the days spent at the front. Glancing round the office, he surmised it was a foreman's room in peacetime, the warehouse beyond the hallway and this room the responsibility of the supervisor that had been housed in the small space.

To the side of the desk was a number of rolled blankets, and Hausser realised the man slept in this room, the office a safe choice, having no windows with the rest of the building surrounding it. The two storey building provided adequate cover for the small room, the first floor above containing materials and stock for the factories nearby.

The major broke his contemplation, dropping the papers he had been reading back onto the desk. 'Major Schenk seems to hold you in high regard, Leutnant. His message requests you are returned to his unit as soon as practicable.' The major looked across at him, his eyes sparkling in the candlelight, a smile forming on his face. 'I am happy to make your acquaintance, it's just a pity it's under such circumstances.'

Hausser nodded, 'Yes, I agree, perhaps a drink under a warm Italian sky would be more suitable?' An ironic smile forming on his face.

The major grinned, 'Ah......now that would be a more agreeable situation, glad to see you are able to keep a sense of humour even now.' He slapped his knee, reaching down behind the desk and retrieving a half filled bottle. 'Would you like a glass of Schnapps?'

Hausser smiled warmly, 'Yes please, then I think I should get to my men.'

The major nodded, retrieving a couple of glasses, holding the rims of the tumblers between two fingers. Placing the glasses on the table, he uncorked the bottle and poured ample quantities of the clear liquid into each tumbler. Grabbing one of the tumblers, the major raised the glass, 'Prost! Leutnant Hausser, to you and your unit's success!' He then downed the glass in one, closing his eyes and twisting his head as he swallowed the strong liquid.

Hausser gingerly picked up the glass and raised it in return, sipping from the tumbler, the liquid nearly overpowering his taste buds. He coughed once as he swallowed, smiling at the major as the warmth spread through his stomach.

Major Slusser topped up his glass, grinning at Hausser's somewhat reserved drinking. Splashing a top up into the younger man's glass, he sipped his own and leant back in his chair. Clearing his throat, he picked up one of the pages from the desk in front of him. 'So, Hausser, let's get to your men. We have assigned a small number of stragglers and 'homeless' troops to you. Survivors from the Russian *maelstrom* if you like. They are of mixed nationalities, but they seem good men. It's only about a platoon strength, maybe slightly larger, but it will do for the meantime until you re-join your unit. We may get you some more in due course.'

Hausser nodded, sipping from the tumbler again, his senses warming as the alcohol spread through his body. He noticed the major's face was becoming slightly flushed, the effects of the Schnapps beginning to become apparent.

The major glanced up at him, ensuring the younger man was keeping up with him, looking back at the paperwork, he continued. 'You may have some language problems, but I understand some of your existing men can speak other languages, so hopefully you can get by.' He leant forward, picking up his glass again, swigging greedily from it. 'Now to your duties. We face the Russian 62nd Army on the banks of the river where they have a narrow bridgehead, held throughout the entire battle I may add. Although I would love to push them into the water, this is unrealistic with the current *turn* of events.'

Hausser nodded, 'Yes I imagine.'

Major Slusser reached for his tunic pocket, retrieving a battered pack of cigarettes. Placing one between his teeth, his offered the packet to Hausser, leaning forward, he placed his elbows on the desk either side of the paperwork.

The younger commander leant forward to light the major's cigarette, retrieving one for himself from the packet.

The major drew on the lit cigarette and continued, smoke spilling from his mouth as he talked, 'The Russians are being supplied from the other side of the river regularly, probably at night. I predict they will become increasingly active in the next few weeks as they realise we are vulnerable. It is my....*our* job to ensure they do not succeed in breaking out. Do you understand

Hausser?' The major's eyes narrowed as he looked up at the younger officer, drawing on his cigarette again as he watched him intently.

Hausser lowered his glass, looking back at the major across the desk, slightly startled at the man's directness, 'I understand Sir. If they break out, this will create further havoc in the city and extra strain on the army.'

Major Slusser smiled, his face now fully flushed with the alcohol he had consumed, 'Exactly. It is imperative we contain the 62nd Army until a relief effort gets here and stabilises the front. Unfortunately, as we are now on the defensive we will have to guess or gain intelligence where and when the Russians will attack.' He leant forward, topping up Hausser's glass.

Hausser nodded further, beginning to warm to the major's manner, understanding and presentation of the situation. Drawing on his cigarette, he sipped from his glass again.

The major raised his tumbler and swigged from it in response, then continued, 'That is where your unit comes in Hausser, and my need for you. We are quite thinly stretched and have very few reserves at present. I need a 'fire brigade' to reinforce any sector they attack in. Your 'new' unit provides this, allowing me to rotate the front line troops and create a reserve, if only a small one. At least now if they attack, I can move the extra men in to support the defenders.' The major looked curiously at him, his eyebrows raised awaiting a response.

Hausser smiled warmly, a mixture of his understanding of the major's intent and the alcohol, 'I understand Sir.'

The major smiled back at him, 'Good, thank you Hausser. Now, in a moment, I will get my adjutant to accompany you to your men. Tomorrow morning you should move up and relieve a section of the front….probably tomorrow night. Keep an eye out for the enemy moving troops up or any suspicious activity. That could be the clue we need to their intent.'

'I will Sir,' Hausser replied. Draining his glass. 'Where is it we will head in the morning?' The quantity of alcohol was more than he was accustomed to and he felt his insides turn uncomfortably as the strong liquid descended towards his stomach. A stronger warmth began to slowly spread through his body, the alcohol landing on a relatively empty stomach.

The major leant back in his chair again, his eyes slightly bleary from the drinking. He paused, a tired sigh coming from his lips, 'You will take up positions in front of the Red October Tractor Factory.'

As Hausser trudged through the iced snow, his stepping slightly uncoordinated due to the alcohol, he considered the challenges ahead. The adjutant next to him indicating a warehouse door some one hundred metres away. Their boots crunched across the ice, the snow still falling around them. The rattle of gunfire from the nearby frontline caused the men to instinctively lower their heads. Shells burst in the city to the south as they walked across the ice covered delivery yard.

Reaching a single doorway to the side of the wide front double delivery doors, a sentry unfamiliar to Hausser saluted and opened the door for him. The adjutant turned, bidding the young commander farewell and beginning the return route to the major, the promise of a warming drink to welcome him back hastening his walk. A broad grin crossed his face abruptly as he trudged away from the damaged warehouse, the hoarse cheer from within the building behind him causing some amusement.

Chapter Nine: To the Front!

Hausser walked slowly along the line of soldiers, his head thumping from the previous night's consumption and his injury. Examining the soldiers one by one, he considered their ability as a fighting unit. The men were of several different nationalities, some Romanians, Hungarians and the rest, German soldiers. All escapees of the Russian offensive or stragglers from units that had escaped the pocket, their fate perhaps not as lucky. He could see from the expressions on their faces that they had all experienced a great deal and that morale was low. Lacking friends and countrymen, not knowing if their comrades were alive or dead, or even having witnessed their friends killed had eroded the men's' resolve.

Their bedraggled national uniforms, dirty and torn had seen better days, and the inspection he had organised simply emphasised the situation they found themselves in from their presentation. He counted twenty nine men in total in addition to the men that had escaped along the riverbank, bringing their fighting strength to forty two soldiers.

Stepping back, he turned to Tatu, 'What weapons do we have as a unit?'

Tatu stroked his moustache, his hangover intense from a nights drinking. The vodka provided by the major allowing the men some respite from reality and creating some camaraderie as they had all drunk together. He turned his head towards Hausser, 'Twenty nine rifles, nine sub machine guns, including our own, one MG34 with six belts of ammunition and a Russian DP-28 machine gun with five drums of ammunition, Sir!' He barked, the Romanian intent on presenting discipline to the on-looking men.

Hausser smiled at the Romanians retort, realising his intent. He paused, thinking for a second, 'Grenades?'

Tatu stepped forward indicating to the boxes to his right, 'Fifty six grenades in total, a mixture of different makes, Sir!'

Hausser rested his hands on his MP40, the strap round his neck, turning he nodded at Meino, 'Soldat Meino, please go to the Major and request additional warm uniforms for the men, I want them all in the same. If he has to strip rear echelon staff, then so be it. We can give them our discarded clothing.' Hausser thought for a second. 'Also, ask if he has any more weapons he can *donate* to his new unit please.'

Meino nodded, a grim expression on his face, 'Yes Hau…Sir!' He turned and marched from the building, a smile crossing his face in embarrassment.

Distant gunfire broke the mood in the warehouse, the soldiers jumping slightly at the noise, the front on that morning having been reasonably quiet. Three separate explosions in the distance, further south of them indicated the start of a firefight between two units, the gunfire becoming more constant.

The wide building had sustained considerable damage, the rear roof section having collapsed inwards. The men stood in what would have been the front of the warehouse, with a small office on the right side. Occasionally, snowflakes or a cold breeze would drift through the building from the hole in the roof at the far end of the building, the soldiers hunched slightly against the temperatures in the early morning light.

Hausser turned to Tatu again, 'How many rounds per rifle?'

The Romanian smiled slightly, 'An average of eight clips per man Sir!' His pleasure at foreseeing the young commanders questions apparent.

Hausser nodded slowly, turning back to face the men. Raising his voice he addressed them, 'I want to split you into three groups, your squads. One will be led by Tatu here,' he indicated to the Romanian quartermaster next to him. 'Another by Meino whom has just left, and he third by……' He paused considering his options, 'The third squad will be led by myself.' He turned his head to look at Udet and 'Hase' to his right, stood in the second line, 'You two will be with me, and double as runners.' Indicating to Petru next to them, 'You are with Tatu and Nicu my friend, and the Italians with Meino.' The soldiers nodded in response. Hausser coughed, the cold air catching his throat, 'Right, form into your squads, men!' He turned to look at Tatu, indicating for him to come to the side with him with a nod of his head.

The soldiers began being moved into three separate groups by Petru, Udet and Luca, a low murmur of voices as they chose individuals for each group, placing those who had friends with each other and selecting others for their weapons and preferences. A couple of the Hungarians protested when Udet tried to split them up, so he relented and placed them in Hausser's squad, as one spoke Romanian. The other Hungarians were placed in Tatu's squad as one in that group spoke a little Romanian.

Hausser sighed as he stood with Tatu at the side of the warehouse, out of earshot. 'Well my friend, what do you think?' His face inquisitive.

Tatu looked him straight in the eye, 'Let's hope the Russkies do not attack today, we need to get to know these men a little first. Yes they are all soldiers, but of differing ability I guess.'

Hausser nodded, 'Yes, I agree. Once they get to know each other, they will become more experienced and be able to work effectively as a group, until then we can expect casualties if we come under attack. Only when they stop thinking about their last unit and start thinking of this one will they become good. The longer we have, the better they will get.' He turned, seeing the soldiers were now formed into three squads.

The small door to the warehouse opened and Meino entered the building, walking briskly towards Hausser and Tatu. He stopped in front of them, slightly out of breath, a grin on his face, 'The major says you have a damn cheek Hausser, but he will have some uniforms for you in about an hour.' He paused, his expression surprised as he looked across at the three groups of assembled men, then continued. 'He says he has no weapons to give you, but he will get some more ammunition delivered with the clothing and uniforms....he also requests you move up when you are ready.'

Hausser nodded, smiling, 'Excellent. He is a good commander.' He looked across at the groupings of men, indicating to them. 'Meino, you have one of the squads. I will talk to them briefly first, then get your men to search the warehouses for material, I want the equivalent of scarves for their mouths and cloth to wrap on their hands and feet. It will be cold out there and we need them prepared. The rest of us will head out, understood?'

Both men nodded in response, their adrenalin beginning to rise in anticipation. Hausser turned and walked a couple of steps towards the assembled men, his hobnailed boots clicking on the warehouse floor. Placing his arms loosely over his MP40, he looked up, seeing the men before him were assembled in three groups, with four soldiers stood at the front of each squad.

He paused, surveying the soldiers before him, their faces expectant. Raising his voice, he glanced back at Tatu before speaking, 'We are soon to move up and occupy positions in front of the Tractor factory, facing the Russian positions. Although we are a new unit, the Russians do not know that. If they suspect, we will be the target for any attack.' He paused, looking across the grim faces, 'Stay together at all times, and keep your heads down. There are Russian snipers active in the area and they will not hesitate to shoot any one of you.'

He looked across to Udet and 'Hase' in his squad, his mood reflective, 'The army is in a bit of a position here in Stalingrad, but this should not be affecting us. The Luftwaffe is flying in supplies and there is a relief effort underway. Our job...' He looked across the men's faces, his voice becoming more determined, 'Our job is to defend this sector of the front. That is all we have to do. What goes on behind our position is nothing to do with us, we simply hold on and stop the Russians, understand?'

There was a brief pause as the soldiers absorbed the information, then a mixed murmur of 'Jawohl, Herr Leutnant!' spread across the warehouse.

Hausser nodded acceptingly, a cool breeze drifting through the large storage area, 'Good, let's move out. My squad first, the rest following.' He raised his hand, indicating to Udet and 'Hase'. Both men stepped to the front of the group, turning to the squad behind them and indicating for them to follow. The men in the third squad began taking their rifles from their shoulders as they walked forward. Hausser turned and marched briskly to the small side door, pulling his scarf up around his mouth.

Opening the door, he glanced briefly outside, then slipped through the opening, turning to his right. One by one the soldiers followed, bracing themselves against the cold early morning air. Hausser slipped round the side of the building, following the written directions he had been given the previous night. Passing a sentry, he nodded a greeting, the man stamping his feet in the snow. Proceeding down the side of the building, he could hear the sporadic gunfire getting louder as he neared the end of the wall on his right hand side.

Glancing around the corner of the warehouse, he looked down the narrow street, parallel to the river he considered. Opposite and to the left was an alleyway between two damaged buildings, and he realised this was the route to take from his instructions. He glanced back down the street, the buildings broken and shattered on either side. Seeing only a couple of German figures in the distance, he jogged across the snow, the surface frozen above the cobblestones. As he reached the wall opposite, he slipped into the narrow passageway, a shell burst to the south startling him. He reached up and lifted the strap of his weapon over his head, brandishing it in both hands.

He turned, seeing 'Hase' run across the street to join him at the entrance to the alleyway, the soldier half crouched. Behind him, the soldiers lined up along the side of the warehouse, their weapons now in their hands. The men were glancing around cautiously, the fear rising on their faces.

'Hase' looked into his face as he arrived by his side, a brief smile crossing his face. Hausser looked at him, his voice lowered, 'Are you alright, my friend?'

'Hase' nodded, his eyes wide, 'Yes Sir.' Hausser watched him as the soldier looked round, checking the street further. Then he turned and gestured to the other soldiers to cross. Hausser patted him on the shoulder, and jogged into the alleyway, lowering his body to a half crouch as he realised the front line was becoming nearer.

'Hase' watched as the young commander moved along the alleyway between the two buildings, his heart pounding. He then looked back down the virtually empty street. He had felt contented when Hausser had returned to them, his initial fear being overcome. A fear of loneliness in his own country that had confused him until he realised he had become an outcast through one decision, the decision to survive when the two men had first met. Over the three days they had been separated, he had struggled with several emotions, mostly guilt. Then the commander's return had eliminated this, the realisation his own nationality was unimportant in this struggle now, just his loyalty mattered…and survival. He had pushed the uneasy thoughts from his mind, understanding he had mentally struggled with his own feeling of identity, but that this was confirmed with Hausser's return, he was simply a soldier in the commander's unit, a loyal one. This had comforted him, realising his loyalty was to this man, not any country any more. That this was his unit.

Udet stopped next to him, startling him from his thoughts. He glanced back down the alleyway, seeing the commander beckon to him at the corner, he pushed himself out from the wall and ran after the officer, his head ducked, holding his rifle in his right hand. A muffled burst of machine gun fire and sporadic rifle shots echoed out in front of them, beyond the broken buildings. As he reached the young commander, the alleyway stopped at a junction, a damaged building in before them. The alley continued to the left and right, coming to a sharp bend on either side after twenty to thirty metres. Broken masonry and bricks lay on the ground, the buildings having been hit several times during the weeks and months of battle. The alley to the right seemed to lighten at the end, he looked round as Hausser went left, the officer placing his back along the wall as he approached the turn in the alley, his machine gun held upright in front of him.

'Hase' turned as Udet and other soldiers approached him at the junction, their boots crunching on the frozen snow. He held his left hand out to stop them, watching Hausser for instructions. He watched as the commander ducked his head out quickly into the turn in the alleyway, checking the next part of their route, his breath held. Hausser moved back behind the safety of the wall he leant against and turned to look at him, his left hand gesturing him forward, the officer's eyes wide with adrenalin.

'Hase' ran forward, stopping just behind Hausser, the light in the alleyway dim from the buildings on either side. He nudged the young officer, gaining his attention, indicating he should go first. Hausser scowled, then nodded briefly, realising the man was right. 'Hase' scrambled round the officer on the rubble and turned the corner in the alley, running forward half-crouched.

A burst of machine gun fire made him look up instinctively, hearing the sound loud to his front. The short distance to the end of the alley was in virtual darkness, the high walls on either side reducing the light significantly. He slipped on rubble and slates fallen from the roofs on either side, stopping just before the end of the passageway. The morning light was stronger beyond his position, and he pushed himself against the wall, wary the front was close.

The alleyway ended at the junction to another wider street, broken and damaged buildings and warehouses on either side. To the right was another junction, a street extending away from him, towards the river. To either side the street extended for some distance and he could see numerous entrenchments dug into the road surface, catching a glimpse of the tops of helmets in some of the foxholes. The defensive positions placed facing streets and lanes leading from the river.

Looking into the distance, he could see smoke rising from the damaged buildings on the horizon, the Russian positions overlooking some of the streets before him. His breathing heavy, he realised his heart was beating hard in his chest, a feeling of nausea rising within him.

A short distance in front of him was the entrance to a trench, dug into the road, a slope leading into the man-made cover declining away from him. He glanced to either side, out from the alley, his mouth dry with excitement. Then pushed himself forward and slipped on the slope, his heart beating loudly as he scrambled to his feet. To the front of him a couple of rifle shots rang out in the crisp morning air, the noise only some fifty metres away. The trench split in two after a short distance, the left turn seeming to enter the basement of the building opposite as well as stretch off along the walls of the damaged structure towards the firing positions in that direction, the right bending round and along the street, zig-zagging to link the fox holes and machine gun positions to the south.

He crouched in the cold, roughly dug trench, breathing heavily. Thinking this must be the second or third defensive line from the front, the few reserves resting. He turned and waved back down the alleyway, seeing Hausser acknowledge him in the gloom of the passage.

In the distance, on top of one of the smoking buildings, a young Russian soldier crawled forward, his body low to avoid being detected from the German positions below. The bit his lip as his leg scratched against some roof tiles, the top of the building now open to the elements apart from some broken roof supports. Grasping his sighted rifle, he pushed it slowly forward until the muzzle was just before the broken brick of the front wall, the attic he was now lying in mostly destroyed by shellfire. Moving his head to the sight, he slowly began to survey the scene of broken buildings and streets before him, searching for a target.

As the smoke and dust drifted in the air around him, his open eye became accustomed to the sighted magnifier he squinted through, the sight dirty round the edges. The rifle was wrapped in cloth, partly to protect the weapon, but also to reduce the noise when the rifle fired, reducing the likelihood someone could pinpoint his position. Knowing the light was coming from behind him, he kept low, moving some debris around his weapon to steady it further.

The crumps of artillery fire to the south startled him, his reaction to look back through the sight, searching for a German soldier that may look out to see where the artillery landed. Moving the weapon slowly, he scoured the defensive positions below him in the distance, then moved further back to a road, seeing black lines across the snow, indicating further trenches. Realising a shot of that distance would indeed be very fortunate to hit its target, he considered he should fire above any enemy he could see to compensate for the distance and gravitational pull on the bullet.

Hausser advanced carefully along the alley, reaching the end and glancing out to either side cautiously. His exhaled breath condensed, he realised the morning temperature was not rising much, the cold beginning to settle for the day. Seeing the emplacements to either side, he darted forward, down the slope and into the trench to join 'Hase'. His breath laboured, he nodded to him, 'I think I will go first now, any challenge from the soldiers here could result in you getting shot.' He grinned briefly, pulling the scarf up over his mouth again, the material having slipped down.

'Hase' smiled back, removing his helmet. He pulled the balaclava up from around his neck and replaced his metal headwear. 'It will be a cold day Hausser, I hope we get the extra clothing for the men.'

The officer nodded thoughtfully, turning to indicate for Udet and the other men to follow, hearing their boots slip and slide on the debris in the alleyway. 'Best move forward now, stay close to me 'Hase', I will do the talking. Keep your head down.'

'Hase' nodded grimly, pulling his scarf up over the balaclava, his eyes darting back across he wide street, seeing the soldiers beginning to fill the passageway as they waited for the officer to indicate for them to proceed. Hausser slipped past him and he turned to follow, the frozen earth to either side of him rough and hard as he brushed his shoulder against the walls of the trench.

Across the defensive works and destroyed and damaged buildings, the Russian sniper had seen some movement out of the corner of his eye as he slowly moved his sight across the terrain. Moving his rifle back to study the area, he stared through the sight, glimpsing part of a dark passageway between two recently damaged walls of a roofless building. He scowled as he realised he had a very narrow and limited view of the alleyway due to the obstructions from the damaged building before it. Watching the darkness in the passageway intently, he strained his eye at the scope to try and determine any movement, his breathing shallow.

Through the narrow gap between the damaged walls, the Russian jumped as he saw a German helmet move across his view, Udet sprinting across the road and into the trench. The Russian sniper drew breath, raising the muzzle of the rifle slightly to compensate for the distance. Seeing another brief movement, he squeezed the trigger, the rifle kicking back into his shoulder.

The bullet flew across the destroyed landscape, over damaged buildings and trenches, the projectile clipping the side of the damaged wall in the opening he had been staring through. Udet turned in the trench as he heard the scream behind him, the Hungarian soldier following him falling backwards, his hands clutching the air as his rifle clattered onto the iced surface of the road.

The man fell backwards, blood pouring from his throat, the bullet cutting through his wind pipe. Udet's eyes widened in shock, ducking into the trench. In desperation he pushed 'Hase' to the floor of the trench, shouting at the men in the alleyway, 'Stay back, sniper!'

Hausser had turned as he heard the screams, the frustration clear on his face as he realised the wounded man had no chance of survival.

The soldier struggled as he lay on the road, his hands around his bloody throat, his body convulsing in panic as he went into shock, the blood pouring from his deep wound. The soldiers in the alleyway backed away in terror, watching as the dying man stretched his hands out towards them, his eyes begging for help.

Tatu forced himself through the group of men in the alleyway, shaking his head in disgust as he reached the front of the group and saw what was before them, the soldier in the road now beginning to twitch as his body was starved of oxygen, the blood filling his lungs.

Hearing bursts of machine gun fire in the distance as German gunners sprayed the buildings at the top of the riverbank, he reached into his jacket for a smoke grenade, pulling the pin and tossing it over the street, the canister landing just before the broken buildings on the other side of the road. As the dense smoke rose into the air, he prodded the Hungarian soldier next to him, 'Take another man and clear the body, he doesn't deserve to be left there.'

The soldier nodded, grabbing the man next to him as Tatu lower himself to a crouch and ran into the road. Stopping briefly at the twitching mortally wounded soldier, then continuing into the trench, he nodded grimly at Hausser to continue, then turned and indicated for the other soldiers to cross.

As the men cautiously ran out of the alleyway, their bodies lowered, they heard the 'puffs' of mortars to the left as the gunners fired a salvo towards the smoking buildings in the distance.

Walking round to the left, his body lowered, Hausser looked despondently into the entrance to the building to his right, the opening smashed into the foundation wall. Seeing the basement illuminated, he dipped his head inside, noticing two German soldiers sat on boxes on either side of an oil lamp to his left. Two passageways lead away from the large room, one towards the river and the other to the south. Raising his right leg, he stepped though the opening, startling the soldiers. They stood up abruptly, the boxes falling backwards, both snapping to attention. Hausser saluted, both man returning the gesture, his voice low, 'Morning gentlemen. How are things?'

Both soldiers wore greatcoats, gloves and balaclavas, their clothing worn and dirty. The soldier on the right scratched the side of his cloth covered face, seeing the disgruntled look on the commander's face, 'The front seems quiet this morning, Herr Leutnant.'

Hausser nodded, 'Good. Are you men resting?'

The soldier nodded, 'Yes Sir, we had sentry duty during the night.'

The officer lifted the strap of his MP40 onto his shoulder, 'We are moving up to take up positions in front of the Tractor Factory, I presume it's further to the north?'

The soldier nodded, seeing another German soldier step into the basement behind the officer. 'Yes Sir.'

Hausser smiled under his scarf, 'I have a number of men with me, but they have limited warm clothing, can they wait in here until I find the position, then come back for them?'

The soldier stepped forward, 'Yes Sir, there is plenty of room, the passageways lead off to other trenches.' His eyes lightened, 'The extra bodies may warm the place, this is a fall-back position.'

The officer nodded, 'Good.' He turned indicating to Udet who had pushed his head through the opening. 'Udet, bring the men in here to wait, we will go on ahead and find the positions. Hopefully by the time we come back, Meino will have arrived with the extra clothing.'

Udet nodded, his eyes glinting in the light, 'Yes Sir.' His head disappeared back through the opening and they could hear him outside, 'You men, in here. Sit together to keep warm, the commander will go on ahead.'

As the men began to clamber through the opening, Hausser turned back to the great coated soldier, pointing at the passageway to towards the river, 'Should I go this way?'

The man nodded, 'Yes Sir, when you get to the trenches, turn to the north. That's the second defensive line. Don't go any further forward, the Russkies are shooting at any movement.'

The officer nodded, adjusting his helmet, 'Thank you. 'Hase', Udet, follow me.'

The soldier spoke again, 'Sorry Sir, may I suggest something?' The room was beginning to fill with men, the soldier raising his voice to get the officer's attention.

Hausser had reached the entrance to the passageway, he spun round, his eyes quizzical, 'Yes of course.'

The soldier stepped forward, pointing at his shoulder, 'Best remove your epaulettes and insignia Sir, the Russian snipers are targeting our officers.'

The young commander's eyes widened in surprise, 'Er...yes, thank you, I will.' He nodded, and turned abruptly, disappearing into the passageway towards the river, his free gloved hand rising to his shoulder. Udet and 'Hase' were stood at the opening, as he passed between them, they turned and followed the officer, their boots echoing across the basement.

Chapter Ten: The Red October Tractor Factory

Udet followed Hausser down the narrow passageway as it continued for some distance before widening into a larger storage area, some twenty metres long. Wounded lay on either side of the wide area and the three soldiers began stepping carefully forward between outstretched legs and discarded equipment. The misery in the room was almost overpowering, the bitter and forlorn moans filling the area. He glanced at several, his expression hidden beneath his scarf, the blood soaked bandages covering a man's face, the broken and shattered limbs, the exposed stomach and chest wounds. A young soldier was crying to his left, his shoulders shaking uncontrollably, his hands covered in blood from his thigh wound, the liquid soaking down his combat trousers and dribbling onto the cement floor.

A muffled explosion shook the building, the noise coming from above them, plaster and cement dust falling from the ceiling. Udet looked to the left, through an opening, glimpsing further casualties inside the similar sized room, most of the soldiers more severely wounded, others lying still, lifeless, their eyes staring if open. Blood covered the floor as two uniformed medics busied around the wounded attempting to attend to them with limited resources, their unshaven faces stressed with the days and weeks of the consequences of heavy fighting. Several candles lit the two rooms, the only warmth, the light flickering across the dirt and blood smeared walls and broken men's faces.

Udet's eyes were becoming moist as his emotions welled up within him, realising the difference between these men and himself was simply where he stood, what he did, how long his luck would hold.

The three men passed through the doorway at the end, arriving in another similar sized room at a right angle to the previous, a hole in the wall to the left at the end leading to another trench. Hausser turned to Udet and 'Hase' beckoning to the left hand side, out of sight of the room they had just passed through. He looked at them individually, seeing Udet was the most affected from look in his eyes. Placing his hand gently on his shoulder, he moved closer to both of them, his voice lowered but firm, determination in his eyes.

'It is difficult, but I need you two to concentrate. If you are distracted, then there is a chance you may end up in one of those rooms. Do you understand?'

Udet sniffled under his scarf, 'Y…Yes Sir!' He blinked several times to clear his eyes.

Hausser turned to 'Hase', checking to see if he understood the meaning of what he had said, he saw the soldier nodding, his eyes stern, seeming to supress his emotions. The young commander decided not to repeat the message in the man's language, observing he seemed to have grasped the conversation. 'Good, now Udet, I will send you back to get the men. Do not bring them through the wounded, can you find another way?'

Udet nodded, his voice soft, eyes wide, 'Yes Hausser, sorry.'

Hausser smiled beneath his scarf, trying to raise the young soldier's spirits, 'Macht nichts!' He patted his shoulder, 'It's a natural reaction.' He turned as a soldier scrambled through the hole in the wall, dragging his rifle behind him, snowflakes flurrying around the man.

The soldier looked up, nodding, his eyes tired, 'Leutnant Hausser?'

The young commander nodded, 'Yes, what is it?'

The soldier saluted casually, his dirt caked uniform and unshaven features the signs of some considerable time on the frontline, 'I have come to collect you Sir. Escort you and your men to the right section of the front.'

Hausser pursed his lips, saluting back. 'My men have no warm clothing as yet, shall we proceed to our positions and I will send back for them?' A burst of muffled gunfire echoed through the opening, the soldiers tensing in response.

The man at the opening nodded uncomfortably, unperturbed by the gunfire, 'Yes Sir, follow me please. Keep you heads down, the Russians in this sector are good shots.' He turned abruptly, ducking back through the opening.

An explosion outside the opening threw dirt and snow through the hole in the basement wall. Hausser walked to the opening, bending to look out, seeing the soldier further down the trench beckoning him.

Hausser ducked under the broken masonry on top of the opening, emerging half crouched into the trench, the cold air enveloping him as he moved. Behind him, Udet and 'Hase' crouched to negotiate the hole, their breath held. A shell burst to the south caused them to duck instinctively, the chatter of machine gun fire and rifle shots across the immediate vicinity rising in intensity. Udet slipped through the hole in the basement wall and approached Hausser, his body half hunched. The young commander turning and advancing further down the deep trench, glancing up at the soldier before him and a junction ahead.

'Hase' peered cautiously into the distance towards the river after he slipped through the opening, seeing the broken open topped buildings and the many smoke plumes rising into the sky. Looking round, the scenes extended as far as he could see to the south and north. The buildings immediately before them were of fewer stories than the ones in the distance, the many lower warehouses and factories supplying the taller storage buildings for distribution of their goods to boats on the river. The river being a major supply artery between the south and the north of Russia before the German forces reached the west bank three months previously.

Beyond these taller buildings he saw nothing but the snow clouded sky, indicating the start of the land declining to the river only some three hundred and fifty metres away. Small flashes from the far buildings indicated rifle and machine gun fire from the Russian Sixty Second Army positions, the Red Army holding some of the taller buildings at the top of the slope, the sound of the shots reaching him a second later.

The trenches snaked through and between the buildings, the elaborate network linking forward positions to the secondary and third defensive lines. Attacks and counterattacks had reduced many of the buildings to shells, their roofs torn, walls punctured or shattered. Some buildings had been completely flattened, the only signs of their previous existence being a lone chimney or half destroyed wall, the bombing, shelling and rocket fire having been falling upon the factory district for weeks.

Hundreds of frozen bodies lay amongst the ruins, sharing their existence with the living. Some were buried in collapsed buildings, others shattered and broken in the open, having been hit by bullets and shellfire, the remainder lay in the sewers below. Russian and German corpses finding a common place for a final resting place in the northern ruins of Stalingrad's factory district.

The bodies were not all soldiers, civilians and hastily formed worker units attempting to hold or resist the German invader also lay amongst the dead, their inexperience or innocence no match or protection from the advancing Germans and their heavy weaponry.

'Hase' remembered the stories from the advance in August. As the Wehrmacht neared the city and reached the river to the north, the worker battalions had responded en-masse to their forced conscription. Hastily formed from the employees of the factories, they had apparently walked out confidently at first, spurred on by the political officer's words of encouragement, of impending heroism and victory. They faced a strong experienced army with tanks and machine guns that could fire between 800 and 1500 rounds per minute, precision designed for killing and killing as many victims as possible. Most of the innocent defenders were overwhelmed and slaughtered in the street and factories they had worked in only days previously. Most of the political officers had then escaped, back across the Volga.

Hausser turned in the junction in the trench ahead, 'Hase! Come on!' He looked curiously at the soldier stood by the end of the trench, urging him on.

'Hase' shook his head, breaking his thoughts and focussing on the commander to his front, 'Coming Sir!' He ran forward half-crouched towards the Hausser and Udet.

They turned left to the north, walking slowly along the trench, stepping across discarded equipment and bullet casings. Snowflakes fluttered to the ground from the overcast sky, a cold breeze sweeping in from the river and the east bank, unimpeded by the shattered buildings. The men's breath began to become condensed as they walked, half crouched. Shells burst to the north and south across the devastated landscape, the rattle of machine guns and sporadic rifle shots heard in the distance, towards the river.

Turning right, following the trench, they passed under railway tracks, the sleepers below them on the trench floor, the frozen wood creaking as their weight descended onto it through their boots. Then they moved to the side, pushing against the wall of the trench as two soldiers approached them, carrying a wounded man, his eyes closed tightly. Both his hands were pressed across his stomach wound, his dirty uniform stained deep red, and a thin blood trail left behind him.

The trench continued for some distance before splitting. They turned left, once again heading to the north. As they walked down the trench, they passed firing positions and bunkers, dug into city streets and underneath buildings. Sheltering inside were dishevelled soldiers, their uniforms dirty below their unwashed and unshaven faces, the signs of exhaustion and stress on their faces. Bullet fire whipped above them as they stepped carefully over discarded boxes and bullet casings, the items frozen into the earth on the floor of the trench.

Their exhaled breath condensed, the snowflakes slowly drifted to earth around them. At a bend in the trench, turning more to the north east, they passed under a knocked out Panzer IV tank, the tracks gone from the steel wheels. The armoured vehicle had been hit several times with small anti-tank projectiles, the scars across its armoured plate indicating a number of direct hits from several attackers. Glancing out above the trench briefly, Udet saw a destroyed Russian T34 tank some distance away across the destroyed landscape, the vehicle charred from a heavy fire. The two tanks having duelled in the streets some weeks ago as the supporting infantry attempted to assist in taking out the enemy vehicle, the conclusion leading to both steel warriors being destroyed, and both their crews killed.

Continuing in the trench, they passed many emplacements, the infantry within all of similar appearance to the previous sights. Most were subdued, several indicating a greeting through a briefly raised hand or grim nod, their faces covered by scarves or a few lucky ones, with balaclavas.

They progressed through many junctions in their journey, some other trenches heading to the forward positions, others to emplacements of supply areas. Udet paused by one smaller narrow trench, leading off to the left. The smaller trench lead to a lower, almost circular emplacement and he noticed the steel cylinders standing almost upright on the frosted ground of the emplacement. The mortar crews sat in improvised shelters on the emplacements edges smoking, their fire support role now limited to defensive fire only with the rationing of ammunition. The grim realisation that they would soon be joining the ranks of infantrymen etched on their dirt covered faces.

Udet turned, following 'Hase' and Hausser, his pace increased to narrow the distance. As he got within three metres of the back of 'Hase', a shout from a position to their right startled them, 'Enemy aircraft! Take Cover!' Ducking instinctively, Udet glanced to the right, looking towards the river.

As he stared at the smouldering buildings in the distance, he could just make out the black dots beyond the damaged structures at the top of the riverbank. As he watched, he became aware that 'Hase' and Hausser were now next to him, crouched in the trench, their breathing heavy in the cold temperature.

The dots seemed to be moving slowly, the aircraft flying low and directly towards them. As they watched, the dots began to get bigger, a shaft of light hitting one of the cockpit and sparkling in the distance. Then the aircraft disappeared as they swooped down before the buildings on the skyline, the roar of engines sweeping across the terrain as they crossed the Volga.

Udet could hear the crew of a nearby machine gun frantically loading their weapon, then the planes swept over the smouldering buildings in the distance, the rising smoke swirling around them as the pilots pushed their controls to lower the front of their aircraft. Tracer bullets soared up from the defensive positions as the German gunners desperately tried to target the six aircraft, their machine guns firing controlled bursts.

Hausser pushed the two helmets next to him down into the trench and the planes roared down from the high buildings, beginning to level out to start a strafing run. The soldiers' guide dropping to the ground and covering his head with his hands.

The wings of the IL-2 Sturmoviks flashed as their pilots fired across the defensive positions, the bullets splattering across the broken ground in rows across trenches and bunkers throwing snow and frozen dirt into the air. Four of the planes dropped their bombs, the explosions rising up behind them as they flew, throwing debris and broken men upwards and outwards.

Udet looked up from his position, lying on his back on the floor of the trench, his hands over his face as the earth and debris fell around them from the explosions. Through his fingers, he saw the flash of the planes as they flew across their position, the red stars on their wings blurred with their high speed.

The roar of the low flying aircraft was deafening as the pilots opened their throttles in anticipation and pulled back on their controls, the aircraft rising into the air just above the soldiers cowering in the trenches. As they rose, the rear gunners on the planes opened fire, the smaller calibre bullets impacting around the trenches and positions as the planes started to bank to the right, turning to the north.

Udet started to rise from his position, freezing as Hausser shouted fiercely at him, 'Stay down, they will come back!' Startled, he dropped back onto the floor of the trench. The sounds of moaning and the desperate calls for 'Medic' sounded across the defensive positions as Udet closed his eyes, the terror rising within him. The machine gun fire from the positions continued as the planes banked round to the north, turning to use up the remainder of their ammunition, their plan to fly along the trenches.

Hausser looked round desperately, trying to see somewhere to shelter as he anticipated the pilots plan, seeing the planes in the distance. From behind them, a 20mm quad cannon opened fire from the shelter of a broken factory wall, the anti-aircraft fire adding to the machine gun tracers rising from the ground.

Udet stared in awe as he saw the planes begin to bank sharply and head back towards them from the north, his heart rate rising and eyes opening in shock, the planes heading directly towards their position. Hausser rose to a crouch in front of him, blocking his view and raising his MP40 in desperation. Udet grabbed 'Hase's' shoulders, pulling him along the trench, away from the aircraft, aware of the futility as he felt the panic beginning to grip him.

The six planes were turning in the distance to fly in two waves, three aircraft positioning to begin the first strafing run with the remaining planes behind them. As the first three planes began to swoop down towards the trenches, their guns began to blaze again, Hausser started backing down the trench, firing his MP40 towards the oncoming aircraft. Bullets splattered on the ground some three hundred metres in front of them, the dirt and debris on the ground being thrown into the air.

As the lead pilot's eyes narrowed, seeing the German soldiers in the trenches running for cover, his rear gunner shouted, his voice rising in panic across the cockpit, 'Enemy fighters!' The pilot yanking the stick sharply to the left, the Sturmovik banked dramatically towards the river, some fifty metres above the devastated landscape. The aircraft behind their flight leader followed suit, their guns still firing. The red stars on the wings shooting past as their pilots opened their throttles again, the planes gathering speed as they began to level out.

Hausser looked in disbelief as the planes swept away from them to the right, the engine roars filling the land around them. The noise was deafening, the engines screaming as the pilots attempted to push their machines to maximum speed. Udet froze in the trench, looking at the aircraft as they began to level out, their rear guns opening fire across their position, then towards a new threat. Hausser glanced to the left, following the fire from the rear gunners. Three ME109 German fighters swooped down from over the buildings to their left, their screaming engines on full throttle as they neared their prey, the slower Russian aircraft. Having seen the Russian aircraft from their high level patrol, the German pilots had taken the opportunity to pounce, dropping to just above the factory buildings to conceal their approach, nearly skimming the broken rooftops as they closed the distance on their targets.

The lead German fighter's guns blazed at his targeted Sturmovik, the impact of his bullets on the Russian ground attack aircraft clearly audible as the Russian pilot began to weave his plane to reduce the chances of being hit. Debris from the targeted aircraft broke off and shot across the landscape, eventually falling onto the positions below. Aware his plane was heavily armoured, the Russian kept flying low, spinning his wings to a vertical position to sweep between two of the higher buildings on the skyline in an attempt to lose his pursuer. The other Russian aircraft rising over the smouldering buildings and following their flight leader out over the Volga.

The lead ME109 soared dramatically, almost vertically up into the air, the Russian ground fire from beyond the buildings targeting him directly. The small calibre anti-aircraft guns placed on the edge of the river opening fire to defend the Russian bridgehead. The two German fighters to either side of their Schwarm leader banked to the south and north as Russian machine guns opened fire from the smouldering buildings.

Udet watched the flash of speckled silver and black crosses on the wings of the German fighter as it banked south, then heard the engine cough, a thin smoke trail begin to flow behind the fighter as the pilot fought to control his damaged aircraft. Udet began to rise in the trench, fascinated by the pilot's efforts, the damaged plane slowing and banking round south of them, the dark thin smoke trail flowing behind it.

Then hands grasped him roughly, startling him, pulling him back down into the trench. The force surprising him, he tried to turn as a bullet zipped overhead, hitting the ground behind the trench. Falling onto the ground with the force, he realise 'Hase' had dragged him down, aware the young German was exposing himself to sniper fire in his fascination.

Lying on the cold floor of the trench again, Udet looked down to see 'Hase' lying beyond his boots, a grin on his face. The young German lowered the back of his helmeted head to the ground, relief sweeping over him. Then he heard the breathless, familiar voice of Hausser, 'Shall we continue when you two are finished your nap?' Hearing the young commander clip a new magazine into the base of his weapon.

They then advanced along the trenches for some time, perhaps forty minutes, they struggled to make speedy progress through the many twists and turns of the defensive system. Ever step was carefully considered due to the debris in the trenches, the spent bullet casings, broken equipment and discarded used supply containers. The fear of exposure to an enemy sniper preventing the many obstructions from being collected outside the trench walls. The temperature remained below freezing, the bitter conditions adding to the seemingly slow erosion of their motivation, their aching backs from the uncomfortable position they were forced to advance in now causing considerable lumber pain.

At yet another turn in the trench, turning north once again, the lead soldier guiding them stopped, turning to Hausser, he pointed into the distance, 'Do you see the chimney, Herr Leutnant?'

Hausser nodded, looking at where the man was pointing, seeing a lone thin chimney of considerable height standing in the distance. Around the chimney were shells of buildings, their roofs destroyed, the exterior walls standing erect against the elements, their surfaces potted and punctured from the fierce fighting. 'Yes, is that the Tractor Factory?'

The soldier nodded, 'Yes Sir, the Russkies stopped producing tractors there and changed to tanks some time ago. They were driving them out from the production line to face us at one point, until we took their beloved factory.' He grinned, the strain showing again in his eyes. Then he seemed to become distant, the smile fading, 'We lost many of our men taking the objective.'

Hausser looked at the man, seeing he was near to breaking point, 'I will send one of my men back for the others, they should have their clothing by now.'

The soldier nodded again, 'It will not take long now Sir. He looked past the commander to the two soldiers behind him, 'If you lose your bearings, just ask someone for directions to the lone chimney, they should all know that.'

Udet and 'Hase' nodded as Hausser turned to face them, 'Udet, go back and get the others please. Keep your head down and move more to the west.' He indicated with his right hand, 'Moving that many men through the trenches we have been in will take too much time.'

Udet nodded, 'Yes Hausser, I will try and get back to you as soon as possible.' He nudged 'Hase's' arm as a farewell greeting and turned in the trench, running back the way they had come, his body lowered.

They moved forward again, keeping a distant eye on the chimney. Slowly it got nearer, the circular brick construction beginning to rise up before them. With it to the left stood the shell of a tall tower, not as high as the chimney. The red brick building virtually cut in two with only half of the structure still standing to the height of four floors, its exposed upper floors open to the elements, the red bricks pitted and torn.

As they got nearer, 'Hase' could make out the different buildings that made up the tractor works. A long factory building, probably the main production area, with several other blocks and smaller buildings surrounding it. All were heavily damaged, their roofs incomplete or broken by shellfire. Metal girders and frames stood between and adjoined some of the buildings, the equipment and machinery for moving heavy metal machine parts and vehicle frames.

They began to pass soldiers their guide recognised as they entered the large complex, the man nodding or greeting people, their gestures warm and friendly. Hausser realised the reason for their friendly welcome relatively quickly, these men would probably be expecting to be relieved by him and his small improvised unit.

Rubble and broken bricks covered the roads and paths around the buildings as they exited the trench system. Their guide leading them between buildings from the trench exit and into a damaged administrative building on the outer edge of the complex. The building was nearly square and had been white in the past, but now presented a dark grey colour to the world, the exterior walls pock marked with the scars of battle.

Climbing some stairs wearily, the soldier that had lead them through the factory district indicated for them to turn to the left at the top of the staircase. Hausser turned around the wall at the top of the stairs, walking into a relatively wide open plan office space capable of accommodating probably four desks, the furniture shattered across the wooden floorboards. One desk remained intact on which a radio was situated, the operator sitting before it, his headphones over one ear. In the corner facing the river with their backs to them, binoculars held to their eyes, an officer and Major Slusser were knelt before a sandbagged broken and charred window.

Chapter Eleven: Overview

The Major glanced over his shoulder, 'Ah, Leutnant Hausser, good to see you, are your men ready to take up their positions?'

Hausser walked forward, lowering himself as he approached the window, 'They should be with us soon, Sir. I have sent back for them, they were waiting for warmer clothing.'

Major Slusser nodded slowly, 'I see, I was hoping they would be here by now.'

Hausser's eyes narrowed, 'They should not be long now. What's the situation, Sir?'

The Major indicated to the officer next to him, 'This is Hauptmann Gerstle, he is commander of the unit you will be replacing.' He turned his eyes to the captain, 'Hauptmann, will you advise us of the situation please?'

The captain turned, looking Hausser up and down, nodding a greeting, the tiredness on his unshaven face apparent, 'Good to see you Leutnant, we have been manning this sector of the front for a number of weeks now.' He turned back to the window and raised the binoculars to his eyes, clearing his throat, 'In my opinion, the Russians are up to something, I expect we will hear from them really soon. They seem to have changed their tactics from simply defending to more ambitious ideas. More aggressive sniping, movements at night, etc.' He lifted the glasses above his head, offering them to Hausser, 'Here.....you take a look.'

Hausser moved further forward to between the men, taking the binoculars from the man's hands and raising them to his eyes. As he raised the glasses to his eyes, he looked out through the damaged window, snowflakes fluttering through the opening. Seeing the building they were in was placed towards the back of the factory complex, he moved the glasses further towards the river, observing what seemed to be the front line of trenches interspersed through smaller outbuildings, some fifty to one hundred metres in front of the complex. There was a section of land before these trenches, the snow covered earth pitted and burnt with the weeks of fighting, the buildings in the area more severely damaged than others.

The captain paused, waiting for Hausser to adjust the binoculars, 'Look to the far right, at the top of the riverbank, do you see the four storey damaged building?' Sporadic rifle shots echoed in the distance an indication of the tenseness on the front line.

Hausser squinted through the glasses, moving along the damaged and destroyed buildings some two hundred metres from the edge of the factory, 'Ah, yes I see it.' Observing the large broken four storey brick block, the roof destroyed.

'The Russkies seem to use that as a collection point, sending out men to sweep and scout the area. The obstructions in the middle provide some cover, but we have seen an increase in their activities in the last day.' The captain stopped talking, allowing Hausser to take in the terrain.

Major Slusser moved his glasses to study the block, 'Do you think they are preparing for an attack?'

Hauptmann Gerstle nodded, 'The only conclusion I can make. Due to the trenches and works they have completed on the wide riverbank, beyond our line of vision, we are unable to gain intelligence as to whether they bring troops up or not. It is a difficult position, they are able to increase their men in a particular area quite considerably ready for an attack without us being forewarned. The first sign we will have is when they initiate the attack.'

The major lowered the glasses from his eyes, turning to look at the captain, 'I see, not the best position to be in.' He glanced round at Hausser, 'We attempted to take the riverbank a number of times, but the Russkies are very determined defenders, beating us back each time. We took the building in question two or three times, but they threw everything at us to retake it before we could consolidate. To be honest I am not surprised, it holds an excellent view of their positions, if we had taken that and the adjoining buildings, they would probably have lost this section of the river.' He looked down, becoming reflective, 'Still, I think it is too late now, our orders are to hold our current positions and await the relief effort.' He looked round at Hausser, 'What's your view?'

Hausser nodded slowly, still studying the terrain. He looked through the field glasses at the other three or four storey buildings adjacent to the building they had been discussing. All were to the south of the main building and had been severely damaged, smoke rising from a number of them, their windows and jagged outlines exposed to the elements. 'They have an elevated position over our front line in that building and the ones further to the south, but the broken buildings and obstructions in between should provide some interruption to continuous sniper fire onto our men. Unfortunately, they will also prevent us from seeing the attack break, if indeed they attack out from those buildings.'

The major smiled briefly, 'If you were them, Hausser, would you attack that way?'

Hausser thought for a second, then a faint smile passed across his face, 'Yes I would.' He looked north of the building they had been discussing, seeing the buildings to be lower and more severely damaged. The ground between the lines in that area more open. 'Still, the ground is too obstructed to use many tanks, is it mined, tripwires?'

The captain nodded, 'Yes, that's the problem, the Russkies seem to have a fondness for our mines, they are better than theirs. They come out every night and remove some, cut our tripwires.' He grinned ironically, 'Determined bastards!'

A smile briefly crossed Hausser's face, 'Interesting, the sign of an impending attack. I will have them placed in depth just before the trench line, perhaps dig the trenches deeper, then fragmentation from the explosions won't hit our men.'

Hauptmann Gerstle turned to look at him, 'Good luck with the digging, the ground is now so solid due to the frost you will need to use grenades! It must be colder than last year, Herr Leutnant.' He paused, wiping his nose, 'Then you have the sewers, they are quite active down there. You will have to place men underground to stop them infiltrating our rear. That is the most soul destroying thing for the men, they just hate it.'

The officers turned as they heard boots on the stairs behind them, seeing a breathless Udet appear at the corner of the room, the surprise on his young face evident as he saw the three officers. Snapping to attention, he saluted formally.

Major Slusser nodded to him, raising his hand to his helmet, 'Yes private?'

Udet swallowed hard, 'Soldat Udet, Sir. Reporting our unit is ready to be deployed Sir!'

The major nodded, turning to Hausser, 'It seems your time at the front is here, Herr Leutnant. This situation concerns me so I am moving my headquarters here to oversee this sector. You will have close support if needed. Hauptmann Gerstle's men will be held in reserve for the next few days, but they will be close by if we need them.'

Hausser lowered his binoculars, looking at the Major, 'Yes Sir. I shall move the men up immediately.' He turned to the captain, 'Thank you for the situation report, Captain.'

The senior officer nodded, the captain leaning forward grasping his arm, 'Take care out there Leutnant, I feel the Russians will be coming soon. Give it another hour, and move your men up under the cover of darkness only, otherwise the Russians will start shelling.' Their eyes met and Hausser saw the seriousness in the captain's expression.

'Yes, Thank you,' he lifted his hand to his helmet and rose from his knelt position, turning he moved half crouched towards Udet, indicating for him to head back down the stairs. Realising the room seemed darker now, the light of the late afternoon beginning to fade.

The major called after him, 'Stay close to the radio Hausser, and keep me updated of anything that happens.'

'Hausser stopped at the wall, half turning, he grinned, 'Yes Sir, you will be the second to know!' Then he disappeared from view, the sound of boots descending the wooden stairs echoing round the silent room.

Major Slusser turned to Hauptmann Gerstle, his expression grim, 'Get a few of your men to sandbag the windows and barricade the doors of this building when they are fully relieved. I want additional fire-points and emplacements prepared along this line, this building in the centre, impregnable. Your men will man this line if....when the Russians attack Hausser, understand? The Russians will pay for every metre.........in blood!'

Chapter Twelve: Croatian ingenuity

The forty plus men moved swiftly through the darkness, stopping at cover points and waiting for others to catch up. Using two main paths through the factory complex, they stepped cautiously forward, their weapons at the ready. Their boots crunched unnervingly on the iced snow, their exhaled breath condensed as it forced its way through their scarves and balaclavas.

Hausser moved up, advancing in the middle of the group, escorted by Udet and 'Hase', his men behind him following their progress. To the right moved Meino and his squad, with the Italians, Luca and Alessio. His squad had picked up additional supplies on Hausser's instructions and they were slowed by the extra rolls of barbed wire and flares he had told them to collect. Tatu and Petru took the left position, moving swiftly but cautiously along towards the side of the main heavily damaged factory building.

As the men moved forward, the first snowflakes began to fall for the night, becoming thicker as they progressed, the clouds above dropping a heavy snow fall as they slowly progressed across the sky. Hausser was relieved that the snow would provide additional cover, but this also provided an additional challenge to keep the men together. In unfamiliar terrain there was a chance some would stray past the forward positions, becoming disorientated in the heavy snow fall.

He began to stop more frequently, gathering the men together and ensuring there were no stragglers. As night had fallen, the temperatures had dropped further and he was keen to get all the men into the forward positions before the conditions deteriorated further.

As the soldiers moved alongside the large main factory building, the large dark structure high above them to the left, they passed several defensive positions. The soldiers manning the emplacements braced against the temperatures, their candles or improvised lights covered from the snow and to prevent light escaping, thus preventing markers for any Russian observers.

Meino was struggling to keep his men together on the right, the Hungarians in his charge resentful of being put under Croatian leadership. He hissed instructions into the darkness, seeing only snowflakes and silhouettes, reminding them of the importance of staying together. Luca and Alessio had opted to carry the extra rolls of barbed wire and flares and were slowed by their burden, following directly behind Meino.

The Croatian soldier looked to the left and saw the end of the large shadow above them, as they passed the Tractor factory, realising it must only be a number of metres before they reached the trenches. Moving slowly forward he called out quietly, the unnerving feeling of disorientation beginning to enter his mind. After about three minutes he began to become concerned, considering he must have covered almost fifty metres, then he heard a faint response to one of his calls, the word, 'Heir!' drifting through the snowfall towards him. Skirting a low damaged wall, he almost fell into the forward trench, slipping on the edge when it loomed up before him.

As he slipped downwards into the trench, hands grasped his uniform, preventing him from falling, two soldiers of the 305th Infantry Division grinning as he regained his stance in the trench. Thanking them he moved up and down the trench for some distance, inspecting the area he was to defend, ensuring all his men had reached their destination. The trench turned at an angle directly opposite the tall buildings he had seen in the distance, the broken and shattered blocks Hausser had advised the Russians occupied. He realised he had a position of about one hundred metres to defend with only twelve men, a daunting and unnerving prospect, making him slightly uneasy.

He slowly made his way along the trench towards the front of the Tractor Factory to report to his concerns to Hausser, passing soldiers as they briefed the new arriving unit on the situation and their individual positions. He reached a small low accommodation block, the trench entered the building through an opening in the basement wall. He cautiously climbed through, finding the officer speaking with Hauptmann Gerstle, the room lit by dim candlelight, the light flickering across the walls.

He stepped forward, stamping his feet from the cold and dusting the snow from his uniform with his spare hand, his other grasping his MP40. As the officer and captain turned to look at him, he stood more sharply, saluting, 'All men in position Sir. I have to report the section we cover is extensive for the men I have under my command. We are nearest the enemy positions and will require reinforcement if attacked.'

Hausser nodded grimly, 'I understand, I will move one of the machine gunners to your sector and a couple of riflemen to compensate.' The commander thought for a second, 'The other machine gun will be placed in the building above us as it has a good line of fire.' He turned to Hauptmann Gerstle, 'Can I also have your heavy weapons please?'

The captain smiled under his scarf, 'We only have one MG34, set up in the factory roof above us, but I see I have a lot more men.' He considered for a second, 'I will leave it there for you, but you will have to man it. That gives you three MGs for a front of about three hundred metres Leutnant.'

Hausser nodded, 'Good, thank you. That should be an excellent deterrent.'

The captain continued, 'There is also a good sniping position in the remains of the factory roof, do you have a suitable man?'

Hausser thought for a second, then his eyes lightened, 'Yes, perhaps........have you a sighted rifle for him?'

Hauptmann Gerstle nodded, 'I think we have a spare, our sniper is quite proficient and organised.' He smiled slightly, 'He will be reluctant to give up his spare weapon, but under the circumstances.....'

Hausser nodded, 'Good, then we have a man for it.' He turned back to Meino, 'Get the Italians to place extra wire, flares and some Russian grenade traps out in the ground in front of your position. That should hold the enemy for a while, or even persuade them to move around you, exposing them to extra fire.' A grin formed on the officer's face, 'Once they are finished, send young Luca to me, it's time to see if his shooting is as good as his cooking!'

Meino nodded slowly, a smile briefly crossing his face, 'Yes Sir. I will get it done now.' He turned abruptly, heading back for the opening in the wall behind him.

Hausser called after him, 'I will have the squads rotated every couple of hours, that should reduce their exposure to the cold. They will spend one third of their time in the building.'

Meino turned his head as he stepped through the opening, the cold air enveloping him again, 'Thank you Sir, I will tell the men.'

He passed through the hole in the wall and began to walk back down the trench, passing the mixed nationalities of soldiers as he went, the snow now falling heavily. As he progressed, his breathing becoming laboured, he noticed the unit they had come up to relieve was beginning to leave, the troops having changed positions with the new arrivals in the variety of firing positions. He stopped briefly to exchange a few words with a corporal that was preparing to depart.

Luca and Alessio turned to look at him as the Croatian arrived back at their position, the Italians' faces solemn beneath their scarves, knowing full well what the squad commander would want them to do. Sitting opposite each other in the trench, both were smoking heavily, knowing the dangers of the task at hand.

Meino crouched down before them, accepting the lit cigarette Alessio offered him, his hand outstretched towards him. Lowering his scarf, he took a deep draw on the cigarette, the Croatian began to talk in a whisper, 'Once we have finished our smoke, we will head out and bolster the wire defences in front of our position, specifically around the bend in the trench.' He indicated further along the trench with the hand holding the cigarette, 'One of us will have to crawl out to the edge of the defences and set up more flare and grenade traps. The cylinder grenades are best, so leave any stick grenades behind.'

Luca smiled, patting his knapsack, 'I have brought a couple of Romanian grenades and three or four Russian *Limonka* ones, will they do?'

Meino's eyes widened, 'Good, quite resourceful of you young Luca, we will use those then. I have a couple too, how about you Alessio?' The Italian raised his hand in the gloom, showing three fingers, his expression strained. Meino nodded, his expression becoming serious again, reaching into his tunic pockets, he produced three half used rolls of twine, 'Use this to attach to the pins on the grenades and stretch the cord out before the wire. Do the same with the flares. Remember, the cord must be taut, but not too much, the snow lying on top of it will set them off otherwise.'

Both Italians nodded slowly, the smile fading from Luca's face as he drew on his medicated cigarette again. 'Are there any traps out there already?'

Meino shook his head, 'Probably not many according to the previous occupants, they have always been told to keep the ground clear to attack....that has changed now.' He glanced round, making sure the other soldiers were in position, 'We must get beyond the wire and out into the land beyond. Then we split up and move to either side, chose your spots carefully.' He rose slightly, glancing over the trench wall, seeing the snow was falling very heavily, turning to face the men again, he indicated with his head, 'Right, let's go! We meet back in the middle after placing the items, then we return to the trench, understand?'

Slowly the three men made their way along the trench, their breath beginning to freeze on their scarves. After about ten metres, they reached a small junction leading to the left in the trench, the gradual slope ascending up to ground level. Meino indicated to the soldier guarding the gap their mission was about to commence, and the man whispered along the line to hold fire. Lowering to their hands and knees, they proceeded up the slope and out into the land before the frontline trench, the snow iced beneath them.

A broken wall was on their right and reaching the end of it they lowered themselves to their stomachs and began to crawl below the first lines of wire, the sharp steel needles just above their heads. The wire obstacles had been placed to a depth of about twenty metres and was about a metre high. Iced snow hung to the wire, and they began to feel the cold seep through their uniforms and gloves. As they emerged from the shelter of the broken wall, a bitter breeze enveloped them, the cold seeming to almost take their breath away.

Luca moved slowly off to the right with Alessio in the centre and Meino to the left. They crawled forward, their hearts beating loudly in their chests, their breath held. As the snowflakes fell around them, the grooves their bodies made in the snow as they progressed began to become covered behind them, a thick veil of cold snow lying across the frozen landscape.

Meino hissed to his right, 'Stay within five or ten metres so we can hear each other.'

Luca swallowed, the cold beginning to restrict his breathing. He moved cautiously forward, dragging his knapsack with his left hand, his rifle in his right. He slowly began to turn to his right, away from the others, his aim for the area in front of the bend in the trench. Moving slowly between the thin poles that had been placed a couple of weeks earlier, the barbed wire wrapped around them. Occasionally the uniform on his shoulders would catch on the wires above and he would drop back slightly to free himself, before proceeding again. He could feel and hear the scraping across the top of his helmet as he pushed forward, the needles of the wire resisting his movement.

After about ten minutes he reached the edge of the wire, leading out into the empty terrain beyond. He could see the shadows of broken walls and the foundations of buildings before him, their original structures reduced from weeks of shelling, leaving only heaps of rubble and the occasional outline indicating where a building had once stood. The broken remains were now covered in a blanket of snow, the ice breaking and splitting the structures further as the temperature rose and fell dramatically.

Crawling further forward, he stopped next to a pile of rubble, leaning against the cold broken brick. Looking to his left, he thought he could just make out the shadow of Alessio crawling forward. Swallowing and exhaling, he hissed towards the shape, 'Alessio?'

The shadow stopped, then turned slightly, 'Luca, what is it?'

Luca breathing was heavy, 'Just checking, I don't want to lose you out here!'

Alessio smiled under his scarf, his fondness for his countryman strong, 'Just think of the beaches in Sicily, Luca and get the damn grenades put up!'

Luca grinned briefly under his scarf, remembering the holiday the two of them had spent together as teenagers, travelling to the southern Italian island for a week to explore their homeland. He raised his hand slightly, and turned back, beginning to crawl forward again. His breath was becoming short and he prayed to himself that he would not have another asthma attack.

Reaching the foundations of a small building, he considered this a good place to position his first trap. As he crawled round the structure, he eventually found what used to be the doorway, the opening now only about half a metre tall. Looking through the opening he could just make out the remains of the walls that had once bordered the rooms, now reduced to nothing more than an outline on the ground. Piles of broken masonry and bricks lay around the structure and he struggled to reach the doorway without contorting his body.

He reached forward, wrapping the twine around the grenade and attaching it to the broken doorframe. Once he had accomplished this, pulling it tightly to hold the grenade in place, he reached for his bayonet and twisted it through the twine, breaking the strand. He could feel his heart beating loudly as he moved slightly to attach the cord around the opposite frame. Tying this he stretched the cord across the opening to the grenade, allowed some extra twine, cutting it once again with his bayonet. His hands were shaking as he slowly slipped the twine through the pin of the grenade, realising that if the pin was pulled, he would be lucky to get away in time with the metal *Limonka* attached to the doorframe. Steadying himself, and taking a deep breath, he tied the twine loosely and backed away from the item, mentally noting to himself 'four grenades to go, one flare.'

Luca placed the items slowly, trying to make a mental note of the positions and working around in an arc in front of the corner of the trench. The final grenade was placed between two small walls, wedging the last *Limonka* in some rubble and stretching the twine across the gap between the debris. He then began to crawl back along the arc, mentally trying to check his route every two or three metres. The snow was still falling heavily as he progressed, a blanket of white covering all his previous tracks, disorientating him. Concern rose within his chest as he realised all the broken buildings seemed to look the same in the snow flurry. He passed a doorway, leaning forward in the gloom, trying to determine if this was where he had placed the first grenade, the heavy snow fall now blanketing the entire area. Shaking his head in frustration, he continued crawling forward until he reached the position he believed he had seen Alessio at previously, his visibility now reduced to two or three metres.

But Luca was alone, his heart beating hard in his chest, the fear of disorientation rising within him. The snowflakes fell all around him, his exhaled breath causing them to swirl before landing on the ground. Had he strayed out from the position he thought he was at? He slowly moved around, turning his body and staring desperately into the darkness, seeing only the near shapes of broken walls and debris in the gloom. He decided to wait for a while, allowing his countryman and Meino time to return. After two or three minutes, he began to become increasingly concerned, wondering whether to return to the trench and wait for them. He whispered out in the darkness, 'Alessio?' Then crawled forward a few metres to see if his countryman was returning.

He waited, hearing nothing. Then he whispered again, his voice slightly louder, 'Alessio? Meino?' There was no response, then a shuffling to his right made him freeze, catching his breath. He slowly turned towards the sound, pulling his rifle silently forward with his right hand.

Breathing heavily, his chest wheezing, he felt the nausea rising within him, a fear of the unknown beginning to overcome him, his mind racing. As he raised his rifle, he determined to whisper again, 'Alessio?' He jumped as a burst of machine gun fire erupted in the darkness before him, some ten metres away. The bullets splattered around him in the iced snow, his back arching as they punctured his uniform and the back of his ribs, his rifle firing as his fingers clenched. As he twisted onto his back, he felt the pain sweep through his body, six bullets having entered his back. He lay still, his breath in short gasps, the agony spreading across his torso. His chest heaved as he began to struggle for air, his exhalations beginning to become shorter, the air condensing above him. The snowflakes drifting downwards towards and into his open terrified eyes. The pain increased, his mind becoming clear in his terror, the realisation he could not move, or feel his legs. He heard a burst of fire from beyond his boots, Meino's MP40 firing into the darkness above his body. Rifle cracks followed from above his head, then a machine gun burst from beyond his boots again.

As the bullets zipped through the air above him, Luca's mind slowly filled with images of home. His smiling mother, the beach, meals together with his sister and her husband, his mother and father in their home. The sun through the trees in their small garden where he used to play, then they seemed to grow distant, further away, tinged with darkness. Tears welled up in his eyes as he realised it was all to end here, a bitter twisted frozen hell, thousands of miles from his beloved Italy. Then darkness filled his vision, his breath short and sharp for a few seconds, then nothing.

Meino and Alessio had waited for some time, becoming concerned about the missing Luca. Lying in the iced snow, they had whispered his name every now and then, trying to provide some guidance for him if he had got lost in the darkness. They had considered several times that they may be in the wrong place, having both perhaps become disorientated. They had both 'jumped' instinctively when they heard the burst of fire, the distinctive noise of a Russian PPSH machine gun. Scrambling apart across the snow, they had sought cover behind debris and fired out into the darkness, aiming high to avoid hitting Luca if he was in front of them. Bullets had whistled back, hitting the debris and broken shells of the buildings around them, forcing them to push themselves lower into the frozen rubble for cover.

The Russian patrol having strayed too near the German lines in the dark, covered their retreat. Firing wildly towards the enemy line then moving, attempting to avoid return fire if their position was identified. The MG34 in the factory roof opened fire, spraying small bursts across the terrain, blinded by the falling snow.

Meino turned, the panic rising within him. Shouting towards the trench behind them, 'Nicht Schiessen! Nicht Schiessen!' Afraid the infantrymen in the front trench would open fire in unison with the MG34, potentially hitting them.

The soldier in the trench awaiting the three soldiers' return shouted to either side to prevent the scared men from firing. Warning them of allied soldiers to their front, before the trench.

As the return fire subsided, Meino indicated to Alessio to return to the trench with his hand, the Italian nodding. As Alessio began to crawl back towards the front line, his mind was filling with dread. The fate of Luca unknown, he feared the worst.

Meino waited until the MG34 stopped firing from the factory in the distance to his left, the landscape slowly returning to silence. The Russian infantry patrol retreating back across the ground they had been sent out to sweep for enemy activity. He slowly crawled forward, heading for the spot where he had heard the initial machine gun burst. The snow was falling heavily, seeming to be even heavier than before, the flakes coming to rest all around him. He held his MP40 tightly in both hands as he edged forward, his breathing heavy, forcing the exhaled breath through the freezing scarf across his mouth.

As he progressed, he saw the shadow of a low destroyed building wall emerge through the snowfall, the debris on the ground before him. Pushing his left arm forward, it hit an object that moved slightly, his breath catching in his mouth as he realised it was a boot. As he drew alongside the body, his fears were realised, Luca lay dead, his rifle and knapsack by his side.

The Croatian lay there for a minute, the frustration and bitter sadness rising within him. Then slowly Meino gathered the knapsack, lifting the bag over his head and wrapping the strap of the rifle around Luca's limp arm to his shoulder, thrusting the Italians hands under his belt. Pushing himself to the foot of the body, he began pulling the lifeless soldier back towards the frontline. It took him nearly one whole hour to complete the grim task.

Situation Report: 305th Infantry Division to Sixth Army Headquarters

Date: December 11th, 1942.

Limited enemy incursions or attacks on the front line before the Tractor Factory. Casualties sustained from sniper fire continue all along divisions section. Sniper activity increasing, sapping morale. Food and ammunition supply situation becoming critical. Request immediate increase in supplies.

There was no reply.

Historical Overview: December 11th, 1942

Since the encirclement was completed, the Russian Army launched two major attacks, one against the south of the encircled army, the other against the northwest, the Germans believing both were beaten back. But the objective was to discover the defenders strength, not for territorial gain.

Out on the steppe, the Russian Army is preparing two lines of defensive positions, one line facing inwards against the defenders of Stalingrad and the other facing outwards in an attempt to prevent any relief effort from the German Army outside.

After the Russians captured the German Sixth Army's main supply base at the Chir railhead, the army encircled within Stalingrad are relying of the German Air Force, the Luftwaffe, to supply the pocket by air. The Luftwaffe needing to supply the surrounded Army's ammunition, food and other supplies. Stores are limited within the pocket, with only an estimated two or three days of food remaining. The Sixth Army begins slaughtering their horses for food. Horses that are already slowly starving.

The Russians believe they have encircled approximately 70-80,000 soldiers, the true number is closer to 300,000 men. The temperature is dropping….each day, sometimes by the hour.

The Russian Winter of 1942 had arrived, this was to be one of the most vicious and coldest winters on record.

Chapter Thirteen: December the Twelfth, 1942

Several days had passed. Hausser cautiously clambered over the debris in the factory, the cold wind blowing through the severely damaged structure, biting at his clothing. Slowly crossing the main production floor, he stepped over broken bricks and damaged metal pieces scattered across the ground. Glancing to his right, he could see the engineering workshops at the far end of the building, their view partly obstructed by broken heavy machinery, rubble and the flurrying snowflakes. Crumps of explosions and the cracks of sporadic rifle fire crept across the frontline from the north and south, the nervous defenders opening fire on any shadow or movement before them.

Climbing over a broken conveyor, he stepped through broken machinery and made towards a doorway in the middle of the large building. The broken glass and shattered wood crunched beneath his boots as he walked into a small corridor with offices on either side. Emerging from the gloom, the air was bitterly crisp that afternoon as he trudged across a cement yard towards the administrative building. Nodding to the soldier stood just inside the doorway, he made for the staircase, climbing the stairs wearily and turning into the office he had stood in a week before.

The floor was now cleared and the windows sandbagged, providing some cover from the bitter winds that swept through the factory district. In the middle of the room was a repaired table with a couple of maps across it. Several makeshift chairs of boxes and repaired workshop stools sat around the centrepiece, with a small side table housing the radio and operator. The room was lit with several candles, providing quite an eerie effect across the walls and sandbags as the naked flames flickered in the slight air movement.

Major Slusser looked up at him from the table, the man stood on the other side, leaning over the maps, 'Ah, Leutnant Hausser, good to see you. We are just waiting for Hauptmann Gerstle and the other company commanders before we start. Help yourself to a cigarette.' The major indicated to the side table with several cigarette packets next to the radio.

Hausser saluted, 'Thank you Major, how are we today?' He walked over to the radio, nodding to the operator who was listening intently to radio traffic through his headphones.

The major straightened up, his face grim, 'I am getting annoyed at the activity in the sewers further along the line. The Russians seem to be getting rather ambitious. Several fire fights have broken out, but we have held them, inflicting some casualties in one of their bigger incursions.' He lifted a cigarette and lit it, 'They are trying to get behind us and we can't let that happen, they could interrupt our supplies and cut us off. They must be stopped.'

Lighting his own cigarette, Hausser nodded thoughtfully, hearing boots on the stairs to his left. He turned to see Hauptmann Gerstle reach the top of the staircase, two other officers behind him, they nodded a greeting and turned to salute the major, stiffening their stances.

Major Slusser indicated for the men to approach the table, 'Have a seat gentlemen, and let me update you on events.'

The officers assumed seating positions on the makeshift chairs, leaning forward to look at the maps. The major leaned back, stretching, then clearing his throat, his eyes lightening, 'I have good news gentlemen, Von Manstein has attacked from the southwest, driving through the Russian 51st Army. Hoth's tanks are making good progress we are told. The radios are jammed, but despatches were flown in to us by the Luftwaffe informing us of the situation.'

Grins broke onto the faces of the tired officers around the table, their moods heightening with the news, Hauptmann Gerstle slapped his knee, 'Excellent news, Major, this is just the boost the men need.'

One of the other officers leant forward, placing his elbows on the table, 'If I may ask, Sir, how long before they break through to us?'

The major's eyes sparkled in the candlelight, 'I do not know, not long I hope. Apparently more divisions are coming from the western front with the view of re-establishing our positions along the Volga. This time, we may destroy the Russian Bear once and for all.' He paused, allowing the happiness of the officers subside, letting them offer a variety of possible situations that could emerge, watching their grins widen.

He noticed Hausser was quieter, his mood more subdued. Puzzled, the major raised his hands to quieten the other men, 'Leutnant Hausser, is there something troubling you?'

Hausser looked down at the map, his eyes seeming tired, and his expression solemn, 'We have a long way to go yet I think. Yes, we have hope but the supply situation is grim and I cannot see the Russians giving up their grip of us here without a fight. The weather is getting worse and now favours the defender, Hoth's tanks may take some time to get here. What shall we do in the meantime?'

Major Slusser nodded, seeing the other men become more subdued as they considered what Hausser had said. 'Yes, I think you may be right. Rations were cut again three days ago, the reductions will be passed on to the men tonight. We have better prospects now though, so let's have a look at our position and see if we can improve our defences.' The major stood back, running his hand across his face. Turning to the radio operator, he nodded to him, 'Can we have some drinks please Gunther?' The operator nodded, removing his headphones and rising from his position, he headed towards the stairs.

The major turned back to the officers, 'Now, let's start with the casualty figures for the last week.'

Hausser stumbled on the broken bricks, his return journey to the forward command post made more difficult in the fading light. The small amount of vodka he had consumed had warmed his stomach, but was now reacting with the bitter air, causing him to feel slightly drunk.

His mood was grim, the casualties weighing heavily on his mind. His own unit had lost six men, including the cheerful Luca, depressing him considerably. Sniper fire had increased in the last two days and this had increased his uneasiness, the Russians becoming more organised. They had heard the enemy at night, moving in the cover of darkness, probably scouting their positions out in the land before them. He had considered sending out a patrol to confront them, but had decided against it, the men being too inexperienced and too few in number.

Slowly he progressed through the broken factory, carefully stepping over obstacles and through the devastated equipment. Shellfire and dive bomber attacks had obliterated most of the contents of the large building, with destroyed machinery and production parts lying all across the area.

Reaching the far wall, he gingerly stepped down the decline leading to the trench that went beneath the building wall, leading out to the small accommodation block that housed his command post. He could hear talking above him in the rafters of the building, Alessio attempting to make conversation with the machine gunner placed just under the roof.

The young Italian had offered to take Luca's place as sniper and he had disagreed at first, his concern for the man's ability apparent. Alessio had argued convincingly to be given the opportunity and to avenge his countryman's death. Hausser had eventually given up the argument, agreeing reservedly, stating that he would take the position in turns with Nicu, the better shot assuming the role more permanently. He smiled briefly as he recalled Udet's face, the expression of rejection when he had refused his eager request to try the position. The young soldier's regret being clearly reversed in his expression when Hausser had asked him to consider how cold it would be up in the roof of the factory.

Entering the trench, he passed a soldier coming the other way, the men turning to the side to allow each other to pass. The Hungarian nodded recognition beneath the material wrapped round his mouth, raising his hand in a relaxed salute. Hausser had saluted back, seeing the man was carrying the food supply boxes from a successful trip to the forward command post, now returning the containers to the broken offices across the factory for the following day.

The cold air swept across him as he passed through the foundation wall of the factory, exiting into the exposed part of the trench before it entered the accommodation block some one hundred metres away. The trench twisted back and forth with a couple of junctions leading to the north or south positions. As he walked, his head began to feel clearer, becoming more adjusted to the bitter cold. He looked up, seeing the stars beginning to become clear above him, the sharpness of the lights eerily beautiful in the night sky. A beauty that meant only one thing for the soldiers in the trenches that night, the temperature would sink to an almost unbearable level. He considered rotating the men more frequently that night and issuing any additional clothing he could find as he approached the entrance to the command post. A couple of flashes to the south distracted him briefly, the Russian shells exploding in the air before the defensive positions, their lights fading as the glowing shrapnel fell to earth.

Stepping through the opening in the foundations to the building, he glimpsed Tatu to his left in deep conversation with Petru and Nicu, their unit's time in the buildings almost drawing to a close. Several other soldiers sat around the room, having just finished eating. Some were smoking, others chatting in subdued voices, their spirits lowered as they realised the time to venture back into the cold was approaching. He stamped his feet on the cement basement floor as he entered, dusting off the moisture that had crystallised on his uniform, his helmet frosted.

He stepped towards the three men, 'So what's the situation?'

Tatu spun round, his expression angry, 'It's the rations, Hausser, they are not enough for the men!'

The young commander nodded grimly, noticing the other men around beginning to take notice, their conversations ending. 'I agree, but we have no choice at present until the supply situation improves.'

Tatu indicated for him to come to the side, his expression grave. He lowered his voice, 'Herr Leutnant, I am a quartermaster, the men will starve on these food levels over time. There must be more, surely?'

Hausser shook his head, 'I understand your concerns. I have spoken to the Major today regarding this, there is no more food available. If we stay on these rations, then we will survive until the relief effort gets here.'

Tatu shook his head in exasperation, his voice rising again, 'Relief effort? We have been cut off for over two weeks, we are now eating the horses.....' He raised his hands above his sides in exasperation, 'This is madness!'

Hausser's eyes narrowed, his voice rising in frustration, 'Tatu! Pull yourself together, this is unacceptable!' He placed his hands on his hips, glaring at the sergeant.

Tatu lowered his arms, his face becoming crestfallen as he realised his position. His eyes filled with sadness, 'Yes, Hausser, you are right. I am sorry. It's just in all my time making sure the food is fit for the soldiers, I have never served up rubbish like this.....I' His anger rising again.

Hausser interrupted, his voice firm, raising his tone to ensure the rest of the men in the room could hear, 'General Hoth attacked the Russians earlier as part of the relief effort, his tanks have smashed through enemy positions and he is driving towards Stalingrad as we speak.'

Tatu's eyebrows rose, his expression frozen for a second, 'Really? That is fantastic news.' Seeing an opportunity to redeem himself, he turned, looking across the startled soldiers, their expressions lightening, 'Do you hear that men? German tanks are coming!'

A hoarse cheer circled the room, the soldiers outside in the bitter cold turning to look in curiosity.

Hausser raised his arms for the men to be silent, 'They are on their way, but we have to hold our positions until they arrive. The rations are all the Sixth

Army can spare to ensure we all survive until the tanks get here, we must get used to them, simple as that!'

Tatu looked back at Hausser and nodded, 'I understand Herr Leutnant, but now we know they are coming, we can survive on this rubbish for a few days.' He turned back to the staring soldiers, raising his voice slightly, 'I will prepare a menu for you all for when the relief effort gets here with our new supplies!'

Grins and smiles circled the room, the soldiers' spirits heightened by the charismatic declaration.

Hausser turned as he saw the soldiers look to his left, seeing the Hungarian that he had passed earlier in the trench enter the basement through the hole in the foundations. The man was breathing heavily, his eyes wide, 'Herr Leutnant!'

The officer nodded, his adrenalin beginning to surge, 'Yes, what?'

The Hungarian soldier looked startled, 'The sniper, Alessio. He says the Russians are moving a lot in their buildings.'

In the trenches, the soldiers ducked down, pressing themselves into the frozen earth, their hands over their heads. Willing the ground to allow them to go deeper. They had just heard the distant thumps from across the Volga. The sounds of heavy artillery firing.

Chapter Fourteen: In the cold of the night.

Alessio's eyes widened as he saw the flashes in the distant darkness, across the river. The young Italian had become increasingly nervous as he had seen movements in the buildings at the top of the riverbank, shadows moving across the naked flames of flickering candles. Watching through the small pair of field binoculars he had been provided with, he had observed movement within the buildings and soldiers moving down into the forward trenches in numbers. The distance in the darkness was too great for him to consider a shot with his new rifle, the figures not clear and in cover.

As he had lowered the glasses, he had become startled by the distant flashes across the Volga on the horizon. Their sight mesmerising, he hesitated to consider the target, the flashes broken by the trees in front of the artillery position.

Hands grabbed him roughly, the machine gunner pulling him from his position in the rafters of the factory. The German gunner shouted in his ear, pulling him towards the boxes and machinery that were stacked as a makeshift set of steps to their raised position, 'Get down into the trench!'

Explosions and flashes on the positions outside spurred him from his inaction, the two soldiers stumbling and slipping down the improvised steps, they landed roughly on the rubble at ground level. The gunner grabbed the back of Alessio's padded jacket, propelling him towards the slope declining towards the trench that led under the building walls.

Shell bursts outside showered dust and debris down upon them, the explosions on the outside wall and roof dislodging already broken masonry and tiles. As they reached the hole in the foundation wall, bricks and tiles crashed into the outside trench before them, a cloud of dust and snow flying through the opening, engulfing them. Coughing and raising their hands to protect their faces, they fell to either side of the hole, pushing themselves against the walls for cover.

Outside, the shells fell in front of the trenches, the blasts lighting up the darkness, virtually blinding in contrast to the darkness. Debris and dirt flew

126

into the trenches, hitting the soldiers cowering or lying with their faces in the snow for protection. The ground shook as numerous shells fell across the line all along the factory district.

Major Slusser rose from his seat at the table as he heard the thumps in the distance, turning to look out of the sandbagged window. As the shells flashes burst all around the forward positions, he grabbed a steel helmet, placing it on his head. Turning to the radio operator, he barked, 'Get downstairs for cover!'

The operator needed little encouragement, having already picked up his helmet, he grabbed his rifle and made for the staircase, the major behind him collecting his MP40. As they descended the wooden staircase, their boots cracking on the cold wood, Hauptmann Gerstle turned into the staircase at the foot of the stairs, almost colliding with the descending men. His face was flushed with alcohol, his helmet at an angle, he had been drinking with some soldiers in the next door building after the briefing.

Major Slusser glared at the captain's uniform, the tunic unbuttoned at the collar, his subordinate's eyes wide and glazed, 'Gerstle, you are a disgrace!' The major pushed him roughly in the chest, 'Why are you not with your men?'

Hauptmann Gerstle swayed with the push, grasping the major's arms to steady himself, 'B...but we are in reserve, Sir...'

The major pulled the man's face towards him, his eyes narrowed, lips pursed, 'There is no reserve now you fool! You have left your men, you coward!' He pushed him away, the captain toppling backwards, landing roughly on the rubble covered floor. A shell hit the outside wall of the building, dust falling from the ceiling. Major Slusser stared in contempt at the Hauptmann at his feet, 'I should have you shot for this!' He hesitated for a second, thinking, then he raised his hand, pointing determinedly at the captain, 'You are unfit for duty and relieved of your command!' He moved his outstretched arm to the radio operator, 'Stay with Gunther here, I am assuming command of your men!' The explosions outside were getting louder, beginning to approach the building. Turning to the radio operator, the officer glaring, he raised his voice further, 'Find a heavy MG! Get it set up upstairs when the shelling stops, the Russians are coming, and lots of them!'

In the forward command post, flashes from the explosions outside were eerily casting shadows through the openings. The soldiers of Tatu's squad, huddled in the basement for protection listened to the screams and explosions outside, their terror rising. Tatu stood up right next to Hausser as the shells hit the roof of the small accommodation building, the defenders from the ground level running down the stairs into the cellar. Dust clouds billowed down the stairs behind them as the roof of the small block collapsed inwards in the centre.

Tatu nervously ran his hand across his moustache, raising his voice in the dust filled cellar, 'Stay calm, they can't get us down here!' He glanced at Hausser, the young commander nodding to him in support, 'Get ready for when it stops, check your weapons.......we are going out then!'

For a few minutes, the shells rained down on and around the front line in the factory district. Any soldiers not in cover or in the trenches would be very lucky to survive such a bombardment. Broken walls collapsed, trench sides fell inwards, bunker roofs imploded onto the occupants. Firing positions disappeared under collapsing walls and as a result of direct hits, communication cables were severed. All along the sector, the German defensive positions were targeted to maximum effect. Two soldiers bringing up ammunition to the front line were blown to bits as a shell landed before them, their bodies shattered against the force of the intense blast.

As the last few shells fell, the defenders slowly raised their heads from underneath their hands, thankful for their individual survival. The shouts for 'medic' and moaning of the wounded filled the air as the sound of the last explosion faded across the front. There was a brief silence, then the smiles of survival dissipated as a distant low pitched screeching was heard to the east, the soldiers ducking back down into their trenches and desperately covering their heads once more.

Hausser turned to Tatu, his eyes widened at the sound, 'Katyushas!' He leant out of the opening into the trench, his shout startling some of the defenders beginning to rise for cover, 'Get down, Katyusha Rockets incoming!' The commander's eyes met with a young Hungarian lying on the floor of the trench some ten metres away, his face contorted in terror. The line of sight was broken as the officer tilted his head, hearing crumps from his right, the west. German artillery was returning fire, their limited and rationed stock of ammunition being utilised to make a limited show of strength to the Russians. The young commander shouted, his voice straining in the cold, before ducking back into the command post, 'Alles in Deckung! Artillerie!'

Major Slusser had just left the safety of the administrative building as the shellfire had died down, heading across the iced path in the direction of the reserve trench. He looked across at the sky to the east as he heard the distant low pitched screeching, seeing the distant lights soar into the dark air on the other side of the river, the flames from the rockets seeming to slow as they levelled out and flew towards their positions. Swallowing hard to subdue the remaining vodka in his stomach, he started to run, the cold air whipping at his uncovered face. Reaching the entrance to the trench, he slipped down the slope, seeing some of the German infantry lined in front of him, glancing pensively out towards the incoming rockets.

Multiple trucks had launched their rockets from the east bank, aimed at the factory district, the rockets soaring up over the freezing Volga River. As the propelled shells levelled out and began to slowly lose altitude, experienced troops would watch the smoke trail to predict the approximate landing area, the rockets hitting the ground in clusters due to their narrow alignment on the launch vehicle. Once determined, the experienced soldier would know he had a limited time to move, and move very quickly if he was in the line of fire.

About fifty metres south of the forward command post, 'Hase' was watching the rockets as they began to lose height, realising the nearest would fall around the trench further to his right. Turning, he shouted a warning, calling the men towards him, but it was clear from their expressions that they did not understand or even hear. Udet, next to him, realised what 'Hase' was doing and also called out, some of the infantry rising and running towards them, their bodies lowered in the trench as the rockets began to fall to earth.

'Hase' forced Udet down onto the floor of the trench, falling on top of him, pushing his helmet forward to shield his face. The flames rose up to the south of them as the rockets exploded, the warm blast wave flowing along the trench engulfing them. The blast threw debris, broken bricks, rocket fragments and snow into the air, the shrapnel propelled upwards and outwards cutting through anyone who was not in cover. Three soldiers, two German and one Hungarian were hit directly as one rocket landed in the trench between them, the force of the blast killing them instantly, their bodies shattered and blown into the air. The rest of the salvo of rockets landed either side of the trench walls, the deadly shrapnel and debris zipping through air with the force of the explosion, cutting through the bodies of any soldiers that were not in cover.

As the shrapnel and debris lost momentum and fell to earth, a quantity landed amongst the other soldiers cowering beneath the trench walls. The metals pings as shrapnel collided with their helmets, their hands over their faces. Shell fragments and debris fell on their shoulders and legs inflicting some scratches and bruises. Some soldiers near the blast in the trench suffered from perforated ear drums, the blast wave having nowhere to escape to once it had entered their ear canals. Further disorientated shouts for assistance echoed across the devastated terrain.

'Hase' pushed himself upwards and backwards, unbalanced, he grasped at the trench walls to steady himself, knowing the Russian infantry would have used the salvo of rockets as cover to start the approach to their positions. Dirt and snow fell from his uniform as he straightened up, the shrapnel that had fallen on top of him dropping from his body. He glanced around frantically, his senses disorientated. Seeing the other soldiers slowly rise from the snow, dusting their uniforms down, confusion on their faces, he quickly looked out over the trench wall to the east. Squinting into the darkness, the torn land before the trench seemed still, the dissipated smoke and dust clouds seeming to hang in the freezing air. Glancing back, his eyes darted around the trench, instinctively and desperately searching. The smell of scorched earth and material was almost overpowering in the close confines of the trench. He hesitated, catching a glimpse of what he had been searching for, a flare lying some five metres away on the floor of the trench.

Udet was spitting snow from his mouth, pushing himself up with his hands. Rising to his knees, he reached for his rifle, the weapon lying nearby on the trench floor. As he rose from his position, they heard the puffs of flares up and down the line, the projectiles rising into the air before their positions. Most soldiers looked up, seeing the items twist in the night sky, the light beginning to cascade from the projectiles onto the torn terrain below.

There was a brief chilling silence, the lights beginning to fall to earth as they reached their highest trajectory. Then a rifle crack startled them, the sound coming from the factory roof. A burst of machine gun fire from the same location signalling the presence of enemy soldiers in the land before them. 'Hase' turned back to the front of the trench raising is rifle, with Udet next to him. Thirty metres in front of them, a flare exploded, one of the last surviving trip wires being triggered.

Hausser and Tatu were leading the men from the forward command post along the trench, dispersing them amongst the existing squad. Machine gun fire erupted from the south of their position, then further along the line, the gunners seeing moving shadows in the darkness as the flares fell to earth. To the north of them, on the other side of the forward command post, rifle shots echoed out as Meino's squad fired out into the night.

They heard the 'puff' of smoke grenades just in front of the trench, a sign the Russian infantry were preparing to attack. Udet bit his bottom lip, the tenseness almost too much. As the smoke rose, flashes in the distant buildings made the soldiers duck down instinctively as the Russian machine guns opened fire all across the factory section. Bullets whizzed overhead and splattered against the broken buildings behind them, the gunners firing high initially to gain the distance.

Tatu and Petru passed behind 'Hase' and Udet, patting them on the shoulders, the Romanian quartermaster's voice determined, 'Make every shot count!' Then he continued down the trench shouting encouragement at the other soldiers. Nicu pushed between Udet and 'Hase', raising his rifle above the trench, both soldiers side stepping to make room for the young Romanian. Turning to either side, the young Romanian winked at both, his features seeming almost childlike and innocent in the situation that was evolving. To the left, they heard Hausser shouting instructions, then the words were drowned out as machine guns fired on either side, the tracer bullets scything into the rising smoke.

Bullets splattered across the ground in front of the trenches, the Russian machine guns raking the front line. 'Hase' ducked down grasping one of the stick grenades from his belt, unscrewing the base of the cylinder, he pulled the cord and lobbed the grenade out into the smoke. He breathing heavy, watching the object rotate in the air until it disappeared into the white shroud in front of them, a distant 'crump' as it exploded followed immediately by screams. Nicu reached down repeating the action, then Udet shouted desperately to the soldiers either side, 'Grenades!' Throwing his own into the smoke.

The noise of explosions, machine gun and rifle fire was almost deafening, the bullets zipping through the air in all directions. As the soldiers tensed in the trench, they heard the distinctive squeal of tank tracks in the distance, through the smoke, their collective adrenalin and terror rising in response.

Grenades bounced on the ground before them, the Russian infantry throwing their explosives before launching an attack. Most grenades stopped just before the trench, the elevated frozen earth and sandbags in front of the defensive positions preventing the explosives from rolling further, stopping them from bouncing into the trenches.

The soldiers in the trenches ducked down, the explosions throwing dirt and sandbags into the trench on top of them. More smoke grenades landed before the trenches, the 'puffs' as the grenades detonated sending more smoke clouds across the land before the defensive positions.

'Hase' glanced over the trench wall, seeing nothing but smoke. He could hear the whine of tank tracks in the distance, across the terrain, but considered it would be difficult for the tanks to get in too close to the trench due to the many obstacles. A 'whoosh' shot over his head, the explosion behind him, the tanks opening fire. His fear rising, he glanced up and down the trench, seeing soldiers rise from their crouched positions and raising their rifles over the trench wall.

Hearing the machine guns firing in bursts to either side, 'Hase' checked his weapon. A cry from the right startled him, the voice desperately calling 'Medic' as the soldier tried to help his comrade, hit in the face by grenade shrapnel, blood pouring across his features.

Udet struggled to his feet next to him, raising his rifle. They froze, hearing the distant call of 'Hurrah!' The Russian infantry commanders urging their men forward, having now discounted the tank support. A shell whistled overhead as if to emphasise one of the tank crews' frustration, the projectile hitting the outside of the factory wall.

The 'Hurrahs' grew in volume as the Russian infantry rose up from the cover and ground in the smoke in front of the trenches. The remaining German and Romanian soldiers straining their eyes into the smoke before them for movement, their weapons raised and ready.

'Hase' stared into the smoke, the clouds billowing across the terrain in front of him, bullets splattering across the ground before the defensive position. His hands were shaking as he raised his rifle to his right eye, then he saw movement, a shape in the white cloud, a man running towards him. He squeezed the trigger, the rifle jolting backwards into his shoulder, the silhouette falling backwards into the rubble.

More shadows moved in the smoke, the rifles across the line cracking as infantrymen fired into the thick grey clouds obscuring their sight. Grenades bounced over the trench wall, the Russian infantry throwing them as they advanced. Some defenders ducked momentarily, others did not, too afraid to let the attacking infantry closer, realising they had to prevent the attacking infantry from overwhelming them.

The grenade explosions wounded several defenders, the shrapnel flying at high speed across the defensive line, hitting soldiers in their faces and shoulders. Several grenades fell into the trenches, some being thrown back out in the seconds the defenders had to catch or pick up the primed explosive. Others exploded, killing or wounding nearby soldiers as they desperately tried to move away from the explosions.

The shapes in the smoke increased dramatically in number, the main body of the Russian advance now approaching the trenches. 'Hase', Udet and Nicu fired in unison at the shadows, then the Russian infantry broke through the clouds of smoke, the grey and brown uniforms swarming towards the trench.

'Hase' gritted his teeth and fired again, hearing the machine guns on either side now firing continuously. Bullets sprayed through the air around them, the figures before the smoke being cut down as the machine guns moved desperately from side to side. Behind him, 'Hase' heard a deeper burst, an MG42 heavy machine gun firing from the first floor window of the administrative building.

As the MG34's on either side stopped, their gunners desperately pushing new ammunition canisters onto the top of their weapons, the Russian infantry were upon the trench, soldiers dropping onto the defenders. Rifle shots became more sporadic as the fighting became hand to hand in the forward positions.

'Hase' fell backwards as a Russian soldier jumped into the trench on top of him, his rifle rising up as the man bore down on him, catching him beneath his jaw, breaking it with a crack. The man fell onto the floor of the trench, screaming, his hands rising to his shattered jaw. 'Hase's' eyes widened as Nicu brought his hand down hard onto the Russian's chest, the flash of his bayonet ending the man's life in an instant.

Udet fired at point blank range at another Russian leaping towards him, the man's body doubling up as the bullet hit him, killing him before he landed in the trench.

Nicu rose from his crouched position, having now attached his bayonet to his rifle, thrusting it upwards into the side of a Russian attacking the man to his right. The man screamed, falling sideways away from him before the position.

Hausser saw his three squad members struggling further along the trench, some fifteen metres away, Udet glancing frantically towards him. Rising from his crouched position, the young commander fired his MP40 at the advancing Russians, then shouted encouragement to the men surrounding him. Pushing towards Udet and 'Hase', he clicked a new ammunition cartridge into the base of his machine gun, noticing some of the Russian infantry struggling with the wire in front of his position.

Hausser pushed forward, firing sporadic bursts over the trench wall, the bullets whipping past him. Seeing another wave of Russian infantry burst through the gape in the wire, he bit his lower lip, realising the situation was becoming desperate. He fired another burst, four Russian soldiers dropping back across the tangled wire.

He was now about five metres from the three men as he fired again, emptying the machine gun magazine at the advancing enemy. He stooped, attempting to reload as he saw Russian infantry dropping into the trench before him, turning to attack Udet, with 'Hase' beyond him.

'Hase' was knocked to the floor of the trench as a Russian jumped down from behind him, hitting him with his rifle on the shoulder. 'Hase' twisted on the ground, looking up, seeing the enemy soldier lifting his weapon to hit him. Nicu thrust forward above 'Hase', the bayonet entering the Russians stomach, the man falling backwards in agony.

Udet had turned to face the Russian attacking 'Hase', then was knocked forward, a Russian behind him jumping onto his back as he dropped into the trench. Udet fell to his knees, a cry of frustration coming from his lips, the weight bearing down on him. The body behind him heavy as the Russian slipped down his back, Udet's hands clawing for the sides of the trench in a desperate attempt to support himself. Then the weight fell to the side as Hausser fell upon the Russian soldier from behind, hitting him with the butt of his unloaded machine gun. The Russian screamed in pain and rolled in the trench as Hausser raised the weapon to bring it down again with a crunch.

Udet frantically tried to raise his weapon, another Russian dropping into the trench before him, blocking him from 'Hase'. The man turned, the glimmer of a smile of his face as he saw the German soldier on his knees. He raised his PPSH 41 machine gun, then fell backwards as 'Hase' shot him in the back, the blood splattering across Udet's helmet.

Machine gun bullets zipped over the top of the trench, the gunners lowering their aim to try and prevent further Russians getting into the defences. High in the factory roof, Alessio was furiously aiming and firing his sighted Kar 98 rifle from his position. As the smoke began to clear, he could see the flashes from at least three Russian T34 tanks in the area between the lines, the tanks now waiting for the trenches to be cleared before moving forward.

Pulling the bolt back on his rifle, he raised it to his eye again, firing at the swarm of Russian soldiers before the front line trench. A man fell, then he frantically pulled the bolt back again, raising the rifle to his eye once more. More flares rose into the sky, fired from behind the German line, the machine gunners keen to target the attackers more effectively.

The machine gunner next to him, placed another ammunition holder on top of his MG34 machine gun, the adrenalin pulsing through his body. He double checked the barrel of the gun was behind the factory roof, avoiding the Russian tanks from seeing his muzzle flashes directly, then lowered himself backwards, moving his eye to the sights. As he looked, the smoke dissipated further and he saw a group of Russian infantry approaching the trench, he moved the weapon slightly to point just in front of the group and pulled the trigger. Bullets flew across the terrain, straight at the position he aimed at, cutting down most of the infantry as they ran into the fire.

'Hase' fired out from the trench, felling one of the Russians running towards him, a group of around twenty rising up from cover. He swallowed, considering running, then discounting it, realising the decision would be fatal, he would be shot in the back. He reached to his belt for a grenade, ducking as bullets splattered across the front of the trench, running his hand across his belt in panic, his eyes widened as he realised there were no grenades left. Biting his lip, he heard Udet and Nicu fire either side of him before ducking back. He pulled the bolt back on his rifle, realising the gun was empty, he rose up ready to confront the enemy. Looking in awe out over many Russian bodies, the MG34 from the factory and MG42 behind him having fired low into the advancing Russian squad.

Tatu was some fifty metres south of Hausser and his men, shouting at the soldiers before him, their firing temporarily holding the Russian infantry in the destroyed buildings. He had jumped out of the trench and was now lying in the remains of a doorway behind the defensive line, using his weapon to pick off anyone who got through. His fear was rising, knowing they were fighting in the trenches to either side of his section. The chances of being overwhelmed now becoming high, a fall-back position unlikely with the strength of the Russian attackers. He knew a defender that tried to disengage and retreat to a new defensive line now would lose a lot of men, the attackers firing into the back of the retreating unit.

Raising his machine gun, he fired a burst into the darkness as several troops in the trench reloaded. Seeing Russians in the pulsing light of the flare above them, he fired again, the enemy ducking back into cover.

Fearing the worst he shouted for the men to throw their last grenades, a few small dark obstacles rising into the air as a result. As the explosions flashed in the darkness before their position, he swallowed hard, realising the Russians would now throw everyone forward.

He tensed, clipping a new magazine drum under his weapon. Then he heard the crumps in the distance behind him, his spirits rising. German artillery was firing from outside the city in support, expending in excess of their daily ration to bolster the front line.

Udet froze as he heard the whoosh of shells passing over their heads, the subsequent explosions throwing men and equipment into the air before them as the darkness seemed to turn to day. The shells landing dangerously close to the front line, decimating the Russian infantry still advancing across the terrain to attack. The heavy artillery destroying one of the Russian tanks in the land before them, its turret being blown into the air as the tank disintegrated, the heavy artillery shell a direct hit on the T34.

The flames and fire from the explosions rose high into the air, Alessio instinctively pulled his face away from the sights of his weapon, his eyes hurting at the contrasting light from the darkness in the magnified sight. Blinking as the light subsided, he lifted the rifle again, inserting another ammunition clip into the weapon.

Udet stood transfixed, staring at the explosion, then froze as he saw the many figures and silhouettes rising before the lights, jumping across broken and devastated walls as they advanced to towards them. The next wave of the Russian attack was on its way, forced forward by its commanders. Udet turned, shouting in panic, 'More Russians coming!'

Tatu swallowed as he heard the distant alert, hearing the machine guns starting to fire again, the bursts changing to continuous fire. He leant forward, shouting desperately, 'Continuous fire, bring them down!' Petru glanced round, Tatu seeing fear in his eyes, then they mellowed. Tatu spun round, looking to see what his countryman had seen, then a fleeting grin formed on his face, seeing the German infantry advancing cautiously towards them through the rubble.

Major Slusser was half crouched, his left arm raised as he urged his men from their positions. He ran forward shouting, spurring the soldiers from the reserve positions onwards, his MP40 in his right hand, 'Keep down, get into the forward positions! Drive them back!'

He ducked as a shell burst to his left, the dirt falling across his face and uniform. Stopping by the side of a damaged wall, he crouched, urging the soldiers forward again with his left hand. Glancing back, he saw the cloud trails rise into the sky from about six hundred metres away. 'About time!' He whispered to himself.

The German Nebelwerfer unit had received the major's desperate order to fire some moments earlier, the rocket battery commander demanding a repeat of the instruction as his men loaded the heavy rocket launchers. He received in response,

'Fire immediately on map coordinates supplied. Russian attack threatening to break through into the factory district. Defensive line being overwhelmed with several incursions. Ammunition rationing temporarily suspended. Fire when ready. Major Slusser's command.'

Running from his defensive bunker, the artillery commander started shouting at the crews around the rocket battery, realising if the Russians broke through, his unit would be in their line of advance. Receiving the all clear from his subordinate, he stood back, watching the crews move away from their weapons. He raised his hand, dropping it immediately, 'Fire!' As the fuel ignited in the rockets, the crews shielded their eyes, the rockets shooting from their firing cylinders and accelerating away across the landscape into the darkness, the smoke trails soaring into the cold sky. The wheeled guns jolted backwards as they fired, then settled between their wheel blocks.

The Nebelwerfer battery commander turned, the crews looking at him expectantly, his eyes wide with excitement, 'Reload.......Quickly!' His exhaled breath condensed in the cold air.

Hausser looked over his shoulder, seeing the smoke trails lit at the end, the fuel burning beneath the rockets. As the rocket trails approached, he started shouting at his men again, 'Incoming defensive fire, take cover!'

A wall of flame rose into the air some thirty to one hundred metres before the trenches as the rockets landed amongst the advancing Russian infantry. Bodies were blown apart, broken limbs thrown into the air as the rockets exploded in clusters across the ground.

The surviving German and Romanian defenders in the trenches, still firing at the enemy in front of them, gasped at the spectacle of destruction, the flames tearing upwards into the night sky.

Major Slusser moved forward at a crouch, urging the men around him into the frontline trench. As the German reserves dropped into the trench, he saw Leutnant Hausser stood further down the defensive line to his left. He jumped down into the trench and ran towards him, jumping over and around the bodies lying of the trench floor.

Hearing distant whistles through the darkness, a signal for the Russian attack to end, Hausser's relief was evident to the major, his shoulders sagging, the young commander started to move up the trench in front of him, beginning to check the wounded.

The shouts of 'Medic!' filled the frontline as soldiers struggled with their injuries. The moaning beginning to increase as the gunfire subsided. The cracks of rifle fire continued along the front as defenders fired after the retreating Russian infantry.

In the factory roof, Alessio fired several times, aiming at the Russian officers once he saw the infantry beginning to fall back. He grinned as one ducked behind some debris, his bullet ricocheting near the officers head, 'See how you like to be targeted instead!' he whispered to himself.

Major Slusser caught up with the more junior commander, grasping Hausser's shoulder. 'We drove them back Hausser, well done.'

Hausser turned abruptly, his face grim, his eyes narrowed in hatred, 'Yes, but we lost a lot of good men in the process. They can replace theirs, we cannot!' He then turned back, trudging along the trench, shouting over his shoulder, 'They will be back!'

The Major's eyes widened in surprise at the response, seeing Udet and 'Hase' look round at him from the trench wall, surprised at their commanders aggressive response. Major Slusser moved forward after Hausser along the trench, seeing he was walking behind the new and existing soldiers of the frontline, the junior commander beginning to check the condition of his men and their defences.

'Leutnant Hausser, wait there!' The major's raised voice was firm. As he caught up with the now stationary officer, Hausser slowly turned to face him again. The major's expression becoming softer as he saw that Hausser's face seemed completely despondent. 'Look, you and your men did well, we drove them off. I will pull your unit back from the front for a couple of days, give them a rest. I just have one more effort to ask of them.' The major seemed to be almost pleading and Hausser's mood lightened in sympathy, realising his frustration was with the war, not the major.

He turned, looking the major in the eye, his voice low, 'What do you want us to do?'

Chapter Fifteen: Forward Planning

Major Slusser drew greedily on his cigarette, looking across the table at Hausser, 'So, Leutnant, this is the plan.'

Hausser looked down at the roughly drawn map, his expression grim, 'Very well, let me recap so far. We enter though two different manholes. Sweep the tunnels beneath the front lines for Russian infiltrators and drive them back if possible. Are the tunnels flooded?'

The Major shook his head, swigging from his glass, the dust falling from his uniform, 'No, the only way the tunnels can flood is from the reservoir outside the city. We have secured this, so there is no danger there.' He leant forward pointing at the darker lines on the map extending towards the river, 'These are the tunnels that can flood if the gates are opened at the reservoir. The water will rise in the rest of the system, but the force is so strong the water usually only passes along these routes.'

Hausser nodded, running his hand through his matted hair, 'I see. So where are the Russians now?'

The Major pointed to areas towards the river marked on the map, 'The Russkies hold these sections, mostly the lower sections, but they know the system well, where as we do not, so they keep finding ways though.'

Hausser raised a cigarette to his lips, lighting it and blowing smoke to the side, 'What if they attack in force when we are down there?'

The Major leant back, drawing on his cigarette again, 'I have decided to end this underground game once and for all. It has cost too many men so far, the soldiers hate the fighting and darkness down there, it is destroying morale. I also have to deploy men underground that could help us up here, and that is crucial.'

Hausser nodded slowly, sipping from the glass the major had provided he glanced at the man before him, seeing he wished to continue, 'Please go on Sir.'

The Major swigged from his glass again, 'Whilst you are sweeping the tunnels, I will get engineers to place explosives in these areas…..' He leant forward again, pointing to several crosses on the creased map, 'When you have successfully pushed the Russians back, we will blow the side tunnels, blocking them and preventing the Russians from advancing. This will channel any advance into specific tunnels that I know I can defend successfully.' He looked up at Hausser again, 'The situation at present is precarious, if the Russians get behind in force us through the tunnels, then they may cut us off. Supplies are low enough as it is without disruption, if they are successful in getting into our rear it will cause panic and jeopardise the entire northern sector as they push reinforcements through. Difficult I know, but if they succeed, I have not got the men to hold the factory section and fight a rear-guard action. We may lose the factory district all together. This is the main supply route for the units north and north west of here.'

He stood back, his face grim, draining his glass and indicating to the radio operator, the man rising from his seat and retrieving another bottle of vodka. The operator topped up the Major's glass and then moved round the table towards Hausser, the young commander raising his hand to indicate he did not want any more. The sounds of distant gunfire and an explosion could be heard, a Russian patrol opening fire on German positions two hundred metres south of the administrative building.

Turning back to look at the map, Hausser frowned, 'I don't like the idea of having explosives blow up our only means of retreat. How will you know when to order the detonations?'

The Major smiled briefly, 'I imagined you would be concerned, I have given strict orders for the explosives not to be blown until you and your men are out of the sewers, or we know that you are safely in one of the tunnels not to be blocked.'

Hausser looked solemnly across at Major Slusser, 'When do you want us to start?'

The major smile broadened, 'Immediately if you could, I have a feeling the Russians may be planning their next move as we speak. They have failed above ground tonight, they may try below ground as well.'

Hausser grimaced, sighing, 'Very well, I will go and get my men.' He leant over, picking up his helmet, his face grim.

The Major saluted, 'Thank you Hausser, this will secure our sector I hope. If we don't do it now, it will cost lives later, and maybe the entire position. Use the men that are there already if you need to.'

Hausser raised his hand in salute, 'We will do our best Sir.' He turned abruptly on his heels, walking to the stairs.

Hausser blinked as he looked down at the crudely drawn map provided by the Major's radio operator, the candlelight flickering across the rough paper it was drawn upon. 'So, we enter here, and work our way along these two routes.' He drew his gloved finger across the map, following the drawn lines, glancing up at Tatu, 'What do you think?'

Tatu drew his hand across his moustache, his eyes tired, 'Who will lead each group?'

Hausser sighed, 'We have lost quite a few men, eleven dead and five wounded. That leaves us with about twenty one men in total, including us. We split into three squads, using one in reserve. I will lead one, you lead the second. Meino, you will lead the smaller third squad of three men and assist the engineers, that's the reserve. We will leave Alessio in the front as a sniper for practice, he seems to be beginning to excel at the role now.'

Tatu eyebrows rose, 'Eight men in an enclosed space?'

The young commander nodded, 'We will leave one sentry at the junctions along each route to cover our rear and for a fall-back position if required, completing the sweep with just the squad leader and three or four men. Then

144

use the reserves to rotate and provide some respite until the order is given to leave and block the tunnels concerned.'

Tatu nodded, a grim smile forming on his face, 'Yes that could work. We will need to have men nearby to reinforce if they attack, where will we position them?'

Hausser pointed at two areas on the roughly drawn map, 'These look sufficient to house the reserve. We can place any extra ammunition we can get there too.'

Meino leant forward, studying the drawing, 'Issue any sub machine guns to the forward men, this is not rifle territory. Then we have a good start to drive the Russkies out.'

Hausser nodded with Tatu, 'That's good enough. We don't have a flame thrower, but must consider they do, so let's brief the men on how to take them out. Extra grenades for all, we sweep the area and drive them back, retreat and set trip wires before our positions and hold back for them to blow the tunnels. No delay fuses on the trip wires, instant detonation in case they counterattack.'

Tatu and Meino looked at Hausser directly, the Croatian speaking slowly, 'Right, when do we start?'

Hausser looked down at the map, 'The 62nd Army has just been driven back, so their commanders will probably be looking to redeem themselves. I believe this is where they will look.' He leaned forward pointing at several sections of the crude map. 'Give them another thirty minutes to organise themselves, then they may come in shooting. They will probably come in here, here and here. Moving across and through these two main sections and trying to move to our rear. We do not have enough men to stop a large attack, so the Major says we can use the men down there already to bolster our numbers.'

Tatu looked down, studying the map, 'Are we to blow some of the tunnel sections, force them into concentrated areas?'

Hausser nodded, 'Yes, that's the plan, the sooner we drive the Russians back and blow the tunnels, the sooner we are out of the sewers.' He looked at the Croatian, 'Meino, do you want to ask the major politely to hurry up with the engineers and explosives? He seems to like you.'

Meino sighed, smiling, 'Very well, strange the relationship that builds between someone that will inherit an Inn and an officer that likes to drink!'

Tatu and Hausser laughed, the strain on their faces dissolving for a few seconds.

Meino grinned back with determination, 'I will go and ask him now.'

Hausser nodded, the smile falling from his face. Looking down he pointed at an intersection on the map. 'Bring anything you can get here, then come and find us along the routes. You and your men will be in reserve to begin with.'

Meino's eyes narrowed, 'Right, I will try and get back in twenty minutes, it will be close if the Russians come when you think.'

Hausser nodded, his face becoming darker, 'If they come, we will hold them until you bring any explosives. Be quick, my friend.'

Meino nodded, turning and walking swiftly from them towards the opening in the wall of the damaged building, some forty metres south of the administration block. He looked back as he climbed through the hole into the outside trench, raising his hand, 'See you in the sewers, gentlemen!'

Chapter Sixteen: Into the darkness

Tatu slipped into the shaft leading to the sewers, his PPSH 41 slung over his back. Slowly descending the cold metal steps, he screwed his face up as the smell of excrement and decay swept into his nostrils. Petru entered the manhole above him, stepping carefully down the ladder above his countryman carrying a lantern. Reaching the bottom of the ladder they stepped across from the bottom rung onto a small walkway at the side of the wide drainage channel, avoiding the putrid water.

As his soldiers descended the ladder behind them, Tatu walked forward boldly, keen to reach the small group of German troops already positioned in the sewer system. The tunnel was relatively wide, a main shaft for the adjoining pipes and tunnels to deposit their rainwater and sewage into. The brick built sewage system stretched the length of the city along the Volga River, extending from the northern factory district to the southern housing suburbs, the many tunnels seeming to mostly run parallel or at right angles to the river and the system's exit pipes. Several separate sections for remote city areas also supplemented the larger city system.

The Romanian quartermaster stopped at the intersection of the tunnels, some twenty metres from the ladder, the light from the oil lantern Petru was carrying having diminished too much for him to continue. His exhaled breath condensed in the cold he turned impatiently, watching as Petru waited for the group of five other soldiers to descend the ladder. Nicu was the last to gingerly step onto the slimy walkway to the side of the half frozen polluted water of the drainage channel.

They walked slowly towards Tatu at the end, taking their weapons from their shoulders, their faces pensive. Tatu indicated for them to increase their pace with his hand, his impatience evident, the sounds of their boots echoing off the walls of the tunnel. Petru saw the grim look on Tatu's face and increased his walking speed. As he drew level with his countryman, Tatu turned and walked to the left, his large jacket rising as he swung round. Lifting his machine gun from his shoulder, he saw a dim light emanating from a narrower tunnel to the right and crouched to enter it, his boots cracking through the thin ice on the surface of the slurry in the passageway.

Tatu swore under his breath as he felt the cold seep through the stitches in his boots, the chilling change on his feet almost causing him to draw breath as his body temperature reacted to the freezing cold water. As he reached the end of the small narrow tunnel he glanced back, seeing the shadows in the tunnel behind him, Petru following the soldiers with the lantern. Glancing round the corner to the right, into a wider tunnel, he saw the source of the light, a candle flickering on the next corner with murmured voices beyond it.

As the nearest soldier stopped behind him, Tatu indicated for him to wait, his finger raised to his lips for silence. Slipping round the corner, the quartermaster approached the light cautiously, his ears straining to listen. Hearing German voices, he grinned at his caution and glanced round the corner where the candle stood, seeing the two German infantrymen at the end of this narrow tunnel. He turned, indicating for the soldiers behind him to approach.

Leaning out into the tunnel, Tatu called softly to the Germans, 'Freund!' The soldiers stopped talking abruptly and spun round, the candle next to them flickering with the movement. Seeing Tatu in the tunnel a grin passed across one of their faces, the prospect of leaving the enclosed dark space clearly elating him. The quartermaster emerged into the side tunnel and advanced half crouched towards them.

Gunfire echoed around the walls, Tatu seeing the Germans at the end tense and duck down, their rifles raising towards the direction of the sound. Then he heard more shots, the rattle of a sub machine gun mixed with the cracks of rifle shots. A scream in the distance, the noise echoing off the slime covered bricks.

As the quartermaster reached the two infantrymen he looked to his right, the sporadic gunfire continuing along with the screaming. 'Where are they?' He hissed at the two Germans. Seeing the infantrymen were crouched behind a small wall of sandbags, placed up to the edge of the drainage channel.

148

The soldier pointed, the fear on his face, 'Along in the next tunnel, that's the forward position, it's beyond the front line above.'

Tatu nodded, 'Good, stay here, cover any retreat.' He glanced round, seeing that Nicu was behind him with four Hungarians and Petru. 'Get ready men.'

Tatu ran forward, rounding the sandbags, the foul water splashing around him. Further gunfire echoed across the tunnels, the screams becoming more desperate. As he reached the turning in the tunnel he glanced round the corner quickly, seeing gun flashes at the end of the narrow passageway, some thirty metres away.

Turning he indicated to Petru for them to separate, to continue further down the wide tunnel, his thought to move in on the fighting from two directions. As the soldiers passed him, he grasped Nicu's arm, beckoning him to follow. Pushing himself into the narrow side tunnel, he lunged forward, the poisoned water splashing around him. He advanced slowly, half crouched along the tunnel, raising his PPSH 41 before him. The gunfire got louder as he approached the end, becoming almost deafening in the enclosed narrow space.

The screams intensified as he began to approach the end, moving to the left side of the passageway, he realised the gunfire was coming from the right. Reaching the intersection, he heard closer fire and ducked his head out quickly to look. Before him to the left was another small sandbagged section, some five metres away, a German infantryman firing a burst of his MP40 above it. Lying next to him was another infantryman writhing in the slurry of the drainage channel, his hands clutching his stomach. Blood flowed down the channel, the dirty water propelling it along the slight decline in the wide passageway towards the steps at the end, some twenty five metres away.

Tatu looked down the tunnel as it sloped away from them into the darkness. Seeing some movement in the darkness at the end he realised the Russian infantry were preparing to attack, probably awaiting for the defending soldier to reload. The quartermaster ducked back In, clenching his grip on his weapon, the screaming filling his ears. He glanced at Nicu, then grasped the

149

grenade in his jacket. The firing stopped abruptly and Tatu pushed himself from the wall, tossing the grenade forward as he lunged from the passageway, the small round metal sphere bouncing off the surface of the round tunnel roof before landing and rolling down the slope towards the steps.

The German infantryman spun round in shock, his eyes wide with fright as Tatu crashed to his knees next to him. Shouts in Russian echoed across the walls, then the grenade exploded at the top of the steps, showering dust and polluted water across the width of the tunnel. Having seen the grenade, the Russian troops had ducked back into cover, their opportunity to attack passing as the German soldier used the opportunity to replenish his weapon.

Tatu leant forward and roughly grasped the heavily wounded infantryman's shoulder, heaving him back behind the sandbags, the injured man pushing with his feet. The quartermaster pulled him behind them, resting his helmeted head next to the sewer wall, the man bleeding heavily from his stomach wound, his eyes closed in pain.

Tatu nodded to Nicu across the tunnel, then fired a burst of his PPSH over the sandbagged wall. Nicu lowered himself to the floor of the tunnel, gritting his teeth as his body came into contact with the frozen slime on the bricks. He crawled forward, the screams of the wounded man echoing across the walls around him. Reaching the edge of the wider tunnel, he cautiously pushed his rifle out to point towards the steps.

As he lined his eye up on the sights of the weapon, he saw a helmet move across the darkness below the steps, the rifle kicking back into his shoulder as he squeezed the trigger. The shot echoed through the tunnels, hitting the sloped wall behind the Russians dislodging grime and frozen excrement, the bullet missing its target.

Tatu turned to the infantryman next to him, hissing, 'Where are the other soldiers.......the forward position?'

The soldier shrugged grimly, 'They caught us by surprise, and there was no firing from the next position.' He glanced round at his moaning countryman,

150

indicating with a jerk of his head, 'Kurt was running up the steps when he got hit, I covered him until he crawled back here.' The man turned and started to comfort his wounded countryman, checking his open stomach wound, 'We need to get him out of here.'

Tatu glanced at the wounded man, the blood dripping onto the iced bricks of the tunnel, his voice low, 'We will hold here, drag him out when I start firing.'

The soldier nodded grimly, the man moaning loudly as he lifted him to push his arms through the man's arm pits, ready to drag the man out of the line of fire.

Tatu looked round as Nicu fired again, responding to movement in the darkness at the foot of the steps. Firing bursts from other areas in the sewers echoed across the bricked walls as firefights broke out throughout the tunnel system.

The quartermaster leant forward, hissing, 'Now!' He lifted his machine gun above the sandbags, firing a burst down the tunnel. Hearing the man groan behind him as the soldier dragged him across the iced bricks and into the narrow side passage, the blood leaving a trail across the tunnel floor as they struggled past Nicu.

Further gunfire exploded across the tunnel walls as the Russians at the foot of the steps returned fire, their bullets whipping along the wide tunnel, dust and grime falling from the ceiling, the Russians ducking into cover again.

More distant gunfire continued, a muffled explosion broke the gunfire as an unfortunate soldier ran through a tripwire somewhere along the tunnels, the screams and shouts of wounded and desperate men filling the sewage system. All along the dark underground sewers the Russian 62nd Army probed the makeshift defensive positions, the soldiers sometimes fighting hand to hand in freezing stagnant and polluted water.

Petru was breathing heavily, the sounds of sporadic gunfire echoing around him. He had initially thought he could move around the Russians Tatu had engaged, attacking them from a different direction, but the tunnels were not joined. He had advanced cautiously along the first wide tunnel, turning into smaller tunnels that he thought would lead towards Tatu, but this had proved futile and he had become disorientated, losing his way. Now he could see the uneasiness beginning to form in the eyes of the Hungarian soldiers with him, the grip on their weapons tight, their breathing laboured. They were lost.

As he slowly advanced along the narrow tunnel they were in he could hear them whispering to each other behind him, some voices excited, others more firm. He stepped into deeper frozen liquid as they approached the end of the tunnel, the sounds of running water getting louder. Glancing out into the next passageway, he could hear distant firing to the left, but realised the water was running from that direction, the depth now over his boots. To the right, the tunnel seemed to open into an underground area and he considered moving towards it, the noise of the water louder there. Turning, he sighed as he realised he now only had two men with him, the others having left the group, deserted them. The soldier behind him shrugged and looked at him apologetically, the light from the lantern flickering across his face.

He indicated for them to turn round unsure of how deep the flowing water was, the freezing liquid around his feet persuading him to try and find his way back towards Tatu. The soldier before him nodded, slowly shuffling his boots round in the slime on the floor of the tunnel. Gunfire and flashes burst across the tunnel, the man in front of him being propelled backwards onto him. Petru fell backwards into the slurry as the man's weight hit him, the soldier in front of him being hit several times by the burst from a machine gun at the end of the passageway. Petru went under the freezing water, then broke the surface spluttering, the water in his nose. Then he held his breath in terror, bracing for another burst of machine gun fire.

He lay there for a second, the man above him thrashing around briefly, then the soldier slowly became still. The weight of two men on top of his lower legs, Petru was pinned to the floor of the tunnel, the putrid freezing water lapping around his head, his face pushed just out of the liquid next to the head of the man above him to breathe. He could feel the strain on his neck muscles, the pain intense as he stretched upwards for the foul oxygen. The freezing water now covered his body, the pain of the intense cold forcing him to blank his mind, fearful of the panic rising within him. He could hear talking in Russian at the far end of the narrow tunnel, the enemy initially considering checking the bodies, but fearful of what may be in the darkness and water, the lamp having been extinguished.

Petru cleared his mind. Forcing away the urgency, almost panic to push the body above him away, realising this would result in a further burst of gunfire. With the loud running water beyond his head, he slowly began to wriggle himself free from the two bodies above him, his arms and legs screaming in pain from the weight and freezing water. Pushing himself against the body, his head began to emerge from the side tunnel into the rushing water, the strong current rising over his mouth and eyes. He held his breath again, pushing harder to free himself, his boots sliding against the sides of the narrow passageway in a desperate attempt to break away. With the foul water rushing around him, he thought he could hear gunfire, then just the rush of water. He pushed harder, feeling his arms and legs gradually becoming numb in the freezing cold water. A realisation his oxygen level was lowering as his mind began to scream at him to breathe, but he could not open his mouth, the turbulent water cascading over his face.

Inside Petru, his determination and hatred for the war rose up, his desperation becoming panic, he kicked out and pushed in one final effort to free himself, the momentum moving the bodies slightly, freeing him and sliding him into the flowing water. His head rose above the liquid and he heard himself cough and splutter, the inhale of air loud, seeming distant as he struggled with consciousness. The freezing water current pulled him down the tunnel, the noise of running water getting louder as he spluttered and gasped in the tunnels torrent. His body was bumped and scratched on the bricks beneath him, then suddenly he felt himself falling backwards, head first. He was engulfed in freezing water, feeling the grime and slurry rush across his face. He closed his eyes and mouth, his body still desperately short of air. He twisted in the freezing cold water, pushing his head upwards and kicking out against the drag of his uniform, his face emerging on the surface.

Hausser stopped in the wide passageway, hearing the gunfire echo across the walls around him, unable to determine which direction it came from in the labyrinth of tunnels. Udet and 'Hase' stopped next to him, half crouched in the sewer tunnel, their weapons held before them, a Romanian soldier holding the lantern aloft a metre behind them. The three listened, straining their ears to try and sense the distance and direction of the echoing shots.

Exhaling heavily, Hausser shrugged and began moving cautiously forward again, the six soldiers with him following him closely, their nerves taut. Reaching the end of the tunnel they were in, they slowly moved down a ramp at the end towards a junction, the light from the lantern behind him diminishing as he slipped silently down the decline. Stepping onto the lower level, the young commander lifted his hand to indicate for them to stop, pushing his boots forward with his MP40 clenched menacingly, he approached the corner at the junction. Glancing quickly to either side, he indicated for the men to follow as he turned left into a narrower passageway, the bricks iced on either side. Before him, he could see snowflakes drifting into the tunnel from an open shaft some five metres away, the colder air from outside enveloping him as he approached.

Leaning forward, he glanced upwards, seeing the darkened sky above the open manhole, his exhaled breath condensed. The stars sparkled down at him in the freezing air, their intensity almost breath-taking. Seeing the manhole was clear, he indicated for the men behind him to proceed, raising his weapon to point at the opening. The soldiers increased their steps as they passed under the shaft to the manhole, stepping deliberately across the ice and patch of frozen snow on the brick floor of the sewer. As they reached the end of the passageway, Hausser side stepped beneath the opening, his eyes concentrated on the manhole above him. Then he turned and caught up with the other soldiers.

Approaching the next junction, the sporadic gunfire was getting louder, the fighting in other areas of the sewers intensifying as the Russians reinforced their attack. An explosion echoed through the brick built passageways some distance away, followed by screaming, the soldier caught in the explosion losing a limb.

Checking the routes either side of the junction, Hausser turned right, followed cautiously by the other soldiers their weapons stretched out before them. They found themselves in a wider tunnel, the gunfire significantly louder from the end they faced, some ten metres away. Flashes illuminated the walls at the next junction, indicating someone was firing just around the corner, the rattle of the machine gun bursts a familiar sound.

The fleeing Hungarian infantryman slipped as he turned the corner in front of them, his boots losing their grip on the iced bricks. Falling roughly, the MP40 fell with a clatter onto the floor of the sewer. Ignoring his fallen weapon, he scrambled towards them on his hands and knees, attempting to rise to his feet, propelling himself forward and away from his pursuers. Udet lunged forward, grabbing the man and pulling him roughly to the right wall as Hausser and 'Hase' raised their weapons.

The Hungarian was terrified, his eyes wide and breathing in sharp rasps, desperately attempting to pull away from Udet, to run further from the passageway behind, to escape. The young German struggled with the man, until his frustration became unbearable and he let his grip loosen. The panicked soldier broke free pushing Udet to the side, the German falling onto one knee. The terrified Hungarian ran back behind them into the tunnel, his panic driving him away into the darkness beyond. As he passed one of his countrymen in the group, the soldier shouted at him in his native language to stop. But it was to no avail, the man could not hear anyone, he continued running in terror.

Hearing shouting in Russian and boots on the brick surface of the tunnel to their left, Hausser and 'Hase' lowered themselves to a crouch, the other soldiers following suit, their weapons pointed at the corner. Udet briefly watched the man disappear into the darkness, then turned raising his rifle towards the corner despondently.

The footsteps approached the corner, the sounds of several pairs of boots on the brick floor of the sewer. Gunfire and explosions from grenades echoed through the tunnels as the fighting heightened further into the dark sewage system.

The first Russian infantryman ran round the corner, his bayoneted rifle held at waist height. Two more infantry appeared behind him as Hausser opened fire, the first soldier to emerge spinning round with the bullets impact, the rifle falling from his grasp. Udet and 'Hase's' rifles cracked as the other two Russians fell backwards, their screams of surprise as they impacted on the hard frozen floor of the sewer echoing across the curved walls of the tunnel.

Hausser ran forward, hearing further boots scraping in the tunnel to the left. Jumping over the outstretched bodies of the dying men, he kicked a rifle away from one of the wounded soldiers, the injured man reaching out for the weapon. Crouching at the corner, Hausser fired another burst from his machine gun blindly down the passageway, hearing further screams as the bullets hit the advancing enemies in the confines of the tunnel. The soldiers fell to the floor of the tunnel, their weapons clattering onto the brick surface. Leaning out briefly, he saw two man lying in the tunnel only two metres from the corner. Behind him, his men inspected the wounded and dying enemy, moving their weapons out of reach.

Hausser moved into the side tunnel, pushing one of the Russians back with his boot as he tried to rise, the blood pouring from his mouth. Stepping over the other prone man, the Russian grabbed his ankle, his eyes pleading. The commander checked the tunnel ahead was empty and bent down to the wounded soldier, blood beginning to soak through the man's tunic. The soldier was quite young, his eyes blue and wide with shock. Hausser bit his lip as the youngster grasped his tunic, his lips moving to try and speak to the German.

The Russian youth looked up at the commander, tears in his eyes as he tried to speak, his voice broken as he choked back his emotion. Hausser placed his hand beneath the man's head, lifting it slightly from the floor of the tunnel as the dying soldier coughed, the young commander horrified the soldier was so young.

The young Russian soldier looked up at Hausser, his eyes pleading as he realised that his life was ebbing away. The commander looked down at him, his whisper going unheard by the men behind him, tears beginning to form in his eyes, 'I am sorry.' The other soldiers stood behind him, grimly and warily watching the other Russians lying on the tunnel floor as they fought for life.

The youth coughed and nodded slightly, blood beginning to run from his mouth and nose, he spluttered, his eyes closing for a second, 'We will all die here…..' His grip loosening on Hausser's tunic, his head falling backwards as his eyes became lifeless.

Hausser gently lowered the young soldier's head to the floor of the tunnel, rising to his feet despondently. Lifting the strap of his weapon onto his shoulder, he glanced round, then grimly stepped over the body in the passageway, advancing further down the dark tunnel.

As he stepped forward, holding his MP40 held at waist height, he felt the nausea in his stomach. His hatred of the endless fighting rising within him. The sounds of gunfire were getting louder as he reached the end of the passageway, hearing the noises coming from the right. He looked out quickly, seeing the next wider sloped tunnel was empty, cold water running down the centre drainage section of the passageway.

Stepping over the drainage gully, he advanced cautiously along the left wall, his body still half crouched. Udet moved along the right wall, his rifle held before him as they approached another junction in the tunnel. Behind them, 'Hase' and the other members of the group followed warily, the poor light from the lantern flickering across the walls.

Glancing round the next corner, Hausser moved into the narrow tunnel, hearing the noises of gunfire now only a short distance away. The water splashed across the walls as he pushed his boots through the slime. Reaching the end of this narrow passageway he leant out briefly, seeing a German soldier knelt next to the corner on his right, his attention on the next passage. To the left, he saw another junction, the sounds of water running in the tunnel. Indicating for the soldiers to split, he considered the Russians must have come from the left side tunnel. Looking down, he realised the water in the passageway was flowing into a grill on the floor of the tunnel.

The startled infantryman at the corner glanced round, a brief smile crossing his face as he recognised the uniforms. He nodded to Hausser, 'We are falling back, Sir. The Russians are too strong.'

Hausser approached him slowly, 'How long have you been here?'

The soldier shook his head, 'Only a few seconds, I am going to cover the remains of our group as they retreat.' He tensed as firing further down the tunnel system erupted again.

The commander indicated to the other tunnel with a twist of his head, 'Where does that lead?'

The soldier shrugged, 'Not sure, but there is a central section nearby where the water collects before going out to the river. All the pipework leads there, then the water is released towards the Volga.'

Hausser's eyebrows raised in curiosity, 'So the Russians are entering the system on a lower level than us?'

The soldier nodded, 'I think so. I am no sewer expert, but that's what it seems.'

The commander nodded thoughtfully. 'How many men are you with?'

The soldier glanced back down the passageway nervously, 'Five, they are up ahead. The Russians are using grenades and flamethrowers to clear us out. We just have not got the numbers to hold them.'

Hausser wiped the scarf across his mouth, 'I see. You and your men try and hold here until we have finished a sweep of the other tunnels.'

The soldier nodded slowly, his expression grim. 'Yes, Herr Leutnant.'

Hausser turned, indicating to one of the Hungarian soldiers with them, 'Stay with him.' The soldier nodded grimly, moving forward. Hausser looked across the other soldiers, 'The rest come with me, we will check the other tunnels.'

Tatu changed the magazine of his PPSH 41 as he glanced across at Nicu, the younger soldier lying at the corner, his rifle pointing at the steps. Clipping the new ammunition drum into the base of the weapon, the quartermaster hissed across the wide tunnel, 'Any grenades?'

Nicu shook his head, looking back down the sight of his weapon, 'Petru and the others were carrying them.' The movement at the foot of the stairs seemed to have ceased, but both soldiers could just hear the Russians talking in hushed voices at the end of the wide tunnel.

They both tensed as they heard further movement at the foot of the steps, the scraping of boots and some louder whispers. Tatu raised his head cautiously above the sandbags, his ears strained to listen. Gunfire broke out further across the tunnel network preventing him from determining sounds below the stairs. Placing the barrel of his machine gun on top of the makeshift barrier, he ran his spare hand across his moustache nervously.

As the echoes of gunfire subsided, he strained to listen again, the sounds of running water in the tunnels now the only noise. Looking across at Nicu, the younger soldier shrugged, whispering, 'Have they gone?'

Tatu smiled deviously, a twinkle in his eyes, whispering back, 'There is only one way to find out....' He straightened his back, the muscles across his shoulders tight. Raising his voice, he spoke loudly down the tunnel, his voice questioning, 'Hey Russkie?'

The sounds of running water in the tunnel continued, the sporadic cracks of rifle fire and bursts from machine guns in the distance. Tatu looked across at Nicu, a confused expression on his face. The quartermaster turned further, examining the tunnel behind them. Seeing the drainage tract bending away to the left with the tunnel, he realised they were in a corner section of the sewer.

Tatu breathed hard, rising from his crouched position, raising his voice further, 'Hey Russkie?' He lifted the machine gun from the sandbags, cradling the magazine drum in his left hand. The sounds of running water continued in the tunnel, with distant gunfire the only other noise.

Nicu's eyes widened at the quartermaster's movement, hissing, 'What are you doing?'

Tatu glanced across at him and winked, then lunged round the sandbags, running to the top of the steps and jumping down. Nicu scrambled to his feet, seeing the quartermaster land on the floor of the tunnel below the steps and drop to a crouch.

Leaning forward, Tatu glanced from side to side cautiously as he approached the corner, seeing there were no enemy soldiers on the end of the tunnel. At the left corner, he stopped, resting his back against the wall, exhaling heavily, his heart racing. Then he ducked his head out quickly checking the tunnel.

Nicu slowly approached the top of the steps, the grip on his weapon tight, an exasperated look on his young face, 'What did you do there?'

Tatu turned his head, smiling briefly, 'It's what I would have done. This is a bottleneck, if we block them for too long, they will retreat and try to find somewhere else.' He wiped his nose on his sleeve as the younger Romanian descended the steps, 'Now, let's go and find the others.'

Hausser was scrutinising the map with contempt, the light from the lantern flickering across the worn page. Looking at Udet, he exhaled in frustration,

160

the air condensed before him. 'I don't know which village idiot drew this, but it's not much help.'

Udet grinned, his right eyebrow rising at the unexpected humour, 'So....we are lost?'

A flicker of a smile crossed Hausser's face, 'Pretty much so. Let's hope the defenders we left stay where they are so they can show us the way out.' He slapped Udet's shoulder, 'Your role to remember the route!'

Udet's eyes fell, mentally recounting the two tunnels they had just crept through, his voice subdued, 'Thank you, Herr Leutnant.' The three Hungarians and 'Hase' stood behind him grinning as they began to realise what must have been said.

Hausser walked forward to the next corner, screwing the makeshift map up in his gloved hands and dropping it to the side of the tunnel. Glancing into the next passageway quickly, he grasped his machine gun and disappeared into the opening, the stench rising into his nostrils once more.

Udet stepped towards the passageway, hearing the commander whisper back impatiently, 'Please bring the light when you are ready, gentlemen.' The young German scowled and lowered his head, stepping into the darkness, extending his hand to receive the lantern.

The foul stale water splashed across their boots as they stepped along the small side tunnel, the light flickering across the walls before Hausser. As he approached the end, he slowed his pace, seeing a faint light ahead flickering across the walls.

Reaching the corner, Hausser felt the grate of a metal grille beneath his boots, hearing a low murmuring and moaning. Hausser stole a glance round the corner, towards the light. Seeing a prone German soldier lying by the side of the wide tunnel with two other soldiers crouched over him, he stepped out, shaking his boots. The nearest soldier spun round raising his rifle, then lowered the weapon, a brief smile forming on his face. Then the smile dropped.

Hausser straightened up in the wide tunnel, stepping towards them. Then he noticed the soldier lying on the floor of the tunnel was bleeding and walked briskly to the three men. 'How is he?' He enquired.

The second soldier looked up, his eyes saddened. He shook his head slightly, attempting to conceal the expression from the wounded man. Hausser turned to the men with him, indicating to one of the Hungarians, 'Adel, have a look, see what you can do.'

The older Hungarian stepped forward, dropping to a crouch to look at the soldier. The half-conscious wounded man groaned as the Hungarian ex-medical student began to examine him.

Hausser indicated for one of the soldiers to come to the side, 'Were the Russians here?'

The soldier shook his head, tiredly removing his helmet, 'No, one of the secondary positions. They surprised us, hitting Karl. There was no warning fire from the forward position.'

The commander nodded slowly, 'Right, who is manning the position now?'

The soldier looked at him, 'Two Romanians, one has a big coat.' He grinned thoughtfully, 'A very big coat.'

Hausser smiled fleetingly, 'The old fool is nearby then......' Noticing the soldier looking curiously at him, he continued, 'Erm, he is one of my men. Where are they exactly? We are lost.'

The soldier turned, pointing to an opening further down the tunnel, 'Go down there......follow the trail of blood.'

Adel rose from his crouched position and approached the commander, his voice a whisper, 'We need to get him out of here, Sir, or he will die.' The man was late thirties with darkened eyes, his thin frame complimented by his bushy black hair and beard.

Hausser nodded solemnly, 'Very well, go with him Adel. Come back as soon as you get him to the medic station and wait for us near the entrance.'

The man nodded, turned and stepped back to the wounded man.

The commander looked across at the other soldiers, 'Let's go, Tatu is ahead, he may need our help.' He pointed to the entrance some metres away.

'Hase' and Udet moved towards the passageway further down the wide tunnel, brief grins forming on their faces. They crouched to enter the narrow tunnel, Udet holding the lantern before them.

Hausser moved in behind them, cautious of their eagerness, 'Go slower and be careful. Remember the Russians are ahead.'

Udet and 'Hase' paused at the end of the passageway, realising their potential error. Gunfire could be heard through the tunnels, the fighting getting nearer.

The group cautiously moved through the maze of tunnels, the stench nearly overwhelming in places. The darkness seemed to close in on each individual man as they progressed, their senses heightened by the close proximity of the gunfire, expecting to emerge into a firefight after each corner. The lantern provided only minimal light, the slight glow casting shadows across openings and the contours of the bricks around them in the tunnels. The illumination stretched only so far, the soldiers straining their eyes in attempts to see beyond the light's penetration, searching for the signs of a waiting enemy or threat. Each man fought his own deepest fears in the dark, desperate to avoid their own violent personal demise in sewers beneath the brutalised freezing city. The terror of individual pain or death in the enclosed misery of this darkened environment playing on their minds.

The soiled water seeped through the stitching in their boots, the freezing cold liquid numbing their feet and slowly eroding their resolve. Entering another narrow passageway, Hausser was becoming increasingly concerned that they had strayed even further from the exit and were now hopelessly lost. Initially they had followed the wounded man's trail of blood, with droplets in places and smudges in others. Reaching a wider section of the tunnel system with a small sandbagged defensive position, they had found a larger section of blood smeared across the brick floor of the tunnel. The discarded magazine drum from the Romanian quartermaster's PPSH 41 machine gun and spent bullet casings indicating the scene of a brief skirmish.

Moving forward, they descended the steps in front of the sandbagged position, leaving one lonely soldier next to the candlelit defence. His solitary vigil for defence and a potential fall-back position, but also as a potential guide towards the exit.

Hausser glanced into the tunnel on the left, seeing the water ripples glinting in the light from the lantern, the surface of the liquid broken several times. The commander screwed his face up in disgust as he considered what was in the water, then realised the items were moving in a specific direction. His eyes widened as he saw the six rats emerge from the water at the other end, the liquid glistening on their fur. A shiver went down his spine, realising the rodents were extremely well fed. He sighed heavily as he determined there were no clues required as to their diet.

'Hase' moved in front of the commander into the narrow passageway, Udet following. Pushing their boots into the water, they heard louder gunfire burst out further into the sewage system, then an explosion. As the water seeped into 'Hase's' boots once more, he slowly advanced down the narrow tunnel, hearing the other soldiers enter the passageway behind him. Approaching the end of the tunnel, he stopped, straining his ears in an attempt to listen into the sewer before him.

The sound of running water to the right was interspersed by the faint sound of squealing seemingly to the left. He turned and retrieved the light from Udet behind him. Feeling another metal grille beneath his boots, the water surging downwards beneath him, he stole a glance out into the next tunnel, seeing the bodies lying on the cold surface of the sewer floor. There were several Russian and German corpses scattered across the tunnel, the victims of a bitter hand to hand fight. To the left were a similar number of bodies, the light casting shadows across the walls and floor. He tensed as he saw a

164

couple of the bodies seem to move, considering briefly there may still be some wounded amongst them. Then he caught his breath as he realised the numerous rats amongst the prone figures, gorging on the lifeless bodies. The figures twitching as the rats gnawed on tendons and muscles that still exuded warmth.

The nausea rose within him as he considered the rodents lust for blood and warm meat. Gripping his rifle tightly, he edged cautiously into the tunnel, the water splashing around his boots as he stepped out of the polluted liquid. His eyes widened in horror as he realised the rats were not perturbed by their presence, the rodent's natural fear of man no longer evident. Several of the vermin eyed him defiantly, their eyes flashing in the light. A couple rose onto their haunches to sniff the air, their front teeth bloody.

Beside him he noticed Udet was observing the vermin closely, his rifle pointing towards them. Their joint realisation that the Russians were no longer the only enemy, but the bitter environment itself and their survival within the confines of the devastated city above. With those thoughts, a strange alien affinity with the rodents' fragile city existence was established.

Chapter Seventeen: Friend or Foe?

Hausser cautiously emerged from the passageway, his eyes widened at the sights around him. Pushing the soldiers forward, he hastened them to the right, preventing them from further dwelling on the gruesome sights around them.

Moving towards the sounds of running water, they heard the sounds of sporadic gunfire getting slightly nearer. Cautiously descending the slope at the end of the wide tunnel, they stepped back into the freezing water, the polluted liquid now rising above their ankles.

'Hase' moved to the left towards the sounds of gunfire, following the current and pushing his boots gingerly through the thick liquid. He hesitated, glancing round and seeing Hausser nodding to him, indicating for him to continue. 'Hase' glanced further into the darkened passageway before him, then walked forward into the tunnel, his eyes straining to see beyond the dim light from the lantern.

As the light faded in the passageway as 'Hase' advanced with the lantern, Udet proceeded into the tunnel behind him, following the flickering light in front of him. Stepping cautiously, he noticed several rats passing him through the water, the rodents swimming towards the bodies to their rear.

As 'Hase' approached the end of the passageway he could feel the cold water moving in his boots each time he stepped, the battle between his body temperature and the freezing liquid continuing. Reaching the corner, he held his breath, seeing a faint light filtering across the walls from the left. He clenched his Kar 98 rifle tightly in his left hand and ducked his head out into the narrow tunnel before him.

The next tunnel was of similar width to the one they stood in, the level lower, the water flowing vigorously from right to left, the current swirling stronger as the water from their tunnel joined it. Seeing a flickering candle in an alcove on the right at the bend of the passageway, he hesitated nervously, turning his head as a body floated past on the current, the frozen corpse's face contorted in pain. The body continued in the torrent's flow disappearing from view as it floated round the bend in the tunnel.

'Hase' cautiously pushed his feet forward at the junction of the passageway, gingerly feeling for any steps or a slope beneath the dark water's surface. As his boot slipped on the edge of the slope, he pushed his foot downwards, feeling for the floor of the tunnel. Udet grasped the back of his tunic to steady him, understanding his actions.

Feeling the brick floor of the tunnel beneath his boot, 'Hase' moved forward slightly, placing his weight through his leg. The frozen torrent tugged as his boots, the undercurrent strong. Udet tightened his grip on the back of 'Hase's' tunic, feeling the soldier struggle against the water's force. 'Hase' half turned, his back against the corner of the junction as he edged out into the torrent.

Hausser leant forward across Udet, taking the lantern from 'Hase', seeing the soldier beginning to shiver with the cold as the water seeped through the combat trousers above his boots. 'Hase' nodded his thanks, his teeth beginning to chatter beneath his scarf. Raising his rifle, he stepped sideways into the tunnel, his back pressed against the wall. Bracing himself against the flowing water, he could feel the cold clinging to his legs, the sensation seeming to pierce his flesh with the freezing liquid.

He edged along the tunnel, the sensation of the undercurrent tugging at his legs almost overpowering. Seeing the other soldiers slowly follow him from the side tunnel, he pushed himself further along the wall, allowing them room.

As 'Hase' began to follow the wall round the bend, the force of the flowing water moved from the side of his legs to the front, almost pressing him against the wall, the water rising to his crotch as the current was forced to turn in the tunnel. He felt his body begin to shiver in addition to his teeth chattering, his exhaled breath condensed as the temperature in the passageway dropped further.

Pushing his numb legs sideways, he forced them through the silt accumulated on the bend, the progress slowing as the slurry seemed to suck at his boots. With the water pressure and the slurry on the floor of the tunnel, his progress lowered, his cold legs now edging along the wall.

His eyes widened in horror as he saw the group of rats swimming towards them in the torrent, their fur glistening in the water. As his arms were raised holding his weapon above the water, he froze, considering striking out at them as they approached. Then the rodents turned in the torrent, swimming past him into the darkness, his relief apparent as he exhaled condensed air heavily.

Gunfire echoed across the walls from ahead, startling them. 'Hase' stopped then glanced round, seeing the suffering on the other soldier's faces, their bodies beginning to shake with the cold, their teeth chattering. Now all five of the men lined the wall, their arms raised to protect their weapons, their progress slow as they edged through the raging water.

As 'Hase' turned the bend in the tunnel, he felt the water pressure resume on the side of his legs, his feet moving more freely. Becoming more wary of his shaking due to the freezing water, he tried to turn slightly, beginning to wade through the fast moving liquid, forcing his numb body from side to side to increase his pace. He felt the torrent ease as the soldiers behind him adopted his tactics, their bodies forming a makeshift breakwater for him.

Squinting into the darkness, he could not make out the end of the tunnel. The light from behind him flickered off the water as it surged in front of him, seeming to increase in momentum. Staring forward as he pushed himself through the liquid, his fear began to rise, the darkness seeming endless before him.

He heard a soldier thrash in the water behind him as he slipped, Hausser grasping the man and steadying him before he slipped beneath the surface. 'Hase' realised the cause of his fear, the consideration an enemy may lean into the darkness ahead and open fire. The water noise was now intense around them in the narrow tunnel, the surface of the polluted liquid beginning to carry debris past them at higher speed.

'Hase' struggled forward, the other soldiers pushing themselves through the polluted water, their tenseness beginning to transform into panic at the realisation they could not turn back. As he pushed forward, his body now shaking uncontrollably with the cold, he realised the water was now above his belt, the water level rising rapidly in the narrow tunnel.

Hausser realised at the same time that the level was increasing, determining it was now too late for them to turn back, his fear becoming almost intoxicating, 'Keep moving!' His urgent shouts went virtually unheard with the increasing volume of the water around them. The soldiers now collectively aware of the rising water.

'Hase' felt the water reach his chest, raising his rifle higher to prevent it becoming unusable. As the weapon grated on the sloped roof, he turned it in his hands, the barrel pointing forward as the brick ceiling prevented the weapon from being held above either side of his body.

Moving the rifle to one hand, be began to use his free arm to assist his progress, moving it with his body. The water was now just below his chest, his body becoming increasingly numb as he pushed himself through the water. Hearing some of the men groan behind him, he realised panic was beginning to set in as they collectively tried to push against the current, a current that was becoming stronger.

As he spluttered, the water rising dramatically before dropping back below his chin, he saw a flicker of light ahead, his heart racing in his chest. He pushed himself further, the water tugging at his legs and body. As the water rose to just under his chin, he thought he saw a helmeted head duck into the tunnel towards them, in front of the dim light.

His body tensed as the dim light got nearer, his mind becoming clear, his ears waiting for the sound of gunfire. 'Hase' thought of warning the others behind him, but realised they could do nothing, the water restricting any reaction. Closing his eyes briefly, he felt the water surge over his chin, the light

169

seeming closer. As he opened his eyes, another helmet ducking into the tunnel on the opposite side to the first, the metal glinting in the poor light. His legs were now being pulled upwards by the force of the water as it gained speed rapidly. Closing his eyes again, realising he could no longer resist the undercurrent, his mind admitting defeat. He relaxed his numb leg muscles, allowing the water to lift them from the sewer floor, the water beginning to propel him forwards.

'Hase' braced himself as he rapidly approached the light, hearing louder rushing water as his ears cleared the surface of the poisoned liquid in the tunnel. As his body surged forward with the gushing water, he relinquished fighting the current, allowing it to push him towards the light. Feeling the scraping of the walls as his shoulder hit the brickwork, he gritted his teeth, his body turning in current of the water to face the tunnel behind. As the freezing water rose, he saw the soldiers behind him fighting against the undercurrent, individually reaching out for the walls desperately as they lost their footing, the force of the accelerating mass of liquid too strong to resist.

Udet closed his mind to what was happening, the freezing temperature having numbed him. As his boots lost contact with the bricks below, his body was propelled forwards, briefly glimpsing 'Hase' disappear some metres before him. The flickering light was now only metres away and he glimpsed metal in the distance before the water rose up over his face and he closed his eyes instinctively, awaiting for what would happen, his breath held.

'Hase' felt hands attempted to roughly grab him from the left, scratching his arm and back, then the grip was torn away with the force of the water. He felt himself falling, the world spinning for a second as he dropped downwards. Feeling water explode around him as he landed in the deep reservoir, then the sensation of being pushed downwards as the weight of the water falling from above forced him further into the murky depths. Momentarily, he felt his body drift, his mind darkening and becoming relaxed, unable to feel the freezing water around him. He felt a blow to his back, then side, then he was hit briefly several times, his mind twisting to presume the impacts were bullets. He felt his body drifting downwards, weight tugging on his limbs, pulling him into the darkness, his body limp and numb. The pain from the impacts was bruising, his mind considering the cold was dulling the pain of the impacts. He smiled briefly, thinking he would not die in extreme pain at least, that fate was perhaps treating him kindly at the end.

Then his mind screamed at his to survive, to kick out and fight the weight dragging on his body, his soaked uniform adding considerable weight. Kicking his boots hard, he felt them hit a wall, then make contact with a solid obstacle. He pushed his feet against the underwater step, feeling his body drift upwards in the water, his conscious urgency to breathe turning into panic. Forcing his numb legs to move, he opened his eyes briefly, seeing the dim light above him through the muddied water. Kicking again, the light perhaps seemed to get bigger, his mind becoming confused, his sight dimming slightly. Feeling the pain in his limbs lighten, a sensation of warmth seemed to slowly filter into his body, his view of the light dimming further.

Then he felt his body move, the warmth beginning to surge through him. His body moved again, his mind struggling to understand what was causing the movement, the warmth seeming to beckon him. Then he closed his eyes, feeling his uniform stretch across his body briefly. Then he was moving, faster and faster, his eyes drifting open, the light accelerating towards him. The water exploded around him once more as his head burst above the surface. He heard the sound of a large wheeze as his body sucked in air, then another, the air restricted by the water in his throat and lungs. As he wretched and coughed, he felt the warmth recede, his mind seeming to reach out in an attempt to capture the heat, to retrieve it. He felt his body jerk as he coughed more, his limp body being moved in the freezing water. 'Hase's' body spun round as he neared a low platform, seeing the hands reach out for him from above. His body rose slightly from the water as the hands gripped his uniform tightly, then he dropped back. More hands grasped his shoulder and uniform and he jerked upwards from the water, still retching and sucking in air. He looked down as his body rose out of the polluted liquid, seeing the water cascade off his uniform and boots. Further beyond his feet, he saw a helmeted head, the gloved hands pushing him from the water. The helmet rose upwards, the concerned face of Udet below the steel headpiece, the water in the reservoir over his shoulders.

Hearing splutters to the right, 'Hase' felt his upper body landing on metal, then he was turned over roughly, his helmet hitting the metal walkway. Feeling a knee placed hard on his back, pressing downwards, his stomach and insides feeling trapped. Then he felt the liquid rise within him, his mouth opening as water poured from his body. As he vomited, he sucked in air, the gasps weak initially then becoming stronger. The pressure on his back was intense as he lay there, struggling for air, his chest wheezing and gasping. Then he felt a body land on top of his left side, the knee lifting off his back, the pressure lightening.

He coughed and spluttered, the exertion having completely drained him physically. Feeling the body on his left roll to the side, a hand placed on his side, he slowly rolled over onto his back, breathing sharply and heavily, his chest painful. His body shaking with the cold and his teeth chattering, he cautiously opened his eyes looking up at the stained bricks above him.

His eyes slowly adjusted to the dim light, his body jerking as the warmth began to slowly fight its way back into his limbs. Then a helmeted head appeared above him, looking down, the face of the shadowy figure seeming to smile broadly.

'Hase's' body jerked as he coughed violently again, raising his head and spitting the foul tasting phlegm from his mouth. He lowered his head again looking up at the smiling face looking down on him, then a flicker of recognition went through his mind at the eyes above the dirty scarf in the dim light.

Nicu was grinning at him beneath the scarf, 'We wondered if you would come.' The Romanian stated, kneeling down above him, his expression becoming concerned. 'We need to get you warm.' Beginning to unbutton his tunic quickly. As 'Hase' lay there, he could hear the distant gunfire echoing through the tunnels, looking up at Nicu, the young Romanian had understood his concerns. He had whispered to him gently as he removed his tunic, 'We are holding the Russians back, so we are safe here for the time being.'

Pushing himself up painfully onto his elbows, 'Hase' slowly pulled himself backwards, extracting his legs carefully away from the water's edge. Looking round slowly, he saw the reservoir was quite large, metal gantries on several levels surrounding the deep water storage area. Several candles flickered on the metal walkways, the lights casting shadows that danced across the walls with the movement of the water. Around the gantries sat several Russian residents sheltering from the ravages of the city above, their clothes worn and faces grim. Most were elderly, but two small children were amongst them seeming fascinated by the soldiers' actions. Five passageways exited the large spacious man-made brick cavern on two levels, with a number of drainage pipes around the room feeding the mass of water below them. The noise of the rushing water was continuous, both from the passageway and some of the piping. The cold air in the wide space seemed to cling to the human presence, adding to the misery felt by the residents.

Nicu had removed most of his uniform, providing him with a large number of makeshift rags to wrap himself in, mostly provided by the startled residents, the rest from a small storage cupboard next to the reservoir. The young Romanian had then helped him stand and moved him to sit with a small bedraggled group of refugees sheltering in the large man-made storage area, the fighting driving them from the tunnels.

As 'Hase' cautiously sat down, his body wrapped snugly in the many layers of rags and blankets, the elderly man and lady next to him had moved closer to him. Placing their arms around him for warmth, the man removed his jacket and placed it over 'Hase's' shoulders. The woman had tears in her eyes as she began rubbing his numb arms vigorously. Speaking in hushed Russian to the elderly man on the other side of him, 'Such a young man, so far from home. They are too innocent to die here.'

Realising the elderly couple presumed he was 'just another' German soldier, he remained quiet, his teeth chattering uncontrollably as he sat there. The elderly woman gradually stopped rubbing his arm and held him to her, her body shaking as she cried, 'You are just like my young Marat, fighting for something you no longer understand.' She sobbed.

'Hase' watched as Nicu had begun twisting the uniform material to squeeze as much water from it as possible. His body was still shivering, but less than before. The jolts less violent as the warmth from the couple pressed closely to him began to filter into his.

Across the corner of the reservoir from him, one of the Hungarian soldiers was grinning, his elation at escaping the water alive evident. He looked past the soldier, the water gushing from the tunnel opening and downwards, into a wide and spacious area. The soldier lay on a metal gantry, the water bubbling below him. Beyond the falling water he saw a Romanian soldier frantically rubbing Udet's legs in urgency, attempting to rejuvenate warmth, concern on the Romanian's face.

He was still shivering as the Nicu returned the damp uniform and felt body length underwear, lying it gently across his still numb legs. Nicu knelt before him, studying him as his shivering became lighter, smiling at the elderly couple either side of him, 'Thank you.'

They nodded in response, their faces lined with the exhaustion and hardships they had experienced. The woman slowly turned, retrieving a small bundle from behind her. Unwrapping the cloth slowly, she produced some small crusts of bread from the bundle, offering them to 'Hase' and Nicu in her outstretched hand. Both soldiers shook their heads, the thought of taking the bread from the elderly couple abhorrent to them.

Nicu raised his hand, shaking it and indicating for the elderly woman and her husband to eat. In response, she smiled briefly, offering the small snack across 'Hase' to the elderly man. The man shrugged, glanced at 'Hase' then extended a hand slowly, retrieving a morsel of bread and placing it in his mouth. As he chewed slowly, he smiled at Nicu.

Chapter Eighteen: Trapped

'Hase' gingerly started to dress himself, wary of the stares of the many Russian civilians in the reservoir. Seeing his embarrassment, the elderly couple slowly stood up and placed themselves in front of him, shielding his body as he slipped back into the damp felt underwear. Lifting his combat trousers over his knees, he could just hear gunfire above the flowing water from one of the passageways to the right.

As he buttoned his tunic, Tatu emerged from the darkness of the tunnel, a smile crossing his face as he recognised the soldiers spread amongst the Russian civilians for warmth on the gantries. Nodding at Hausser, the Romanian quartermaster moved towards him, descending a set of metal steps. He then walked under the mass of falling water before climbing more of the gantry steps, the studs on his boots clicking on the metal walkway.

Hausser raised his eyes as Tatu stood over him, the commander twisting Udet's uniform to squeeze water from the fabric. 'We will have to move Hausser, the Russians seem to be moving more men up in the tunnels.' Tatu grinned as he observed the young commander dressed in civilian clothes, blankets placed across his shoulders.

Hausser glanced back at the material in his hands, then looked at Tatu, ignoring his amusement, 'Do you know the way out?'

Tatu shook his head, his face becoming grim, his hand running across his moustache, 'No, the only safe way out I know is full of water.' He indicated to the waterfall behind him, 'I have checked the other tunnels, but there are Russian infantry in each of them. I don't know the system, so we may attack in the wrong direction and be in here for days. We are holding them for now, but if they attack in force...well, that will be it I think.'

The commander rose to his feet, a blanket falling to the walkway. Thinking for a second, he turned to Tatu, his face grave, 'Most of our weapons are waterlogged, so will not be reliable now. We need to find a way out.......and quickly, to save the men.'

Hausser shuffled past Tatu, handing the uniform to Udet sitting shivering against the wall. He turned sharply, his eyes narrowing, 'Where are the controls to empty the reservoir?'

Tatu shifted his stance, pointing across the wide room, 'There are some hand wheels over there in the corner on the lower level, but that still does not give us a way out.'

The commander nodded, turning to face the walkways above he raised his voice, speaking Russian, 'Please help us, we need a way out of here, can anyone tell us the way?'

The Russian civilians looked at him suspiciously, hesitancy and caution on their faces.

Hausser coughed, then spoke again, 'Please tell us the way out of here if you know one.'

Behind Hausser, the elderly man next to 'Hase' slowly raised his hand, his wife beginning to sob in fear. 'Hase' slowly lowered himself before the woman, nodding at the elderly man, his voice soft, 'Don't worry, he is a good man, he will not harm you.'

The woman's eyes opened wide as she recognised his Ukrainian accent, the tears beginning to flow from her eyes, 'You are Russian, but why?'

'Hase's' eyes became moist, he swallowed hard, placing a hand on her shoulder as she shook, her head dropping to look into her lap, 'He saved my life and the lives of my men, I owe my loyalty to him now.'

The woman slowly raised her head, her eyes defiant, her voice low, 'But you are a traitor to your country now, yet so young...' The tears rolled down her cheeks as she wept and 'Hase' realised she was crying for him, for his predicament.

A tear rolled down his cheek as he knelt before her, his hand on her shoulder. He swallowed again, his throat tight with emotion, a desperation rising within him to tell her the truth, 'Our position was impossible in the Crimea. We

176

were cut off, left to die by the commissars. This commander saved me and my men and a village full of people from destruction.' He leant forward slowly, as the elderly woman sobbed, 'He saved the villagers and refugees, letting us escape to safety as Russian planes bombed the village behind us. That is why I have loyalty to this man, not his country.'

The woman's head rose, her shoulders shaking with emotion as she looked into his eyes. Raising her hand, she grasped his arm tightly, her tear filled eyes staring into him, 'But what will become of you?'

'Hase' held the stare for a second, the tears flowing down his face, he shrugged slightly, his voice a whisper, 'I don't know.'

The elderly lady turned to look at her husband, his eyes wide with the spectacle before him, she nodded to him, 'Show them the way.'

The elderly man stepped slowly round 'Hase', descending the steps from the platform they had been sat on. He stopped before Hausser and Tatu, his hand reaching for his cap and removing it, his eyes lowered. He moved the cap nervously around in his hands, the fear rising within him as he stood before the young commander and Romanian quartermaster.

Hausser leant forward, placing his hand on the old man's shoulder, his voice soft, 'There is no need to be afraid, we mean you no harm.' Explosions could be heard along the tunnels, the Russian infantry trying to dislodge the German defenders with grenades.

The man's head slowly rose, looking the commander in the eye, his expression defiant, 'I am not afraid of you, or your men. There is nothing else your army can inflict on our country that would make me afraid.' His eyes became grave, 'This war will go on for years, the hatred becoming more vicious in its enactment. All there is left is people and how they help each other survive.'

Hausser's eyes widened in surprise at the man's honesty. Tatu, next to him, shaking his head. The commander looked at the elderly man, admiring his bravery. 'Tell me how we can get out please.'

The elderly man stood there, staring at the young commander, 'I will help you because I believe you are good men. Good men need to survive to stem the spread of evil that thrives in this war. Perhaps my helping you is my defiance of the evil........that you can survive and help others.'

Hausser nodded slowly, realising the man had little fear left, his tiredness of the conflict and suffering apparent in his features. Tatu placed his hands on his hips, his frustration rising, 'Herr Leutnant, we have not got time for this!'

Hausser raised his hand indicating to Tatu to stop talking, 'This man will help us, let's let him speak.'

Tatu stepped back, screwing his face up and sighing. 'Very well, you are in command,' he stated despondently.

The elderly man smiled fleetingly, 'I have one request, Herr Commander.' As he looked at Hausser, his eyes widened slightly as he saw the top of the black cross outlined in white around his neck, the blankets hiding the rest of the medal from view.

Hausser's eyebrows raised, 'Please tell me.'

The man shuffled towards him slightly, 'I worked in these sewers and along the river for years. All this water is coming from a flooded reservoir outside the city, it happens every now and then, it will flow for hours. To escape you will have to flood the lower tunnels, the water will subside here and allow you access to a maintenance tunnel, only then you can escape.' The man wiped some moisture from his face with his right hand, 'I ask that you tell the Russians you will flood the tunnels, they can get the civilians out before they drown or are swept out onto the freezing ice on the Volga.'

The commander nodded, thinking. 'How long is this tunnel, and how will we ensure we get away?'

The elderly man sighed, 'You should keep going along the tunnel taking a left, then the second right. There is a ladder there, it will bring you out of the tunnel system avoiding the water.'

Hausser smiled briefly, considering the man may be lying, then discounting it. The elderly man seemed genuine enough, his determination to explain the escape and save the people in the lower tunnels contradicting any motive to trap them. He looked at the man, his eyes staring at the commander, not breaking eye contact. He could see the elderly man wanted reassurance before explaining further. Slowly he nodded, 'Very well, we will give them ten minutes to move the people from the lower tunnels.'

The commander turned to look at Nicu, indicating for his uniform, the young Romanian turning to retrieve it from the handrail he had placed it upon after wringing the excess water from the material. Hausser then looked up at 'Hase', 'Go to the forward positions and shout to the Russians. Tell them we will flood the tunnels in ten minutes and that they should move civilians out.' He hesitated, considering what he was doing, his eyes looking round at the assembled Russian civilians, 'Tell them we have civilians in here too and that we will not harm them.' He turned, indicating to Udet, 'Go with him.'

'Hase' nodded, pausing for Udet to come with him, the young German buttoning his damp tunic.

Turning back to the elderly man, Hausser smiled, 'It is done, please show me where this tunnel is.'

The man turned slowly, pointing into the water by the wall below them, 'The hatch is down there. The access is from a small platform which you take that ladder to.'

Tatu spun round, seeing the metal rungs set into a recess in the wall, a small walkway above leading to it. He turned back to the man, 'How do we release the water?'

The elderly man smiled, knowing the Romanian was not fond of the plan, his distrust evident, 'The controls to open the flood gates are over there.' He pointed across the room, 'In the corner. You must wait before opening the gates, this level of water will drown or kill everyone below this area between here and the river.'

179

Tatu nodded, a glare on his face, 'Yes I know, I just want to make sure you know what you are talking about.' He mounted the steps from the platform, walking briskly on the metal gantries round the large reservoir, heading towards the point the man had indicated to. Reaching the far end of the large room, he stood on a wide platform, becoming indistinguishable in the darkness around him.

There was a short pause, then Tatu's voice boomed across the reservoir, 'Herr Leutnant, he is telling the truth, the controls are here.'

Hausser turned to the elderly man, his voice a whisper, 'Thank you, we will do what you ask.' He indicated to 'Hase' to continue. Turning to face the reservoir, he called across to Tatu, 'Go and tell the Russians in another tunnel, I want to make sure more than one gets the message. Place 'trips' as we retreat.'

In the darkness he heard an emphasised 'tut', then Tatu's strained voice, 'Oh, very well.' The Romanian emerging from the darkness and disappearing into the nearest tunnel.

'Hase' passed Hausser on the metal platform fastening his belt, Udet rising to join him after tying his boots. As they climbed the steps leading to the next level, Nicu handed Udet his rifle, the two men's weapons lying at the bottom of the reservoir after their experience in the waterfall.

Hausser began to place his feet through the legs of the damp felt underwear, the blankets dropping from his shoulders. Looking round in slight embarrassment, he saw the numerous Russian civilians averting their eyes as he pulled the underwear up around his waist.

As 'Hase' and Udet slipped into one of the tunnels, the sound of running water receded as gunfire echoed through the passageways. Moving forward cautiously, they advanced along a tunnel parallel to the river, turning left towards the Volga as the passageway bent round. They could hear shouts in the distance as the defending Hungarian infantry held their positions further forward of where they were. The voices sounding alarmed as the defenders realised the Russians were moving into the sewers in force.

Edging forward to the next dark corner, Udet hissed to the infantryman hiding behind the sandbags in the next passageway, 'Where is the front position?'

The soldier turned sharply, fear in his eyes, the candle at his feet flickering in the movement, 'Just ahead, the Russians are getting ambitious, we have lost two men.'

'Hase' moved past the man, nodding to him as he did so. Nearing the next corner, he saw a boot at the bend in the tunnel, the dead soldier having been hit as he retreated. Stooping down and lowering himself to his knees, he grasped the dead soldier's discarded rifle, pulling the bolt back to check the chamber. The Kar 98 rifle holding only two rounds, he cautiously leant forward and stretched to the man's belt for more ammunition. Bullets flew through the tunnel above him as the Russians opened fire on the German position ahead. He ducked down instinctively, startled by the fire, his heart beating faster in his chest.

Udet knelt at the corner, his exhaled breath condensing in the cold passageway. Ducking round the corner, he saw 'Hase' delicately pulling bullet clips from the dead soldier's ammunition pouches. Beyond him, he could see the two Hungarian soldiers cowering behind another sandbagged position as the bullets flew overhead. Dirt and debris fell from the curved ceiling of the tunnel as he edged forward into the passageway behind 'Hase', his rifle raised.

'Hase' had retrieved the dead soldier's ammunition, swallowing hard as he had taken the bullet clips from the corpse, the blood from the man slowly extending across the floor of the passageway. Stuffing the clips into his damp tunic pockets, he crawled past the corpse, making his way gingerly forward towards the sandbags and cowering soldiers.

One of the Hungarians turned to face him, indicating with his right hand for 'Hase' to stay low. Udet crawled behind him, reaching into his tunic to check for the twine he had been given earlier. As he grasped the thin cord, he smiled to himself briefly, seeing three circular grenades lying before to the sandbags ahead, the light from a dwindling candle glowing on their smooth surfaces.

As 'Hase' reached the frightened Hungarians there was a lull in the gunfire. Udet shouted from behind him nudging 'Hase's' buttocks, 'Hey Russkie!'

There was a pause, then a muffled voice echoed through the tunnel, the Russian infantryman hiding behind the next corner, some thirty metres away down a decline in the passageway, 'What Fritz?' The Russian smiling briefly at his broken German, his PPSH 41 held tightly in his hands, the machine gun barrel warm for the firing.

'Hase' coughed, clearing his throat, emphasising his Ukrainian accent, he shouted, 'We have civilians from the city! We do not want to harm them, but we need to flood the lower tunnels to save them, the water is rising too fast.' He rubbed the back of his neck nervously under his helmet with his hand, considering the lie was necessary to convince the Russians in front of him.

The Russian's eyes widened in astonishment as he heard his native language, the Ukrainian accent startling him. The six infantrymen behind him in the tunnel looking at each other in confused surprise.

'Hase' shouted again, 'Did you hear me?'

There was a pause, then the Russian infantryman replied, his tone suspicious, 'Yes.....I hear you..... Why should we believe you Fascists?'

'Hase' paused, then shouted again, his tone firm, 'You have ten minutes to move your men and civilians to safety, then we flood the lower tunnels, understand?'

The Russian infantryman hesitated for a second, then turned to the soldier next to him, whispering, 'Go and tell the captain. Get him to clear the tunnels quickly.' He turned back to face the corner, raising his voice, 'Very well Fascist, but this will not save you. There is no mercy for your army in this city now! We will give you ten minutes, then we will come and get you!'

'Hase' turned to Udet, indicating with his hand that the Russians had understood. Udet nodded and leant forward, picking up one of the grenades and carefully attaching one end of the twine to the pin. Retrieving one of the sandbags, he wrapped the rough string around the bag, then leant out, dropping the bag at the other side of the passageway, moving back into cover quickly behind the makeshift obstruction.

Indicating for the Hungarians to retreat to the corner, he bit through the twine, attaching the end to another grenade. Pausing as the Hungarians crawled back behind them, he then wedged the grenades into the sandbagged wall, ensuring the twine was stretched across the passageway. Indicating to 'Hase', they both crawled backwards from the barrier, their hearts beating loudly in their chests.

The Russian soldier glanced round the corner, seeing the isolated sandbags beyond a body in the tunnel, he smiled knowingly. Hearing distant shouting in the tunnels towards the river, he realised the soldiers were moving civilians out of the lower tunnels, his smile broadening. He considered his captain to be somewhat of an idiot, but at least not that stupid, to ignore such a warning.

Reaching the corner in the tunnel, 'Hase' waved at the Hungarian soldiers, pushing them back to the last sandbagged barrier. The Hungarians smiling as they moved further from the Russians, the two of them moving briskly away from the corner.

'Hase' then turned to Udet, indicating for him to leave, the young German initially shaking his head, then reluctantly turning and walking back towards the reservoir. The firing was now distant in the tunnel system, the battle now further along the line. 'Hase' knelt next to the corner, hearing the sound of Udet's boots recede in the passageway, then they stopped as the young German turned the next corner, heading back to the reservoir to update Hausser.

As he knelt there, listening to the sounds of dripping water and distant gunfire, 'Hase' thought of the elderly lady and their brief conversation. Guilt overcoming him, he considered if his parents or even grandparents would be as understanding or non-judgemental as the old lady in the reservoir. It was one thing to condemn the communists in front of him when he was a young boy, but would they understand him or his reasoning for fighting against his fellow Russians?

Thinking back, he realised the decision he had made in the Crimea to help Hausser had brought him to this point. A decision made in seconds that had decided his fate of months of loyalty and fighting for the invading Germans and their allies, had changed the direction of his life dramatically. Could he change what he was now? He realised he could not, the Russians, his countrymen, would now shoot him on the spot if he surrendered, perhaps even torture him first if the commissars got hold of him.

Pushing the thoughts from his mind, his resolve and determination to continue heightened, the loyalty to one man overriding his country and background. The conclusion to his thoughts.......he would have died back in the Crimea had he not made the decision, and so would many innocent others. In some confused way, the betrayal of his country and his actions since were justified for the survival of his men and the inhabitants of the village.

He glanced round the corner as he heard movement, the shuffling beyond the sandbagged barrier. He realised the Russian infantry were beginning to consider the makeshift position before them may be unmanned. Gripping the rifle tightly, he raised it to his shoulder. He squeezed the trigger, the shot loud in the passageway as it hit the roof of the tunnel above the sandbags, the Russian infantry ducking back behind the corners for cover at the base of the ramp.

Distant footsteps in the tunnel behind him made him turn, seeing the Hungarians glancing at him cautiously from behind the next sandbagged barrier. Behind them, to the left, Udet's face appeared from the side passageway, indicating with his hand for him to come to him.

'Hase' backed slowly from the corner, then turned, walking with renewed determination towards Udet. As he reached the sandbags, he indicated for the Hungarians to retreat further, back into the reservoir. Udet shook his head in frustration at him, then crouched next to him at the barrier, his voice a whisper, 'Alright 'Hase', we will be the last to leave...again.' The young German beginning to grin as he prepared another grenade, slipping the some twine around the top of the explosive.

'Hase' shrugged next to him, not understanding the words, but grasping the meaning. Then he slapped Udet's shoulder with the back of his hand, a smile forming on his face. Udet leant forward using a sandbag as he had done before, wrapping the twine around it and stretching the string across the passageway. 'Hase' watched over his friend, his rifle leant across the top of the sandbagged barrier.

Back in the reservoir, Hausser glanced up at the Russian civilians on the gantries above him as he buttoned his damp tunic, the dishevelled and dirty faces glancing back and forth between the soldiers cautiously. Considering the time to leave was approaching, he began to make his way across the walkways and platforms to the controls for the flood gates. Slowly the elderly man followed him, smiling grimly at the other Russians as he passed them in an attempt to ease their concerns.

As Hausser reached the walkway that led to the control platform, he paused, awaiting the elderly Russian to catch him up. Hearing footsteps in the passageway below him, he looked down as a soldier entered the reservoir. Grinning as he recognised Tatu, he stamped on the walkway to get his attention. Tatu looked up, startled, a grim smile forming on his face, 'The men are ready Hausser......the Russkies seem to be moving people out of the lower tunnels.'

Hausser nodded, 'Good, can you come up and give me a hand?'

Tatu nodded, proceeding to the metal staircase to his left. Climbing the metal steps, he emerged onto the platform behind Hausser, turning to proceed towards the commander. Hausser waited for him, the elderly Russian next to him, the young commander speaking as he turned to the controls, 'How is Petru?'

Tatu looked at him, smiling, 'Shivering. It's a good job the Russians in here picked him out of the water, or he would have frostbite or drowned.'

Hausser nodded grimly, 'Let's hope he doesn't.' Turning to the Russian, he smiled to alleviate the elderly man's concerns, 'Show me which control opens the flood gates please.'

The Russian nodded, moving past him and stopping next to a metal handle, 'Winding this will open the gates, then you have to open the hatch over on the other side of the reservoir.' He pointed across the wide expanse of freezing water, 'It's just there, next to the ladder. Open that, climb down and you are in the maintenance tunnel.'

Hausser looked across the dimly lit room, seeing the metal ladder set into the wall as it descended into the water. He nodded, looking at the man, 'Thank you.'

The elderly Russian nodded, a melancholy look in his eyes, 'I wish you well commander and thank you for sparing us.'

Hausser smiled briefly, 'It's the least we could do, you have helped us survive and for that you have my thanks.'

Tatu stopped next to Hausser, slightly out of breath from the climb, 'Shall we open it now?' An impatient look on his face.

Hausser looked round at the room, the Russian civilians all watching him, sighing at their misery, he nodded, 'Let's get out of here.'

Tatu stepped forward, grasping the metal handle, his arms tensing. Pulling on the lever, the handle would not move, the mechanism half frozen. Hausser slipped the strap of his MP40 over his shoulder and grasped the lever next to Tatu, heaving the cold metal with him. At first the handle wouldn't move, then a grating sound from the gears slowly released the frozen cogs and the lever moved gradually clockwise.

The grinding and squealing of the gears echoed across the chamber as they slowly turned the lever. Hausser glanced down at the freezing water, through the metal mesh platform. Seeing a couple of bubbles rising to the surface of the water, he applied more pressure to the lever, his arm muscles straining. He glanced at Tatu, 'Pull harder!'

The Romanian quartermaster grunted as he tensed his muscles, the lever beginning to move more freely. Further bubbles rose to the surface of the water next to the front wall, the metal doorway from the reservoir beginning to rise. Both men applied more pressure, their arm muscles straining to move the handle quicker.

Hausser looked down again, seeing larger bubbles on the water's surface, then a large explosion of air on the water's surface next to the wall as the metal doorway began to open, a larger air bubble escaping from the drainage tunnel. Further large bubbles broke the water's surface as the handle moved further, then the sound of rushing water filled the wide room, the water beginning to flow through the open metal hatch into the declining flood tunnel, gathering speed.

Turning the lever several more times, Hausser and Tatu could see the water surface bubbling furiously as it was sucked through the open metal doorway, the drainage tunnels beyond filling with the freezing liquid as the wall of water increased speed on the declining tunnels towards the river.

Tatu removed one hand from the lever, grasping the rope that hung from the wall next to it and wrapping it round the handle, the extra makeshift brake effective. Slowly removing their hands from the lever, both men smiled in satisfaction as they saw the metal did not move, the cogs locking the gate open with additional support from the taut rope.

Looking down, Tatu saw that the water level was slowly dropping, the walls above the surface of the liquid wet from where the water had been, the gate fully open allowing the foul liquid to escape. A smile spread across his face, 'That's the first challenge, now let's get to the maintenance hatch.'

Hausser turned next to him, heading for the stairs to the platform. The elderly Russian stepped back, 'There is no need to rush, the water will take some time to lower enough.'

Hausser stopped, spinning round, his eyes wide, his voice rising, 'Some time? How long?'

The elderly man backed away, seeing the young commander's frustrated anger, his body beginning to shake, 'May-Maybe ten minutes, perhaps longer.'

Hausser's eyes narrowed, realising he was scaring the man he lowered his voice, 'I understand, that may be too long for us though.' He turned to Tatu, 'Get the men to stay in the tunnels and tell them to hold their positions, we are not out of here yet.' He turned back to the elderly Russian, 'Please move your people to the higher walkways, it may make them safer from gunfire.

Tatu nodded in agreement, glaring at the elderly Russian, 'Ten minutes only, or you will be swimming to the Volga!' He ran to the steps, hearing muffled rifle shots from the tunnels.

Hausser looked at the elderly Russian, shrugging, 'Let's hope the water drops then.' He started descending the steps to the next platform, making his way round to the lever for the maintenance hatch. The elderly Russian started indicating for the civilians on the lower levels to move higher.

As Tatu advanced down the tunnel he had used previously, high in the reservoir, he heard the shooting ahead. Cautiously, he approached the next corner, hearing the rifle cracks loud in the next passageway. Ducking into the passage to check the way ahead, he saw Petru and a German soldier at the next corner, firing towards the left.

Crouching to approach them, Tatu took his PPSH 41 from his shoulder. As he reached his countryman, Petru glanced round smiling a greeting, 'How long before we move?'

Tatu shook his head, 'Another few minutes, can we hold?'

Petru nodded briefly, then glanced back down the dark passageway, 'The Russians are getting ready to attack.......perhaps we can hold a while longer.' He raised his rifle firing into the darkness, the shot cracking across the tunnel walls. Leaning back behind the corner, he turned again to Tatu, 'I don't feel too good, I think I may have swallowed too much water.'

Tatu grinned fondly at his friend, 'There is still plenty back in the reservoir if you want some more.'

Petru's eyes widened, a smile forming on his face, 'Perhaps on the way out!'

The German soldier next to them held his hand up for them to be quiet, 'Listen!'

Straining their ears, Tatu's eyes opened wide as he heard the clicking at the end of the passageway, 'Flame thrower! Fall back!'

They backed away from the corner as a 'whoosh' surged down the tunnel, the jet of flame billowing past before them into the tunnel on the right.

Tatu shouted, 'Back to the next corner!' Raising his machine gun in one hand, he reached for a grenade in his overcoat pocket. Grasping the last remaining Romanian grenade, he pulled it out of his large leather jacket, gripping it in his left hand.

Another jet of flame surged past the junction they had just left as they reached the corner behind them. As they backed round the corner, he offered the grenade to Petru, his countryman pulling the fuse. Tossing the grenade along the passageway, Tatu watched as it bounced on the brick floor of the tunnel, coming to a rest at the corner of the junction. Ducking back, the blast wave seemed to shake the tunnel, fragments of dirt and debris falling from the brick ceiling.

As Tatu leant back out, the smell of the explosion was strong in his nostrils, the smoke from the blast hanging in the tunnel. He squinted to try and see into the darkness, then ducked back as a wall of flame shot towards him down the right hand side of the tunnel, closing his mouth as he pushed Petru to the floor of the passageway.

As the flame receded, the stench of chemicals caught in his throat. Pushing himself upwards, he fired blindly into the tunnel, only extending his right arm to the corner. Turning to the other two, he screamed, spittle hitting their faces, 'Back to the next corner, I will hold here!'

The German soldier turned and ran down the passageway, dropping to his knees and turning at the next corner. As Petru backed away, Tatu glanced at him, their eyes meeting, the fear passing between them. Then his countryman turned and ran back to the kneeling German infantryman, his rifle raised towards Tatu.

The Romanian quartermaster fired again into the tunnel, then ducked out quickly to see. Seeing a Russian soldier writhing at the junction clutching his stomach, he pulled back, running half crouched towards Petru. Machine gun bullets splattered across the walls of the tunnel he had just left, the Russian infantry firing blind into the tunnel. The moaning of the wounded Russian soldier as his countrymen pulled him to safety echoing off the walls.

Feeling his adrenalin rise further, Tatu skidded to his knees before Petru, indicating to the German soldier, 'Get back to the reservoir and tell Hausser we can't hold them!'

The German nodded, wide eyed beneath his helmet, he spun round and ran into the darkness, slipping on the frost of the tunnel floor as he turned the last corner before the reservoir. Falling on one knee, he glanced back at them, fear on his face, then lunged forward disappearing out of sight.

A grenade dropped into the passageway at the end, both Tatu and Petru ducking back into the next passageway as it exploded, the dust and dirt flying past just in front of them. Tatu leant out, firing a burst of his machine gun, the flashes from the muzzle of the weapon illuminating their faces.

Another grenade bounced off the right wall of the tunnel and they ducked back in, the blast throwing more debris past them as they crouched in the side passageway. Tatu ducked out, firing again, the burst from his weapon splattering against the wall at the end of the tunnel. Then he glimpsed the flash of light on the wall as the flamethrower advanced towards the corner. 'Back!' He shouted in almost panic as flames shot along the right wall towards them, the chemical smell pouring through the passageways.

Backing away, the flame hit the end of the tunnel in front of them, burning fuel spitting towards them from the impact. Tatu instinctively turned, shielding them both with his jacket, then shaking and slapping the back of his jacket to dislodge or extinguish any burning fuel.

Petru's eyes were wide with fright, dragging his countryman towards him as he backed to the corner. Hearing Russian voices in the next tunnel, Tatu raised his weapon, firing another burst at the corner where he had just knelt, the bullets ricocheting off the brick, dislodging dirt and debris that flew across the tunnel.

Dropping to his knees at the corner, Petru raised his rifle ready to fire at any Russian looked into the passageway. Tatu backed round the corner slowly at a crouch, his weapon held pointing before him. As he leant against the cold bricks, he could hear the frightened voices of the Russian civilians in the reservoir behind him, their panic rising. Grabbing Petru's shoulder, he pulled him from the tunnel, pushing his countryman before him.

Another grenade bounced into the passageway before Tatu, the grenade rolling towards him. Pushing himself back, Tatu fell against Petru as the grenade exploded just the other side of the corner, showering them with debris and dirt from the ceiling. Their ears ringing, Tatu turned to move to the reservoir, hesitating as he saw Hausser advance towards them a stick grenade in his right hand. Turning back, he raised his own weapon as Hausser pulled the fuse on the grenade and tossed it at an angle into the next tunnel, the grenade bounding out of sight towards the junction.

Screams of alarm from the tunnel and the scraping of boots as two Russians tried to turn and flee the explosion that followed, then the blast and further screaming. The dust and smoke from the grenade billowing down the tunnel.

Further shouting in Russian, then bullets whipped across their front in the passageway before them, the Russian soldiers providing cover fire to drag the two wounded men away.

Hausser slapped Tatu's shoulder, 'Time to leave old man, get to the maintenance hatch.' Tatu turned, hesitating and shaking his head, unable to hear the command, his ears ringing. Hausser grabbed the shoulder of his jacket, dragging him backwards, 'Go!'

Flames surged into the tunnel at the end, fuel spitting into the passageway they were in. The three soldier's instinctively jumping back as the intense heat emanated towards them. Backing to the reservoir itself, Hausser shouted into the tunnel, 'Russkie, these are your people with us!'

There was a short silence, then the flame surged up the end of the tunnel again. Hausser dropped to his knee at the edge of the reservoir, raising his MP40 to point into the tunnel, 'Get to the maintenance hatch!'

As Tatu and Petru ran across the walkways, their boots clunking on the metal floors, soldiers emerged from other passageways, fright on their faces. Tatu looked across at the water on the other side of the reservoir, seeing the level had lowered sufficiently for the rusted hatch door to be seen, catching his breath as he saw the hatch was only half open. Glancing upwards, he saw the elderly Russian trying desperately to wind the handle that opened the small metal door.

Indicating to Petru to head for the hatch, the Romanian quartermaster grasped the handrails leading up to the platform the elderly Russian was on as Petru passed him to his right, heading for the step ladder. As he reached the ladder set into the wall, Petru turned, beckoning to the soldiers behind him to come forward.

Hausser fired again into the darkness, hearing the clunk of boots on metal to his right as Udet and 'Hase' backed out of the next passageway, firing into the tunnel as they did so. A muffled explosion came from the tunnel, one of the tripwires having been broken.

192

Petru assigned three men to form a makeshift defence on the metal platforms as the remainder of the fourteen men began to raise their rifles over their shoulders to enable them to climb the ladder. Pointing at a German soldier, Petru indicated for him to go first snatching his rifle, the man clambering onto the cold metal rungs and descending quickly. The Romanian turned and tossed the extra rifle to Nicu.

Glancing up, Petru could see Tatu and the Russian 'yanking' the handle as fast as they could to open the hatch, the metal door rising frustratingly slowly, the mechanism squealing as the door rose. Looking down, he could see there was now enough space for a man to slip into the small tunnel and beckoned more soldiers forward as the German below him disappeared into the opening.

Gunfire echoed round the reservoir as the defenders at the opening of the tunnels fired into the darkened tunnels before them. The frightened cries and whimpering of the Russian civilians rising at each gunshot.

Petru glanced up at Tatu, seeing his countryman holding the lever to keep the hatch open. Turning to the men before him, he pushed one nearer the ladder, shouting 'Hurry up, there is no time!' He looked down, seeing the soldiers on the ladder disappear into the opening one by one, their pace painfully slow.

Hausser fired again into the tunnel, realising his weapon was almost empty. He ducked back against the wall pulling a fresh magazine from his belt pouch and attaching into the MP40, pushing the empty canister into the slot in his belt. Flames shot out of the tunnel on the wall opposite, the flamethrower now at the last corner before the reservoir.

The screams of the civilians echoed across the reservoir as the flame receded back into the tunnel, the chemical 'whoosh' leaving burning splatters across the walkway. Hausser gritted his teeth and fired into the tunnel, keeping his body back, pressed against the wall. Looking down in desperation, he saw three soldiers including Nicu aiming up at the tunnels next to Petru, fright on their faces. Three soldiers were still descending the rungs on the ladder, with Tatu on the platform above holding the hatch open.

He drew breath, firing into the tunnel again, then shouted across at Udet and 'Hase', 'Get going now!' The two soldiers glanced across at him startled, then rose from their positions and began running along the metal walkway, descending the first set of steps. Hausser closed his eyes briefly, then forced himself from the wall, firing a burst into the tunnel as he ran across it. Stopping by the next opening, he fired a blind burst into the passageway, then ran across it, his legs pushing him forward on the metal walkway. Reaching the steps, he turned and started to back down them, his weapon raised, jerking it back and forth from each tunnel opening above him.

The moaning of the Russian civilians got louder as he descended the steps, the panic rising within the people as they realised the danger they now faced. Hausser dropped onto the platform below him and backed away, awaiting the first Russian soldier to appear. The rifles cracked behind him as the soldiers saw movement in the tunnels, the gunfire echoing across the brick reservoir walls.

Hausser glanced round, seeing Udet and 'Hase' on the ladder, then froze realising Tatu was still above them. He turned frantically, seeing the elderly Russian raise his hand in acknowledgement, pushing Tatu from the lever and grasping it, the strain on the old man's face. A smile briefly crossed Hausser's face as he saw Tatu's expression as he turned from the lever, pushing his PPSH 41 over his shoulder and beginning to descend the metal steps.

As he passed under the flowing waterfall from the tunnel above, Hausser saw the grenades bounce out of the passageway entrances, dropping to the water below. The explosions throwing the freezing water over the remaining defenders. Screams from the civilians above him echoed round the walls as he ducked down, his hands rising to protect his face.

Rising from his crouched position, he fired into the openings, Tatu firing from behind him. Hausser climbed the last couple of steps backwards, firing controlled bursts as Tatu indicated for the three defenders to move to the ladder. Feeling a hand on his shoulder, he glanced round, realising Tatu was behind him, the Romanian pulling him up the last two steps.

Hausser fired again at the openings, the bursts short as two more grenades bounced through the tunnel entrances, falling into the reservoir and exploding in the water below, the men ducking as the freezing liquid and debris fell on them. The screams from above were becoming continuous as the Russian civilians huddled next to the walls, covering their faces.

Glancing round, Hausser could see the three defenders descending the rungs of the ladder, their boots 'clunking' on the cold steel. He backed towards them, Tatu beside him, their weapons pointed across the reservoir at the passage openings. Firing another burst, Hausser grasped his ammunition pouch for another magazine, his hands shaking.

As Tatu reached out for the first rung of the ladder, his hand missed it, he turned to look and grasp the metal rung. A Russian soldier emerged from one of the tunnels firing his PPSH machine gun, two of the soldiers on the rungs dropping into the water below, their punctured backs arched as they lost grip on the metal rungs. Tatu spun his head round firing with his right hand at the Russian, the soldier toppling over the handrail with his momentum, falling down into the reservoir. Then Tatu backed down the ladder, his machine gun raised.

Hausser bit his lip, forced the magazine into his weapon and raising it, firing into the tunnels on the opposite wall. Turning he looked up at the elderly Russian, 'Danke', he grasped the rung of the ladder and swung himself onto it, holding his machine gun with one hand pointing at the passageways as he descended, his left arm strained as he gripped the upper rungs.

Tatu crouched and backed into the opening, firing a burst at the passageways above, then lowered himself to the floor of the small tunnel to cover Hausser. As Hausser swung himself across and into the tunnel, he spun round, bent double, his weapon raised.

His arms straining, the elderly Russian looked down, seeing the German commander had entered the hatch, the bodies below floating in the water.

The Russian tensed then jumped back, the handle swinging round as the maintenance hatch rolled downwards, plunging the small tunnel into complete darkness.

Hausser turned in the dark, hearing Tatu swear, 'Let's get out of here.' Several bullets clanked against the steel hatch, then there was just the sound of distant sobbing behind the metal plate, the civilians' relief evident as the Russian soldiers entered the reservoir.

Chapter Nineteen: Emergence

The cold water soaked into their damp combat trousers as they crawled up the incline in the tunnel through the darkness, the small tunnel from the hatch being too low to stand or crouch in. Reaching a turning in the narrow passageway, Tatu could see a small light ahead, one of the soldiers using his lighter to illuminate the area. Behind him, Hausser crawled backwards, his machine gun on his back. Distant shouting in the reservoir seemed to indicate the Russians had no appetite for chasing them into the darkness. Hausser hoped the elderly man would be treated well by the pursuing Russians and that they would perhaps not understand the lengths the man had gone to assist them.

The light flickered across the men's faces as some sat in a small storage area, relief at having escaped their pursuers evident on their expressions. Tatu nodded a greeting solemnly to the small group as he arrived in the area, the six soldiers awaiting the men further forward to send news back of having located the exit.

Slipping past the small gathering into the next passageway, Tatu adjusted his machine gun, pushing it under his jacket as protection against the water running down the walls and dripping from the ceiling. Seeing another flickering light just up ahead, Tatu crawled forward beginning to feel claustrophobia with the closeness of the walls and roof of the tunnel. The lower parts of his combat trousers were now soaking wet, the cold seeping into his muscles as he progressed.

Reaching another junction with a dark passageway to the right, he could hear two soldiers whispering in German in the darkness, awaiting the call to move forward. He continued crawling along the passageway for thirty metres. Approaching the flickering light, he saw a Hungarian soldier sat at the next junction, a lighter in his hand. The soldier pointed to his left, indicating the next turning on Tatu's right. As the Romanian quartermaster turned into the next passageway he saw the short tunnel led to a wider room, a further light flickering as he approached the more open space.

Entering the small room, he nodded to Udet and 'Hase', the two of them sat smoking in the dim light next to Petru. Looking to the left, he could just see a small side tunnel, beyond it the rungs of a metal ladder. A dim light illuminating the side room the ladder was in. Indicating with a nod of his head to the soldiers sat in the small room, he moved towards the small opening on his left.

Crawling sideways into the narrow tunnel, Tatu lowered his head to crawl into the small passageway. As he reached the other side, he glanced up, following the rungs of the ladder as they ascended a long shaft. At the top, he saw a thick metal grille some twenty metres above him, with dim daylight shining through the holes in the cover that were not covered in snow.

Rising to his feet, he stretched his back, the journey through the low tunnels stiffening his muscles. Looking down, he noticed Udet crawl through the opening behind him. Then Tatu grasped the rungs on the ladder and started to climb wearily from the sewer.

As he gradually reached the top of the ladder, Tatu listened out for sounds above. Hearing only distant gunfire, he pushed the metal grille above him slowly. The metal cover moved slightly, a creaking sound coming from the worn hinges and slight cracking as the ice around the grille broke. Pushing harder, the grille moved upwards in the recess in the road. Tatu stepped up another rung and pushed the grille open, the cold air hitting his face as the metal obstruction swung upwards, a slight squeal from the rusted hinges as it did so.

Breathing in the fresh air for a second, Tatu climbed another step and cautiously raised his helmet out of the opening.

The opening was at the side of a wide road through the factory district, the damaged buildings on either side some of the numerous warehouses and machine shops for this area. Their roofs were mostly damaged or destroyed, the smoke still rising from some of the smouldering building shells. Turning slowly in the manhole shaft, Tatu could see the road was quite short with a turning at either end, deserted in the cold morning light. Heavy snow clouds moved overhead, the coldness of the dark night slowly giving way to the dim light of a new day.

Hearing footsteps on the rungs of the ladder below, Tatu cautiously clambered out of the shaft, the cold morning air gripping him as he rose to his feet on the side of the street. Turning and bending down, he grasped Udet's hand, assisting him from the shaft, then indicated for him to move to the side of the street, unsure of where they were.

As the soldiers slowly emerged into the light, many blinking to accustom their eyes to the new day, the Romanian quartermaster moved them to the side of the thoroughfare, indicating for them to stay low. Tatu then turned to Udet, 'Have a quick look round would you, I need to know where we are.'

Udet nodded, taking his rifle from his shoulder and walking slowly along the wall of the building they were stood alongside, the iced snow crunching beneath his boots. A shell burst in the distance, the soldiers ducking their heads instinctively. The distant sounds of machine gun fire and rifle cracks spread across the streets as fighting on the front line flared up in the housing districts to the south.

Udet exhaled heavily in relief as he leant against the side of the destroyed factory, the smell of burnt material in his nostrils. Looking back, Udet saw the last of the soldiers emerge from the shaft, Tatu lowering the metal grille back into place. Seeing several of the men looking cautiously at him, Udet glanced briefly into the next street.

Grinning as his caution subsided, he turned back, waving to Tatu to bring the soldiers towards him. Then he stepped round the corner and walked towards the German armoured personnel carrier and Kubelwagen jeep parked by the side of the road.

Chapter Twenty: Attrition

Major Slusser turned to face Hausser, a grim expression on his face, 'It seems you have had quite a night.' He looked the young commander up and down, the stench from the man's dirty uniform wafting across the table. He stared at the young officer's tired eyes, his scratched face unshaven and dirty.

Hausser nodded, removing his helmet slowly, 'Yes, the Russians are certainly becoming more aggressive now we are on the defensive.' Feeling dizzy from the exhaustion, he ruffled his matted hair, looking down at his filthy uniform.

The major looked down at the maps on the table before them, pointing to one of the streets on the paper, 'I have placed men at the exit you used. We were unaware of it until now.' He leant forward and retrieved his glass, a distant explosion breaking the silence, 'What is your unit strength now?'

Hausser sighed, placing his helmet on the table top next to the map, he looked up at the major, 'Sixteen men in total. Fourteen killed, seven wounded and the rest missing, presumed dead in the sewers or blown apart in the attack last night.'

The major studied him for a second, 'You look exhausted, I will move you and your men back for the rest of the day.' He indicated to the seat next to the table, 'Have a seat, Leutnant, before you pass out.'

Hausser slowly lowered himself into the chair, looking up at the major, dark lines beneath his eyes, 'We lost a lot of men last night, please tell me we gained something from it.'

The major turned, looking to the wall of the warehouse office for a second, then he spoke thoughtfully, 'Well, we did not accomplish our ultimate goal, but four tunnels were destroyed. That should be enough to force the Russians into a more limited number of routes if they want to attack. Not nearly as good as I wanted, but we should be able to hold them for the time being, so it wasn't a complete failure.' He turned back, staring grimly at Hausser, watching the Leutnant's head nod, then the younger man moving his position slowly, trying to keep his exhausted body awake. Major Slusser raised his voice, watching Hausser jump slightly, the younger man adopting a deliberate stare at the Major as he spoke, 'General Hoth's tanks of the relief effort crossed the frozen Alksay River this morning, they are now less than forty miles away from the south west of Stalingrad. They will be here in three or four days. Maybe sooner.'

Hausser leant tiredly forward, placing his head in his hands, closing his eyes briefly, his voice distant, 'What difference will that make to the men we lost?'

The major turned sharply, raising his voice in frustration, 'It will mean they did not die in vain. The Russians were prevented from moving behind us in the sewers. Our engineers have demolished some of the tunnels they would have used this morning, I have placed men on the others. We also control the reservoir that caused the flooding, so can do it again if needed, that should stop them, or at least deter them in future.' He stood back defiantly, raising the glass to his lips as he glared at the officer seated opposite him.

Hausser lowered his hands, looking up slowly at the major, his eyes bloodshot, 'Very well, what are my orders?'

The major leant forward again, placing his hands on the table, his right hand leaning on the glass. 'Get some sleep and rest your men, I need you to move up and hold an office block on the southern edge of the factory district, it used to be the local communist party headquarters. That will free up some men to move back to the Tractor Factory.' The major raised his glass again, draining the contents, 'There are no reserves left for me to use at present, but your building is fortified and very robust. I don't expect you will have much trouble.'

Hausser nodded wearily, 'When do you want us to take up position?'

Major Slusser smiled briefly, then looked back down at the map, 'By first light tomorrow.' He reached across for the bottle on the corner of the table, splashing the clear liquid into his glass.

Hausser rose to his feet slowly, saluting wearily, 'Yes Sir, we will be there by first light.'

The major nodded, swigging from his glass, 'Good, I will get my adjutant to locate and bring some drink across for you and your men.' He frowned, 'It's not much, but should ensure you get a restful sleep.' He paused, seeming to think, then looked directly at Hausser, his eyes sparkling, 'Thank you for your efforts Leutnant. I know it has been hard for you and your men, but it has made a difference.'

Hausser's eyes widened slightly, his voice seeming unsure, 'Thank you sir. I will tell the men.'

Major Slusser looked back down at the map on the table, rubbing the back of his neck with his hand nervously. As he heard Hausser close the door behind him, he swigged greedily from his glass again, lowering himself into his chair. Looking around the bare walls of the small office, he sighed loudly, his mind conflicted. Moving the map of the factory district aside on his desk, he stared at the small map beneath it. The red line he had drawn earlier indicating where he considered General Hoth's tanks to be.

He slowly leant back in his chair, his face flushed, swigging from his glass again. Looking at the dirty ceiling in the small room, he spoke softly to himself as he lit a cigarette, 'It seems your tanks may be our best hope now Herr General, in four or five days there may be little food left in this damned city.'

Hausser stumbled across the yard, slipping on the frozen snow. Following the route he had taken some days earlier, he slowly made his way back to the damaged warehouse he and his men were resting in. Behind him, the major's adjutant watched him uneasily. The man carrying a box containing five bottles of vodka, the robust glass containers 'clinking' each time he took a step.

As Hausser trudged through the mid-morning light, his breath condensed before him, he thought of what had happened in the sewer. The confusion that had led to the loss of his men, the Russian civilians cowering in fear from them and then their own countrymen. His mind confused due to the exhaustion, he had smiled when he thought of the bravery of his men, their loyalty in defending the reservoir and fighting against superior numbers. The young Romanian, Nicu, and his efforts in the darkness, helping in comforting the Russian civilians and drying out the soldiers uniforms. The nineteen year old soldier's innocence and youthful loyalty contributing significantly to their survival.

Hausser bit his lip, tasting blood as he thought of the conversation Tatu and he had completed after leaving the sewer. They had been stood next to the Hanomag armoured car discussing the next possible moves of the remaining unit and awaiting Meino to re-join them. Having sent men back into the darkness to round up the stragglers and soldiers they had positioned in defence, the remaining group of soldiers waited, most smoking in their exhaustion. In the distance, a couple of muffled underground explosions had indicated limited success in collapsing a number of the tunnels, but both Hausser and Tatu knew it was not nearly enough to stop the Red Army, their efforts having ultimately failed.

Seeing Petru begin to look for Nicu amongst the surviving soldiers, they had initially smiled warmly between them considering his fatherly attitude towards the youth. The protective instinct that Petru always showed to the young soldier, particularly after the initial assault three weeks previously. Then their eyes had become concerned, realising the Petru could not find the youth, his actions becoming more desperate as he ran between the remaining soldiers. Looking at each other thoughtfully, they both then realised simultaneously what had happened, their eyes widening in shock.

Tatu had lunged towards Petru, pulling him towards them as they began to see him becoming even more desperate to find the young man. Realising Nicu was not with the surviving troops, both Hausser and Tatu had concluded what had happened in the final seconds of the escape from the reservoir. That the young Romanian had been one of the soldiers that fell from the metal rungs into the freezing water, his body slowly sinking into the darkness beneath the surface, his back perforated by machine gun fire as they themselves escaped.

Tatu had held the shaking Petru in a tight hug at the front of the Hanomag as he broke the news to the loving Romanian, the man shaking as the tears fell from his eyes. Hausser had spoken softly to Petru as he described what had happened, the determination and bravery of the young Romanian to help defend their escape. Nicu's insistence another soldier went in front of him on the ladder, the soldier surviving and the young Romanian being killed, the outcome of a simple ladder placing, the young soldier giving the ultimate sacrifice.

Petru had cried uncontrollably at first, advising he looked upon the young soldier as a member of his extended family. That his survival of the initial assault by the Russians had been a sign to him that the youngster should be protected. Tatu had held his countryman to his chest for some time as his friend sobbed, his shoulders shaking with grief for some considerable time. Hausser had eventually given up trying to console Petru and had taken the rest of the troops to report to Major Slusser leaving the two Romanians to their grief and to organise any returning soldiers.

His concern at embarrassing the fatherly Romanian in front of the troops becoming paramount as he saw some of the Hungarians beginning to whisper concerns to each other. Tatu and Petru had followed some time later with the remaining soldiers from the sewers, the grief stricken Romanian isolating himself from the others as he found a place to sit alone in the warehouse, away from the other men.

A shell burst in the distance as Hausser crossed the yard towards the damaged warehouse, the distant sounds of gunfire beginning to become louder as he reached the entrance. The small side door opened with a creak as Hausser pulled the handle, the cold air biting at his body. Stepping aside, he held the door for the major's adjutant, the man nodding his thanks as he stepped through the opening.

As the door closed behind them, Hausser saw the surviving soldiers sat around the wide expanse of the storage area, despondency on their faces. He realised a couple of the men were new additions to the group, their uniforms dirty and torn. Some of the troops were lying asleep, their heads on their helmets on the floor, some having dragged any material from the storage racks to form makeshift beds. In the centre, smoke slowly rose from a small fire burning in an open top oil drum, 'Hase', Alessio and Udet raising hands in greetings from warming themselves around it, their faces grim.

Looking right, Hausser saw Tatu talking to Meino in the small side office, the men sitting on the damaged chairs inside. As he walked over to them, Tatu raised his hand in greeting, the broken glass crunching beneath Hausser's boots. Standing in the doorway, he leant against the frame, the tiredness in his eyes causing him to rub them with his hands, 'We have some Russian vodka for the men.'

Meino smiled weakly, 'Good, something to dull their senses.'

Tatu shook his head, his face stern, 'We will need more than that! This unit is shattered Hausser, what are we to do now?'

Hausser rubbed his torn gloves across the stubble on his face, 'We move up to the line in the early hours.'

Tatu slammed his fist on the table, 'This is madness! We have only eighteen men with the two extra stragglers the Major has provided! What possible difference will we make?' He stood up abruptly, glaring angrily at the commander.

Hausser slowly reached up and removed his helmet, dropping it to the floor, 'This time we go to a block at the outskirts of the factory district. Apparently it is very sturdy and easily defended.'

Tatu blinked hard at him, his voice rising in anger, 'What about food? The rations are now ridiculous, about one thousand calories a day as far as I can work out, what the hell is going on? We will starve to death here soon! Are the German troops getting more?'

Hausser's frustration rose dramatically at the outburst as he glanced round, seeing the seated men behind him in the warehouse beginning to look across. His anger seeming to concentrate as he stood there, staring at the

Romanian quartermaster. He shouted back at the Romanian, 'Shut up! I am in command here and we will follow orders! I want no more defeatism from you, understand?' He continued, his fists clenching, 'The rations are the same across the city. The orders are to move up, so we will...with or without you, do you understand what I mean?'

Tatu's eyes widened in horror, realising his outburst had undermined Hausser's rank in front of the soldiers. Meino jumped up, his MP40 clattering to the floor of the office, his arms outstretched between the men, 'I am sure Tatu was mistaken and did not mean what he said, Herr Leutnant!'

Hausser stared determinedly at Tatu, his eyes narrowed, unshaven face flushed red with anger, 'Well?'

Tatu's eyes dropped, sorrow spreading across his features, 'I am sorry, Herr Leutnant.' His voice fell to a whisper, seeming thoughtful, 'You have only done good things for us, getting us back from the south, but to this? It was not your fault. Nicu and the other men being killed, well that was not you either.' A brief smile spread across his face before fading, 'At least we will be indoors.....well if the building has a roof, which I notice is becoming rare in this city, a new fashion perhaps?' He looked back up at Hausser, a twinkle in his eye.

Hausser stared at him incredulously, then a grin swept across his features, 'Fool!'

Meino smiled in relief, 'Good, let's get a drink.' He slapped Tatu's shoulder, 'We also need to look after Petru, he is in a bad way.'

Tatu nodded, looking at Hausser, 'Yes Herr Leutnant, we need to keep someone with him now, he is really depressed.' He indicated to Meino to leave the office with a jerk of his head. The Croatian stepping past the commander into the warehouse in response.

Tatu sat back down wearily as Meino returned with a bottle of Vodka, depositing on the table and turning to leave, the Croatian nodding to Hausser, 'I will go and sit with Petru for a while.'

Tatu grasped the bottle, 'Come sit with me, my friend, let's have a drink.'

Hausser glanced at the soldiers outside the office, their concentration now on the vodka bottles being passed around, sighing, 'Oh.....very well.' He slumped into the wooden chair vacated by Meino, the seat creaking with his weight. Tatu clenched the cork of the bottle between his teeth, spitting it onto the floor of the office and taking a swig from the fiery liquid, wincing as it entered his throat. Throwing a packet of American cigarettes on the table, he indicated for Hausser to help himself to one, handing him the bottle.

The major's adjutant approached the doorway, leaning on the frame, 'I have arranged for some spare greatcoats to be delivered to you later today. It's all we have.'

Tatu nodded at the smaller man, his uniform immaculate, 'Please take our thanks back to the Major, that will be of immense assistance.' Hausser turned his head, smiling grimly at the officer and nodding.

The adjutant nodded in return, 'Enjoy the vodka gentlemen! I will see if there is any more for later, but supplies are now very short.' He turned on his heels and walked briskly from the warehouse, the door creaking behind him as he exited.

The Romanian quartermaster leant back in the chair, his uniform stained from the night in the sewer, his boots scratched and worn. Pushing his head back, he lit a cigarette and blew the smoke into the air, 'So where is the relief effort, did the red faced major tell you?'

Hausser gave a brief smile, 'Yes.' He swigged from the bottle, straining his eyes as the liquid hit his throat. Glancing out of the broken office window he saw Meino lower himself next to Petru further down the warehouse, away from the other soldiers, the Croatian offering the lonely Romanian a drink.

Tatu leant forward, staring curiously at Hausser, 'So? Where are they?'

Hausser grinned at the man's urgency to know, raising a cigarette to his lips, 'They have crossed the Alksay River, forty miles south west of Stalingrad.'

Tatu smiled, his eyes brightening, 'Good, they are well on their way. Let's hope they are bringing food, and by food, I mean not shitty horse meat!' He grinned widely, 'I have had enough of that now!' He clutched the bottle Hausser held towards him, raising it in a toast, 'To your Herr General Hoth's success! The success of German Panzers driving to the Volga!'

Chapter Twenty One: New Defensive positions

Moving along the side of the street cautiously, Hausser grasped his MP40 before him, his stance slightly crouched. Behind him, seventeen soldiers moved silently through the night, their boots placed carefully on the iced snow to prevent noise. Hugging the walls, they felt the cold breeze envelope them, the air sweeping in from across the Volga river five hundred metres to their left.

Moving south along the streets, they could hear the cracks of rifle shots across to their left, the front line some three to four hundred metres away. The streets were deserted, the piercing cold from the clear dark sky keeping most sentries and soldiers in their dugouts or makeshift positions. The night breeze gripped their greatcoats and exposed flesh, seeming to bite at their skin. The cold air began to gradually form on their coats as condensation, the molecules of water freezing in the low temperature, their overcoats beginning to be covered in a thin white layer of frost.

Their exhaled breath hung in the air, the temperature now well below freezing, their scarves and gloves providing limited comfort against the bitter breeze. The frozen city around them seemed to exude death, the occasional exposed corpse discoloured in the moonlight, each body prevented from decaying in the bitter temperature, the skin gradually greying over the days it was left unattended.

Hausser stopped at a junction, squinting into the distance, a thin mist seeming to hang in the street as the frost grasped it. The illusion of the cloud simply the moon reflecting on the crystalized tarmac, the breeze carrying frozen moisture across the thoroughfare. Unable to make out the end of the street, he hesitated, blinking and wiping the gathering frost from his eyebrows. Seeing a number of soldiers had moved to the right side of the street, he lunged forward. Darting across the side street that was exposed, the lane leading towards the river. The extreme cold seemed to embrace him as he stepped forward beyond the shelter of the building wall, almost taking his breath away.

Reaching the safety of the wall opposite, he turned, looking at the waiting soldiers. Most were crouched, glancing around cautiously. The scarves and other material across their mouths with their almost white ice covered greatcoats creating an almost surreal picture of an advancing unit. He smiled briefly beneath his scarf, thinking of his previous experiences and visions of advancing troops in urban areas, the current spectacle completely remote from what he had seen previously.

Ducking out to look along the street he had just passed, he saw it was empty. Raising his gloved hand, he indicated for the lead soldiers to cross, the men responding by running low across the tarmac, the space between each man approximately 5 metres. Each individual holding his breath as he completed the short exposed distance, the fear of a hostile rifle shot or the burst of machine gun fire running through their minds.

As the troops all completed the exposed run, Hausser retrieved the roughly drawn map from inside his greatcoat, staring down at the paper in the gloom, his eyes gradually becoming accustomed to reading the paper in the moonlight. Looking around briefly, he recognised the area they were in from the adjutant's description, the southern lower parts of the factory district.

Glancing back down at the makeshift map, he turned as the soldier next to him tried to look across the paper, his face rising next to him to look over his shoulder. Udet blinked several times as Hausser looked at him, the temperature misting his vision. The young commander looked back around, then thrust the map into Udet's chest, the young German grasping it with his spare gloved hand. 'Keep close, we are nearly there,' Hausser hissed.

Hausser lunged forwards again, his boots scraping across the iced road surface. His body crouched, he passed the waiting soldiers, Udet behind him. Seeing 'Hase' at the next junction ducking out to look into the street to the river, he stopped beside him. 'Hase' half turned, urging him forward, 'Go, it's clear.'

Hausser sprinted low across the small side street reaching the safety of the next wall and turning, beckoning the men across. On the other side of the main street, Tatu and Petru moved forward, hugging the walls, Alessio behind them, his sniper rifle pointing across and down the side street, their makeshift squad following.

Reaching the next junction, Hausser paused to catch his breath, crouched next to the corner. Two bodies lay in the street before him, the soldiers having been killed by sniper fire from the left side street leading towards the river. Ducking out quickly to look down the street, he saw the street was deserted, a burning building in the distance, the reflection from the flames dancing off the crystalized iced on the road's surface.

Judging by the casualties before him, he realised the front line was now close, just over one hundred metres away, the streets angle having gradually moved them towards the Russians. Several rifle cracks rang out, the sound clear and sharp in the frozen streets, then a muffled explosion. Breathing heavily, Hausser looked up, the tension beginning to spread across his body. The dark sky was beautifully clear, the vision of the stars sharp in the frozen air.

Clearing his mind and looking across the street they were in, he saw with some relief that Tatu and the others had stopped just short of the junction. Glancing round, he recognised the small alleyway opposite from the adjutants description, the path between two burnt out buildings apparently leading to a small square with an ornate fountain. The square set before the building they had been assigned to.

Glancing back across at Tatu, he indicated for them to run across all at once, the fear of a lone sniper looking out down the street from the river rising within him. Tatu raised his hand in agreement, understanding the young commander's wishes. Turning, the Romanian quartermaster indicated for his men to move around him, whispering their intent.

Hausser also turned, calling forward the soldiers behind with a hiss, the troops edging around him. Whispering, he looked into the nervous eyes of the small group of soldiers around him, 'We run together, this side street is exposed to fire from the front line. When I give the signal, all move forward, understand?' The soldiers nodded apprehensively, fear in their eyes.

Looking back across the street at Tatu, he waited for the Romanian to finish briefing the soldiers around him, then saw him indicate he was ready.

The commander raised his gloved hand, the tension mounting in the soldiers as they waited for him to indicate for them to run across the exposed street. As his arm dropped, the troops lunged forward, their boots propelling them across the frozen street.

Hausser ran into the dark alleyway, Tatu behind him, as he stopped by the side the other men joined him. The distant rifle crack was too late to claim a casualty, the bullet whistling past behind them, the Russian sniper having too little time to react. The bullet ricocheted off the building wall at the end of the street, the sound of the distant shot seeming to hang in the freezing air.

The young commander checked the street behind them, ensuring all the soldiers had crossed, then turned sharply, advancing down the alley. The troops followed him slowly, all considering their close encounter with the Russian sniper.

As Hausser reached the end of the alley, he could see the small fountain in the moonlight, the statue damaged from shell fragments. To his left, around the small circular fountain base sat the steps and entrance to the local party headquarters, the solid wooden doors closed and locked. To either side of the entrance, two pillars bordered the three steps rising to the double doors, the front of the building pock-marked from the impact of numerous bullets.

Seeing a light flickering from within, Hausser indicated for the soldiers to wait in the alleyway behind him whilst he approached the entrance. Glancing out, he saw here was a small side window, the light coming from the opening, the silhouette inside the building smoking. He hissed in the darkness, 'Achtung! Freund!'

Movement inside the building as the soldier guarding the entrance raised his rifle, then the response, a determined challenge, 'Kommen sie aus!'

Stepping from the alleyway, he walked cautiously forward. Seeing the sentry acknowledge him, he proceeded half crouched towards the steps. Raising his right boot to ascend the three steps as the door opened slightly, a shaft of candlelight spilling from inside.

The muzzle of a rifle was slowly pushed out of the opening, pointing directly at him, the expression on the frightened soldier's face within clearly very cautious.

Hausser stopped on the second step, declaring himself, 'Leutnant Hausser, 76th Infantry Division. We have come to relieve you.'

The soldier behind the door hesitated briefly, then lowered the rifle, 'My apologies, Herr Leutnant, please come inside.' The door opened, the flickering light cascading from the doorway as the gap became wider.

Hausser stepped forward, indicating for his men to follow him, the young commander slipping through the narrow opening. Straining his eyes to adjust to the light, he dusted the shoulders of his greatcoat, the frozen moisture falling from his heavy jacket.

The soldier before him saluted, lowering his weapon further. Hausser glanced to the left, seeing the young soldier that had been at the small window click his heels formally, his salute stiff and mechanical. The young commander smiled weakly, saluting back, 'How many men have you here?'

'Twenty three,' the soldier replied with a regimented tone. 'Thank you for coming, Sir. We could do with a rest.'

Hausser's eyes widened, 'What's it like here?'

The German infantryman stepped towards him nervously, 'The Russians are in the buildings between us and the river Sir. Their positions are well defended with snipers and machine guns, but they seem to have little appetite to attack at present. We inflicted some heavy casualties on them the night before last, killing several of their officers.'

Hausser nodded slowly, 'I see.' He moved to the side as Tatu pushed the door open wider, stepping inside and shaking his jacket, the frost dropping onto the marble floor in the entrance hall. Several soldiers stepped in behind him, the troops keen to get out of the bitter cold. The entrance hall had been finely furnished and equipped before the arrival of the current occupants, an impressive central staircase leading to the administrative offices on the first floor, the stairs splitting to either side from a middle landing. The ground floor offices of the NKVD accessed from hallways on either side of the building.

Seeing the German soldiers' expressions of surprise as they recognised some Romanian uniform, Hausser walked across to the reception desk, the nails on his boots clicking across the marble tiles. As the soldiers slipped through the doorway behind him, he leant against the sturdy desk, 'We have a number of different soldiers with us. This unit represents the harmony that can be achieved between Germany and her allies. Now where is your commander please?' He turned, the candlelight behind him, his eyebrows raised at the nearest sentry.

The soldier swallowed, nodding, 'Er, yes Sir, I will get him for you.' The young man quickly moved to the central staircase, climbing the steps two at a time.

Hausser turned to look at Tatu, seeing the exasperated expression on his face at what he had just said, he grinned, winking. Tatu shook his head, 'I have heard everything now!' He grinned back, cuffing the back of Udet's helmet as the young German walked past him, his head moving around in awe as he studied the entrance hall with some surprise.

Hausser indicated with his hand to Tatu, 'Let's keep the men in two squads, you lead one, myself the other. Petru and Alessio with you, Udet and 'Hase' with me?'

Tatu nodded, 'That's fine, Herr Leutnant.' His response wary of the remaining German sentry stood next to him. 'Do you want me on the ground floor or the first?'

Hausser thought for a second, 'You take downstairs, I will move between the two with Udet and 'Hase'.' He glanced upwards as he heard boots on the marble stairs. Seeing an officer turn the corner from the left staircase and descend to the middle landing, he raised his hand in salute.

The Captain saluted as he descended the marble steps, his uniform covered in dust, but virtually immaculate by comparison to the dirty and stained combat clothing of the arrivals stood in the entrance hall. He was of similar height to Hausser, his frame thin, with a flushed jovial expression. His face accommodated a large scar of the left cheek, his hair black with greying sides beneath his helmet.

As his boots clicked onto the marble tiles on the ground floor, the captain's eyes widened, taking in the spectacle of the soldiers before him, 'My God, where have you men been?'

Hausser stepped forward, extending his hand, 'Leutnant Hausser, Sir. My men and I have been in the front line for days, then the sewers.'

The captain grinned, his nose twitching, his grey eyes wide, 'The sewers were not far from my mind, Leutnant. Your presence precedes you in that sense.' His grin widened, shaking Hausser's hand, 'Let's place your men around the building, then you and I can have a chat, eh, Leutnant?'

Hausser nodded, 'Yes Sir.' He indicated to Tatu with his right hand to disperse his men on the ground floor, pointing to the corridors leaving the entrance hall on both sides, then turned to face the captain again.

Tatu started barking orders to the men, indicating which side of the building each of them should proceed along. As Alessio stood before Tatu, the Romanian quartermaster smiled briefly. 'Ah, our Italian, go and find a spot you can make a nuisance of yourself from, but keep your head down!' Alessio smiled grimly in response, making his way up the stairs ahead of the men.

The captain turned stepping back towards the staircase with Hausser following, the soldiers walking briskly to either side of him towards their prospective corridors.

The captain turned his face to look at the man next to him, 'I am Hauptmann Ebner, 389th Infantry Division. The command post is upstairs. You will find there is little movement around here, the Russians concentrating their forces further north and south. We blunted their attack here the night before last quite effectively, so I imagine they will lick their wounds for a few days.' He glanced at Hausser, 'Your men can probably have as close to a rest as they can imagine under the circumstances, we have done your work for you.'

The young commander nodded, smiling, 'Thank you Sir, did you lose many men?'

The captain's grey eyes became saddened as they reached the landing, 'Yes, five. Not many I know, but I am very attached to the men under my command, so any loss is regrettable if you know what I mean?' He continued up the stairs to the left, Hausser following behind him. Further down the staircase, Udet and 'Hase' followed, six troops behind them.

Reaching the top of the marble steps, the captain indicated to a room opposite, 'This is where the field telephone is, and I have made my quarters there. You may wish to do the same. The telephone is connected to the Major's headquarters, so if you need anything, just ring. It usually takes around one hour to get here.' He hesitated, thinking for a second, then shrugged, 'Actually, he has only come here once, I always went to him to report.'

Meino slipped past them, winking at Hausser, with three soldiers following. The captain smiling as he saw the gesture, 'Interesting unit you have Leutnant Hausser.' He blinked, rubbing his right eye with his hand, his expression then becoming more serious, 'The telephone wires may be cut if they start shelling. Usually they send someone out quite quickly, the major likes to keep regular contact with the front line units, so they will notice very quickly. He is a good commander, very sympathetic to the soldiers manning the defences.'

He turned walking along the corridor towards the back of the building, stopping after a few metres, the floorboards creaking. Indicating to the blocked windows, he coughed, then spoke, 'As you can see, we have barricaded all the windows, much to the annoyance of the Russian snipers.' Pointing further down the darkening corridor, approximately fifteen metres in length, he continued, 'There are observation or firing points set into each opening and at the end there are two offices with sandbagged windows and machine guns. They cover the approaches and keep the Russians' heads down.' His face became grim, 'There are a couple of blind spots though. Diagonally approaching the corners of the building is outside the arcs of the guns, so you will have to deploy riflemen to keep watch on these routes. The Russians know this and that's how they attacked recently. You can put additional men in the buildings next door, but they are quite exposed and I don't think you have enough.'

Hausser nodded, smiling, 'Thank you Sir, your briefing is very informative.'

The captain nodded, a smirk fleetingly crossing his face, 'I will send runners to notify the units on either side that you do not have enough men to cover the adjoining buildings, which should prompt them to give you some support.' He hesitated, then spoke more softly, aware of the soldiers passing them, 'I have sent out a small patrol to check the surrounding units, so when they return, please advise them to follow us to the warehouse.'

Hausser thought for a second, then looked up, 'Yes Herr Hauptmann. Should we put out patrols?'

The captain shook his head, 'There is little need to be honest it just puts the men in danger. I only did so to ensure I gave you up to date information. The Russians are now virtually static, and you have too few men to risk losing any. Your view of the surroundings is excellent in clear weather, so why provoke casualties? There are tripwires placed in some places before the building, that should give you enough warning if the Russians get too ambitious.'

Hausser smiled, happy not to be sending men outside in the bitter cold, 'Thank you. Is there anything else I should know Sir?'

The captain grinned, his scar rising up as he did so, 'What little supplies you will receive will come every two days in the morning. They will approach from the rear and it is your responsibility to warm the rations downstairs. You are at the end of the supply line from the 389th, so the food has to come quite a distance, it is usually frozen when it gets here.' He walked back towards the Leutnant, 'Still, you won't want for ice in a drink!' He laughed briefly, reaching into his tunic and retrieving a packet of cigarettes, offering them to Hausser.

Hausser looked down at the white packet with a red circle in the middle, the American cigarettes he had seen several days earlier. Looking up, the captain saw the curiosity on the young Leutnant's face.

Captain Ebner smiled again, 'We looted the Russian supplies in the basement and there is also some nice food there. But use it sparingly, we want some when we come back. There are still some cigarettes down there too, it seems the communist hierarchy was perhaps a little more equal than the Russians around them.' His smile widened to grin.

Hausser nodded, 'Thank you Sir that is very kind.'

The captain placed his hand on Hausser's shoulder, 'Well, Leutnant, that is it.' He lowered his voice as his men began to pass him, descending the staircase on their way to assemble in the entrance hall. 'You seem to have some very organised men here, I will take my leave whilst it is still dark. I don't want the Russians seeing up depart, it might give them ideas.'

Hausser smiled briefly, 'There is a sniper aimed at the end of the alleyway, be careful there.'

The captain's eyebrows raised, 'Really? I thought we got him. Oh well, be careful, he is quite a good shot and he doesn't seem to feel the cold.'

Hausser slowly walked down the staircase with the captain, enjoying his company, 'So when do you think you will return?'

The captain started pulling on his gloves, a soldier handing him his overcoat, 'Perhaps a week, maybe longer. I will have a drink with our friend, Major Slusser and discuss it in a while. We have known each other since before the war, so I imagine he will do his best to provide some sort of homecoming for us.'

Hausser grinned, 'He has retreated onto Russian Vodka now, I think the Schnapps is all gone.'

The captain's eyes widened, then he grinned again as he pulled his large overcoat up over his shoulders, 'Perhaps he will have one last bottle saved for an old friend.' They now stood at the bottom of the staircase, the entrance hall virtually full of the captain's troops. The captain looked around, surveying his men and concluding they were all present. Turning to Hausser, he smiled faintly, 'Well, it is time to go, Leutnant. I hope you have a pleasant stay.' The captain raised his hand, saluting Hausser. The young Leutnant returning the gesture.

Turning, Hauptmann Ebner buttoned his greatcoat and took the MP40 one of his men offered him. The door opened and the soldiers filed out, the cold breeze sweeping into the entrance hall and causing the candle to flicker. As all the troops exited the building, the captain stood in the doorway, turning to look at Hausser, 'Place two men on the door at all times, this is virtually their only way in.' He raised his hand in gesture, 'Take care, see you in a week or so.'

Hausser nodded, 'Give my regards to the major please, and be careful.' He saluted as the door closed with a thud behind the captain.

Chapter Twenty Two: Paying the penalty for mistakes

Two hundred metres east of the political headquarters in the basement of a machine shop, the candles flickered. The building above virtually destroyed, the soldiers stood expectantly, the cool air drifting down the staircase at the end of the long room.

The Russian officer stepped along the line of men before him, his eyes scrutinising each man. His uniform well pressed, with red piping and shoulder straps complimenting the red band around his officer's cap. Reaching the end of the line of soldiers, he smiled briefly as he looked into the eyes of the infantryman in front of him, the right side of his face flushed. 'Private Medvedev. Your conduct is no surprise.'

The soldier stared back defiantly, his brown eyes looking straight at the political officer. The officer staring back at him, his lips raised slightly in contempt, 'The soldier that was outwitted by fleeing fascists.' He stepped forward, his face just before the soldier's, 'Losing his men's respect and virtually collaborating with the enemy. I should have you shot now........you coward.' The officer was now only inches from the soldier's face, his smile formed into a sneer.

The officer stepped back, then reached across his body to his holster, the soldiers further along the line glancing sideways, their eyes widening. The officer smiled as he unbuttoned his side holster, looking directly at the face of the soldier in front of him, the man staring back. The officer shook his head slowly, then whipped his hand across from his holster, striking the soldier across the face, the hard slap echoing across the darkened basement they were stood in.

Private Medvedev staggered backwards, his hands sweeping upwards to steady himself as he stumbled into the soldier behind, the man grasping him and preventing him falling. Straightening up, the blood dripping from his nose, he re-joined the line of soldiers, a determined look in his eye as he stared back at the officer in defiance.

The officer grinned, watching the blood drip onto the soldier's tunic, the man's eyes beginning to become moist after the impact to his nose. 'Broken, but still defiant, eh?' He leant forward, prodding the soldier hard in the chest with his fingers, 'It will not be for long, as soon you will be dead, Medvedev.' The officer stepped back, turning at an angle to face the other soldiers. Slowly he raised his hand, pointing into the soldier's face, 'This man is a disgrace to Mother Russia. He fraternised with the escaping enemy soldiers, losing his units weapons and valuable supplies to the fascists.' The officer slowly walked back along the two lines of eighteen men, looking at each soldier closely, 'You have all made mistakes that have jeopardised the safety of our beloved country that is why you find yourselves here, in this penal unit under my command. My job is to give you one last opportunity to serve your country heroically. You may die in the process, or you may survive and go back to your units as free men in the service of your country, understand?'

The soldiers barked their reply in unison, 'Yes Sir.'

The Political officer nodded, smiling at the sergeant stood by the stairs and raising his voice again, 'The fascists have barricaded themselves into our local NKVD headquarters. One of our snipers reports that the fascists have just changed the men in the headquarters, there are new soldiers there, unfamiliar with the building and their surroundings. It is our job to drive them out and hold the building for if and when the fascists counterattack. Do you understand?'

The soldiers stood, facing forward, their voices in unison again, 'Yes Sir.'

The officer placed his hands on his hips, turning to look across the men again. Indicating to the three dead bodies lying in the darkness before the line of men, the blood from the corpses slowly spreading across the dusty floor. 'This was their patrol. The fascists will be awaiting their return. Three more dead Germans in our glorious city, a city we will retake from these invaders.'

He kicked the boot of one of the bodies, 'Make sure you kill more fascists when you enter the building. Those of you that do not kill a fascist will remain in this unit. After you have taken the building, we will send more soldiers to join you. You will then join that unit as free men, do you fully understand?'

The soldiers' eyes widened, their excitement rising at the chance of escaping the penal unit, 'Yes Sir.'

The officer raised his hand to his mouth, placing a cigarette between his lips. Lifting a silver lighter to the end of the cigarette, he flicked the small wheel at the end of the lighter, the spark igniting the petrol within. He sucked on the cigarette, the small flame igniting the end, before extending the lighter in front of him, then flicking the lid shut. Looking across the silver object, he smiled briefly, 'American lighters.' He announced, 'Just like the rations you will receive in the district headquarters once you are successful.' He looked across the soldiers before him again, 'The fascists think they are in a well barricaded building. They are warm and secure, complacent in their new comforts.' He blew the blue/grey smoke across the front line of soldiers, a contemptuous smile forming on his face, 'They do not know that there is another way into the building, one that they will never find, one devised by the NKVD for just such a situation.'

Private Medvedev smiled briefly, his expression hidden in the gloom at the end of the basement. He tasted the sweetness of his blood in his mouth, the liquid flowing from his nose. Considering the Political Officers statement, he thought of the probable reason for another entrance to the NKVD's headquarters, for their own escape if the local inhabitants decided to rise up against communism.

He now despised this officer and the uniform he stood in. They had stood in line as the bewildered German soldiers had been led into the basement by the sergeant at the end of the room. The small patrol having been captured as they became disorientated in the darkness, the soldiers surrendering when they realised they were surrounded by Russian infantry, not even firing a shot in defence. He smiled ironically, not even attempting to kill any of us, trusting they would possibly be treated fairly. They had smiled nervously as they had been lead into the basement, believing they were to simply be asked to give information to the Russian officer, then perhaps taken to the rear, across the

Volga. Their hands tied, they had chatted amicably at first, their broken Russian causing grins amongst the assembled soldiers as they had tried to communicate, stating 'Hitler ist Kaput', 'That they were simply conscripted soldiers.'

They had then realised the real gruesome reason the Political Officer had brought them there as he had arrived, taunting them for a time in front of the assembled soldiers. Without warning, he had slowly cut the throat of the first captive, his hands tied behind his back. The soldier had been little more than twenty years old, the blood flowing from his body as he fought for breath and collapsed to his knees, then onto his back in the cold basement, his body twitching as he slowly died.

Medvedev had requested to speak at that time, trying to challenge the officer for his conduct. He had been slapped across the face and told to be silent, or he would join the captives. He had noticed the uneasiness in the sergeant's eyes, the fear or unwillingness to challenge the officer apparent. Four of the assembled soldiers had been physically sick.

The Political Officer had then walked up and down the line as the other two captives begged for mercy, taunting them and explaining to the assembled audience that this was how German soldiers should die, 'on their knees begging.' That his reasoning for killing the prisoners was to show *his* Russian soldiers that Germans could be killed and to show them how, that they had lacked the will to do this in the past and that that was why they were here, in this unit.

He had then wiped his knife on the tunic of the second captive before stabbing him in the stomach, holding the knife and twisting it as the German, a man of thirty plus years had cried for his wife and child, that he loved them. The officer had then kicked the man to the ground, stating how he had to die knowing the Russians were superior. Placing his boot on the back of the man's head and applying pressure with his foot as the German sobbed, his blood seeping onto the basement floor.

The third captive, a corporal, had pleaded with the Political Officer, asking that he be killed quickly if that was to happen. His pleas of 'Bitte, Bitte' resulting in the officer sneering at him as he kicked him to the floor. The officer kneeling on the man's back as he repeatedly stabbed him, the man finally pleading to be killed. The Political Officer had then gone outside for a cigarette as the mortally wounded men died, their moans chilling the Russian soldiers ordered to remain in their two lines watching the lives slip away. Three more soldiers had retched at that point, the colour draining from some of the others faces, their eyes dropped in shame.

Forcing the thoughts from his mind, he recalled the reason for him standing there in the basement, the arrival of the NKVD officers to the fishing lodge some three weeks earlier, how they had stripped him of his rank. The humiliation of him in front of his men and the penal unit they had gone to supply. How the political officers had ripped his epaulettes from his tunic, reducing him from captain to infantryman in seconds. He bit his lip as he thought of the years he had worked to rise to the rank of captain, gone in an instant. His bitterness complete and epitomised in his hatred for the political officer at the end of the room. A man who had probably never experienced a combat command, or faced the enemy in a battle. Now he knew his years of loyalty had been futile, all the hard work irrelevant.

He smiled again briefly to himself, thinking of the Germans and Romanians that had tricked him when he arrived at the Fishing Lodge. Their treatment of him and the men with him almost fair after what they had probably experienced at the hands of the Russian Army. How he had focussed on the Russian they had had amongst them, his countryman dressed in a German uniform. How he himself had wondered for days why the man would betray his country. He smiled again to himself in irony, perhaps he now knew, perhaps the Russian dressed in a German uniform had experienced something as chillingly similar to himself. He shook himself from his thoughts, realising the Political Officer had begun speaking again and pacing the line of soldiers slowly, the man probably looking for an opportunity to punish him further.

The Political Officer was almost half way along the line again, inspecting the soldiers before him once more. He cleared his throat, spitting on the dusty floor of the basement, '……..So you will understand that sacrifices have to be made for final victory against the fascists. For any man failing to take the objective, only death will await. If you retreat, I will have you shot. If you fail to take the NKVD headquarters, I will have you shot. Do you understand me?'

The soldiers in line stiffened, their voices in unison once more, 'Yes Sir.'

The Political Officer neared the end of the line, his lips curling up in contempt as he approached private Medvedev, 'Comrade Stalin is relying on you to complete this duty for Mother Russia and for that you should be truly grateful. To die for this country is the ultimate honour, to kill fascists is now our duty to Mother Russia. We take no prisoners, and kill all the defenders that do not run in fear.' He stopped once again in front of private Medvedev, indicating to him, 'If this man survives and you have not taken the building, you have my permission to shoot him. I will ensure no charges are brought. Do you understand?'

The soldiers stood facing forward, their voices becoming hoarse, 'Yes Sir.'

The Officer nodded, smiling. He leant forward, whispering to Medvedev, his lips pursed in contempt, 'You see you traitorous scum, even your own country wishes you dead. You are nothing, your history is nothing, and your family will soon disown you. Nobody challenges me, you are nothing but a miserable coward.'

Medvedev clenched his fists beneath his uniformed sleeves, the motion going unnoticed by the officer as he stepped back, smiling into Medvedev's face and blowing smoke across his features. The anger rose within Medvedev, his urge to hit the political officer repeatedly rising. His eyes betrayed him as they narrowed whilst he stared at the officer, the man's eyebrows raising as he glimpsed the reaction of anger.

The officer stepped back further, forcing a smile, fear evident in his eyes, his hand slowly moving to his holster, 'So you still have some fight in your heart, Medvedev. A heart that will not beat much longer I hope.' He turned, walking briskly along the line and indicating to the sergeant, 'There is one hour of darkness left, issue the men with weapons and start the attack. Push eight or ten men through the tunnel and use the rest as a diversion. Once they are inside, we will attack in force.' He turned briefly, looking down the line of troops, then placed a boot on the first step, reaching for another cigarette as he climbed the wooden stairs, adjusting the overcoat around his shoulders.

The officer emerged into the cold night, pulling his overcoat around him. Lighting a cigarette by flicking his lighter again, he blew smoke across the small remaining roofless room of the machine shop, hearing the sergeant below, 'You heard the officer, step forward to collect your rifle. You ten will come with me to the tunnel entrance, the rest wait here for my return. We attack immediately.'

Some one hundred and fifty metres to the northwest, behind the German front line, an Austrian soldier looked through binoculars across the torn landscape. He had crawled carefully into the small remaining space left of the roof of a machine tool workshop, the rest of the building almost completely destroyed. Lying back from the edge of the nearly open rooftop, the binoculars slowly moved across the dark landscape. The obstructions before him of broken boxes and roof tiles restricting view, but also providing considerable cover from any Russians scanning the area. The soldier lay in complete darkness, nearly completely covered by tarpaulin and debris, slowly and deliberately moved across him as he crawled into the position.

As he scanned the devastated area, seeing the flickering lights through cracked and torn walls and windows, he mentally marked potential areas for target, preparing for when the morning light spread across the area. He knew this was the time most soldiers were least alert, their need to relieve themselves or prepare a warm drink creating vulnerability due to distraction.

He smiled grimly beneath his thick scarf as he recalled Major Slusser's personal briefing, instructing him to move freely up and down the front line. As he had wrapped material around his sighted Kar 98 sniper rifle to reduce muzzle flash and the sounds from the weapon, the major had sat next to him sipping from a glass of wine, 'Get out there and terrify the Russians. Make them fear fresh air itself. Your secondary objective is to take out any Russian sniper that exists in the factory area, especially the one in the south, he has inflicted too many casualties and is undermining morale.'

The twenty nine year old Austrian had nodded knowingly as the major had talked, his excitement rising at the thought of stalking an accomplished enemy, studying his tactics and reactions before ending his life. The challenge sending adrenalin shooting up and down his spine as he had considered how to draw his enemy out. As he had successfully targeted enemies in the north, he had studied the scrawled map of the southern front line for three days, marking known casualties and suspected positions of the sniper. He had resisted the initial demands of the major to move into the area immediately, explaining he wanted to study his adversary first before killing the Russian. On the previous evening, he had finally reported to the major that he now understood the Russian's tactics and would venture to the south in the early hours to begin the one to one battle. His prediction that the Russian would be dead by the following evening exciting the major considerably.

In the early hours, he had silently followed the group of German and Romanian soldiers as they moved cautiously south, creeping to this predetermined position in the bitter cold unnoticed. Mentally noting the Russian sniper shot as the soldiers in front of him had successfully crossed a street. After a painfully slow movement into position, careful not to dislodge or move any items to provide evidence to an opposing sniper, he was finally settled in his position, scanning the terrain with his binoculars.

He froze, noticing a slight and very faint flicker of light as he slowly moved the glasses, the possible indication of an enemy's position distracting him. Adjusting the binoculars slightly, he moved the glasses back to where he had seem a slight disturbance in the freezing air. Then he saw some distortion in the air again, the exhaled cigarette smoke rising from a roofless position. Slowly and deliberately, he placed the binoculars on the tiles next to him, silently collecting and raising his rifle. He smiled and he slowly pushed the muzzle of his rifle cautiously and quietly through the tarpaulin in front of him, lowering his head to allow his right eye to look through the magnified sight, holding his breath in his nostrils.

Chapter Twenty Three: The NKVD District Headquarters

Hausser had walked along the left corridor on the ground floor, checking the soldiers were in their positions and familiarising himself with the building layout. Seeing that most of the windows were well barricaded on the left side, he cautiously entered the front ground floor office nearest the river. The room was full of filing cabinets, most lining the walls, with a central rectangular set in the centre. Tatu stood with Petru in the wide room, covering the width of the building, chatting to the two Romanian soldiers he had positioned in the room. Turning, the Romanian quartermaster nodded to Hausser, a smile forming on his face, 'This is a good defensive position Herr Leutnant, the walls are thick and the windows well protected.'

Hausser grinned, 'Good, let's hope the Russkies think the same and don't bother attacking.' He beckoned to Tatu and Petru to join him in the corridor outside.

Tatu held up his hand, walking to the many filing cabinets in the room, 'Take a look at this first please, Herr Leutnant.' He pulled open one of the drawers, showing the many files inside. 'These are files of civilians of interest in this area, it seems the NKVD were keen to monitor the population in the area.'

Hausser looked round the room, the wide area lit only by three candles sitting on top of the many filing cabinets, the drawers itemised in alphabetical order. He sighed, 'It seems the Russians also watch over their population then, not all are as equal as others in the communist state it seems.'

Tatu nodded, his face grim, 'This is the worst one.' He stepped to the centre block of cabinets, pulling open a drawer in a set marked 'Special Interest'. It seems they executed most of this cabinet as we arrived, most of them here in this building I guess. Bastards!'

Hausser pursed his lips, realising the building had thick walls for more than one reason. He pushed his machine gun round onto his back, the strap slipping from his shoulder. Readjusting it, he lifted one of the files from the cabinet carefully, opening the card cover and inspecting the contents. A picture stared up at him from the front page, the man's face badly bruised and cut. Dropping it back into the cabinet with disgust, he turned to Petru, 'How are you holding up my friend?'

Petru looked at the floor, his face solemn, 'I will be alright, Herr Leutnant. Nicu's death was a shock, but we must carry on. It's best to concentrate on survival now, perhaps we can think about the fallen once we are out of this city.' He eyes drifted upwards, looking directly at the young commander.

Hausser placed a comforting hand on the soldier's shoulder, 'Good, let's do that. He was a brave young man, self-sacrificing for the benefit of the unit. One day we will have a proper funeral for him, but he will not be forgotten.'

Petru smiled grimly, 'Thank you Herr Leutnant that means a lot to me.' He averted his eyes, looking towards the flickering candle behind the young commander.

Hausser patted his shoulder, then indicated for the two men to follow him into the hallway. Stepping out of the room, he turned to face them, 'There is apparently a basement in this building with some additional supplies.' He smiled briefly as he saw the two Romanians' eyes widen, smiles forming on their faces. 'I don't imagine there will be much, but go and check these supplies and see if you can muster up a good meal for the men for tomorrow, that should cheer them up.'

Petru smiled broadly, 'I think it must be my turn to cook.' He indicated to Tatu, 'He puts too much spice in everything...ruins it for everyone!' He grinned, seeing Tatu's face fall.

Hausser winked at Tatu, 'Bet you didn't know that until now.'

Tatu shrugged, looking at Petru with mock disdain, 'Why did you not tell me before?'

Petru grinned, 'I have a feeling this may be our last chance of a good meal for some time, I don't want you ruining it with too much spice.' He stepped past Hausser, 'I will go and find these supplies, and plan the meal.' Turning to look at Tatu, 'You can come one you finish sulking.' He walked off grinning, heading for the corridor on the other side of the building.

Tatu looked at Hausser, 'He is becoming very outspoken. Not sure I like the new Petru as much.'

Hausser grinned, running his hand across the stubble on his chin, a half beard now adorning his face, 'He is still your friend, don't be so sensitive.......he is only joking with you.' He leant forward, lowering his voice, 'Find where their interrogation room is in the building, I presume they must have had a couple of prison cells as well. They are all probably in the basement to reduce the noise from the beatings, have a look and give me a shout, we may have use for the cells if we get any prisoners.'

Tatu nodded grimly, 'I will have a look, then help Petru.' He grimaced, 'Too much spice indeed, cheeky chef!' He strode past the young commander, heading after Petru.

Hausser checked back into the room they had just left, seeing the two Romanians stood by their assigned windows. Continuing along the outskirts of the ground floor, he walked down the corridor on the opposite side of the building, noticing a staircase leading down into the basement on his right in the centre of the building. Hearing a muffled argument below, he smiled to himself, hearing Tatu question Petru as to how much spice and herbs he would use for each of their country's dishes.

As he reached the end of the corridor, emerging back into the entrance hall he nodded to the two soldiers by the closed doors, then heard a ringing from upstairs. Realising it was the field telephone, he climbed the steps of the central staircase two at a time, slowing as he heard the ringing stop, a familiar voice answering the telephone.

Climbing the last couple of steps to the left of the central staircase, he heard the conversation to his left, 'Yes Sir, I will go and get him if you like........I understand, Sir......Yes Sir, I will tell him.'

Hausser turned onto the first floor landing, seeing Meino looking towards him nodding, the telephone held to his ear. Then he lowered the handset, placing it back into its cradle.

Hausser walked towards the Croatian, 'Did they not want to talk to me?'

Meino shook his head, 'Just giving information, Herr Leutnant. It was the major's adjutant. He wanted to see that we had arrived in one piece.'

The young commander grinned, raising his eyebrows, 'A social call?'

Meino smiled briefly, 'No, he told me to tell you that he wants to know of any Russian movements in this sector, no matter how unimportant they seem to be.' He paused, mentally recalling the conversation, 'He seemed quite concerned, also stating we should keep alert and not become too comfortable, that the major will visit us over the next couple of days.'

Hausser nodded, stroking his half-beard again, 'I see, anything else?'

Meino's eyes widened, 'Yes, apparently there are a number of Russian snipers in the area. He wanted us to know that the major has sent one of our snipers to eliminate them and provide further support for the line here, and that we should not send out any patrols until this has been achieved.'

Hausser looked at Meino thoughtfully, 'Good, let's hope he is successful, this sniper. Though he may be very cold out here.' He thought further, 'Let's let the men at the front door know in case this sniper comes calling for food or supplies.'

Meino picked up his MP40 from the desk next to the field telephone, glancing round the office it was situated in, 'I think this must have been the office for the local commander.' He smiled, looking at the higher quality desk and chairs in the room, the well painted walls, 'I will go and tell the men on the door now.' The Croatian walked round the desk, the nails on the soles of his boots clicking on the polished floorboards.

As Meino drew level with Hausser, there was a muffled explosion outside, the two men stiffening. Looking at each other, their eyes widening as the machine guns at the end of the corridor burst into life. Hausser moved first, 'Get along the corridor and see what is going on, I will go downstairs and see if the Russians are attacking.'

Meino nodded, lunging forward and beginning to run along the first floor corridor, passing a Romanian soldier squinting through the gap in the window in an attempt to see out into the darkness. Hausser grasped the wooden handrail on the stairs, descending the steps quickly. Reaching the bend, he saw the two soldiers at the front door cautiously peering out into the small square. Muffled rifle cracks could be heard to the north, the unit next door opening fire on any movement before the building.

Shadows moved across the terrain outside, the soldiers of the Russian penal unit launching their assault across the broken ground. Moving from broken walls and doorways the soldiers desperately attempting to find cover from the machine gun fire as they advanced. One unlucky soldier felt the pull of the tripwire across his shin, the explosion almost instant, the concealed twine and grenade removing any element of surprise.

In the large basement, Tatu had been inspecting the three cells that ran along the wall below the front door, leaving Petru in the room opposite, inspecting the meagre stock of supplies by candlelight, considering what to prepare in his head. The Romanian quartermaster had been considering what misery had occurred in the medium sized room before the cells, a lone chair sitting in the middle of the sparsely furnished cement room. He was thinking that perhaps other prisoners had witnessed interrogations, a sinister motivation for their own confessions when Petru hissed at him abruptly, 'Tatu, come here!'

Tatu turned from the miserable rooms, 'What is it?' Moving towards the doorway, the staircase just beyond it, between the two rooms.

'Shhhh!' Petru replied cautiously, slowly grasping the rifle from his shoulder.

Tatu stepped forward, the candle he was holding flickering in the draft. Lowering his voice, a puzzled look on his face, 'What is it?'

Petru was stepping quietly and deliberately away from the back wall of the room, slowly turning his rifle in his hands to point at the rack of supplies. He indicated with a nod to the wall, his voice a whisper, 'Listen!'

Tatu strained his ears, hearing the muffled explosion outside as a soldier walked through a tripwire. Then the machine guns firing above, the sound distant through the building. He whispered, 'I can't hear anything.'

Petru turned his head quickly, glaring at him in the candlelight, 'There is someone on the other side of the wall.'

Tatu's eyes widened, stepping forward. Cursing under his breath as he realised he had left his machine gun on top of the filing cabinets upstairs.

As they watched, the shelves moved forward slightly, the tins and packages shaking on the shelves, shelves they were not intended to be placed on. The wooden backed unit scraped slightly across the floor, the weight of the supplies preventing the unit from swinging open completely, the Russian soldier behind the obstacle straining to push the barrier aside.

Tatu reached down slowly, retrieving his knife from inside his boot, stepping closer to the shelving unit and placing the underside of his foot against the edge of the shelving unit, preventing it from moving further. He indicated for Petru to move to the other side of the shelves, extinguishing the candles. Machine gun fire echoed through the building as the gunners on the upper floors fired out into the destroyed landscape before the NKVD headquarters, the tentacles of a thin mist creeping across the devastated workshops and factories from the river.

The shelving unit shook as the Russian soldier pushed against the wood again, the narrowness of the passageway preventing more than two men from gaining access to the barrier. Another Russian soldier handed his lantern to the man behind and stepped forward to add to the first, the eagerness of the soldiers in the tunnel beginning to subside and transform into frustration.

The unit scraped across the floor again, Tatu placing his shoulder against the corner to resist the movement. The Russian soldiers pushed harder, the unit moving inwards again, the gap widening slightly. One Russian soldier slipped sideways, trying to use his body to lever the shelving unit open. A third Russian soldier now stepped up to the barrier pushing with his hands above his countryman, the shelves moving slightly again, Tatu slipping backwards, his boots unable to grip the cement floor.

A hand appeared on the side of the shelves as the first Russian managed to get his shoulder into the gap, the unit moving again. Then Private Medvedev stepped forward, turning his rifle and bringing the butt across onto the hinges with a crash. Then he raised it again, the rusted metal hinges resisting the first hit.

Tatu turned, indicating to Petru to run for the stairs, his countryman stepping across the room quickly, stopping at the doorway and dropping to his knees, his rifle raised. Tatu raised his knife and brought it down into the shoulder of the Russian soldier pushing between the wall and the shelving unit, the scream as the blade tip entered next to the man's collar bone echoing across the cellar. The wounded soldier pulled back in panic, colliding with the other soldiers pushing, disrupting their momentum. His screams as the blood spurted across the walls and wooden unit startling the other Russian infantry in the tunnel.

Tatu sprung back from the shelves, turning and running to the stairs as the wooden unit toppled forward, the tins and packages falling to the floor, the hinges breaking. As the Romanian quartermaster ran past Petru, the rifle cracked, the bullet flying through the shelved and wooden backing, hitting the middle Russian in the chest. He fell backwards as his ribcage shattered, the fragments piercing his heart and killing him instantly. The wounded Russlan, grasping his bleeding shoulder turned into the tunnel, pushing his countrymen to the side in his desperation to escape to safety.

The shelves crashed to the floor, the contents of some of the tins and packages exploding across the cement as the wood crashed on top of them. Petru pulled the bolt back on his rifle, firing into the mist of flour and dust that had exploded into the air, hitting another Russian soldier in the face, the man's head bucking backwards with the impact, his body falling forwards onto the broken shelves.

Tatu grabbed Petru's shoulder, dragging him from the corner at a crouch as rifle bullets splattered against the wall opposite the tunnel opening. Scrambling towards the top of the stairs, Petru half crouched his rifle pointing downwards, Tatu pulling on his shoulder. The two Romanians saw the muzzles of two Russian rifles appear at the foot of the stairs, the weapons slowly turning to aim at them as the Russian infantry advanced to the corner. Petru fumbled with the bolt on his rifle in panic, his hands slipping across the steel, a sickly feeling surging through his stomach. Tatu's eyes widened in panic as he realised they would not reach the top of the staircase in time, his spare hand dropping the knife and grasping at the wooden steps.

Bullets splattered across the walls of the cellar at the foot of the stairs, the Russian infantry ducking back in panic. Tatu spun round, seeing Hausser stood at the doorway, his machine gun pointing down above them, the muzzle flashing. A startled Romanian appeared next to him in the opening, Tatu's PPSH machine gun in his hand, he fired a burst down into the basement.

Panicked shouts could be heard in the basement, the Russian soldiers realising their rifles were no match against the two machine guns in the confined space. Private Medvedev shouted across the men, 'Retreat into the tunnel, get out now before they use grenades.'

The six Russian soldiers needed no prompting. Heeding the shouts, they turned and ran into the tunnel, scrambling over the supplies and broken shelves. Private Medvedev backed towards the open tunnel, his rifle raised, covering the men's retreat, his aim at the corner of the wall, the foot of the staircase.

As he stepped backwards, lifting his legs over the shelves, his eyes on the corner, he did not know the breathless last man had turned in the tunnel. Remembering the political officer's speech, he raised his rifle, aiming at the figure stepping over the shelves.

The rifle in the tunnel swayed with the soldier's breathing and panic as the figure in the basement slipped on the body lying over the shelves. The rifle cracked and bucked upwards, the figure spinning round as the bullet entered private Medvedev's right shoulder blade, his own rifle crashing to the cement floor of the cellar as it dropped from his grasp. Then the soldier in the tunnel turned and ran into the darkness, his panic overcoming him.

The Russian sergeant quickly climbed the stairs to the roofless room at the top, seeing the light of dawn beginning to creep across the sky above, the room the only part of the building left standing. The Political Officer was stood smoking and listening to the gunfire behind him, an ironic smirk on his face. They could hear the desperate shouts to retreat, the thirty six penal unit soldiers having been unable to overcome the impregnable defence of two machine guns, traps and defensive flanking fire from the adjacent German unit. The fourteen survivors of the attacking penal unit now fleeing.

The sergeant stood before the Political Officer, his breathing heavy, fear in his eyes, 'The men are retreating Sir, there have been casualties. They have machine guns....'

The Political Officer turned slightly, looking at the sergeant, his eyebrows raised. He slowly pulled the collar of his overcoat up, a protection against the morning cold, 'You have a machine gun, don't you.'

The sergeant nodded, his eyes wide, 'Er, yes Sir.'

The Political Officer nodded slowly, 'Shoot them. Shoot all the cowards that retreat.'

The sergeant's eyes widened further, his voice shaking, 'But Sir, the enemy has mach...'

The Officer interrupted, his voice determined, 'Are you questioning my order?' He looked away from the sergeant, over his shoulder towards the high buildings in the distance. Seeing a distant light, he stepped sideways curiously, straining his eyes to look towards the horizon.

The sergeant shook his head fearfully, 'N...No, Si..'

The shot was distant, the high powered rifle immediately withdrawn into the tarpaulin. The muzzle flash concealed deliberately amongst the ruins of the destroyed workshop roof. The material wrapped round the barrel reducing the sound and flash further. The Austrian sniper lowered his head, his dirt covered face touching the cold slate and debris on the destroyed floor of the workshop attic. He slowly exhaled, ensuring no dust rose in the close confines of his position.

The Russian sergeant stood there, his mouth open in mid-word as the Political Officer slowly dropped to his knees in front of him. The bullet had been fired from one hundred and fifty metres away, through a hole the size of a dinner plate in the exterior building wall, a shell puncture from three months before. The bullet had pierced the officers back and penetrated his heart, exiting the front of his chest, his ribcage collapsing.

The sergeant gasped as the officer slumped forward, his face smacking against the broken cement from the roof of the workshop, the blood splattering as the dead man's nose shattered on impact.

The sergeant looked down in bewilderment, raising his hand to his face to wipe the single splatter of blood from his cheek. The officer still held a burning cigarette in his dead gloved hand.

Chapter Twenty Four: The Tunnel

Hausser slowly and cautiously advanced down the wooden staircase, stepping carefully round Tatu and Petru. As he neared the bottom of the steps and the end of the wall, he lowered himself to a crouch, seeing the bullet holes in the plaster above him.

Hearing scraping in the room to his right, he gripped his MP40 tightly, leaning outwards from the wall in an attempt to see into the room. As he descended the last couple of steps, he felt his stomach seem to twist, the caution rising dramatically within him. Glancing quickly round the wall, he glimpsed the Russian soldier struggling amongst the broken shelves and supplies, his low groans an indication he was badly wounded. Surveying the two other bodies in the cellar for movement and checking the darkened tunnel, he jumped forward as he saw the Russian soldier struggling to reach his rifle. The weapon just out of reach on his wounded side, the soldier desperately stretching across his body with his uninjured arm, his teeth clenched in pain. The discarded flickering candle lay just beyond the weapon, the wick struggling to stay alight.

Hausser glanced round to the stairs, nodding to the on-looking Tatu and Petru, then he lunged forward into the room. As he reached the Russian infantryman, Hausser kicked the rifle out of his reach, the man's fingers just touching the weapon, a whine of frustration coming from the man's lips.

Tatu and Petru entered the room behind him, Tatu brandishing his PPSH machine gun and running to the tunnel opening, jumping over the broken wood and scattered supplies. He pointed the weapon menacingly down the passageway, straining his eyes to stare into the darkness.

Hausser turned, indicating to the Romanian behind Petru, 'Get a couple of soldiers down here to guard the tunnel entrance. Bring Adel to look our prisoner over, see what we can do for him. Find out if there are any casualties upstairs.' The soldier nodded solemnly, turning and climbing the stairs from the basement. Turning to Tatu, Hausser saw the Romanian quartermaster nod as an indication he understood to watch the opening.

Hausser cautiously bent down to the moaning Russian, the man's hand over his face as he lay on his side, his spirit seeming broken. Leaning forward, Hausser nudged the man's uninjured shoulder, speaking softly in Russian, his voice urgent, 'You are now our prisoner, where does this tunnel lead to?'

The Russian soldier froze, his surprise at hearing his language apparent. Slowly his hand moved from his face as he cautiously looked up at Hausser, his eyes widening as he began to recognise the German officer, 'Y-You again!' He moaned in contempt, his face strained due to the extreme pain in his shoulder.

Hausser's eyes widened, glancing up and down the Russian's body, checking for further injury. As his face moved back to the man's face, a flicker of recognition went through his eyes, the Russian's face covered in dirt, 'The captain from the Fishing Lodge? But how?'

The Russian slowly rolled over onto his back, gasping in agony, his voice shaking, 'F-Fate certainly has an evil sense of humour.......' He lay on his back, tears in his eyes, 'I-I never thought you would even get to the river, let alone this far...' He winced as jabbing pain darted through his shoulder.

Hausser narrowed his eyes at the man's pain, looking at the deep shoulder wound, 'We have a medic, I will get him to look at your wound.' He turned to Petru, 'Go and see what is keeping them, I need this man to survive!'

Petru nodded startled, turning and walking to the stairs, stopping at the foot of the staircase, seeing the Hungarian beginning to descend from the top step, 'Adel is here, Herr Leutnant.' Boots could be heard on the wooden steps leading to the basement, Adel turning the corner and moving towards the injured Russian. Behind him, a Romanian soldier carrying two lanterns walked into the basement room.

Hausser bent further over the wounded soldier, looking into his face, 'I am Leutnant Hausser, Herr Hauptmann.'

The Russian opened his eyes slightly in surprise, 'I-I am only a private now, they stripped me of my rank when I lost the Fishing Lodge to you and your men. I am in a penal unit.'

Hausser shook his head slowly, a grim smile forming on his face, 'Well as far as I am aware, you are a captured Captain in a private's uniform, therefore entitled to some additional comforts....not that we have many.'

Adel bent down next to the man, concern on his face. He glanced at Hausser, his expression grim, 'It is a deep wound, Herr Leutnant. I will see what I can do.' Turning to the Romanian soldier stood next to him, he looked up, 'Get me some water and bandages...if there are no bandages, just get cloth. We need to stop the bleeding.'

The Romanian soldier nodded, running to the stairs.

Tatu grunted in impatience, 'Herr Leutnant, what shall we do about the tunnel?'

Hausser looked up, realising he was concentrating too much on the wounded man, 'See how well built it is, can we blow the supports, collapse it?' He slowly rose, grasping his MP40 and advancing cautiously towards the opening, 'The least we will do is place some traps, have we any AP mines?'

Tatu shook his head, 'I don't think so Haus...., Herr Leutnant.'

Private Medvedev gasped as the Hungarian pulled his shoulder upwards, placing a bag of supplies underneath it. The Russian struggling to speak understanding their concern, if not the words, 'Th-they will probably not be back for a while, they are terrified. Unless the Commissar forces them, that is.'

Hausser turned pointing at the Russian, 'Can we move him?'

Adel glanced towards Hausser, shaking his head dismissively, 'Not upstairs until he is bandaged.'

Petru interrupted, moving forward and bending to help the injured Russian, 'I will move him into the next room.'

Hausser nodded, 'Good, I don't want him or Adel getting hit by some stray fire from the tunnel.' He glanced across at Tatu, indicating to him to proceed with a jerk of his head. Then he turned back to Petru, seeing the Romanian lift the wounded Russian from the debris on the floor, 'Get a couple of men to move the bodies outside too, Petru.' Seeing the Romanian nod his understanding as he supported the Russian, Adel pressing supply bags against the wounded man's shoulder from either side.

Tatu moved forward cautiously, his boots gingerly stepping onto the makeshift wooden planks on the floor of the tunnel, his frustrated voice a whisper, 'I seem to be spending most of this war underground now...' He slowly stepped over the outstretched legs of the corpse in the tunnel.

Hausser grinned fleetingly, hissing, 'Shut up you old fool, and check the supports.'

Tatu shook his head, moving slowly into the tunnel, cautiously pointing his machine gun before him into the darkness. Reaching the first support pillar, he grasped it, realising it was a heavy rough wooden beam, the support stretching up to the ceiling of the tunnel, with further wooden beams at angles to support the wood of the roof above. The ceiling and walls were panelled with thick planks, preventing the frozen earth on the other side them from falling into the passageway.

Tatu turned his head, hissing back towards the room behind, 'This tunnel was built recently, probably in the last few months, Hausser. It should be relatively easy to collapse the tunnel with explosives, perhaps even with grenades behind the supports.'

Hausser nodded thoughtfully behind him at the tunnel entrance, 'Good, let's ring the major for an engineer just in case. In the meantime we will try and blow these supports.' He turned, indicating to a Romanian soldier that had just appeared at the foot of the stairs, 'Bring a couple of men. Get Meino to come with twelve grenades and then move the remaining supplies upstairs.'

The man nodded grimly, disappearing as he climbed the staircase again. Looking back into the darkness of the tunnel, Hausser could just see Tatu moving in the gloom, 'Best come back my friend, we will guard the opening until there is a chance to blow the supports.'

Tatu backed slowly towards the entrance of the tunnel, assuming a position on the left side, his machine gun pointing into the opening. Nodding to Hausser, he whispered across the opening to him, 'Meino and I will place the grenades further into the tunnel that will clear the building foundations. Then if the ground opens above we can use the machine guns on the first floor to cover the entrance.'

Hausser nodded, 'Good that should create a better defence.' He glanced round as two German soldiers entered the basement, one still wearing a dirty and dishevelled military police uniform. He turned towards them, 'Take as many of the remaining supplies upstairs, we may still have a good meal yet once Petru cooks for us.' He grinned, glancing back and seeing Tatu shake his head.

As the two soldiers began picking up some of the tins and small supply bags scattered across the basement floor, further boots on the wooden staircase behind them caused Hausser to glance round again. Seeing Meino emerge into the dim light carrying a small satchel, he smiled briefly, 'Over here, Meino. Let's see if these grenades can being this tunnel down.'

Meino's eyes widened as he saw the scattered supplies on the floor, then the dark tunnel opening Tatu and Hausser stood before. He nodded, moving forward towards them, averting his eyes as he stepped over one of the bodies. Lifting the strap of the satchel over his shoulder as he retrieved a lantern from the floor, his MP40 machine gun held in his other hand.

As the Croatian approached, Hausser moved forward at a crouch into the tunnel, slipping along the right side, his machine gun before him. Tatu moved in behind him, along the left, the light from the lantern Meino was carrying casting shadows across the tunnel walls and ceiling from the support beams.

After about twenty metres, the tunnel bent slightly to the left. Hausser stopped, looking at the beams on the bend and nodding to Tatu, whispering, 'Would this be a good place?'

Tatu nodded as Meino joined them, the Croatian studying the support beams on either side. Lowering himself, he slipped the satchel from his shoulder, and opened the flap of the bag, delving inside for the grenades. Meino looked up seeing Hausser advance further round the bend, 'I will place six grenades behind each support, three on either side. We attach twine to the primers, then get back as far as we can before pulling them. Understand?'

Hausser glanced back, nodding. Tatu leant forward receiving two stick grenades from Meino. Unscrewing the bases, he tied the primer cable together from the base of the grenades and wedged them behind the support beam to his left. Meino repeated the action on the right, handing Tatu an additional grenade, 'Place this one on the bottom, the weight from above should add to the explosion then.'

Tatu nodded, following the instruction. The next support beams were approximately one metre further forward from the previous two, the additional supports added to strengthen the corner. Replicating their previous placements, Meino handed Tatu two rolls of twine from his tunic pocket, holding the ends of the cord, whispering, 'Unroll these back to the basement. Once you are there, whisper to me, I will attach them. Then we retreat and detonate the grenades from the room.' His eyebrows rose expectantly.

Tatu nodded slowly indicating he understood, running his hand nervously across his moustache, 'I don't like explosives.'

Meino grinned, 'Neither do the Russians.......now go!' He rolled the twine around his boot as Tatu retreated backwards, the cord beginning to extend along the tunnel.

After several seconds he heard a hiss from the basement from Tatu, 'There is no more cord, is that enough?'

Meino looked down, checking the amount of cord around his boot in the dim light, 'Yes.' Turning to look at Hausser further along the darkened tunnel, 'Time to go, Herr Leutnant.'

Hausser backed towards him, staring into the darkness. As the two men drew level, he turned to Meino, 'Will the explosion be instant?'

The Croatian shook his head, 'No, I will let the timers do the job for us, in case there is a problem.'

Hausser nodded, watching the soldier tie the ends of the twine onto the primer cords, occasionally glancing cautiously further into the tunnel to check it was clear. As Meino finished tying the cord to all the grenades, he looked into the Leutnant's face, 'Let's go, and don't stand on the cord!'

Hausser nodded, impressed with the Croatian's workmanship. Both soldiers slowly backed down the tunnel, Meino picking up the lantern as they passed it. Slowly and carefully they stepped backwards along the tunnel, cautious of stepping on the twine.

Emerging back into the basement, Hausser turned to see the bodies and most of the supplies had been removed. Meino carefully took the twine from Tatu, turning to the other two, 'Everyone out of this room please, I will do this.' The Romanian soldier behind them slowly retreated, his eyes widening in excitement.

Hausser and Tatu nodded, backing away from the tunnel opening. Reaching the wall of the room, they moved behind it, sheltering on the stairs, hearing the wounded Russian groan in the room behind them. Hausser turned, hissing across the basement into the next room, 'There will be an explosion shortly, brace yourselves.'

Adel replied, sighing, 'Yes, Herr Leutnant. Not sure if our prisoner will hear it clearly, he has drifted unconscious with the pain.'

Hausser glanced back into the room, seeing Meino move to the left side of the tunnel opening, the end of the twine in his hands. The Croatian turned to look at him, his eyebrows raised, 'Ready?'

Hausser nodded, slowly retreating behind the wall, his breath held. Then he heard boots on the cement floor of the room as Meino lurched towards them, the Croatian running past into the next room.

There was a massive blast, the sound heightened in the enclosed space of the basement. Two smaller muffled explosions followed, a dust cloud billowing across the room and engulfing the soldiers on the stairs and in the room beside them. Then there was silence.

Tatu and Hausser coughed the dust from their mouths and throat, hearing some coughing in the room beside them. Slowly Hausser stepped cautiously down onto the concrete floor on the basement, glancing into the dust filled room.

He strained his eyes to see through the dust clouds as the particles slowly fell to the concrete floor. Moving forward slowly, he bent down and picked up a lantern, approaching the dark opening on the wall of the basement. Then his eyes widened, a grin forming across his face as he saw the blockage further down the tunnel, the frozen earth and wooden beams having imploded into the passageway. The tunnel now sealed with debris.

Chapter Twenty Five: Recoil.

As the morning light had slowly spread across the sky, the Austrian sniper had lain motionless behind his tarpaulin cover. The cold breeze from the Volga enveloping him in the morning light, he had slowly moved his blankets around him, his inaction adding to the cold in his muscles. Shell bursts and rifle cracks echoed across the landscape from north and south, motivating him further, the sounds the perfect camouflage for his hunt.

Determining he would remain in the destroyed machine shop roof for most of the morning, he had scanned any possible target points through the telescopic sight on his Kar 98 rifle. As the dawn had arrived, he had noticed some of the Russian soldiers in the distance moving amongst their defences, but decided to hunt his ultimate prize, the Russian snipers, before targeting simple infantrymen. Smoke rose from some positions, the sign of previous shelling or smouldering combustible remains.

Scanning the broken landscape before him, he had squinted through the sight as he investigated possible hiding places for his adversaries. He had smiled to himself as he saw one possible spot, even thinking he may have adopted it himself had the roles been reversed, a faint smile spreading across his face as he saw a slight glint in the morning light from beneath the destroyed lorry.

The damaged vehicle had been abandoned, the driver killed by shell fragments at the explosion before the lorry as he had driven the vehicle towards the river, desperately trying to escape the advancing German army some months earlier. Lunging into the shell crater, the vehicle had turned onto its side, the dead driver lying in the vehicle cab for the last three months, his body initially decaying before the winter frosts had set in.

A small gap between the edge of the crater and the underneath of the lorry had remained, the inexperienced Russian sniper adding obstacles around the opening as protection. The Austrian had smiled as he realised the man's one mistake. One small gap had been filled by a crate, the wooden box probably having fallen from the vehicle. The position was used by snipers and forward artillery observers, the occupants becoming complacent with the position, the Austrian considered.

Having studied the base of the vehicle and the neatly placed obstacles around it, he considered the items were too neatly placed in the surrounding maelstrom of destruction. Seeing shadows in the small gap between the vehicle and the shell crater, he determined the position was now occupied.

He leant slightly forward, his eye moving closer to the end of the telescopic sight. Licking his lips, his finger extended towards the trigger, aiming he rifle just above and to the right of the slight gap between the crate and broken cement section from the pavement. His experience telling him this would compensate for the distance and slight breeze.

He lowered his breath, the shallow intakes and exhales steadying the weapon further as he awaited any movement. His finger squeezed the trigger slightly as he saw a shadow dart across the opening, the high powered weapon jolting back into his shoulder. He slowly pulled the rifle muzzle back behind the tarpaulin in reaction to the shot.

The bullet flew across the landscape, clipping the corner of the crate and entering the shoulder of the forward artillery observer, the man screaming in shock and pain as he was propelled backwards, blood splattering across the underside of the vehicle above him.

The young Austrian exhaled slowly against the broken floor beneath him, ensuring no dust rose from his action. Then he lay there for some seconds, regaining his composure.

Slowly the rifle muzzle pushed through the tarpaulin again, the young man squinting through the sight. Seeing the new trail blood on the underside of the vehicle, he slowly moved the rifle to the left, scanning north of the lorry. He glimpsed the tops of helmets running towards the overturned vehicle along a trench, realising soldiers were running to help the wounded man. The rifle muzzle moving slowly back to his previous position in anticipation.

Another shadow moved across the opening, his finger squeezing the trigger again, the bullet passing between the obstacles and hitting an infantryman in the chest as he bent down to help the wounded artillery observer. The soldier was killed instantly as the high velocity bullet tore through his body, the soldier falling dead next to the writhing artillery observer. The other two infantrymen backed away from the overturned lorry in terror, their bodies lowered in the trench, the man's screams loud in their ears as he began to bleed to death.

The Austrian's cheek was once again pushed against the upper floor of the broken machine shop, a grim smile crossing his face as he thought to himself, 'That should flush you Russian snipers out, let's see who is the better hunter now.' More rifle cracks and explosions echoed across the landscape from either side as the young man realised that this may prove to be a very profitable day.

Chapter Twenty Six: Orders are orders.

Hausser smiled briefly in frustration, listening to the major talking on the other end of the field telephone, his voice slightly slurred.

The major continued obviously highly agitated, static crackling across the line, '....so I explained to your Major Schenk that you were needed here, that your position was relatively safe and that you would be there for a number of days.' The Major drew on his cigarette, his hands shaking, glancing across at Hauptmann Ebner, the captain staring back through bloodshot eyes. 'It appears, your major friend has acquaintances at Sixth Army headquarters, so I have to release you and your men at short notice. This is not on, Hausser, I am very annoyed!'

Hausser sighed, 'I understand Sir...I can assure you Major Schenk will probably have good reason if he wants my men and I back...' He paused as the major interrupted.

'Really? I certainly hope so. This position in the factory district is imperative to hold for the safety of the divisions to the north, every man is needed.' The major swigged from his glass again, indicating for Hauptmann Ebner to top it up with a wave of his hand. He lowered himself into the chair behind him, stubbing his cigarette out, 'Anyway, you said you had a combat report, tell me.'

Hausser looked up as Meino approached the entrance to the office, speaking back into the telephone handset, 'Yes Sir, we drove back a Russian attack earlier this morning, they came through a tunnel into the basement and sent infantry across open ground before the building. They suffered heavy casualties. We lost two men to sniper fire, the Russians were targeting the defenders windows.'

The major stood up again, glaring at Hauptmann Ebner, 'Tunnel, what tunnel?' The captain's eyes widening in surprise in front of him.

Hausser spoke softly, looking across the room at Meino, 'The NKVD must have dug the tunnel some time ago, Sir...perhaps an escape route. Anyway, we have demolished it now.' He smiled faintly, 'Unfortunately, some of the extra supplies were destroyed in the skirmish, so we have moved them upstairs.' He thought for a second, 'Perhaps if you would like to visit us later today we can provide you with a small sample of our Romanian *chef's* cuisine?'

The major smiled in surprise, a glint forming in his eye, 'You have a damn cheek, Leutnant! Still, who am I to turn down such an invite? I will come with my adjutant and the captain here, as long as the Russians don't ruin the little farewell party for us in the interim. I will transfer my command post to your location for that time.'

Hausser nodded slowly, 'Yes Major, will we expect you in a few hours?'

The major settled back in his seat, 'Dusk Hausser, I will come as the day ends. Damn Russian snipers, I hope my man can thin their numbers, he comes highly recommended.' He winked at the captain opposite, 'Is there anything you need? The new unit will be taking over your stocks of ammunition.'

Hausser smiled to himself, 'We will need some more grenades, Sir. We used twelve in demolishing the tunnel.' He thought for a second, 'We also have a prisoner. He is wounded, but I will try and get some information for you.'

The major grinned, 'Good Leutnant, get the information, then shoot him, we don't have enough supplies for our own men, let alone prisoners.'

Hausser's eyes narrowed, 'But Sir, he surrendered to us.......'

Major Slusser interrupted again, his voice rising, 'Don't question my commands Leutnant. He is the enemy, we shoot them, that's that, understand?'

Hausser gritted his teeth, 'Very well, Sir.' He changed the subject quickly, 'Is there any news of Hoth and his tanks to give the men?'

The major swigged from his drink again, 'Perhaps when we meet Hausser, until then there may be changes in the situation. I will see you this evening, goodbye.'

The phone clicked loudly in Hausser's ear as the major slammed down the handset. Slowly he lowered the telephone into its cradle, looking up at Meino, 'Well, the major is coming this evening and it looks like we are heading back to the 76th Infantry Division.'

Meino nodded, his face dropping, 'Are they.....?'

Hausser cut in, 'Yes......they are outside the city of the steppe, so it will be a little colder I presume. Until then we maintain our defence here.' He picked up his MP40 from the desk, 'I am going to see how our prisoner is doing and perhaps get some information from him.' He walked round the desk, passing Meino as the Croatian stood aside. Hausser turned, looking at him, 'Tell Petru to cook for us this evening. Not much, we need to preserve the supplies for the next unit, but enough for a little farewell to the factory district.'

Meino nodded, a smile forming on his face, 'That will be well received, we have all lost weight in the last couple of weeks, the rations are not enough, Herr Leutnant.'

Hausser nodded solemnly, 'I know, but a good meal before the men trek out into the snow will boost morale I think. Hopefully the major has some good news from the relief effort to tell us as well, we might not be out in the snow for too long with a little luck.' He backed away, turning to descend the stairs as he felt the bannister rail behind him.

Descending the stairs, he thought of the Russian prisoner. The soldier had certainly experienced very bad luck and Hausser was becoming increasingly uncomfortable with shooting an unarmed man whom had surrendered. His thoughts drifted back to the elderly Russian in the sewer reservoir, the man's reasoning for helping them impressing him, but also making him consider an obligation to the belief the old man expressed. Slowly an idea began to form in his mind as he stepped down the marble central staircase.

Nodding to the two infantryman at the door, he turned and headed for the steps to the basement, his mind beginning to focus solely on his idea.

Chapter Twenty Seven: Luck of the Austrian

The light was fading as dusk slowly set across the landscape. The Austrian shivered as he felt the temperature drop further, his lack of movement adding to the cold across his body. He felt his stomach rumble, the cold rations he had eaten earlier in the day insufficient to sustain his concentration, feeling a dull pain across his forehead from his hunger.

His count for the day so far had risen to nine, the Russian infantrymen falling as he had picked them off, a brief careless movement as he watched costing them their lives. He was frustrated at not having killed the Russian sniper he had promised Major Slusser, the man elusive through his absence.

Pinching the bridge of his nose, he slowly and carefully lowered his face to the floor in the roof of the machine shop, tiredness in his eyes. After a few seconds, he carefully lifted his head, moving his eyes back to the sight of his weapon and surveying the landscape again, hoping his long day of patience would be rewarded.

As the muzzle of the rifle slowly crossed the torn terrain between his position and the higher buildings on the skyline, he stifled a yawn, his mind tired from the day's hunting. His thoughts wandered, thinking of the rations he could perhaps gain from the local NKVD Headquarters, the major having advised they were in German hands.

Then he froze, his well-trained mind focussing as he saw movement in a trench north of the overturned lorry he had gained two victories at earlier in the day. A Russian soldier was slowly moving along the trench, his helmet clearly visible even in the diming light. He smiled beneath his scarf, his mind discounting a shot, knowing it was a decoy to lure him out, to betray his position. His heart beginning to beat faster as he realised a Russian sniper was stalking him, using the poor infantryman as bait. His revulsion for the tactic he had experienced across several Russian cities was only overcome by the excitement as he realised his enemy was indeed in the area, awaiting his reaction.

Slowly and more cautiously, he moved the muzzle of his rifle across the terrain, feeling the adrenalin sweep through his body. Knowing if he could only find the sniper's position, then he would await the man's frustration or complacency to set in, that then he would have a shot.

The Russian had been awoken from his deep sleep earlier than usual, the commissar shaking him roughly to gain his focus. He had been advised there was a German sniper in the area that was picking off men and that the less experienced snipers could not locate him. The Political officer had ordered him to go out and find the German and kill him, before his exploits began to undermine the troops' morale.

With the emergence of a new German sniper, the vodka ration had been withdrawn from the front line troops in the area, preventing soldiers from making mistakes after clouding their judgement when faced with a cunning enemy.

Struggling to force himself awake, the Russian sniper known as Ruslan had splashed his face with iced water to gain further alertness, struggling through the trenches as Russian infantrymen covered themselves for the night's frost. He had then wiped gun oil across his features, the liquid reducing any sign of his skin in the darkness.

He had talked through his prospective positions with the commissar, advising him he could only watch until the German took another shot and that he may have already moved on, the search becoming fruitless. The commissar had advised that he would create an opportunity for the sniper, dragging a bewildered soldier from a penal unit and allowing him to drink three or four men's vodka rations before ordering him to make his way up and down the front line, the man promised freedom if he accomplished it four or five times.

The Russian sniper, in his late twenties had protested initially, then realised it was pointless as the commissar offered him the opportunity of taking the unfortunate soldier's place in the penal unit. Trudging out with the drunken soldier, he had told him to stay down if he was hit, and to limit the exposure of his head. The man had replied that he would do his duty to his country and keep moving, that the German would never hit him.

The Russian sniper had shook his head in frustration, realising the inexperienced soldier's reasoning was faulted. They had then reached the taller buildings on the skyline and the drunken soldier had progressed into the trenches merrily swigging from his remaining supply, concealing his fear.

Carefully moving to his predetermined observation position, the sniper had begun to look over the landscape cautiously through his binoculars, the light beginning to fade. He had made a mental note of some of the positions he considered possible for the German sniper and had then retrieved his sighted rifle, moving forward slowly to assume his own position. Unaware the commissar had sent out another man to also hunt the German, that he himself had also become bait.

The Austrian momentarily pulled his head back from the rifle sight, checking the heavily clouded sky and strength of the slight breeze as he looked out over the snow covered landscape. Lowering his head again, he began to check his predetermined spots, the places a sniper would be tempted to utilise.

He watched as the drunken soldier struggled along the Russian lines, seeming to swig from a bottle as he did so. The infantryman was half crouched, moving along the Russian unit deployed to the front line for the night, the soldiers shaking their heads as he passed, grateful they were not taking his place.

The Austrian sniper realised that sooner or later someone would take a shot at the soldier, the careless man offering too much of a target for the German soldiers on either side of him to resist. He licked his lips again, his heart beating hard in his chest as he realised this may also tempt the Russian sniper to fire in retaliation.

Then he caught his breath, glimpsing what he thought was some movement as he scanned the terrain. Squinting through the telescopic sight, he felt the tiredness in his eyes as he looked into the side street along the wall of one of the tall buildings on the horizon. To the left of the narrow lane was a shell crater, breaking the road into the sewer pipe below. As he watched, his eyes widened as he saw the slight movement of the rubble before the crater. His heart beginning to race as he realised a rifle was very carefully being pushed into position.

Considering the distance was perhaps too far, he determined is was worth one shot before retiring for the night, the light fading further. Raising the muzzle of the rifle slightly, he aimed for just above and to the right of the shell crater, compensating for the distance and breeze. The edge of the crater was just visible in the bottom of his sight as he began to adopt shallower breaths, steading the weapon.

His heart nearly missed a beat as he glimpsed further movement, the tiny dark shape rising from the crater edge. Sucking in air through his nose, he just glimpsed an object in the crater, the top of a sniper's head. He tensed, his mind conflicted, was this to be the best shot? Then he relaxed again, his extensive training overcoming his doubts. He waited, watching the position for his prey to move, perhaps provide a better shot, realising he now had limited time with the fading light.

The Russian sniper moved uncomfortably in the cold shell crater, the breeze in the alley seeming colder than the previous night. He had very carefully pushed his weapon forward, so as to limit his exposure, the broken cement and earth around him perfect cover as he slowly edged up the incline of the crater, the hole in the sewer roof behind him. Cautiously he moved his rifle into position, then inched his head forward towards the sight on the weapon. His upper body and head was covered in a grey and white cloak allowing him to blend into the surroundings, reducing the chances of detection. He smiled as rifle cracks to either side of him signified his countrymen's caution, the perfect cover for him to fire. Exhaling slowly, he had learnt to control his breathing in the freezing temperatures, preventing his detection.

Inching his face forward to the sight, he slowly raised the butt of the rifle to allow him to look across the front lines and into a street in the distance, a successful hunting area for him as German troops had moved across the far end behind their lines. He smiled faintly as he wondered how many fascists would try and cross the street this night.

Then there was a distant crack, his body jerked and rolled sideways, slipping down the slope of the crater and falling into the putrid water below. The surging current pushed his lifeless corpse forward, the slope in the tunnel adding to the speed of the water as the body was propelled towards the Volga.

The smoking muzzle of the Scoped Kar 98 rifle pulled back behind the tarpaulin, the angle of elevation from the first floor to the shell cater in the distance just sufficient to take a successful shot. The Austrian smiled briefly, having seen the spurt of blood as the bullet passed through the Russian's camouflaged cloak over his head. He pushed his head onto the cold floorboards below him, exhaling heavily. The day's work was done.

Slowly he shuffled his body sideways, heading towards the broken rear walls of the building, his exit from his spot. Hearing his stomach rumble again, he thought of what food he may be able to convince the nearby unit to relinquish to him. Smiling in the near darkness, he considered Major Slusser's elation at the news, the targeted Russian sniper's death achieved in the few last minutes of the day.

Ruslan lay under his camouflaged cloak, supplied to him the day before as a reward for his total enemy tally mounting to beyond ten. He had scanned the German lines from his vantage point for some time, having little to target, the

German troops opposite fully aware of the capabilities of the Russian snipers in the area.

As the drunken Russian soldier had completed four of his journeys across the front line, the commissar had instructed him to complete another two, determined to flush the German sniper out of hiding. Completing these, Ruslan had grinned in irony at the Commissar's obvious frustration, hearing him berate the soldier some ten metres behind him for 'not trying hard enough!' Then allowing the man to return behind the buildings on the horizon in despair, realising he was no longer fit to make the journey again with the alcohol he had consumed.

Ruslan had then resumed his vigil, unaware that he was now the only Russian sniper in the area, the man sent to use him as bait now lying broken on the frozen iced banks of the Volga. Ruslan's position, lying in the side of a destroyed warehouse building some thirty metres behind the front line had produced no results. Considering he should move positions, he had pondered which position would perhaps provide a better vantage point for his hunt, postponing this as he had heard the crack of a high powered rifle some distance away, slightly to the north.

Staring through his telescopic sight, he had thought of a number of spots, then decided on one further north, an elevated position in a warehouse roof, dangerous during daylight, but effective at night time.

He had stiffened as he saw a figure run across the street in the distance, squeezing the trigger more in desperation than confidence, his view of the street limited due to his angle. He had smiled as he thought he may have clipped the running man, his steps having altered with his shot, the figure stumbling.

Slowly, he pushed himself backwards across the rubble, removing himself from the small gap in the foot of the wall he had pushed his rifle muzzle through. Rising to a crouch behind the wall, he turned and crept away from the position into the darkness, his mind decided on his new vantage point to the north.

Chapter Twenty Eight: The Last Supper

Hausser's eyes widened as he saw Petru checking the two cooking pots before him, the steam from the cooking circulating the enticing aromas of the food through the building.

Petru turned, nodding to him, 'There was not much fuel left for the stoves, but I think we should have quite a feast.' He grinned at the young commander, pointing to a wooden box at the side of the small kitchen, 'I didn't touch that box, not sure if I should have?' His eyebrows rose.

Hausser glanced across the dirty kitchen, the small space used for feeding the NKVD and their prisoners. Seeing the smudged printing on top of the nearby box, 'Nur fur Deutsche Soldaten' (only for German soldiers). He shook his head, 'It doesn't matter. So what have you made?'

Petru stirred one of the cooking pots with his bayonet, 'There were several tins of American food, so I have used some of them. American beef and some sausages from tins, with some rice I found. It's not much, but we should be able to feed the men and the major.

Hausser nodded impressed, 'Good work, Petru, let's hope the major likes it.' He turned as he heard voices downstairs, the familiar accent of the major echoing around the entrance hall. He stopped fleetingly at the door, 'It seems our guest has arrived, I will send the men in in two's to pick up their food. Is it ready?'

Petru shook his head, maybe another ten minutes, I will get Meino to bring the food along to your office, Hausser.' He grinned sheepishly, 'He is your waiter for the evening.'

Hausser smiled warmly, the thoughts of a good meal enlightening him, 'Good, thank you.' He slipped from the room making his way to the stairs.

As he descended the central staircase, he smiled as he saw the major with his adjutant, Hauptmann Ebner raising his hand in greeting. The major was wearing an infantry overcoat, probably to confuse any snipers and was talking to the sentries in front of the door.

The major turned as Hausser stepped onto the ground floor, his face broadening into a smile, 'Ah, Leutnant Hausser, good to see you. Are we all ready for our little meal? It certainly smells good.'

Hausser nodded, smiling wearily, 'Yes Major. Would you like to come up to the office?'

The major grinned, 'Yes, that would be good. I need to be near the telephone, there is news coming in from across the city tonight.'

Hausser's eyes widened, 'Good news?'

The major looked at him, his smile faltering slightly, 'Some good, some bad. Perhaps it will get better as the evening progresses.' He walked towards Hausser, the men beginning to climb the stairs together, the major glancing at him as he unbuttoned his greatcoat, 'Did you get much information from our prisoner?'

Hausser shook his head, 'He was from a penal unit, losing his rank a couple of weeks ago. He only seemed to know we were surrounded and that they were keen to keep harassing the line, preventing us from deploying more troops out onto the steppe.'

The major sighed, 'Yes, well they seem to be doing that a lot.' They turned the corner in the staircase, climbing the last few steps to the first floor, 'Regrettable business having to shoot him, but there is just no food. I trust you managed the job?'

Hausser nodded solemnly, 'Yes sir, his body is outside in the square with the others.'

The major smiled slightly, 'Good, one less Russian to worry about then.' He turned at the top of the stairs walking into the office and sitting himself down on the other side of the desk. 'So, tell me about the position here gentlemen.' He glanced between Hauptmann Ebner and Hausser.

The captain spoke first, 'Well we did not know about the tunnel, but the lines of fire from the building are good and we should be able to hold out for some time. Well, at least until the relief effort arrives.'

The major nodded, indicating for his adjutant to deposit a bottle of Vodka on the table before him, next to the flickering candle, 'I have brought a couple of bottles for you and your men to have a last drink in the city with us.' He glanced up to the adjutant, 'Please give the other two bottles to the men, it will keep their spirits up.'

He leant forward, indicating for the two officers on the other side of the desk to have a seat. Looking at Hausser, he continued, 'So, some troops will arrive in the next few hours, enough to relieve you and your men. Unfortunately there are limited soldiers available, so I will have to keep the men I gave you to bolster our numbers.'

Hausser nodded slowly, 'Yes Sir.'

The major's eyebrows rose, his lips becoming pursed, 'So how many men will you be taking out to join Major Schenk?'

Hausser thought for a second, his eyes saddening, 'I think it is about nine, Major. They are all that remains of the soldiers from the river bend.

The major nodded, pulling the cork form the vodka bottle and pouring three measures into the glasses that the captain had placed before him, 'I see, not many.' He leaned back, swigging from one of the glasses thoughtfully, 'Your unit has suffered a lot of casualties, Leutnant. I am sorry for your loss.' He stared at the young commander thoughtfully.

Hausser nodded grimly, 'Thank you sir, it has been hard. I just hope we have helped you in some way, then their loss will not be completely in vain.'

The major smiled thoughtfully, then sipped from his drink indicating for the two men to do the same, 'Yes you have. We have had quite an adventure for your short time here.' He reached inside his greatcoat pocket, retrieving some cigarettes and dropping them onto the table, 'Please help yourself gentlemen.'

Meino appeared at the door behind them, carrying three steaming mess tins, 'Am I alright to enter?'

The major indicated to him to proceed, his face lightening, 'Of course, please come in. Have we completed the cooking?' He grinned across at Hauptmann Ebner, 'The service here is impeccable, no waiting at all!'

The captain grinned as an aluminium mess tin was placed in front of the major, then himself, 'Not too sure about the waiter's uniform.' He grinned. Meino placed the last mess tin before Hausser and handing three spoons out, winking at the young commander.

The major lifted his spoon to his lips, blowing on the food before slipping it into his mouth, his eyes widening in delight, 'This is very good. Tell me, is this *chef* coming with you out to the steppe?'

Hausser nodded, smiling, 'Yes Sir, he is one of my best men.'

The major smiled back, 'Well our loss, Major Schenk's gain I think. Let us hope he safely survives this mess.'

The officers ate as the food was passed around the defending soldiers in the NKVD Headquarters. Upon completion of the small meal, and scraping their mess tins, the major sat back, raising his boots onto the table edge. He looked across at Hausser, the man sipping from his drink, 'I will be sorry to lose you Leutnant, you and your men have proved very useful here.'

Hausser smiled weakly, 'Thank you sir.'

The major swigged from his drink, lighting a cigarette, and staring at the men reflectively, 'The relief effort has apparently experienced some problems, advancing only a small distance further. It seems the Russians are throwing more men in front of them in attempts to stop General Hoth and his tanks.' He shrugged as he saw the two men's eyes fall, 'I am still confident they will get here though, we will have to destroy these Russian forces sooner or later, and perhaps Hoth will do it for us?'

He leant forward stretching his glass out to the captain, the man rising to top it up. He looked up as a soldier approached the doorway limping, 'Ah, my sniper, how did you get on?'

The Austrian winced as he leant against the doorframe, 'The Russian sniper will not bother you again. He is dead sir.'

Major Slusser's eyes sparkled, a broad smile spreading across his face, 'Excellent! Well done young man.' He indicated to his leg, the smile falling from his face, 'Are you alright?'

The Austrian nodded grimly, 'Yes sir, flesh wound I think.' Seeing the two junior officers before him staring at him.

Hausser rose from his seat, 'I have a medic, Adel. He can take a look at your leg if you like.' Seeing Meino in the corridor outside, he gestured to the Croatian, 'Meino, can you take this man to Adel please.'

Meino nodded, approaching the soldier in the doorway, grasping the man's arm, 'Let's get you some food too.' He grimaced as he grasped the sniper's arm, 'You seem very cold.'

The young Austrian smiled weakly, leaning on Meino next to him, 'Thanks, that would be welcome, I am very hungry!'

The major grinned, turning his attention back to Hausser, 'Right, Leutnant, let's discuss your route back to Major Schenk shall we?'

Chapter Twenty Nine: The Freezing Journey

Tatu and Petru moved slowly through the deserted streets, the darkness causing him to progress cautiously. Behind them, the seven soldiers moved forward, their greatcoat collars pushed up under their helmets. Having been moving for over one hour in the cold, the troops were beginning to regret their new posting out onto the Russian steppe.

The heavy snow clouds were obscuring the stars and moon, turning their journey through the streets to the west of the factory district into virtually complete darkness. The few flickering candles and lights from lanterns in the buildings nearby casting shadows across the pavements and roads as they progressed.

Udet kept close behind Tatu and Petru, his keenness to reach the end of the bitter and miserable journey spurring him forward. The sounds of sporadic shellfire and occasional shot in the darkness slowly became more distant behind them as they progressed through the dark streets towards the edge of the city.

'Hase' and Hausser moved behind the others, checking the streets to either side for signs of life. Occasionally they would see lone sentries or vehicles parked in the side streets, the cold beginning to filter through their uniforms as they progressed. With the heavy cloud cover, the temperature was not as low as expected, the soldiers having covered their faces and hands before departing the NKVD Headquarters.

Occasionally, the moon would break through small openings in the clouds, providing some additional light. Alessio moved in the middle of the group with Meino, accompanied by one Romanian soldier and a German military policeman, the only remaining survivors from the storage towers on the southern side of the city.

As the soldiers progressed, their exhaled breath condensing in the coldest hour of the night, many considered their future. The concerns about the relief effort and their future survival, the loss of comrades and countrymen at the forefront of their thoughts, suppressing their moods.

As the hours passed, and the dawn slowly filtered across the sky, the small group began to reach the outskirts of the city. The smaller damaged and destroyed dwellings of factory workers and labourers becoming more miserable and limited in their appearance as they progressed.

As the buildings became more spaced out, becoming small hamlets and groupings of single storey dwellings, they realised they were beginning to leave the city behind them. The iced snow becoming thicker as the less travelled track they ventured along heading out from the city outskirts.

After a further hour, there were very few buildings, the snow stretching out for as far as the eye could see on either side. The white expanse occasionally broken by a small farm or grouping of buildings in the distance.

By mid-morning, the soldiers were becoming weary, the previous night's vodka and lack of sleep beginning to sap their motivation. Each step was forced through iced snow, the men dragging their feet along the track. The route was used infrequently, the jeeps and lorries transporting supplies using roads to and from the two airfields to the south.

To the left, south, they began to see aircraft flying low in the distance, the planes gathered in small groups. Hausser had explained that these were JU52 transport aircraft, coming into land at Gumrak airfield, the planes full of supplies and ammunition for the troops in the city. Smaller planes flew amongst them, the fighter escorts desperately trying to protect the transports from the roaming soviet fighters patrolling the skies in the land between the Sixth Army and the main German front line, over one hundred miles to the west.

As the soldiers trudged onwards, they watched the planes to their left lower in the sky as they slowly came into land. Once all the planes had landed, there would be a lull for some time whilst the aircraft unloaded their supplies, the skies then clear apart from the patrolling fighters. Then some of the critically wounded from the pocket would be loaded onto the transports, before the planes lumbered down the runway, rising slowly into the air in the distance as they carried their heavy loads. Beginning their perilous flight back to the safety of airfields nearly one hundred and fifty miles to the west, a three hundred mile round journey.

Unbeknown to the watching soldiers, four kilometres to the north, the return flight was just as dangerous as the incoming journey. German fighters from the pocket would escort the lumbering JU52 transports out beyond the front lines and above the Russian positions. The slow transport aircraft would attempt to gain as much height as possible, without causing their precious, seriously wounded cargo to freeze to death. This altitude would offer them some protection from the roaming Russian fighters and Russian anti-aircraft fire from the ground, the Red army moving more and more guns into the area to furnish the corridor the planes flew along. The fighters of the Luftwaffe from outside the pocket would attempt to intercept the Russian fighters and escort the returning aircraft back to safety. Usually the German fighter pilots would try and escort planes out, then meet the previous group's returning aircraft in one flight, thus conserving fuel.

Reaching a small rise in the track as it meandered over a hilltop, the soldiers saw a crossroads in the depression before them, some three hundred metres away. Several soldiers were stood at the intersection, the sentries occupying a small hut and sandbagged defences surrounding the crossroads.

As the soldiers began to descend the slope, a Kubelwagen jeep skidded into view on the left, following the more travelled track running south to north, the jeep carrying orders for a unit on the northern outskirts of the pocket. Behind it, a couple of Opel Blitz lorries moved into view from behind another white slope, their engines revving on the incline as they carried the supplies received from the airfield in the south to the units in the north. The journey to Gumrak having deposited the critically wounded for assessment by the doctors at the airfield, a crude triage system deciding whether a wounded man gained a place on a departing flight or not. Those unfortunate soldiers deemed unfit to travel, or likely to die in the air were moved into the hangars of the airfield to await their personal fates.

Hausser moved forward to join Tatu as they approached the checkpoint. Seeing a military policeman look in their direction, nudging one of his colleagues to assist him.

As he approached the two soldiers, the military policeman, a man in his forties, leaned forward, placing his hands on the sandbagged wall before him.

Hausser saluted, wary the soldier would not immediately distinguish his rank from the greatcoat he was wearing. The military policeman raised his right hand in a relaxed fashion, glancing sideways as the first lorry approached the checkpoint. The military policeman's eyes narrowed as he looked at the bedraggled soldier before him, his voice official, 'Rank and unit? Have you your papers soldier?'

Hausser grinned in irony at the preposterous situation, the checkpoint in the middle of nowhere and the man's attitude, 'Leutnant Hausser, 76th Infantry Division. These are the remains of my men.' He indicated behind him, reaching inside his greatcoat, retrieving the orders Major Slusser had issued to him.

The man looked down at the paper, grimly, 'You must understand, Herr Leutnant, There are many men trying to escape the city. It is our job to ensure they go back to the front. Where have you and your men been?'

Hausser raised the strap of his MP40 back onto his shoulder, the leather having slipped as he extended his arm towards the soldier. He smiled faintly, 'We were supporting the 389th Infantry Division in the factory district.' He looked round at the eight bedraggled men stood waiting behind him, 'There were a few more of us then.'

The man extended his hand, giving Hausser back his orders, his tone nonchalant, 'The army is in a difficult situation, Herr Leutnant. Sacrifices will ensure our overall victory.'

Hausser's eyes narrowed, his tiredness and frustration at the man rising, 'I think we have perhaps sacrificed quite enough to be questioned by a *chain dog*! Now let us past and I expect a proper salute this time!'

The military policeman's eyes widened and he clicked his boots together, the man next to him duplicating the act, his voice becoming more subordinate, 'M-my apologies, Herr Leutnant, I did not mean to speak disrespectfully. Obviously...' He pointed to the state of the men before him and their uniforms, 'Obviously you men have been through a great deal...er, I did not mean to question that in any way.' He raised his right hand mechanically to his helmet in salute.

Hausser saluted him in return, his voice tired, 'I understand you have your job to do soldier, but a little compassion to the men that are from the front lines may not go amiss.' He saw the military policeman nervously swallow, 'Now, please tell me where we are.'

The policeman nodded uniformly, 'Yes, Herr Leutnant.' He stretched his hand out to Hausser's right, 'To the north is the 60th Motorised Infantry Division. They are held in reserve to support the units on the front line.' He paused as Hausser nodded, the Leutnant's exhaled breath drifting past his face, 'To the south Gumrak airfield. If you continue west following this track, you should reach the 76th Infantry Division by nightfall.' His colleague nodded in agreement next to him, his eyes nervously darting across the men in front of him.

Hausser sighed raising his hand, 'Thank you......just relax gentlemen.' He watched as the second lorry skidded on the iced snow behind the military policemen, the other soldiers at the checkpoint moving forward in anticipation that the vehicle may need a push. The lorry jolted forward in the snow, its wheels gaining grip, the vehicle continuing behind the small wooden dwelling house on the crossroads. Hausser smiled warmly at the policemen, trying to calm their nerves, 'Good, I see the road is clear, may we continue?'

The policeman nodded obediently, 'Of course Herr Leutnant, I hope you reach your unit before it gets dark.' The man saluted again nervously, his colleague following suit.

Hausser returned the gesture, indicating for Tatu and the other men to follow as he stepped onto the flattened iced snow of the road, nodding to the military policemen as he trudged past.

As they struggled along the track, leaving the checkpoint behind them, Tatu grinned beneath his scarf, 'You certainly put him in his place, Hausser.'

Hausser smiled thoughtfully, his voice low, 'He was only doing his job. They must be scared, clinging to the stupidity of what they do in this mess? Hoping normality is returned soon.' He turned to look at Tatu, his eyes seeming moist, 'Perhaps Herr General Hoth will return normality for us all, eh?'

Chapter Thirty: Welcome to the cold Russian Steppe

'Ah, our adventurer returns,' Major Schenk stretched his hand out, shaking Hausser's firmly, 'Good to see you my boy. How has it been in the city?'

Hausser smiled at the major warmly, glancing round the bunker, 'It was challenging Sir, but most of us have made it back to you.'

The Major's eyes narrowed, seeing the young commander's discomfort, 'Been busy then, have the Russians been giving you difficulties?'

Hausser nodded, 'Yes Sir, they are quite determined and seemed to have learnt a lot in the last few months. I fear we may have some difficult battles ahead of us.'

The major turned, indicating for him to have a seat, Hausser slumping wearily into the wooden chair before the makeshift table. The major walked round the bench, indicating to the maps on the top of the planks placed over some empty ammunition boxes, 'As you can see we are holding the Russians here on the snow of the steppes, awaiting our relief from General Hoth. It should not be long now, we just need to hold out a little longer.'

Oberleutnant Baumann entered the underground bunker, dropping the tarpaulin curtain back into place that retained some warmth in the strengthened dugout. The major looked up smiling, 'Look Baumann, our Leutnant has returned to us!'

Baumann stepped forward, a wide smile on his face, 'Good to see you *Mr* Hausser, I heard some men had arrived from the city and hoped you were amongst them.'

Hausser stood up abruptly, shaking his friend's hand, 'It took us a while, but we made it in the end.'

Baumann walked past him smiling, 'How was it in the city?'

Hausser slowly lowered himself back into the seat, 'A little grim, but we are holding the enemy.' He turned to the Major, 'Is there any news on the relief effort, Sir? Something to tell the men?'

Major Schenk scratched his nose, nodding, 'Well, General Hoth seems to have been slowed somewhat as the Russians throw their reserves at him, but I am confident he will progress. There are reports from the southern sector that they can see flashes on the horizon, the battle getting nearer. They may even order us to break out and trap the Russian armies, it is a crucial time in the war I think.' He smiled broadly, indicating to his teapot, 'Would you like a drink?'

Hausser nodded, 'Yes please Sir that would be nice. It has been a long walk to get here.'

The major nodded, indicating to the radio operator behind them to prepare some drinks, the soldier rising tiredly from his short wave radio set in response.

Oberleutnant Baumann stood behind the major's chair, smiling at Hausser, 'We have prepared some extra food for you and your men, it's not much, but may compensate for the long walk. How are they holding up?'

Hausser smiled faintly, accepting a cigarette from the major's outstretched hand, 'They are tired, but should be ready tomorrow to join the lines.'

The major shook his head, 'Not necessary my boy, there are other jobs for your men to fulfil, how many have you by the way?'

Hausser grinned ironically, his eyes saddened, 'Eight Sir, not sure what I can accomplish with eight men.' He sipped from the drink the radio operator passed to him, screwing his face up as he tasted the fierce liquid.

Baumann smiled at his discomfort, 'It's the local peasant's brew. Distilled vodka, you will get used to it. I am not sure how they make it, but it is very strong!' He grinned as Hausser coughed.

The major cleared his throat, 'Right, let's give you an update. The Russian army on the steppe before us seems quite strong, but we believe they have had to release troops to the south in attempts to stop Herr Hoth. They are now well dug in and seem determined to sit the battle out until the fight in the south is concluded. We have skirmishes with their patrols occasionally, but mostly we sit here waiting for them to act. Once the relief effort arrives, I am sure we will go over onto the offensive again.' The major sipped his drink, shaking his head and screwing his eyes up as the liquid hit his taste buds.

Hausser nodded, smiling at the major's reaction, 'That sounds interesting. So what shall I do Sir?'

Major Schenk leant forward, looking directly at the young commander, 'Well, supplies are our biggest concern. It appears one of our transports was shot down near our lines just before dark, only a few minutes ago. He must have been damaged or got lost to be so late and trying to make it to Gumrak. We have heard some shooting.' He studied Hausser as the man moved uncomfortably in his chair, 'One of the pilots have made it to our lines and reported there are wounded crew on board and a considerable quantity of supplies. I have posted snipers to keep the Russians away, but I need a small group of soldiers to go out to the plane and retrieve the crew and any supplies, are you and your men up for it?'

Hausser rubbed his eyes, 'We haven't slept for hours Sir, and the men have just walked all the way from the city.'

The major smiled faintly, 'I know, I am sorry my friend. Normally I would not ask, but we need someone to go out there. The snipers report the Russians have not attempted to move towards the downed aircraft yet. It's not too far, maybe three hundred metres from our line, but I don't want to de-man the front line just in case, so will you do it?'

Hausser rose wearily from the chair, his face solemn but determined, 'Very well, Sir. I will get my men. We should do this quickly before the Russians move soldiers out to intercept us.'

The major slapped the table, grinning, 'That's my Hausser! Good man! Move along the forward trench towards the south, speak to sergeant Loris, he is with the pilot that escaped. Once you have completed this, return to me and I will issue you and your men your quarters and rations.'

Hausser saluted officially, 'Yes Sir!' He turned on his heels and walked from the dugout.

Baumann stared at the major, his eyes wide with astonishment, 'Hausser and his men have just walked the width of the pocket to get here, and you send them on a mission?'

The major shook his hand in defence, his eyes defiant, 'Best way to re-focus the man, give him a purpose to reintegrate him with the unit. I don't want him having fond thoughts about the warm city and extra comforts. This will do him good.' He turned glaring at his adjutant, 'Hausser is a 76th Infantry Division man, not some servant of that mad arrogant fool, Major Slusser!'

Hausser walked wearily out of the dugout entrance, then increased his speed as he approached Tatu, his face grim. Passing him, he indicated for him and the seven soldiers to follow, 'Get the men to follow, we are going out to rescue a downed flight crew.'

Tatu's eyes widened in exasperation, 'What? Are you mad?'

Hausser glanced over his shoulder, his eyes defiant, 'Not now Tatu! There are wounded men waiting for us. Get the men to leave all equipment they don't need, and quickly. I am not having any men die as a result of us arguing!'

Tatu nodded, indicating quickly to the soldiers around him as he raised his voice, 'Drop your kit, and move!' He jogged after Hausser, the iced snow cracking beneath his boots.

The soldier glanced from side to side feverishly, his body aching from the confined space he had been hiding in. Seeing the small street was clear, he lunged forward, running across it and dropping to the ground on the other side, the terror within him almost overpowering.

Scrambling along the side of the burnt out building next to him, he gasped as he saw the dark line on the ground in the distance, some twenty metres away. Breathing heavily, he hissed across the flattened landscape before him, 'Don't shoot, friend!'

There was a brief silence, then a voice called back, 'Come out and run quickly, enemy snipers are near here.'

The man was breathing heavily, his heart pounding in his chest with fear, 'On my way!' he hissed back.

The soldier pushed himself upwards, his breath held as he sprinted across the terrain, jumping a low destroyed wall and stumbling, the momentum propelling him forwards. His ears straining desperately for the crack of a rifle or burst of machine gun fire, shots that would probably end his life.

As he dropped into the trench, bullets splattered across the ground behind him, a machine gunner and rifleman in the distance too slow to react in the cold as the figure ran from cover.

His chest heaving and tears of relief flowing down his face, he looked up at the infantryman in front of him, the man staring down into his face. The soldier leaned forward, grasping the man's torn uniform, his voice cautious, 'Who are you?'

The man lying in the foot of the trench looked up, wincing at the pain that swept through him, 'I am Captain Medvedev!' He gasped, 'I have just escaped from the Germans.'

Hausser glanced round, seeing the adrenalin in the eyes of the eight soldiers behind him. Looking back out into the endless white expanse of the Russian steppe before him, he could just see the outline of the large downed plane in the distance, across the darkening gloom. Thin tentacles of frozen mist creeping across the white terrain before them.

Turning, he looked into the eyes of 'Hase' and Udet, seeing them nod to him, their minds resolved to follow their commander. He bit his lip, hissing, 'Let's go!' Pushing his body up the ramp, he darted forward, the soldiers behind him beginning to spread out in the deep snow as they moved cautiously towards the crashed plane.

In the distance, there were flashes on the horizon, Russian artillery opening fire towards the encircled and trapped Germans and their allies on the freezing banks of the Volga.

Sequel Outline:

As the battle in Stalingrad and the southern sector of the Russian Front progresses towards its conclusion, Leutnant Hausser and his men continue their desperate struggle. Now fighting a numerically superior enemy in miserable conditions with limited food and ammunition, their survival becomes more and more uncertain. As desperation begins to become the key motivator to continue, the conditions worsen, becoming a white and frozen hell with temperatures dropping to below minus forty four degrees Celsius.

Outside the city on the frozen steppe, the Red Army begins bolder and more ambitious attacks, smashing into the Italian 8th Army and sweeping it aside, dramatically widening the gap between the encircled city and the German front lines. Now the Luftwaffe have to fly the desperately needed supplies further and in more bitter weather than ever before.

As the defenders cling to the last strands of personal hope, they begin to realise that perhaps no rescue is coming. That the unthinkable may be about to occur to one of the mightiest armies on the planet, a slow and painful death surrounded by thickly iced snow, freezing weather and a bitter, unforgiving enemy. An enemy hell-bent on their complete and utter destruction.

Bloody Kessel will be released later in 2015, portraying the bitterness and attrition experienced in the southern sector of the freezing Eastern Front.

The final struggle for Leutnant Hausser in Stalingrad is about to begin.

In Memory:

This is written in beloved memory of my late father.

Someone whom always encourages you to follow your dreams, promotes happiness and strength as well as helping in everything you wish to achieve is rarely recognised in full until their gift is gone.

Unfortunately, I also lost one of my best friends in 2014, one of my dogs, a Black Lab, Doberman, and Chow cross called Taxi. He was often a troubled individual, having had a very difficult start in life before we met him at Battersea Dogs Home. But was a very loyal, loving and understanding companion in his own way.

It was an honour for me to share over twelve years with him.

Sometimes, it is extremely difficult to fully appreciate the gifts and love others convey on us until they are gone. But with their strong memory and loving experiences they shared and conveyed to us, it becomes easier to appreciate just how uniquely special they were and just how important their affection was. I will miss them both very much.

Contributors:

I would like to thank three of my colleagues for their voluntary assistance with this project.

David Axell has also volunteered some considerable time assisting me with this, the previous book and future projects, talking over additional ideas and potential sub plots. He has also provided valuable input on some of the wording used to assist me in the endeavour to create as close as possible account to reality.

Kara Reed has offered continual encouragement throughout the previous book and the current projects. Listening to ideas and offering ideas on alternatives or additions to existing plot lines. This has been of considerable assistance and I am very grateful for the 'on-call' facility that emerged for me to express ideas and twists as they came to mind.

Juri Heikinen, for his voluntary assistance with some of the most intricate details of this and the previous book geographically. His contributions through searching Russian websites and other Russian language sources for the smallest details I was determined to get exactly correct have been of immense assistance.

Authors Note:

The war in Russia was one of the most brutal history has ever seen. Stalingrad epitomised the brutality and provides the historical background for the story. Although all the units on both sides are historically accurate and placed accordingly across the city and outside, Leutnant Hausser's unit is fictitious. I created the soldiers to try and provide an insight into the many men from several nations that were involved in the struggle. All the units they are sourced from did exist and were at Stalingrad. Likewise, the Russian army was comprised of many different races from across the Soviet Union including Mongolians from the far east of Russia.

In writing this I was very wary of glorifying war, the German invasion of the Soviet Union, the atrocities committed or the acts of some of the Russian soldiers in revenge. The war was terrible, the battle of Stalingrad costing upwards of two million lives.

The ambition of the work is to perhaps provide an insight into the conditions of the time, what affected the men and why they continued fighting. My own fascination of the War in the East stems from the extremes the human spirit will endure when motivated by belief (if misplaced) and the basic urge for survival. As stated, the work is fictitious, but an attempt to demonstrate to the reader my interpretation of what it may have been like. There is little glory in war, only victory or defeat paid for with human life.

The sheer number of innocent men and civilians that died as a result of one, then two men's ambitions beggars belief. The rise of propaganda providing the tools to motivate people to commit atrocities and to keep fighting even when all is clearly lost is nearly incomprehensible in this day and age. Hitler and then Stalin utilised this new tool to deadly effect, being able to produce one message to an entire population in a relatively short space of time was initiated and twisted to deadly effect in World War Two. Both populations were supressed to an extreme, eliminating any democratic argument to what was stated in the media. Today we will question information, even protest…back then there was little option but to obey or face the consequences. We are very fortunate for our current reality.

There were no supermen on either side, simply equal individuals trying to get by. Sometimes their luck would hold, other times it would not. Death was always close by, even seeming to taunt them at times. From the hundreds of accounts and research I have consumed from both sides, I concluded the majority of people were just like us, with personality flaws and insecurities. All had individual beliefs, some righteous, others misplaced, some darker and evil, power through rank enabling them to use this evil against others. I have tried to portray this in these works, avoiding a confrontation involving the SS or National Socialist units until perhaps later. There were no SS formations in the city of Stalingrad on the Volga River.

I hope you enjoy the works I have produced. It has given me a great deal of pleasure devising the ideas, how they would be portrayed and ultimate conclusions. My ambition has always been to create something that is believable, hopefully realistic, portraying history as it may have been. An attempt to place the thirty years spent reading and researching into something anyone can absorb. The times I have awoken in the middle of the night and changed a line or paragraph as I deem it impractical or unrealistic are many.

Ultimately, the work will never be as terrifying or brutal as reality, and for that we must be eternally grateful.

Thank you for taking the time to read what I have created.

17926542R00155

Printed in Great Britain
by Amazon